GIDEON THE NINTH

The Locked Tomb Trilogy

Gideon the Ninth
Harrow the Ninth
Alecto the Ninth (forthcoming)

GIDEON THE NINTH

IX

TAMSYN MUIR

A TOM DOHERTY ASSOCIATES BOOK

NEW YORK

GIDEON THE NINTH

Copyright © 2019 by Tamsyn Muir

Edited by Carl Engle-Laird

A Tor.com Book
Published by Tom Doherty Associates
120 Broadway
New York, NY 10271

www.tor.com

Tor® is a registered trademark of
Macmillan Publishing Group, LLC.

The Library of Congress Cataloging-in-Publication Data is available upon request.

ISBN 978-1-250-31318-8 (trade paperback)
ISBN 978-1-250-31317-1 (ebook)

Our books may be purchased in bulk for promotional, educational, or business use. Please contact your local bookseller or the Macmillan Corporate and Premium Sales Department at 1-800-221-7945, extension 5442, or by email at MacmillanSpecialMarkets@macmillan.com.

First Edition: September 2019
First Trade Paperback Edition: July 2020

Printed in the United States of America

for pT

DRAMATIS PERSONAE

In Order of House Appearance

The Ninth House

Keepers of the Locked Tomb, House of the Sewn Tongue, the Black Vestals

Harrowhark Nonagesimus HEIR TO THE HOUSE OF THE NINTH, REVEREND DAUGHTER OF DREARBURH

Pelleamena Novenarius HER MOTHER, REVEREND MOTHER OF DREARBURH

Priamhark Noniusvianus HER FATHER, REVEREND FATHER OF DREARBURH

Ortus Nigenad CAVALIER PRIMARY TO THE HEIR

Crux MARSHAL OF THE HOUSE OF THE NINTH

Aiglamene CAPTAIN OF THE GUARD OF THE NINTH

Sister Lachrimorta NUN OF THE LOCKED TOMB

Sister Aisamorta NUN OF THE LOCKED TOMB

Sister Glaurica NUN OF THE LOCKED TOMB

Some various followers, cultists, and laypeople of the Ninth

>   *and*

Gideon Nav INDENTURED SERVANT OF THE HOUSE OF THE NINTH

The First House

Necromancer Divine, King of the Nine Renewals, our Resurrector, the Necrolord Prime

THE EMPEROR

HIS LYCTORS

AND THE PRIESTHOOD OF CANAAN HOUSE

The Second House

The Emperor's Strength, House of the Crimson Shield, the Centurion's House

Judith Deuteros HEIR TO THE HOUSE OF THE SECOND, RANKED CAPTAIN OF THE COHORT

Marta Dyas CAVALIER PRIMARY TO THE HEIR, RANKED FIRST LIEUTENANT OF THE COHORT

The Third House

Mouth of the Emperor, the Procession, House of the Shining Dead

Coronabeth Tridentarius HEIR TO THE HOUSE OF THE THIRD, CROWN PRINCESS OF IDA

Ianthe Tridentarius HEIR TO THE HOUSE OF THE THIRD, PRINCESS OF IDA

Naberius Tern CAVALIER PRIMARY TO THE HEIRS, PRINCE OF IDA

The Fourth House

Hope of the Emperor, the Emperor's Sword

Isaac Tettares HEIR TO THE HOUSE OF THE FOURTH, BARON OF TISIS

Jeannemary Chatur CAVALIER PRIMARY TO THE HEIR, KNIGHT OF TISIS

The Fifth House

Heart of the Emperor, Watchers over the River

Abigail Pent HEIR TO THE HOUSE OF THE FIFTH, LADY OF KONIORTOS COURT

Magnus Quinn CAVALIER PRIMARY TO THE HEIR, SENESCHAL OF KONIORTOS COURT

The Sixth House

The Emperor's Reason, the Master Wardens

Palamedes Sextus   HEIR TO THE HOUSE OF THE SIXTH, MASTER WARDEN OF THE LIBRARY

Camilla Hect   CAVALIER PRIMARY TO THE HEIR, WARDEN'S HAND OF THE LIBRARY

The Seventh House

Joy of the Emperor, the Rose Unblown

Dulcinea Septimus   HEIR TO THE HOUSE OF THE SEVENTH, DUCHESS OF RHODES

Protesilaus Ebdoma   CAVALIER PRIMARY TO THE HEIR, KNIGHT OF RHODES

The Eighth House

Keepers of the Tome, the Forgiving House

Silas Octakiseron   HEIR TO THE HOUSE OF THE EIGHTH, MASTER TEMPLAR OF THE WHITE GLASS

Colum Asht   CAVALIER PRIMARY TO THE HEIR, TEMPLAR OF THE WHITE GLASS

Two is for discipline, heedless of trial;

Three for the gleam of a jewel or a smile;

Four for fidelity, facing ahead;

Five for tradition and debts to the dead;

Six for the truth over solace in lies;

Seven for beauty that blossoms and dies;

Eight for salvation no matter the cost;

Nine for the Tomb, and for all that was lost.

ACT ONE

IN THE MYRIADIC YEAR OF OUR LORD—the ten thousandth year of the King Undying, the kindly Prince of Death!—Gideon Nav packed her sword, her shoes, and her dirty magazines, and she escaped from the House of the Ninth.

She didn't run. Gideon never ran unless she had to. In the absolute darkness before dawn she brushed her teeth without concern and splashed her face with water, and even went so far as to sweep the dust off the floor of her cell. She shook out her big black church robe and hung it from the hook. Having done this every day for over a decade, she no longer needed light to do it by. This late in the equinox no light would make it here for months, in any case; you could tell the season by how hard the heating vents were creaking. She dressed herself from head to toe in polymer and synthetic weave. She combed her hair. Then Gideon whistled through her teeth as she unlocked her security cuff, and arranged it and its stolen key considerately on her pillow, like a chocolate in a fancy hotel.

Leaving her cell and swinging her pack over one shoulder, she took the time to walk down five flights to her mother's nameless catacomb niche. This was pure sentiment, as her mother hadn't been there since Gideon was little and would never go back in it now. Then came the long hike up twenty-two flights the back way, not one light relieving the greasy dark, heading to the splitoff shaft and the pit where her ride would arrive: the shuttle was due in two hours.

Out here, you had an unimpeded view up to a pocket of Ninth sky. It was soupy white where the atmosphere was pumped in thickest, and thin and navy where it wasn't. The bright bead of Dominicus winked benignly down from the mouth of the long vertical tunnel. In the dark, she made an opening amble of the field's perimeter, and she pressed her hands up hard against the cold and oily rock of the cave walls. Once this was done, she spent a long time methodically kicking apart every single innocuous drift and hummock of dirt and rock that had been left on the worn floor of the landing field. She dug the shabby steel toe of her boot into the hard-packed floor, but satisfied with the sheer improbability of anyone digging through it, left it alone. Not an inch of that huge, empty space did Gideon leave unchecked, and as the generator lights grumbled to half-hearted life, she checked it twice by sight. She climbed up the wire-meshed frames of the floodlights and checked them too, blinded by the glare, feeling blindly behind the metal housing, grimly comforted by what she didn't find.

She parked herself on one of the destroyed humps of rubble in the dead centre. The lamps made lacklustre any real light. They explosively birthed malform shadow all around. The shades of the Ninth were deep and shifty; they were bruise-coloured and cold. In these surrounds, Gideon rewarded herself with a little plastic bag of porridge. It tasted gorgeously grey and horrible.

The morning started as every other morning had started in the Ninth since the Ninth began. She took a turn around the vast landing site just for a change of pace, kicking absently at an untidy drift of grit as she went. She moved out to the balcony tier and looked down at the central cavern for signs of movement, worrying porridge from her molars with the tip of her tongue. After a while, there was the faraway upward clatter of the skeletons going to pick mindlessly at the snow leeks in the planter fields. Gideon saw them in her mind's eye: mucky ivory in the sulfurous dim, picks clattering over the ground, eyes a multitude of wavering red pinpricks.

The First Bell clanged its uncanorous, complaining call for beginning prayers, sounding as always like it was getting kicked down some stairs; a sort of *BLA-BLANG... BLA-BLANG... BLA-BLANG* that had woken her up every morning that she could recall. Movement resulted. Gideon peered down at the bottom where shadows gathered over the cold white doors of Castle Drearburh, stately in the dirt, set into the rock three bodies wide and six bodies tall. Two braziers stood on either side of the door and perpetually burned fatty, crappy smoke. Over the doors were tiny white figures in a multitude of poses, hundreds to thousands of them, carved using some weird trick where their eyes seemed to look right at you. Whenever Gideon had been made to go through those doors as a kid, she'd screamed like she was dying.

More activity in the lowest tiers now. The light had settled into visibility. The Ninth would be coming out of their cells after morning contemplation, getting ready to head for orison, and the Drearburh retainers would be preparing for the day ahead. They would perform many a solemn and inane ritual in the lower recesses. Gideon tossed her empty porridge bag over the side of the tier and sat down with her sword over her knees, cleaning it with a bit of rag: forty minutes to go.

Suddenly, the unchanging tedium of a Ninth morning changed. The First Bell sounded *again: BLANG ... BLA-BLANG ... BLA-BLANG ...* Gideon cocked her head to listen, finding her hands had stilled on her sword. It rang fully twenty times before stopping. Huh; muster call. After a while came the clatter of the skeletons again, having obediently tossed down pick and hoe to meet their summons. They streamed down the tiers in an angular current, broken up every so often by some limping figure in vestments of rusting black. Gideon picked up her sword and cloth again: it was a cute try, but she wasn't buying.

She didn't look up when heavy, stumping footsteps sounded on her tier, or for the rattle of rusting armour and the rusty rattle of breath.

"Thirty whole minutes since I took it off, Crux," she said, hands busy. "It's almost like you want me to leave here forever. *Ohhhh shit, you absolutely do though.*"

"You ordered a shuttle through deception," bubbled the marshal of Drearburh, whose main claim to fame was that he was more decrepit alive than some of the legitimately dead. He stood before her on the landing field and gurgled with indignation. "You falsified documents. You stole a key. You removed your cuff. You wrong this house, you misuse its goods, you steal its stock."

"Come on, Crux, we can come to some arrangement," Gideon coaxed, flipping her sword over and looking at it critically for nicks. "You hate me, I hate you. Just let me go without a fight and you can retire in peace. Take up a hobby. Write your memoirs."

"You *wrong* this house. You *misuse* its goods. You *steal* its stock." Crux loved verbs.

"Say my shuttle exploded. I died, and it was such a shame. Give me a break, Crux, I'm begging you here—I'll trade you a skin mag. *Frontline Titties of the Fifth.*" This rendered the marshal momentarily too aghast to respond. "Okay, okay. I take it back. *Frontline Titties* isn't a real publication."

Crux advanced like a glacier with an agenda. Gideon rolled backward off her seat as his antique fist came down, skidding out of his way with a shower of dust and gravel. Her sword she swiftly locked within its scabbard, and the scabbard she clutched in her arms like a child. She propelled herself backward, out of the way of his boot and his huge, hoary hands. Crux might have been very nearly dead, but he was built like gristle with what seemed like thirty knuckles to each fist. He was old, but he was goddamn ghastly.

"Easy, marshal," she said, though she was the one floundering in the dirt. "Take this much further and you're in danger of enjoying yourself."

"You talk so loudly for *chattel*, Nav," said the marshal. "You chatter so much for a *debt*. I hate you, and yet you are my wares and inventory. I have written up your lungs as lungs for the Ninth. I have measured your gall as gall for the Ninth. Your brain is a base and shrivelled sponge, but it too is for the Ninth. Come here, and I'll black your eyes for you and knock you dead."

Gideon slid backward, keeping her distance. "Crux," she said, "a threat's meant to be 'Come here, *or . . .*'"

"Come here and I'll black your eyes for you and knock you dead," croaked the advancing old man, "and then the Lady has said that you will come to her."

Only then did Gideon's palms prickle. She looked up at the scarecrow towering before her and he stared back, one-eyed, horrible, baleful. The antiquated armour seemed to be rotting right off his body. Even though the livid, over-stretched skin on his skull looked in danger of peeling right off, he gave the impression that he simply wouldn't care. Gideon suspected that—even though he had not a whit of necromancy in him—the day he died, Crux would keep going anyway out of sheer malice.

"Black my eyes and knock me dead," she said slowly, "but your Lady can go right to hell."

Crux spat on her. That was disgusting, but whatever. His hand went to the long knife kept over one shoulder in a mould-splattered sheath, which he twitched to show a thin slice of blade: but at that, Gideon was on her feet with her scabbard held before her like a shield. One hand was on the grip, the other on the locket of the sheath. They both faced each other in impasse, her very still, the old man's breath loud and wet.

Gideon said, "Don't make the mistake of drawing on me, Crux."

"You are not half as good with that sword as you think you are, Gideon Nav," said the marshal of Drearburh, "and one day I'll flay you for disrespect. One day we will use your parts for paper. One day the sisters of the Locked Tomb will brush the oss with your bristles. One day your obedient bones will dust all places you disdain, and make the stones there shine with your fat. There is a muster, Nav, and I command you now to go."

Gideon lost her temper. "You go, you dead old dog, and you damn well tell her I'm already gone."

To her enormous surprise he wheeled around and stumped back to the dark and slippery tier. He rattled and cursed all the way, and she told herself that she had won before she even woke up that morning; that Crux was an impotent symbol of control, one last attempt to test if she was stupid enough or cowed enough to walk back behind the cold bars of her prison. The grey and putrid heart of Drearburh. The greyer and more putrid heart of its lady.

She pulled her watch out of her pocket and checked it: twenty minutes to go, a quarter hour and change. Gideon was home free. Gideon was gone. Nothing and nobody could change that now.

* * *

"Crux is abusing you to anyone who will listen," said a voice from the entryway, with fifteen minutes to go. "He said you made your blade naked to him. He said you offered him sick pornographies."

Gideon's palms prickled again. She'd sat back down on her awkward throne of rocks and balanced her watch between her knees, staring at the tiny mechanical hand that counted the minutes. "I'm not that dumb, Aiglamene," she said. "Threaten a house official and I wouldn't make toilet-wiper in the Cohort."

"And the pornography?"

"I did offer him stupendous work of a titty nature, and he got offended," said Gideon. "It was a very perfect moment. The Cohort's not going to care about that though. Have I mentioned the Cohort? You do know the Cohort, right? The Cohort I've left to enlist in . . . *thirty-three times*?"

"Save the drama, you baby," said her sword-master. "I know of your desires."

Aiglamene dragged herself into the small light of the landing field. The captain of the House guard had a head of melty scars and a missing leg which an indifferently talented bone adept had replaced for her. It bowed horribly and gave her the appearance of a building with the foundations hastily shored up. She was younger than Crux, which was to say, old as balls: but she had a quickness to her, a liveliness, that was clean. The marshal was classic Ninth and he was filthy rotten all the way through.

"Thirty-three times," repeated Gideon, somewhat wearily. She checked back on her clockwork: fourteen minutes to go. "The last time, she jammed me in the lift. The time before that she turned off the heating and I got frostbite in three toes. Time before that: she poisoned my food and had me crapping blood for a month. Need I go on."

Her teacher was unmoved. "There was no disservice done. You didn't get her permission."

"I'm allowed to apply for the military, Captain. I'm indentured, not a slave. I'm no fiscal use to her here."

"Beside the point. You chose a bad day to fly the coop." Aiglamene jerked her head downward. "There's House business, and you're wanted downstairs."

"This is her being sad and desperate," said Gideon. "This is her obsession . . . this is her need for control. There's nothing she can do. I'll keep my nose clean. Keep my mouth shut. I'll even—you can write this down, you can quote me here—*do my duty* to the Ninth House. But don't pretend at me, Aiglamene, that the moment I go down there a sack won't come down over my head and I won't spend the next five weeks concussed in an oss."

"You egotistical foetus, you think our Lady rang the muster call just for you?"

"So, here's the thing, your Lady would set the Locked Tomb on fire if it meant I'd never see another sky," Gideon said, looking up. "Your Lady would stone cold eat a baby if it meant she got to lock me up infinitely. Your Lady would slather burning turds on the great-aunts if she thought it would ruin my day. Your Lady is the nastiest b—"

When Aiglamene slapped her, it had none of the trembling affrontedness Crux might have slapped her with. She simply backhanded Gideon the way you might hit a barking animal. Gideon's head was starry with pain.

"You forget yourself, Gideon Nav," her teacher said shortly. "You're no slave, but you'll serve the House of the Ninth until the day you die and then thereafter, and you'll commit no sin of perfidy in *my* air. The bell was real. Will you come to muster of your own accord, or will you disgrace me?"

There was a time when she had done many things to avoid

disgracing Aiglamene. It was easy to be a disgrace in a vacuum, but she had a soft spot for the old soldier. Nobody had ever loved her in the House of the Ninth, and certainly Aiglamene did not love her and would have laughed herself to her overdue death at the idea: but in her had been a measure of tolerance, a willingness to loosen the leash and see what Gideon could do with free rein. Gideon loved free rein. Aiglamene had convinced the House to put a sword in Gideon's hands, not to waste her on serving altar or drudging in the oss. Aiglamene wasn't faithless. Gideon looked down and wiped her mouth with the back of her hand, and saw the blood in her saliva and saw her sword; and she loved her sword so much she could frigging marry it.

But she also saw her clock's minute hand ticking, ticking down. Twelve minutes to go. You didn't cut loose by getting soft. For all its mouldering brittleness, the Ninth was hard as iron.

"I guess I'll disgrace you," Gideon admitted easily. "I feel like I was born to it. I'm naturally demeaning."

Her sword-master held her gaze with her aged hawk's face and her pouchy socket of an eye, and it was grim, but Gideon didn't look away. It would have made it somewhat easier if Aiglamene had made a Crux out of it and cursed her lavishly, but all she said was: "Such a quick study, and you still don't understand. That's on my head, I suppose. The more you struggle against the Ninth, Nav, the deeper it takes you; the louder you curse it, the louder they'll have you scream."

Back straight as a poker, Aiglamene walked away with her funny seesawing walk, and Gideon felt as though she'd failed a test. It didn't matter, she told herself. Two down, none to go. Eleven minutes until landing, her clockwork told her, eleven minutes and she was out. That was the only thing that mattered. That was the only thing that had mattered since a much younger Gideon had realised that, unless she did something drastic, she was going to die here down in the dark.

And—worst of all—that would only be the *beginning*.

* * *

Nav was a Niner name, but Gideon didn't know where she'd been born. The remote, insensate planet where she lived was home to both the stronghold of the House and a tiny prison, used only for those criminals whose crimes were too repugnant for their own Houses to rehabilitate them on home turf. She'd never seen the place. The Ninth House was an enormous hole cracked vertically into the planet's core, and the prison a bubble installation set half-way up into the atmosphere where the living conditions were prob-ably a hell of a lot more clement.

One day eighteen years ago, Gideon's mother had tumbled down the middle of the shaft in a dragchute and a battered hazard suit, like some moth drifting slowly down into the dark. The suit had been out of power for a couple of minutes. The woman landed brain-dead. All the battery power had been sucked away by a bio-container plugged into the suit, the kind you'd carry a transplant limb in, and inside that container was Gideon, only a day old.

This was obviously mysterious as hell. Gideon had spent her life poring over the facts. The woman must have run out of juice an hour before landing; it was impossible that she would have cleared grav-ity from a drop above the planet, as her simple haz would have exploded. The prison, which recorded every coming and going obsessively, denied her as an escapee. Some of the nun-adepts of the Locked Tomb were sent for, those who knew the secrets for caging ghosts. Even they—old in their power then, seasoned necromancers of the dark and powerful House of the Ninth—couldn't rip the woman's shade back to explain herself. She would not be tempted back for fresh blood or old. She was too far gone by the time the ex-hausted nuns had tethered her by force, as though death had been a catalyst for the woman to hit the ground running, and they only got one word out of her: she had screamed *Gideon! Gideon! Gideon!* three times, and fled.

If the Ninth—enigmatic, uncanny Ninth, the House of the Sewn Tongue, the Anchorite's House, the House of Heretical Secrets—was nonplussed at having an infant on their hands, they moved fast anyway. The Ninth had historically filled its halls with penitents from other houses, mystics and pilgrims who found the call of this dreary order more attractive than their own birthrights. In the antiquated rules of those supplicants who moved between the eight great households, she was taken as a very small bondswoman, not *of* the Ninth but beholden to it: What greater debt could be accrued than that of being brought up? What position more honourable than vassal to Drearburh? Let the baby grow up postulant. Push the child to be an oblate. They chipped her, surnamed her, and put her in the nursery. At that time, the tiny Ninth House boasted two hundred children between infancy and nineteen years of age, and Gideon was numbered two hundred and first.

Less than two years later, Gideon Nav would be one of only three children left: herself, a much older boy, and the infant heir of the Ninth House, daughter of its lord and lady. They knew by age five that she was not a necromancer, and suspected by eight that she would never be a nun. Certainly, they would have known by ten that she knew too much, and that she could never be allowed to go.

Gideon's appeals to better natures, financial rewards, moral obligations, outlined plans, and simple attempts to run away numbered eighty-six by the time she was eighteen. She'd started when she was four.

2

THERE WERE FIVE MINUTES to go when Gideon's eighty-seventh escape plan got messed up fantastically.

"I see that your genius strategy, Griddle," said a final voice from the tierway, "was to order a shuttle and walk out the door."

The Lady of the Ninth House stood before the drillshaft, wearing black and sneering. Reverend Daughter Harrowhark Nonagesimus had pretty much cornered the market on wearing black and sneering. It comprised 100 percent of her personality. Gideon marvelled that someone could live in the universe only seventeen years and yet wear black and sneer with such ancient self-assurance.

Gideon said, "Hey, what can I say? I'm a tactician."

The ornate, slightly soiled robes of the House dragged in the dust as the Reverend Daughter approached. She'd brought her marshal along, and Aiglamene too. A few Sisters were behind her on the tier, having sunk down to their knees: the cloisterwomen painted their faces alabaster grey and drew black patterns on their cheeks and lips like death's-heads. Dressed in breadths of rusty black cloth, they looked like a peanut gallery of sad old waist-high masks.

"It's embarrassing that it had to come to this," said the Lady of the Ninth, pulling back her hood. Her pale-painted face was a white blotch among all the black. Even her hands were gloved. "I don't care that you run away. I care that you do it badly. Take your hand from your sword, you're humiliating yourself."

"In under ten minutes a shuttle's going to come and take me to Trentham on the Second," Gideon said, and did not take her hand from her sword. "I'm going to get on it. I'm going to close the door. I'm going to wave goodbye. There is literally nothing you can do anymore to stop me."

Harrow put one gloved hand before her and massaged her fingers thoughtfully. The light fell on her painted face and black-daubed chin, and her short-cropped, dead-crow-coloured hair. "All right. Let's play this one through for interest's sake," she said. "First objection: the Cohort won't enlist an unreleased serf, you know."

"I faked your signature on the release form," said Gideon.

"But a single word from me and you're brought back in cuffs."

"You'll say nothing."

Harrowhark ringed two fingers around one wrist and slowly worked the hand up and down. "It's a cute story, but badly characterised," she said. "Why the sudden mercy on my part?"

"The moment you deny me leave to go," said Gideon, hand unmoving on her scabbard, "the moment you call me back—the moment you give the Cohort cause, or, I don't know, some list of trumped-up criminal charges . . ."

"Some of your magazines are very nasty," admitted the Lady.

"That's the moment I squeal," said Gideon. "I squeal so long and so loud they hear me from the Eighth. I tell them everything. You know what I know. And I'll tell them the numbers. They'd bring me home in cuffs, but I'd come back laughing my ass off."

At that, Harrowhark stopped working her scaphoid and glanced at Gideon. She gave a rather brusque hand-wave to the geriatric fan club behind her and they scattered: tottering, kissing the floor and rattling both their prayer beads and their unlubricated knee joints, disappearing into the darkness and down the tier. Only Crux and Aiglamene stayed. Then Harrow cocked her head to the side like a quizzical bird and smiled a tiny, contemptuous smile.

"How coarse and ordinary," she said. "How effective, how crass. My parents should have smothered you."

"I'd like to see them try it now," said Gideon, unmoved.

"You'd do it even if there was no ultimate gain," the Lady said, and she even seemed to be marvelling at it. "Even though you know what you'd suffer. Even though you know what it means. And all because . . . ?"

"All *because*," said Gideon, checking her clock again, "I completely fucking hate you, *because* you are a hideous witch from hell. No offence."

There was a pause.

"Oh, Griddle!" said Harrow pityingly, in the silence. "But I don't even remember about you most of the time."

They stared at each other. There was a lopsided smile tugging at Gideon's mouth, unsuppressed, and looking at it made Harrowhark's expression slide into something even moodier and more petulant. "You have me at an impasse," she said, and she sounded grudgingly amazed by the fact. "Your ride will be here in five minutes. I don't doubt you have all the documents and that they look good. It'd be master's sin if I employed unwarranted violence. There is really nothing I can do."

Gideon said nothing. Harrow said, "The muster call is real, you know. There's important Ninth business afoot. Won't you give a handful of minutes to take part in your House's last muster?"

"Oh hell no," said Gideon.

"Can I appeal to your deep sense of duty?"

"Nope," said Gideon.

"Worth a try," admitted Harrow. She tapped her chin thoughtfully. "What about a bribe?"

"This is going to be good," said Gideon to nobody in particular. "'Gideon, here's some money. You can spend it right here, on bones.' 'Gideon, I'll always be nice and not a dick to you if you come back. You can have Crux's room.' 'Gideon, here's a bed of writhing babes. It's the cloisterites, though, so they're ninety percent osteoporosis.'"

From out of her pocket, with no small amount of drama, Harrowhark drew a fresh piece of parchment. It was paper—real paper!— with the official letterhead of the House of the Ninth on the top. She must have raided the coffers for that one. The hairs on the back of Gideon's neck prickled in warning. Harrow ostentatiously walked forward to leave it at a safe middle point between them both, and backed away with hands open in surrender.

"*Or*," said the Lady, as Gideon slowly went to pick it up, "it could be an absolutely authentic purchase of your commission in the Cohort. You can't forge this, Griddle, it's to be signed in blood, so don't stuff it down your trousers yet."

It was real Ninth bond, written correctly and clearly. It purchased Gideon Nav's commission to second lieutenant, not privy to resale, but relinquishing capital if she honourably retired. It would grant her full officer training. The usual huge percentage of prizes and territory would be tithed to her House if they were won, but her inflated Ninth serfdom would be paid for in five years on good conditions, rather than thirty. It was more than generous. Harrow was shooting herself in the foot. She was gamely firing into one foot and then taking aim at the other. She'd lose rights to Gideon forever. Gideon went absolutely cold.

"You can't say I don't care," said Harrow.

"You don't care," said Gideon. "You'd have the nuns eat each other if you got bored. You are a psychopath."

Harrow said, "If you don't want it, return it. I can still use the paper."

The only sensible option was to fold the bond into a dart and sail it back the way it came. Four minutes until the shuttle landed and she was able to make hot tracks far away from this place. She'd already won, and this was a vulnerability that would put everything she'd worked for—months of puzzling out how to infiltrate the shuttle standing-order system, months to hide her tracks, to get the right forms, to intercept communications, to wait and sweat—into jeopardy. It was a trick. And it was a Harrowhark Nonagesimus trick, which meant it was going to be atrociously nasty—

Gideon said, "Okay. Name your price."

"I want you downstairs at the muster meeting."

She didn't bother to hide her amazement. "What are you announcing, Harrow?"

The Reverend Daughter remained smileless. "Wouldn't you like to know."

There was a long moment. Gideon let a long breath escape through her teeth, and with a heroic effort, she dropped the paper on the ground and backed away. "Nah," she said, and was interested to see a tiny beetling of the Lady's black eyebrows. "I'll go my own way. I'm not going down into Drearburh for you. Hell, I'm not going down into Drearburh if you get my mother's skeleton to come do a jig for me."

Harrow bunched her gloved hands into fists and lost her composure. "For God's sake, Griddle! This is the perfect offer! I am giving you everything you've ever asked for—everything you've whined for so incessantly, without you even needing to have the grace or understanding to know why you couldn't have it! You threaten my House, you disrespect my retainers, you lie and cheat and sneak and steal—you know full well what you've done, and you know that you are a *disgusting* little *cuckoo*!"

"I hate it when you act like a butt-touched nun," said Gideon, who was only honestly sorry for one of the things in that lineup.

"Fine," snarled Harrowhark, now in every appearance of a fine temper. She was struggling out of her long, ornate robes, the human rib cage she wore clasped around her long torso shining whitely against the black. Crux cried out in dismay as she began to detach the little silver snaps that held it to her chest, but she silenced him with a curt gesture as she took it off. Gideon knew what she was doing. A great wave of commingled pity and disgust moved through her as she watched Harrow take off her bone bracelets, the teeth she kept at her neck, the little bone studs in her ears. All these she dumped in Crux's arms, stalking back to the shuttlefield and presenting herself like an emptied quiver. Just in gloves and boots and shirt and trousers, with her cropped black head and her face pinched with wrath, she seemed like what she really was: a desperate girl younger than Gideon, and rather small and feeble.

"Look, Nonagesimus," said Gideon, thoroughly unbalanced and now actually embarrassed, "cut the bull. Don't do—whatever you're about to do. Let me go."

"You don't get to turn and leave quite so easily, Nav," said Harrowhark, with palpable chill.

"You want your ass kicked by way of goodbye?"

"Shut up," said the Lady of the Ninth, and, horrifyingly: "I'll alter the terms. A fair fight and—"

"—and I leave scot free? I'm not that stupid—"

"No. A fair fight and you can go *with the commission*," said Harrow. "If I win, you come to the muster, and you leave afterward—*with the commission*. If I lose, you leave now—*with the commission*." She snatched the paper from the ground, pulled a fountain pen from her pocket, and slid it between her lips to stab it deeply into her cheek. It came out thick with blood—one of her party tricks, Gideon thought numbly—and signed: *Pelleamena Novenarius, Reverend Mother of the Locked Tomb, Lady of Drearburh, Ruler of the Ninth House.*

Gideon said, feeling idiotic: "That's your mother's signature."

"I'm not going to sign as me, you utter moron, that would give the whole game away," said Harrow. This close, Gideon could see the red starbursts at the corners of her eyes, the pink smears of someone who hadn't slept all night. She held out the commission and Gideon snatched it with shameless hunger, folding it up and shoving it down her shirt and into her bandeau. Harrow didn't even smirk. "Agree to duel me, Nav, in front of my marshal and guard. A fair fight."

Above all else Harrowhark was a skeleton-maker, and in her rage and pride she was offering an unfair fight instead. The thoroughbred Ninth adept had unmanned herself by starting a fight with no body to raise and not even a bone button to help her. Gideon had seen Harrow in this mood only once before, and had thought she would probably never see her in this mood again. Only a complete asshole would agree to such a duel, and Harrowhark knew it. It would take a dyed-in-the-wool douchebag. It would be an embarrassing act of cruelty.

"If I lose, I go to your meeting and leave with the commission," said Gideon.

"Yes."

"If I win, I go with the commission now," said Gideon.

Blood flecked Harrow's lips. "Yes."

Overhead, a roar of displaced air. A searchlight flickered over the drillshaft as the shuttle, finally making its descent, approached the wound in the planet's mantle. Gideon checked her clock. Two minutes. Without a moment's hesitation, she patted the Reverend Daughter down: arms, midsection, legs, a quick clutch around the boots. Crux cried out again in disgust and dismay at the sight. Harrow said nothing, which was more contemptuous than anything she *could* have said. But you didn't get anywhere through softness. The House was hard as iron. You smashed iron where it was weak.

"You all heard her," she said to Crux, to Aiglamene. Crux stared back at her with the hate of an exploding star: the empty hate of pressure pulled inward, a deforming, light-devouring resentment. Aiglamene refused to meet her gaze. That sucked, but fine. Gideon started digging around in her pack for her gloves. "You heard her. You witnessed. I'm going either way, and she offered the terms. Fair fight. You swear by your mother it's a fair fight?"

"How *dare* you, Nav—"

"By your mother. And to the floor."

"I swear by my mother. I have nothing on me. To the floor," snapped Harrow, breath coming in staccato pants of anger. As Gideon hastily slipped on her polymer mitts, flipping the thick clasps shut at the wrists, her smile twisted. "My God, Griddle, you're not even wearing leather. I'm hardly that good."

They stepped away from each other, Aiglamene finally raised her voice over the growing noise of the shuttle: "Gideon Nav, take back your honour and give your lady a weapon."

Gideon couldn't help herself: "Are you asking me to . . . *throw her a bone?*"

"*Nav!*"

"I gave her my whole life," said Gideon, and unsheathed her blade.

The sword was really just a gesture. What ought to have happened was that Gideon raised a booted foot and knocked Harrow ass-over-tits, hard enough to prevent the Lady of the Ninth embarrassing herself by getting up over and over and over. A booted foot on Harrow's stomach and it would have all been done. She would have sat on Harrow if she'd needed to. No one in the Ninth House understood what cruelty was, not really, none of them but the Reverend Daughter; none of them understood brutality. The knowledge had been dried out of them, evaporated by the dark that pooled at the bottom of Drearburh's endless catacombs. Aiglamene or Crux would have had to call it a fair fight won, and Gideon would have walked away a nearly-free woman.

What happened was that Harrowhark peeled off her gloves. Her hands were wrecked. The fingers were riddled with dirt and oozing cuts, and grit stuck in the wounds and beneath the messed-up nails. She dropped the gloves and wiggled her fingers in Gideon's direction, and Gideon had a split second to realise that it was drillshaft grit, and that she was absolutely boned in all directions.

She charged. It was too late. Next to the drifts of dirt and stone that she had carefully kicked apart, skeletons burst out of the hard earth where they had been hastily interred. Hands erupted from little pockets in the ground, perfect, four-fingered and thumbed; Gideon, stupid with assumption, kicked them off and careened sideways. She ran. It didn't matter: every five feet—every five goddamned feet—bones burst from the ground, grasping her boots, her ankles, her trousers. She staggered away, desperate to find the limits of the field: there were none. The floor of the drillshaft was erupting in fingers and wrists, waving gently, as though buffeted by the wind.

Gideon looked at Harrow. Harrow was breaking out in blood sweat, and her returned stare was calm and cold and assured.

She plunged back toward the Lady of Drearburh with an incoherent yell, smashing carpals and metacarpals to bits as she ran, but it didn't matter. From as little as a buried femur, a hidden tibia, skeletons formed for Harrow in perfect wholeness, and as Gideon neared their mistress a tidal wave of reanimated bones crested down on her. Her booted foot knocked Harrow into the arms of two of her creations, who carted her easily out of harm's way. Harrowhark's unperturbed gaze disappeared behind a blur of fleshless men, of femur and tibia and supernaturally quick grasp. Gideon used her sword like a lever, showering herself in chips of bone and cartilage and trying to make each cut count, but there were too many of them. There were just so many. Replacements rose even as she pulverized them into rains of bone. More and more cannonballed her down to the ground, no matter in what direction she lurched, from the fruits of the morbid garden Harrow had sowed.

The roar of the shuttle drowned out the clattering of bones and the blood in her ears as she was grabbed by dozens of hands. Harrowhark's talent had always been in scale, in making a fully realised construct from as little as an arm bone or a pelvis, able to make an army of them from what anyone else would need for one, and in some far-off way Gideon had always known that this would be how she went: gangbanged to death by skeletons. The melee melted away to admit a booted foot that knocked her down. The bone men held her to the earth as she reared up, spitting and bleeding, to find Harrow: tucked between her grinning minions, pensive, serene. Harrowhark kicked Gideon in the face.

For a couple of seconds everything was red and black and white. Gideon's head lolled to the side as she coughed out a tooth, choking, thrashing to rise. The boot pressed itself to her throat, then down and down and down, forcing her back into the hard grit floor. The shuttle's descent whipped up a storm of stinging dust, sending some of the skeletons flying. Harrow discarded them and they rattled into still, anatomical piles.

"It's pathetic, Griddle," said the Lady of the Ninth. Bones were shedding from her minions now after the initial adrenaline rush: peeling off and falling inert to earth, an arm there, a jawbone here, as they wobbled out of shape. She'd pushed herself very hard. Radiating out from them was a circle of burst pockets in the hard ground, like tiny exploded mines. She stood among her holes with a hot, bloody face and trickling nosebleed, and indifferently wiped her face with her forearm.

"It's pathetic," she repeated, slightly thick with blood. "I turn up the volume. I put on a show. You feel bad. You make it so easy. I got more hot and bothered digging all night."

"You dug," wheezed Gideon, rather muffled with grit and dust, "all night."

"Of course. This floor's hard as hell, and there's a lot to cover."

"You *insane creep*," said Gideon.

"Call it, Crux," ordered Harrowhark.

It was with poorly hidden glee that her marshal called out, "A fair fight. The foe is floored. A win for the Lady Nonagesimus."

The Lady Nonagesimus turned back to her two retainers and raised her arms up for her discarded robe to be slipped back around her shoulders. She coughed a small knot of blood up into the dirt and waved Crux off as he hovered about her. Gideon lifted her head, then let it fall back hard on the grit floor, dazed and cold. Aiglamene was looking at her now with an expression she couldn't parse. Sympathy? Disappointment? Guilt?

The shuttle connected its docking feet to the ground, crunching hard into the floor. Gideon looked at it—its gleaming sides, its steaming engine vents—and tried to pull herself up on her elbows. She couldn't; she was too winded still. She couldn't even raise a shaking middle finger to the victor: she just kept looking at the shuttle, and her suitcase, and her sword.

"Buck up, Griddle," Harrowhark was saying. She spat another clot out on the ground, close to Gideon's head. "Captain, go and tell the pilot to sit and wait: he'll get paid for his time."

"What if he asks after his passenger, my lady?" God bless Aiglamene.

"She's been delayed. Tell him he'll stand by on my grace for an hour, with apologies. My parents have been waiting long enough, and this took somewhat longer than I thought it would. Marshal, get her down to the sanctuary—"

GIDEON WILLED HERSELF TO pass out as Crux's cold, bony fingers closed around one of her ankles. It nearly worked. She woke up a few times to blink at the monotonous light that illuminated the lift down to the bottom of the main shaft, and stayed awake when the marshal dragged her like a sack of rotten goods across the bottom of the tier. She felt nothing: not pain, not anger, not disappointment, just a curious sense of wonder and disconnect as she was hauled bodily through the doors of Drearburh. She stirred to life for one last escape attempt, but when he saw her scrabbling at the threadbare carpets on the slick dark floor Crux kicked her in the head. Then she did pass out for a little while, for real, only waking up when she was heaped onto a forward pew. The pew was so cold her skin stuck to it, and each breath was like needles in the lung.

She came to, freezing, to the sound of the prayers. There was no spoken invocation in the Ninth service. There was only the clatter of bones—knucklebones, all threaded on woven cords, notched and worn—worked by nuns whose old fingers could pray on them so swiftly that the service became a murmurous rattle. It was a long, narrow hall, and she had been dumped right at the front of it. It was very dark: a rail of gas-discharged light ran all around the aisles, but it always lit like it didn't like the idea and glowed dismally. The arches overhead had been dusted with bioluminescent powders that sometimes trickled down as pale green glitter into the nave, and in all the radiating chapels sat speechless skeletons, still dusty from the

35

farming. Squinting blearily over her shoulder, she saw that most of the sanctum was skeletons. It was a skeleton party. There was room in this deep, long channel of a church for a thousand, and it was half full of skeletons and only very pockmarked with people.

The people mostly sat in the transept, veiled nuns and solitaires, shaven heads and cropped, the weary and scant inhabitants of the Ninth House. Mostly priests of the Locked Tomb, now; there hadn't been soldiers or military friars since she was very young. The only member left of that order was Aiglamene, who'd left her leg and any hope of getting the hell out of here on some far-off front line. The clatter in the transept was occasionally interrupted by a wet, racking cough or the haggard clearing of somebody's throat.

In the apse was a long bench, and there sat the last handful of the nobles of the House of the Ninth: Reverend Daughter Harrowhark, sitting modestly to the side, face dusted with a handful of luminescent powder that had stuck to the blood trails coming out her nose; her ghastly great-aunts; and her parents, the Lord and Lady of the House, the Reverend Father and the Reverend Mother. The latter two had pride of place, before the altar, side-on to the congregation. Crux had the honour of sitting on a chair in one of the dank chevets amid a sea of candles, half of them already out. Next to him sat the only house cavalier, Ortus, a wide and sad Ninth youngster of thirty-five, and next to Ortus sat his lady mother, an absolutely standard Ninth crone who kept fussing at his ear with a handkerchief.

Gideon blinked so that her vision would stop wobbling and focused on the apse. They hadn't managed to cozen her inside Drearburh for a good two years, and she hadn't seen the hideous great-aunts nor the Lord and Lady for a while. Blessed Sister Lachrimorta and Blessed Sister Aisamorta were unaltered. They were still tiny, their faces still tight, grey-painted dribbles, and as the Ninth was free from miracles, they were still blind. They had black bands tied over their faces with white, staring eyes painted on the front. Each preferred to pray two sets of beads, one string in each shrivelled hand, so they sat there clicking a four-part percussion with their suspiciously agile fingers.

Ortus hadn't changed either. He was still lumpy and sad. Being the primary cavalier to the House of the Ninth had not for eras been a title of any renown. Cavaliers in other Houses might be revered and noble men and women of long genealogy or particular talent, frequent heroes of Gideon's less prurient magazines, but in the Ninth everyone knew you were chosen for how many bones you could hump around. Ortus was basically a morbid donkey. His father—cavalier to Harrow's father—had been an enormous, stony man of some gravity and devotion, with a sword and two huge panniers of fibulae, but Ortus wasn't made in his mould. Coupling him to Harrow had been rather like yoking a doughnut to a cobra. Aiglamene had probably focused her frustrations on Gideon because Ortus was such a drip. He was a sensitive, awful young man, and his mother was obsessed with him; each time he caught a cold he was swaddled and made to lie still until he got bedsores.

The Lord and Lady she looked at too, though she honestly didn't want to. Lady Pelleamena and Lord Priamhark sat side by side, one gloved hand placed on a knee, the other joined to their partner's as they prayed simultaneously on a string of ornate bones. Black cloth swathed them toe to neck, and their faces were mostly obscured by dark hoods: Gideon could see their pale, waxy profiles, streaked with luminescent powder, the mark of Harrow's handprint still visible on both. Their eyes were closed. Pelleamena's face was still frozen and fine as it had been the last time Gideon had seen her, the dark wings of her brows unsilvered, the thin fretwork of lines next to each eye uncrowded by new. Priam's jaw was still firm, his shoulder unstooped, his brow clear and unlined. They were utterly unchanged; less changed, even, than the shitty great-aunts. This was because they'd both been dead for years.

Their mummified faces did not yield to time because—as Gideon knew, and the marshal, and the captain of the guard, and nobody else in the universe—Harrowhark had frozen them forever. Ever the obsessive and secretive scholar, she had derived at great cost some forgotten way of preserving and puppeting the bodies. She had found a nasty, forbidden little book in the great Ninth repositories of nasty, forbidden little books, and all the Houses would have had a collective aneurysm if they knew she'd even read it. She hadn't executed it very well—her parents were fine from the shoulders up, but from the shoulders down they were bad—though she had, admittedly, been ten.

Gideon had been eleven when the Lord and Lady of the House of the Ninth had slipped into death in sudden, awful secret. It was such a huge bag of ass how it had happened: what she'd found, what she'd seen. She hadn't been sad. If she'd been stuck being Harrow's parents she would have done the same years ago.

"Listen," said the Reverend Daughter of the Ninth, rising to stand.

The enthroned Lord and Lady should have taken charge of the sacred ritual, but they couldn't, because they were mega-dead. Harrowhark had handily gotten around this by giving them a vow of silence. Every year she added to their penitents' vows—of fasting, of daily contemplation, of seclusion—so blandly and barefacedly that it seemed inevitable that someone would eventually say *hang on a minute, this sounds like . . . A LOAD OF HOT GARBAGE,* and she'd be found out. But she never was. Crux covered for her, and so did Aiglamene, and the Lord's cavalier had helpfully decided to die the day that Priam died. And so Gideon covered too, hating every moment, saving up this last secret in the hopes that with it she could extort her freedom.

All prayer beads stopped clacking. The hands of Harrow's parents stilled unnaturally in unison. Gideon slung her arms around the back of her pew and kicked one foot up atop the other, wishing her head would stop ringing.

"The noble House of the Ninth has called you here today," said Harrowhark, "because we have been given a gift of enormous import. Our sacred Emperor—the Necrolord Prime, the King of the Nine Renewals, our Resurrector—has sent us summons."

That got asses in seats. The skeletons remained perfectly still and attentive, but a querulous excitement arose from the assorted Ninth congregation. There were soft cries of joy. There were exclamations of praise and thankfulness. The letter could have been a drawing of a butt and they would have been lining up thrice to kiss the edge of the paper.

"I will share this letter with you," said Harrowhark, "because nobody loves their people, their sacred brothers and sacred sisters, as the Ninth House loves her people—her devotees and her priests, her children and her faithful." (Gideon thought Harrow was slathering it on pretty thick.) "If the Reverend Mother will permit her daughter to read?"

Like she'd say no with Harrow's hands on her strings. With a pallid smile, Pelleamena gently inclined her head in a way she never had in life: alive, she had been as chill and remote as ice at the bottom of a cave. "With my gracious mother's permission," said Harrow, and began to read:

"ADDRESSING THE HOUSE OF THE NINTH, ITS REVEREND LADY PELLEAMENA HIGHT NOVENARIUS AND ITS REVEREND LORD PRIAM HIGHT NONIUSVIANUS:

"Salutations to the House of the Ninth, and blessings upon its tombs, its peaceful dead, and its manifold mysteries.

"His Celestial Kindliness, the First Reborn, begs this house to honour its love for the Creator, as set in the contract of tenderness made on the day of the Resurrection, and humbly asks for the first fruits of your household . . .

("My name is listed here," said Harrowhark, simpering modestly, then with less enthusiasm: "—and Ortus's.")

"For in need now are the Emperor's Hands, the most blessed and beloved of the King Undying, the faithful and the everlasting! The Emperor calls now for postulants to the position of Lyctor, heirs to the eight stalwarts who have served these ten thousand years: as many of them now lie waiting for the rivers to rise on the day they wake to their King, those lonely Guard remaining petition for their numbers to be renewed and their Lord above Lords to find eight new liegemen.

"To this end we beg the first of your House and their cavalier to kneel in glory and attend the finest study, that of being the Emperor's bones and joints, his fists and gestures . . .

"Eight we hope will meditate and ascend to the Emperor in glory

*in the temple of the First House, eight new Lyctors joined with their
cavaliers; and if the Necrolord Highest blesses but does not take, they
shall return home in full honour, with trump and timbrel.*

"There is no dutiful gift so perfect, nor so lovely in his eyes."

Harrowhark lowered the paper to a long silence; a real silence,
without even the hint of a prayer knuckle clacking or a skeleton's
jaw falling off. The Ninth seemed completely taken aback. There was
a wheezing squeal from one of the pews in the transept behind
Gideon as one of the faithful decided to go the whole hog and have
a heart attack, and this distracted everyone. The nuns tried their
best, but a few minutes later it was confirmed that one of the her-
mits had died of shock, and everyone around him celebrated his sacred good fortune. Gideon failed to hide a snicker as Harrowhark
sighed, obviously calculating inside her head what this did to the
current Ninth census.

"I won't!"

A second hand disturbed the community tomb as Ortus's mother
stood, finger trembling, her other arm draped around her son's shoulders. He looked completely affrighted. She looked as though she
were about to follow the faithful departed to an untimely grave, face
frozen beneath her alabaster base paint, black skull paint slipping
with sweat.

"My son—my son," she cried out, shrill and cracked; "my first-
born sweet! His father's endowment! My only joy!"

"Sister Glaurica, please," said Harrow, looking bored.

Ortus's mother had wrapped both arms around him now, and
was weeping fully into his shoulder. Her own shook with very real
fear and grief. He looked wetly depressed. She was saying, between
sobs: "I gave you my husband—Lord Noniusvianus, I gave you my
spouse—Lord Noniusvianus, do *you* demand my son of me? Do you
demand my son? Surely not! Surely not now!"

"You forget yourself, Glaurica," Crux snapped.

"I know the things that befall cavaliers, my lord, I know his fate!"

"Sister Glaurica," Harrowhark said, "be calm."

"He is young," quavered Ortus's mother, half-pulling him into the safety of the chevet when she realised Lord Noniusvianus would not intercede. "He is young, he is not robust."

"Some would say otherwise," said Harrowhark, sotto voce.

But Ortus said, with his big, sombre eyes and his squashed, disheartened voice: "I do fear death, my Lady Harrowhark."

"A cavalier should welcome death," said Aiglamene, affronted.

"Your father welcomed death unflinching," said Crux.

At this tender piece of sympathy, his mother burst into tears. The congregation muttered, mostly reproachful, and Gideon started to perk up. It wasn't quite the worst day of her life now. This was some A-grade entertainment. Ortus, not bothering to disentangle himself from his sobbing parent, was mumbling that he would make sure she was provided for; the heinous great-aunts had returned to prayer and were crooning a wordless hymn; Crux was loudly abusing Ortus's mother; and Harrowhark stood in this sea, mute and contemptuous as a monument.

"—leave and pray for guidance, or I'll have you, I'll take you off the sanctuary," Crux was saying.

"—I gave this house everything; I paid the highest price—"

"—what comes of Mortus marrying an immigrant Eighth, you shameful hag—"

Gideon was grinning so hugely that her split lips recommenced bleeding. Amid the massed heads of the uncaring dead and the disturbed devout, Harrowhark's eyes found hers, and that disdainful mask slipped in its blankness; her lips thinned. The people clamoured. Gideon winked.

"Enough," snapped the Reverend Daughter, voice like a knife's edge. "Let us pray."

Silence sank over the congregation, like the slowly falling flakes of luminescent dust. The sobbing of Ortus's mother hushed into silent, shuddering tears, buried in her son's chest as he put his doughy arm around her. He was crying soundlessly into her hair. The hymn of the nasty great-aunts ended on a high and tremulous note, never relieved, wasting away in midair; Harrow bowed her head and her parents did too, simultaneous in obedience. The great-aunts nodded their heads to their chests; Aiglamene and Crux followed suit. Gideon stared up at the ceiling and recrossed her ankles over each other, blinked bits of luminescent grit from her eyes.

"*I pray the tomb is shut forever,*" recited Harrowhark, with the curious fervidity she always showed in prayer. "*I pray the rock is never rolled away. I pray that which was buried remains buried, insensate, in perpetual rest with closed eye and stilled brain. I pray it lives, I pray it sleeps . . . I pray for the needs of the Emperor All-Giving, the Undying King, his Virtues and his men. I pray for the Second House, the Third, the Fourth, the Fifth; the Sixth, Seventh, and Eighth. I pray for the Ninth House, and I pray for it to be fruitful. I pray for the soldiers and adepts far from home, and all those parts of the Empire that live in unrest and disquiet.* Let it be so."

They all prayed to let it be so, with much rattling of bones. Gideon had not prayed for a very long time. She looked over the bald, gleaming skulls of the assembled skeletons and the short-haired heads of the faithful Ninth, and wondered what she'd do first when she left for Trentham. The sobs of Ortus's unfortunate mother interrupted the clatter and her less-than-realistic thoughts of doing chin-ups in front of a dozen clapping ensigns, and she saw Harrow whispering to Crux, gesturing at mother and son, her face a painting of bloodless patience. Crux led them off the sanctuary none too gently. They passed down the centre of the nave, Crux hustling, Ortus lumbering, Ortus's mother barely able to stand in her misery. Gideon gave the unfortunate cavalier a thumbs-up as they passed: Ortus returned a brief and watery smile.

Muster broke up after that. Most of the congregation stayed to keep praying at their good fortune, knowing that the Secundarius Bell would be ringing in a scant hour anyway. Gideon would have vaulted up to leave and sprint back to her shuttle first thing, but the skeletons flooded out in neat, serried ranks down the centre of the nave, two abreast, blocking all other progress in their readiness to get back to their snow leeks and the heat lamps of their fields. The disgusting great-aunts removed themselves behind the parcloses to the claustrophobic family chapel off to one side, and Harrowhark ordered her parents' complaisant mummies out of sight to wherever she usually hid them. Back in their lavish household cell, probably, and to bar the door after. Gideon was massaging sprains from her fingers as her sword-master came seesawing down the aisle.

"She lies," said Gideon absently, by way of greeting. "If you hadn't noticed. She never keeps her promises. Not a one."

Aiglamene did not answer. Gideon didn't expect her to. She just stood there, not yet meeting her student's gaze, one liver-spotted hand clutched tight to the grip of her sword. Eventually, she said gruffly: "You have always suffered from a want of duty, Nav. You can't argue that. You couldn't spell *obligation* if I shoved the letters up your ass."

"I gotta say, I don't think that would help," said Gideon. "God, I'm glad you didn't teach me my spelling."

"A soldier's best quality is her sense of allegiance. Of loyalty. Nothing else survives."

"I know," said Gideon, and, experimenting, rose from the pew. She was standing fine, but her ribs ached; one was probably cracked. Her butt hurt from being dragged. She was going to be swollen with bruises before nightfall, and she needed to have a tooth put back in—not by one of the nuns, though, never again. The Cohort would have bone magicians aplenty. "I know. It's fine. Don't get me wrong, Captain. Where I'm going, I promise to piss fidelity all the livelong day. I have lots of fealty in me. I fealt the Emperor with every bone in my body. I fealt *hard*."

"You wouldn't know fealty if it—"

"Don't hypothetically shove stuff up my butt again," said Gideon, "it never does any good."

The lopsided old woman took a scabbard off her back and wearily handed it over. It was Gideon's. Her sword had been sheathed safely inside it. Aiglamene tossed her the abandoned suitcase, to boot. This would be the closest to an apology she would get. The woman would never touch her, and she would never give her a word that had no edges. But this was nearly tender for the captain of the guard, and Gideon would take it and run.

Determined footsteps sounded down the centre aisle, alongside the sound of ancient lace rustling over slick obsidian. Gideon's gut tightened, but she said: "How the hell are you going to get out of this one, Nonagesimus?"

"I'm not," said Harrow, surprising her. The Reverend Daughter's sharp-angled, foxy chin was thrust out, and she still had a thick rime of blood circling each nostril, but with her burning black eyes she looked exalted as a bad bone saint. "I'm going. This is my chance for intercession. You couldn't comprehend."

"I can't, but I also couldn't care less," said Gideon.

"We all get our chances, Nav. You got yours."

Gideon wanted to punch her lights out, but she said instead, with forced jollity: "By the way, I worked out your nasty little trick, jackass."

Aiglamene did not cuff her for this, which was also some sort of apology; she just jabbed a warning finger in her direction. Harrow cocked her chin up in genuine surprise, hood falling away from her dark, short-cropped head. "Did you?" she drawled. "Really?"

"Your mother's signature on the commission. The sting in the tail. If I come clean," she said, "that renders the signature null and void, doesn't it? It buys my silence. Well played. I'll have to keep my mouth shut when I hand that one over, and you know it."

Harrowhark cocked her head the other way, lightly.

"I hadn't even thought of that," she said. "I thought you meant the shuttle."

Alarm bells rang in Gideon's head, like the First and Second Peal all mixed together. She could feel the heat drain from her face, and she was already backing out of the pew, into the aisle, wheeling away. Harrowhark's face was a painted study of innocence, of perfect unconcern. At the expression on Gideon's, Aiglamene had put a hand on her sword, moving herself between the two with a warning stump of the leg.

Gideon said, with difficulty: "*What—about—the shuttle?*"

"Oh, Ortus and his mother stole it," said Harrowhark. "They must be gone already. She still has family back on the Eighth, and she thinks they'll take them in." At her expression, Harrow laughed: "You make it so easy, Griddle. You always do."

* * *

Gideon had never confronted a broken heart before. She had never gotten far enough to have her heart broken. She knelt on the landing field, knees in the grit, arms clutched around herself. There was nothing left but blown-out, curly patterns in the pebbles where the shuttle had passed. A great dullness had sunk over her; a deep coldness, a thick stolidity. When her heart beat in her chest it was with a huge, steady grief. Every pulse seemed to be the space between insensibility and knives. For some moments she was awake, and she was filled with a slow-burning mine fire, the kind that never went out and crumbled everything from the inside; for all the other moments, it was as though she had gone somewhere else.

Behind her stood the Lady of the Ninth House, watching her with no satisfaction.

"I got wind of your plan only last week," she admitted.

Gideon said nothing.

"A week before," Harrow continued. "I wouldn't have known at all, if I hadn't gotten the summons. You'd done everything right. They said I could put my reply on the shuttle I had previously scheduled, if I wanted to write in paper. I will give you your due: there was no way you could have accounted for that. I could have spoiled it before, but I wanted to wait until now to do anything. I wanted to wait . . . for the very moment when you thought you'd gotten away . . . to take it from you."

Gideon could only manage, "Why?"

The girl's expression was the same as it was on the day that Gideon had found her parents, dangling from the roof of their cell. It was blank and white and still.

"Because I completely fucking hate you," said Harrowhark, "no offence."

4

It would have been neater, perhaps, if all of Gideon's disappointments and woes from birth downward had used that moment as a catalyst: if, filled with a new and fiery determination, she had equipped herself down there in the dark with fresh ambition to become free. She didn't. She got the depression. She lay in her cell, picking at life like it was a meal she didn't want to eat. She didn't touch her sword. She didn't go and jog around the planter fields and dream of what days looked like to Cohort recruits. She stole a crate of the nutrient paste they put in the gruels and soups fed to the Ninth faithful and squirted them in her mouth when she got hungry, listlessly leafing through magazines or lying back on her bed, crunching her body into sit-ups to make time go away. Crux had snapped the security cuff back on her ankle and she rattled it when she moved, often not bothering to turn on the lights, clinking around in the dark.

A week's grace was all she got. The Reverend Daughter turned up, as she *always goddamn did*, standing outside the locked door of her cell. Gideon knew she was there because the shadows in front of the little peephole changed, and because it would be nobody else. By way of hello she said, "Fuck you," and switched to push-ups.

"Stop sulking, Griddle."

"Go choke on a dick."

"I have work for you," said Harrowhark.

Gideon let herself rest on the apex extension of her arms, staring down sightlessly at the cold floor, the sweat frosting on her back.

Her rib still hurt when she breathed, and the cuff was heavy on her ankle, and one of the nuns had jammed her tooth back in too hard and it was like the woe of the Emperor every time she sneezed. "Nonagesimus," she said slowly, "the only job I'd do for you would be if you wanted someone to hold the sword as you fell on it. The only job I'd do for you would be if you wanted your ass kicked so hard, the Locked Tomb opened and a parade came out to sing, 'Lo! A destructed ass.' The only job I'd do would be if you wanted me to spot you while you backflipped off the top tier into Drearburh."

"That's three jobs," said Harrowhark.

"Die in a fire, Nonagesimus."

There was a rustle from outside; the light scrape of a pin being pulled from a stud before it was pushed through the mesh of the peephole. Belatedly, Gideon scrambled up to toss it back, as one did a grenade; but the bead of Harrow's earring had landed in her cell, and from that tiny mote of bone sprang humerus, radius, and ulna. A skeletal hand groped blindly at the key in the lock and turned it even as Gideon swung her boot around to smash it into splintery bits. It crumbled away to dust, including the stud. Harrowhark Nonagesimus swung open the door, haloed faintly in the electric lights from the tier, her acerbic little face as welcome as a knee to the groin.

"If you want to do something interesting, come with me," she commanded. "If you want to wallow in your shockingly vast reserves of self-pity, cut your throat and save me the food bill."

"Oh damn! Then can I join your old man and lady in the puppet show?"

"How the world would suffer without your wit," said Harrowhark blandly. "Get your robe. We're going down to the catacomb."

It was almost gratifying, Gideon reflected, struggling with the black folds of her church gown, that the heir to the House of the Ninth refused to walk with her on the inside of the tier: she walked close to the wall instead, keeping pace half a step behind Gideon, watching for Gideon's hands and Gideon's sword. Almost gratifying, but not quite. Harrow could make even overweening caution offensive. After long days with just her little reading lamp, Gideon's eyes stung from the lukewarm light of the Ninth drillshaft: she blinked myopically as the lift rattled them down to the doors of Drearburh.

"We're not going into the inner sanctuary, you recreant," Harrow said as Gideon balked. "We're going to the monument. Come."

The lifts that went down into the foetid bowels of Drearburh were death traps. The ones they entered now, down to the crypts, were especially bad. This one was an open platform of oxygen-addled, creaking metal, tucked behind an iron door that Harrow opened with a tiny chipkey from around her neck. As they descended, the air that rushed up to meet them was so cold that it made Gideon's eyes water; she pulled the hood of her cloak down over her head and shoved her hands up its sleeves. The central buried mechanism that made their pit on this planet possible sang its low, whining song, filling the elevator shaft, dying away as they went deeper and deeper into the rock. It was profoundly dark.

Stark, strong light swamped their landing, and they walked out into the labyrinth of cages filled with whirring generators that nobody knew how to work. The machines sat alone in their carved-out, chilly niches, garlanded with black crepe from Ninth devotees long dead, their barred housings keeping the two at arm's length as they passed. The cave narrowed into a passageway and the passageway terminated in a pitted door: Harrow pushed this open and led the way into a long, oblong chamber of bone-choked niches and bad copies of funerary masks, of wrapped bundles and seriously ancient grave goods.

At one niche, Aiglamene kneeled, having set herself the task of ransacking as many of the wrapped bundles as she could. Instead of a Ninth robe she wore a thick wool jacket and gloves, which gave her the appearance of a marshmallow pierced with four toothpicks of differing lengths. She was wearing a particularly po-faced, battle-weary expression as she picked through around a hundred swords in varying stages of death; next to her was a basket of daggers and a handful of knuckle knives. Some were rusted to hell, some were halfway rusted to hell. She was examining a sword and gloomily rubbing at a bit of built-up plaque on the blade.

"This plan is doomed," she said to them, without looking up.

"Success, Captain?" said Harrowhark.

"They're all archaeology, my lady."

"Unfortunate. What was Ortus preferring, these days?"

"Speaking freely," said Aiglamene, "Ortus preferred his mother and a book of sad poems. His father trained him to fight sword-and-buckler, but after his death—" She gave a somewhat creaking shrug. "He was a damned poor swordsman at his peak. He was not his father's son. *I* would have trained him sword-and-powder, but he said he had the catarrh."

"But his sword must be good, surely."

"God no," said Aiglamene. "It was heavy oil amalgam, and it had a rubber tip. Lighter than Nav's head." ("Harsh!" said Gideon.) "No, lady; I'm looking for a blade in the style of his great-grandmother's. And a knife—or a knuckle."

"Powder," said Harrowhark decidedly, "or chain."

"A *knife*, I think, my lady," her captain said again, with more gentle deference than Gideon had known the old woman possessed. "Knife or knuckle. The knife will be impossibly difficult to adjust to as it is. You fight in a crowd. A chain in close melee will be more of a danger to you than it will to anyone else."

Gideon had long since decided that this was not a good place to be, and that the plans being hatched here were not plans she liked. She started to edge backward, toward the door, picking her path as lightly as possible. Suddenly there was Harrow, squeezing herself between two pillars and draping her arms above her head: long folds of black robe shook down from her arms, making her look like a road-blocking bat. "Oh, Nav, no," she said calmly. "Not when you owe me."

"*Owe* you—"

"Why, of course," said Harrowhark. "It was your shuttle my cavalier ran off in."

Gideon's fist jacked out toward Harrow's pointy nose. Less by design than accident, the other girl stumbled out of the way, half-tripping, dusting herself off and narrowing her eyes as she circled around the pillar. "If you're going to start that again," she said, "here."

She reached down and hauled up one of the discarded blades. It was at least mildly hilarious to see Harrow have to heave with all the might of her, like, three muscles. Gideon took it while the necromancer rubbed fretfully at her wrists. "Try that," she said.

Gideon unsheathed and examined the sword. Long, black pieces of crooked metal formed a decaying basket hilt. A terrifically worn black pommel seal depicted the Tomb wrapped in chains, the sign of the Ninth. The blade itself was notched and cracked. "Only way this kills someone is with lockjaw," she said. "How are you going to get Ortus back, anyway?"

Did Harrow look momentarily troubled? "We're not."

"Aiglamene's too old for this."

"And that is why *you*, Griddle," said the Lady, "are to act as cavalier primary of the House of the Ninth. You will accompany me to the First House as I study to become a Lyctor. You'll be my personal guard and companion, dutiful and loyal, and uphold the sacred name of this House and its people."

Once Gideon had stopped laughing, leaning against the icy pillar and beating on it with her fist, she had to breathe long and hard in order to not crack up again. The beleaguered grimace on Aiglamene's hard-carved face had deepened into an outright sense of siege. "Whoo," she managed, scrubbing away tears of mirth. "Oh damn. Give me a moment. Okay—*like hell I will,* Nonagesimus."

Harrow ducked out from behind her pillar and she walked toward Gideon, hands still clasped together. Her face held the beatific, fire-white expression she'd had the day she told Gideon she was going off-planet: an unwavering resolve almost like joy. She stopped in front of the other girl and looked up at her, shaking the hood from her dark head, and she closed her eyes into slits. "Come on, Nav," she said, and her voice was alight. "This is your chance. This is your opportunity to come into glory. Follow me through this, and you can go anywhere. House cavaliers can get any Cohort position they like. Do this for me and I won't just set you free, I'll set you free with a fortune, with a commission, with anything you want."

This nettled her. "You don't own me."

"Oh, Griddle, but I *do*," said Harrowhark. "You're bound to the Locked Tomb . . . and at the end of the night, the Locked Tomb is me. The nominated Hands are to enter the First House, Nav; their names will be written in history as the new Imperial saints. Nothing like this has ever happened before, and it may never happen again. Nav, I am going to be a Lyctor."

"'Hello, I'm the woman who helped Harrowhark Nonagesimus's fascist rise to power,'" said Gideon to nobody in particular. "'Yes, the universe sucks now. I knew this going in. Also, she betrayed me afterward and now my body has been shot into the sun.'" Harrow came too close, and Gideon did what she had never done in the past: she raised the rusted sword so that its naked point was level with the other girl's forehead. The necromancer adept did not flinch, just made her black-smeared mouth a mocking moue of shock. "I—will never—trust you. Your promises mean nothing. You've got nothing to give me. I know what you'd do, given half a chance."

Harrow's dark eyes were on Gideon's, past the blade pointed at her skull. "Oh, I *have* hurt your heart," she said.

Gideon kept it absolutely level. "I boohooed for hours."

"It won't be the last time I make you weep."

Aiglamene's voice rattled out: "Put that damn thing down. I can't bear to see you hold it with that grip." And, shocking Gideon: "Consider this offer, Nav."

Gideon peered around Harrow's shoulder, letting the blade drop, trashing the miserable thing scabbardless in the nearest niche. "Captain, *please* don't be a proponent of this horseshit idea."

"It's the best idea we have. Nav," said her teacher, "our Lady is going off-planet. That's the long and short of it. You can stay here—in the House you hate—or go attain your liberty—in service to the House you hate. This is your one chance to leave, and to gain your freedom cleanly."

Harrowhark opened her mouth to say something, but surprising Gideon further, Aiglamene silenced her with a gesture. The crappy swords were set aside with care, and the old woman pulled her bockety leg out from underneath her and leant the good one against the catacomb wall, pushing hard to stand with a clank of mail and bone disease. "You care nothing for the Ninth. That's fine. This is your chance to prove *yourself*."

"I'm not helping Nonagesimus become a Lyctor. She'll make me into boots."

"I have condemned your escapes," said Aiglamene. "They were graceless and feeble. But." She turned to the other girl. "With all due respect, you've dealt her too ill, my lady. I hate this idea. If I were ten years younger I would beg you to condescend to take me. But you won't vouchsafe her, and so I must."

"Must you?" said Harrow. There was a curious softness in her voice. Her black gaze was searching for something in the captain of her guard, and she did not seem to be finding it.

"I must," said Aiglamene. "You'll be leaving me and Crux in charge of the House. If I vouchsafe the freedom of Gideon Nav and it is not given to her, then—begging pardon for my ingratitude—it is a betrayal of myself, who is your retainer and was your mother's retainer."

Harrowhark said nothing. She wore a thin, pensive expression. Gideon wasn't fooled: this look usually betokened Harrow's brain percolating outrageous nastiness. But Gideon couldn't think straight. A horrible dark-red heat was travelling up her neck and she knew it would go right to her cheeks if she let it, so she pulled the hood up over her head and said not a word, and couldn't look at her swordmaster at all.

"If she satisfies you, you must let her go," said Aiglamene firmly.

"Of course."

"With all the gracious promises of the Ninth."

"Oh, if she pulls this off she can have whatever she likes," said Harrowhark easily—way too easily. "She'll have glory squirting out each orifice. She can do or be anything she pleases, preferably over on the other side of the galaxy from where *I* am."

"Then I thank you for your mercy and your grace, and regard the matter settled," said Aiglamene.

"How is it settled. I have patently not agreed to this shit."

Both of them ignored Gideon. "Getting back to the original problem," said the old woman, settling painfully back down among the swords and the knives, "Nav has had none of Ortus's training—not in manners, nor in general scholarship—and she was trained in the sword of heavy infantry."

"Ignore the first; her mental inadequacies can be compensated for. The second's what I'm interested in. How difficult is it for a normal swordswoman to switch from a double-handed blade to a cavalier rapier?"

"For a normal swordswoman? To reach the standard of a House cavalier primary? You'd need years. For Nav? Three months—" (here Gideon died briefly of gratification; she revived only due to the rising horror consequent of everything else) "—and she'd be up to the standard of the meanest, most behind-hand cavalier alive."

"Oh, nonsense!" said Harrow languorously. "She's a genius. With the proper motivation, Griddle could wield two swords in each hand and one in her mouth. While we were developing common sense, she studied the blade. Am I right, Griddle?"

"I haven't agreed to stone cold dick," said Gideon. "And I don't care how bad-ass cavaliers are meant to be, I hate rapiers. All that bouncing around makes me feel tired. Now, a two-hander, that's a swordsman's sword."

"I don't disagree," said her teacher, "but a House cavalier—with all her proper training—is a handsomely dangerous thing. I saw the primary cavalier of the House of the Second fight in his youth, and my God! I never forgot it."

Harrow was pacing in tiny circles now. "But she *could* get to the point where she might *believably, possibly* be mistaken for a trained cavalier of the House of the Ninth?"

"The reputation of the Ninth cavalier primary has not been what it was since the days of Matthias Nonius," said Aiglamene. "And that was a thousand years ago. Expectations are very low. Even then, we'd be bloody lucky."

Gideon pushed herself up from the pillar and cracked her knuckles, stretching her chill-stiff muscles out before her. She rolled her neck, testing her shoulders, and unwrapped her robe from around herself.

"I live for those days when everyone stands around talking about how bad I am at what I do, but it also gives me hurt feelings," she said, and took the sword she had abandoned for trash. She tested its weight in her hand, feeling what was to her an absurd lightness, and struck what she thought was a sensible stance. "How's this, Captain?"

Her teacher made a noise in her throat somewhere between disgust and desolation. "What are you *doing* with your other hand?" Gideon compensated. "No! Oh, Lord. Put that down until I formally show you how."

"The sword and the powder," said Harrowhark eagerly.

"The sword and the knuckle, my lady," said Aiglamene. "I'm dropping my expectations substantially."

Gideon said, "I still have absolutely not agreed to any of this."

The Reverend Daughter picked her way toward her over discarded swords, and stopped once she was level with the pillar that Gideon had reflexively flattened her back against. They regarded each other for long moments until the absolute chill of the monument made Gideon's teeth involuntarily chatter, and then Harrow's mouth twisted, fleetingly, indulgently. "I would have thought you would be happy that I needed you," she admitted. "That I showed you my girlish and vulnerable heart."

"Your heart is a party for five thousand nails," said Gideon.

"That's not a 'no.' Help Aiglamene find you a sword, Griddle. I'll leave the door unlocked." With that languid and imperious command, she left, leaving Gideon lolling her head back against the frigid stone of the pillar and chewing the inside of her cheek.

It was almost worse getting left alone with the sword-master. An awkward, chilly silence spread between them as the old woman grumpily picked through the pile, holding each rapier up to the light, pulling rancid strips of leather away from the grip.

"It's a bad idea, but it's a chance, you know," said Aiglamene abruptly. "Take it or leave it."

"I thought you said it was the best idea we have."

"It is—for Lady Harrowhark. You're the best swordsman that the

Ninth House has produced—maybe ever. Can't say. *I* never saw Nonius fight."

"Yeah, you would have only been what, just born," said Gideon, whose heart was hurting keenly.

"Shut your mouth or I'll shut it for you."

Swords rattled into a leather case as Aiglamene selected a couple at hand, shaking a few of the knuckle-knives in to boot. The case creaked and she creaked as she had to tip herself forward, painful with dignity, getting on her one half-good knee in order to pull herself up to stand. Gideon moved forward automatically, but one look from the woman's working eye was enough to make her pretend she'd just been getting back into her robes. Aiglamene hauled the case over her shoulder, kicking unwanted swords back into a niche, yanking the useless sword from Gideon's nerveless hand.

She paused as her fingers closed over the hilt, her haggard face caught up in her consideration, a titanic battle apparently going on somewhere deep inside her head. One side gained the upper hand, and she said gruffly: "Nav. A word of warning."

"What?"

There was something urgent in her voice: something worried, something new.

"Things are changing. I used to think we were waiting for something . . . and now I think we're just waiting to die."

Gideon's heart sagged.

"You really want me to say yes."

"Go on and say no," said her captain. "It's your choice . . . If she doesn't take you, I'll go with her and gladly. But she knows . . . and I know . . . and I think you damn well know . . . that if you don't get out now, you won't even get out in a box."

"So what happens if I agree?"

Breaking the spell, Aiglamene roughly shouldered the leather case into Gideon's arms, slapping it there before stalking back the way that Harrow had left them. "Then you hurry up. If I'm to turn you into the Ninth's cavalier, I needed to start six years ago."

5

THE SECOND LETTER THAT they received care of the Resurrecting King, the gentle Emperor, was somewhat less prolix than the first.

They were lurking in the personal Nonagesimus library, a stone-arched room packed tight with shelves of the musty and neglected books Harrowhark didn't study and the musty, less neglected books that she did. Gideon sat at a broad, sagging desk piled high with pages covered in necromantic marginalia, most of them in Harrow's cramped, impatient writing. She held the letter before her with one hand; with the other, she wearily painted her face with a piece of fibre wadding and a pot of alabaster paint, feeling absurdly young. The paint smelled acid and cold, and working the damn stuff into the creases next to her nose meant sucking globs of paint up her nostrils all day. Harrow was sprawled on a sofa spread with tattered brocade, robes abandoned, scrawny black-clad legs crossed at the ankles. In Gideon's mind she looked like an evil stick.

Gideon reread the letter, then again, twice, before checking her face in a little cracked mirror. Gorgeous. Hot. "I know you said 'First House' like three times," she said, "but I thought you were being metaphorical."

"I thought it would fill you with a sense of adventure."

"It damn well doesn't," said Gideon, rewetting the wadding, "you're taking me to the planet where nobody lives. I thought we'd end up on the Third or the Fifth, or a sweet space station, or something. Not just another cave filled with old religious nut jobs."

"Why would there be a necromantic gathering on a *space station*?"

This was a good point. If there was one thing Gideon knew about necromancers, it was that they needed power. Thanergy—death juice—was abundant wherever things had died or were dying. Deep space was a necro's nightmare, because nothing had ever been alive out there, so there were no big puddles of death lying around for Harrow and her ilk to suck up with a straw. The brave men and women of the Cohort looked on this limitation with compassionate amusement: never send an adept to do a soldier's job.

"Behold the last paragraph," Harrow said from the sofa, "turning your benighted eyes to lines five and six." Unwillingly, Gideon turned her benighted eyes to lines five and six. "Tell me the implications."

Gideon stopped painting and leant back in her chair before thinking better of it, easing it back down to the chill tiles of the floor. There was something a little soggy about one of the legs. "'No retainers. No attendants, no domestics.' Well, you'd be shitted all to hell otherwise, you'd have to bring along Crux. Look—are you really saying that nobody's going to be there but us and some crumbly old hierophants?"

"That," said the Reverend Daughter, "is the implication."

"For crying out loud! Then let me dress how I want and give me back my longsword."

"*Ten thousand years of tradition*, Griddle."

"I don't have ten thousand years of tradition, bitch," said Gideon, "I have ten years of two-hander training and a minor allergy to face paint. I'm worth so much less to you with pizza face and a toothpick."

The Reverend Daughter's fingers locked together, thumbs rotating in languid circles. She did not disagree. "Ten thousand years of tradition," she said slowly, "dictates that the Ninth House should have been at its leisure to produce, at the very least, a cavalier with the correct sword, the correct training, and the correct attitude. Any implication that the Ninth House did not have the leisure to meet even that expectation is as good as giving up. I'd be better off by myself than taking you qua you. But I know how to fake this; I can provide the sword. I can provide a smattering of training. I cannot even slightly provide your attitude. Two out of three is still not three. The con depends on your shut mouth and your adoption of the minimal requirements, Griddle."

"So nobody realises that we're broke and nearly extinct, and that your parents topped themselves."

"So nobody *takes advantage* of the fact that we lack conventional resources," said Harrow, shooting Gideon a look that skipped warning and went straight to barrage. "So nobody realises that the House is under threat. So nobody realises that—my parents are no longer able to take care of its interests."

Gideon folded the paper in half, in half again, and made it into corners. She rubbed it between her fingers for the rare joy of feeling paper crinkle, and then she dropped it on the desk and cleaned paint off her fingernails. She did not need to say or do anything except let the quiet roll out between them.

"We are not becoming an appendix of the Third or Fifth Houses," continued the necromancer opposite. "Do you hear me, Griddle? If you do anything that suggests we're out of order—if I even think you're about to . . ." Here Harrow shrugged, quite calmly. "I'll kill you."

"Naturally. But you can't keep this a secret forever."

"When I am a Lyctor everything will be different," said Harrowhark. "I'll be in a position to fix things without fear of reprisal. As it is, our leverage now is that nobody knows anything about anything. I've had three separate communiques already from other Houses, asking if I'm coming, and they don't even know my name."

"What the hell are you going to tell them?"

"*Nothing,* idiot!" said Harrow. "This is the House of the Ninth, Griddle. We act accordingly."

Gideon checked her face, and put down the paint and the wadding. *Act accordingly* meant that any attempt to talk to an outsider as a kid had led to her getting dragged away bodily; *act accordingly* meant the House had been closed to pilgrims for five years. *Act accordingly* had been her secret dread that ten years from now everyone else would be skeletons and explorers would find Ortus reading poetry next to her and Harrow's bodies, their fingers still clasped around each other's throats. *Act accordingly,* to Gideon, meant being secret and abstruse and super obsessed with tomes.

"I won't have people asking questions. You'll look the part. Give me that," commanded Harrow, and she took the fat stick of black char from Gideon's hand. She tried to turn Gideon's face up to hers by force, fingers grasping beneath the chin, but Gideon promptly bit her. There was a simple joy in watching Harrow swear furiously and shake her hand and peel off the bitten glove, like in seeing sunlight or eating a good meal.

Harrow began fiddling ominously with one of the bone pins at her ear, so with *extreme* reluctance, as of an animal not wanting to take medicine, Gideon tilted her face up to get painted. Harrow took the black and stroked it beneath Gideon's eyes—none too gently, making her anticipate an exciting jab in the cornea. "I don't want to dress up like a goddamn nun again. I got enough of that when I was ten," said Gideon.

"Everyone else will be dressing exactly how they ought to dress," said Harrow, "and if the Ninth House contravenes that—the House least likely to do any such thing—then people will examine us a hell of a lot more closely than they ought. If you look just right then perhaps they won't ask you any tricky questions. They may not discover that the cavalier of the House of the Ninth is an illiterate peon. Hold your mouth closed."

Gideon held her mouth closed and, once Harrow was done, said: "I object to *illiterate.*"

"Pinup rags aren't literature, Nav."

"I read them for the articles."

When as a young and disinclined member of the Locked Tomb Gideon had painted her face, she had gone for the bare minimum of death's-head that the role demanded: dark around the eyes, a bit around the nose, a slack black slash across the lips. Now as Harrowhark gave her a little palm of cracked mirror, she saw that she was painted like the ancient, tottering necromancers of the House: those ghastly and unsettling sages who never seemed to die, just disappear into the long galleries of books and coffins beneath Drearburh. She'd been slapped up to look like a grim-toothed, black-socketed skull, with big black holes on each side of the mandible.

Gideon said drearily, "I look like a douche."

"I want you to appear before me every day, like this, until the day we leave," said Harrowhark, and she leant against the desk to view her handiwork. "I won't cut you bald—even though your hair is ridiculous—because I know you won't shave your head daily. Learn this paint. Wear the robe."

"I'm waiting for the *and*," said Gideon. "You know. The payoff. If you let me have my head, I'd wear my breastplate and use my sword—you're an imbecile if you think I'll be able to fight properly wearing a robe—and I could cavalier until the rest of them went home. I could cavalier until they just made you a Hand on the first day and put sexy pictures of me on a calendar. Where's the *and*, Nonagesimus?"

"There is no *and*," Harrow said, and pushed herself away from Gideon's chair to throw herself back down on the sofa once more. "If it were merely about getting what I wanted, I wouldn't have bothered to take you at all. I would have you packed up in nine boxes and sent each box to a different House, the ninth box kept for Crux to comfort him in his old age. I will succeed with you in tow and nobody will ever know that there was aught amiss with the House of the Ninth. Paint your face. Train with the rapier. You're dismissed."

"Isn't this the part where you give me intel," Gideon said, standing up and flexing her stiff muscles, "tell me all you know of the tasks ahead, who we're with, what to expect?"

"God, no!" said Harrow. "All you need to know is that you'll do what I say, or I'll mix bone meal in with your breakfast and punch my way through your gut."

Which was, Gideon had to admit, entirely plausible.

If Gideon had worried that the next three months would see her in close proximity to the Reverend Daughter, she was dead wrong. She spent six hours a day learning where to put her feet when she wielded a one-handed sword, where to rest (what seemed to her to be) her useless, unused arm, how to suddenly make herself a sideways target and always move on the same stupid foot. At the end of each punishing session, Aiglamene would take her in a one-on-one fight and disarm her in three moves.

"*Parry*, damn you, *parry*!" was the daily refrain. "This isn't your longsword, Nav, you block with it again and I'll make you eat it!"

On the few early days when she had foregone the paint, Crux had appeared and turned off the heating to her cell: she would end up slumped on her tier, screaming with cold, numb and nearly dead. So she wore the goddamn paint. It was nearly worse than her pre-cavalier life, except that as a small mercy she could train instead of going to prayers and, as a bigger mercy, Crux and Harrow were nearly never around. The heir to the House had ordered her marshal to do something secret down in the bowels of Drearburh, where bowed and creaking Ninth brothers and sisters worked hour after hour at whatever grisly task Harrowhark had set.

As for the Lady of the Ninth herself, she locked herself in the library and didn't come out. Very occasionally she would watch Gideon train, remark on the absolute lack of progress, make Gideon strip her paint off her face and command her to do it again. One day she and Aiglamene made Gideon walk behind Harrow, up and down the tiers, shadowing her until Gideon was nearly mad with impatience.

The only dubious advantage to this was that she would sometimes hear snatches of conversation, standing motionless and rigid-backed with her hand on the pommel of her sword and her sightline somewhere beyond Harrow's shoulder. Gideon was hungry for intel, but these exchanges were never very illuminating. The most she got was the day Harrow, too fretful to modulate her voice, said outright: "Naturally it's a competition, Captain, even if the wording . . ."

"Well, the Third House will naturally be the best equipped . . ."

"And the Second will have spent half their lives at the front and be covered in Cohort decorations. It doesn't signify. I don't care about soldiers or politicians or priests. It's a greyer House I worry about."

Aiglamene said something that Gideon did not catch. Harrow gave a short, hard laugh.

"Anyone can learn to fight. Hardly anyone learns to think."

Otherwise Harrow stayed with her books and studied her necromancy, getting leaner and more haggard, crueller and more mean. Each night Gideon fell into bed and was asleep before she could tend her blistered feet and massage her bruised body. On days when she had behaved *very* well Aiglamene let her train with her longsword instead, which had to pass for fun.

The last week before they were due to leave came all at once, like startling awake from a half-remembered and unsettling dream. The marshal of Drearburh reappeared like a chronic disease to stand over Gideon as she loaded her trunk, all of it with old hand-me-downs of Ortus's that could be hastily remade into three different Gideon-sized articles. These reclaimed robes were like her normal clothes, dour and black, but better made, dourer, and blacker. She spent a significant amount of time boring slats into the bottom of the trunk so that she could squirrel away her beloved, deserted longsword, packing it like precious contraband.

Aiglamene had found and reforged the sword of Ortus's grandmother's mother, and presented it to a nonplussed Gideon. The blade was black metal, and it had a plain black guard and hilt, unlike the intricate messes of teeth and wires that adorned some of the other rapiers down at the monument. "Oh, this is boring," Gideon had said in disappointment. "I wanted one with a skull puking another, smaller skull, and other skulls flying all around. But tasteful, you know?"

She was also given knuckles: they were even less ornate, being obsidian and steel set in thick and heavy bands. There were three black blades on the back of the gauntlet, rigidly fixed in place. "But for God's sake don't use them for anything but a parry," said her teacher.

"This is confusing. You made me train empty-handed."

"Gideon," said her teacher, "after eleven ghoulish weeks of training you, beating you senseless, and watching you fall around like a dropsical infant, you are on a miraculous day up to the standard of a bad cavalier, one who's terrible." (This was great praise.) "But you fall apart as soon as you start to overthink your offhand. Use the knuckles to balance. Give yourself options if someone gets inside your guard—though better yet, don't let them get inside your guard. Keep moving. Be fluid. Remember that your hands are now sisters, not twins; one executes your primary action and the other supports the move. Pray they don't watch you fight too closely. And *stop blocking every blow.*"

On the final day the entire House of the Ninth filled the tier of the landing field, and they left room to spare: it was sad to watch their eagerness, their kissing Harrowhark's hem over and over. They all knelt in prayer with the godawful great-aunts as their Reverend Daughter stood and watched, tranquil and bloodless as the skeletons ploughing in the tiers above.

Gideon had noticed the absence of the ex-Reverend Father and Mother, but hadn't thought anything of it. She was too busy thinking about her itchy secondhand clothes and the rapier buckled at her side, and the paint that was now a second skin on her face. But she was still surprised when Harrow said: "Brothers and sisters, listen. My mother and father will not be with you. My father has sealed shut the passageway to the tomb that must always be locked, and they have decided to continue their penitence behind that wall until I return. The marshal will act as seneschal for me, and my captain will act as marshal."

Testament to Harrow's timing for drama, the Secundarius Bell began ringing. From above the drillshaft the shuttle started to make its descent, blotting out the ever-fainter light of the equinox. For the very first time Gideon did not feel the overwhelming sense of dread and suspicion: a pinprick of anticipation curled in her gut instead. Round two. Go.

Harrowhark looked out at the people of the Ninth. So did Gideon. There were all the assorted nuns and brethren; old pilgrims and ageing vassals; every gloomy, severe, and stern face of adept and mystic, of joyless and wasted men and women, of the grey and monotonous population that had made up Gideon's life and never shown her one single moment of sympathy or kindness. Harrow's face was bright with elation and fervour. Gideon would have sworn there were tears in her eyes, except that no such liquid existed: Harrow was a desiccated mummy of hate.

"You are my beloved House," she said. "Rest assured that wherever I go, my heart is interred here."

It sounded like she really meant it.

Harrow began, "*We pray the tomb is shut forever . . .*" and Gideon found herself reciting simply because it was the only prayer she'd ever known, enduring the words by saying them as sounds without meaning. She stopped when Harrowhark stopped, her hands clasped, and added: "I pray for our success for the House; I pray for the Lyctors, devoted Hands of the Emperor; I pray to be found pleasing in his eyes. I pray for the cavalier . . ."

At this Gideon caught the dark, black-rimmed eye, and could imagine the mental accompaniment: . . . *to choke to death on her own vomit.*

"Let it be so," said the Lady of the Ninth House.

The rattling of the assorted prayer bones very nearly drowned out the clank of the shuttle, docking. Gideon turned away, not meaning to make any kind of goodbye; but she saw Aiglamene, hand crooked into a stiff salute, and realised for the first time that she might never see the woman again. God help her, she might never come back. For a moment everything seemed dizzyingly unsure. The House continued on in grand and grisly majesty because you were always looking at it; it continued because you watched it continue, changeless and black, before your eyes. The idea of leaving it made it seem so fragile as to crumble the moment they turned their backs. Harrowhark turned toward the shuttle and Gideon realised with an unwelcome jolt that she *was* crying: her paint was wet with tears.

And then the whole idea became beautiful. The moment Gideon turned her back on it, the House would die. The moment Gideon walked away, it would all disappear like an impossibly bad dream. She mentally staved in the sides of the enormous, shadowy cave and buried Drearburh in rock, and for good measure exploded Crux like a garbage bag full of soup. But she saluted Aiglamene as crisply and as enthusiastically as a soldier on her first day of service, and was pleased when her teacher rolled her eyes.

As they pulled themselves into the shuttle, the door mechanism sliding down with a pleasingly final *whunk*, she leaned into Harrow: Harrow, who was dabbing her eyes with enormous gravity. The necromancer flinched outright.

"Do you want," Gideon whispered huskily, "my hanky."

"I want to watch you die."

"Maybe, Nonagesimus," she said with deep satisfaction, "maybe. But you sure as hell won't do it here."

7

FROM SPACE, THE HOUSE of the First shone like fire on water. Wreathed in the white smoke of its atmosphere, blue like the heart of a gas-ignited flame, it burned the eye. It was absolutely *lousy* with water, smothering it all in the bluest of blue conflagrations. Visible even up here were the floating chains of squares and rectangles and oblongs, smudging the blue with grey and green, brown and black: the tumbled-down cities and temples of a House both long dead and unkillable. A sleeping throne. Far away its king and emperor sat on his seat of office and waited, a sentinel protecting his home but never able to return to it. The Lord of the House of the First was the Lord Undying, and he had not come back in over nine thousand years.

Gideon Nav pressed her face up to the plexiform window of the shuttle and looked as if she couldn't ever get enough of looking, until her eyes were red and streaming and huge migraine motes danced along the edge of her vision. All the other shutters were closed up tight and had been for most of the trip, which had taken about an hour of rapid travel. They had been surprised to find that, behind the plex privacy barrier Harrowhark had coolly slid up the moment they were inside, there was no pilot on board. The ship was being remotely piloted at great expense. There was no clearance for anybody to land at the First House without explicit invitation. There was a button to press if you needed to talk to the remote navigator, and Gideon had been eager to hear another voice, but Harrow had slid the barrier back down with an air of distinct finality.

She looked worn and exhausted, even vulnerable. For the journey's length she had kept her prayer knuckles in her hands and moodily clinked them into each other. In Gideon's comics, Cohort adepts always sat on plackets of grave dirt to ameliorate the effects of deep space and the loss of their power source; trust Harrowhark not to take the placebo. Gideon had warmed herself with the thought that it was the perfect time to kick her ass up and down the shuttle, but in the end, the natural embarrassment of arriving with one's necromancer's elbows on backward saved Harrow's life. All thoughts of ass-kicking had subsided as the approach of the First House reflected light through the open window, light that spilled into the passenger bay in fiery gouts; Gideon had to turn her face away, half-blind and breathless. Harrow was tying a piece of black voile around her eyes, as calm and uninterested as if what hung outside the window was dreary Ninth sky.

Gideon cupped her hands over her eyes to shade them and looked again, getting her fill of the explosive brilliance outside: the velvety blackness of space, with innumerable pinprick white stars; the First, a searing circle of incandescent blue, strewn with dazzling white; and—the outsides of seven more shuttles, lining up in orbit. Gideon gave a low whistle to see them. To an inhabitant of the sepulchrous Ninth House it seemed amazing that the whole thing didn't just combust and crumble into flame. There were other Houses that made their homelands on planets closer to the burning star of Dominicus—the Seventh and the Sixth, for instance—but to Gideon they could not imaginably be anything else than 100 percent on fire.

It was incredible. It was exquisite. She wanted to throw up. It seemed stolid insanity that Harrowhark's only reaction was to slide up the plexiform barrier and hold down the communication button to ask: "How long must we wait?"

The navigator's voice crackled back: "We are securing your clearance to land, Your Grace."

Harrow didn't thank him. "How long?"

"They are scanning your craft now, Your Grace, and we'll move the moment they have confirmed you're free to leave orbit."

The Reverend Daughter sank back into her chair, stuffing her prayer bones into a fold of her robe. Quite unwillingly Gideon caught her eye. The expression on the other girl's face wasn't disinterest or distraction, as she'd assumed; even through a layer of veiling, she could tell that Harrow was near-incapacitated with concentration. Her mouth was pinched in a tight ripple, worrying the black-painted blotch on the lower lip into blood.

It took less than five minutes for the thrusters to creak to life again, for the ship to slowly glide out of orbit. Next to them, in a line, seven other shuttles were drifting to one side, sliding into the atmosphere like dominoes falling. Harrow shook her head back into her hood and pinched the bridge of her nose, and said in tones between pleasure and pain: "This planet's *unbelievable*."

"It's gorgeous."

"It's a grave," said Harrowhark.

The shuttle broke orbit, haloed by coruscating light. This burn-off meant there was nothing to see but sky, but the sky of the First House was the same improbable, ludicrous blue as the water. Being on the outside of the planet was like living in a kaleidoscope. It was a lurching blur for long moments—a whine, as air pockets in the thick atmosphere made the engines scream, a jolt as the craft repressurized to match—and then the shuttle was a slingshot bullet, an accelerating shell. The brightness was too much to bear. Gideon got the impression of a hundred spires rising, choked with green stuff from blue-and-turquoise waters, before she had to squeeze her eyes shut and turn away wholesale. She pressed the fabric of the embroidered Ninth robes to her face and had to breathe through her nose.

"Idiot." Harrowhark's voice was distant and full of badly suppressed adrenaline. "Here. Take this veil."

Gideon kept mopping at her eyes. "I'm all good."

"I said put it on. I'm not having you struck blind when the door opens."

"I came prepared, my sweet."

"What are you even *saying* half the time—"

The glow changed, strobing, and now the shuttle was slowing down. The light cleared, brightened, dazzled. Harrowhark threw herself upon the shutter and slammed it down; she and Gideon stood in the centre of the passenger bay, staring at each other. Gideon realised that Harrow was trembling; little licks of hole-black hair were pasted to her pale grey forehead with sweat, threatening to dissolve the paint. Gideon realised with a start that she was trembling and sweating in concert. They looked at each other with a wild surmise, and then started dabbing at their faces with the insides of their sleeves.

"Hood up," breathed Harrowhark, "hide that ridiculous hair."

"Your dead mummified mother's got ridiculous hair."

"Griddle, we're within the planet's halo now, and I will delight in violence."

A final, thuddering *clunk*. Complete stillness. The seals on the outside were unlatched by some outside force, and as light blazed around the edges of the hatch, Gideon winked at her increasingly agitated companion. She said, sotto voce: "But then you couldn't have admired . . . these," and whipped on the glasses she'd unearthed back home. They were ancient smoked-glass sunglasses, with thin black frames and big mirrored lenses, and they greyed out Harrow's expression of incredulous horror as she adjusted them on her nose. That was the last thing she saw before the light got in.

And then the outside of the First House was open to them, a rush of warm air ruffling their robes and drying the sweat on their faces. Before the hatch had even shuddered to a halt, Harrow, aggravated, had disappeared completely: Lady Harrowhark Nonagesimus, the Reverend Daughter of the House of the Ninth, swept onto the docking ramp instead. Counting five full breaths to mark time, Gideon Nav, Cavalier of the Ninth House, came following behind, praying that her unfamiliar sword wouldn't tangle in her robes.

They were on the enormous, metal-plated dock of what must surely have been the most impressive structure the First House had ever built. It might have been the most impressive structure *anyone* had ever built. Gideon didn't have a lot to go on. Rearing up before them was a palace, a fortress, of white and shining stone. It spread out on the surface of the water like an island. You couldn't see over it and you could hardly see around it. It lapped back in terraces of what must have once been fabulous gardens. It rose up in gracious towers that hurt the eye with their slenderness and precision. It was a monument to wealth and beauty.

Back in its day, at least, it would have been a monument to wealth and beauty. In the present it was a castle that had been killed. Many of its white and shining towers had crumbled and fallen down in miserable chunks. Jungling overgrowth rose from the sea and wrapped around the base of the building, both green slimes and thick vines. The gardens were grey, filmy canopies of dead trees and plants. They had overtaken the windows, the balconies, the balustrades, and clung there and died; they covered much of the frontage in a secretive mist of expired matter. Gold veins shone dully in the dirty white walls. The docking bay must have also been elegant in its era, a huge landing swath that could have held a hundred ships at a time; now ninety-two of the cradles were desolate and filthy. The metal was caked with salt from the water, salt that now assaulted Gideon's nose: a thick, briny scent, overpowering and wild. The whole place had the look of a picked-at body. But hot damn! What a beautiful corpse.

The dock was alive with movement. Five other ships had landed and were expelling their contents. But there was no time for that: someone had come to meet them.

Harrowhark did not care for any herald. She had drifted out like a black ship in sail, a bony figure wreathed in layers and layers of night-coloured cloth with a lace overcloak trailing behind her; adorned with bones, painted like a dead woman, eyes blindfolded with black net. Now she dropped to her knees five paces from the shuttle door and began counting prayers on the knuckle beads in a click-clack monotone. Showtime. Gideon ambled over and knelt next to Harrow on the sun-warmed metal of the dock, her own robes pooling black around her, staring inscrutably at the tint-dimmed chaos of what was going on. The clacking beads made her almost feel normal.

"Hail to the Lady of the Ninth House," warbled a voice delightedly, bringing the count of people who had ever been happy to see Harrow up to three. "Hail to her cavalier. Oh, hail, hail! Hail to the child of the far-off and shadowed jewel of our Empire! What a very— happy—day."

A little old man stood in front of them. He was small and reedy, in the way that reminded Gideon of the oldest of the House of the Ninth, but he had the straightest back and rudest good health of any old man Gideon had ever seen. He was like an old and twisted oak still covered with leaves. He was bald, with a neat, clipped white beard and a golden circlet at his brow. His white robe had no hood and was long enough to brush his calves, and he wore a half-cloak of brushed white wool. Around his waist was a gorgeous belt: it was made of some shimmering gold stuff, and it was embroidered with a multitude of jewel colours in intricate patterns and shapes. They looked like flowers, or flourishes, or both. They looked as though they had been made a thousand years ago and kept in loving perfection. Everything about him was ageless and pristine.

Harrowhark pocketed her prayer beads. "Hail to the House of the First," she intoned. "Hail to the King Undying."

"Hail to the Lord Over the River," quavered the little priest. "And welcome to his house! Blessed Lady of the Ninth, the Reverend Daughter! The Ninth has not visited the First House for most of this myriad! But your cavalier is not Ortus Nigenad."

The slightest pause. "Ortus Nigenad has abdicated his post," said Harrow, from the depths of her hood. "Gideon Nav has taken his place as cavalier primary. I am the Lady Harrowhark Nonagesimus."

"Then welcome to the Lady Nonagesimus and to Gideon the Ninth. Once you have finished your prayers," said the little priest effervescently, "you must stand and be honoured, and come into the sanctum. I am a keeper of the First House and a servant to the Necrolord Highest, and you must call me *Teacher*; not due to my own merits of learning, but because I stand in the stead of the merciful God Above Death, and I live in hope that one day you will call him *Teacher.* And may you call him *Master,* too, and may I call you then *Harrowhark the First*! Be at rest, Lady Nonagesimus; be at rest, Gideon the Ninth."

Gideon the Ninth, who would have paid cash to be called absolutely anything else, rose as her mistress rose. They exchanged glances that even through one layer of veiling and one layer of tinted glass were violently hostile, but there was too much going on to stand and pull go-to-hell faces at each other. Gideon saw other white-robed figures darting to and fro between the shuttles, coming out of open double doors, but it took a moment to realise that these were skeletons in plain white, with white knots at their waists. They were using long metal poles to work the mechanisms that held the shuttles safely coupled to their latches, with that strange lockstep oneness in which the dead always worked. And then there were the living, waiting in twos, awkwardly shuffling their feet next to their ships. She had never seen so many different people—so many people not of the Ninth—and it almost dizzied her, but not enough so that she couldn't pick out when something was amiss.

"I only count six shuttles," said Gideon.

Harrowhark shot her a look for speaking out of turn, but the little priest Teacher cackled as though he were pleased.

"Oh, well noticed! Very good! Yes, there's a discrepancy," he said. "And we don't much like discrepancies. This is holy land. We might be called over-careful, but we hold this House as sacred to the Emperor our Lord . . . we do not get many visitors, as you might think! There is nothing that much the matter," he added, and with a confiding air: "It's the House of the Third and the House of the Seventh. No matter, no matter. I'm sure they will be given clearance any moment now. We needed clarification. An inconsistency in both."

"Inconsistency," repeated Harrowhark, as though she were rolling the word around her mouth like a sweet.

"Yes; the House of the Third will, of course, push the boundaries . . . of course they would. And the House of the Seventh . . . well, it's well known . . . Look; they're landing now."

Most of the other heirs and cavaliers had left their shuttles, and the skeletons were busy pulling luggage out from their holds. The last two shuttles slowly spiralled down to earth, a fresh gust of warm wind scything over everyone as they came to their fluttering rest. Skeletons with poles were already there to greet them, and other living priests, one for each arriving shuttle. They were alive and well, dressed in identical vestments to Teacher's. This made just three priests total, which made Gideon wonder why the Ninth always scored so much geriatric attention. The two new shuttles had both alighted next to the Ninth's, the Seventh's closest and the Third's one over, which was close enough to see who or what was inside as the Third's hatch opened.

Gideon was hugely interested to see three figures emerge. The first was a rather sulky young man with an air of hair gel and filigree, an ornate rapier at the belt of his buttoned coat. The cavalier. The other two were young women, both blond, though the similarity ended there: one girl was tall and statuesque, with a star-white grin and masses of bright gold curls. The other girl seemed smaller, insubstantial, with a sheet of hair the anaemic colour of canned butter and an equally bloodless smirk. They were actually the same height, Gideon realised; her brain had just deemed that proposition too stupid to credit on first pass. It was as though the second girl were the starved shadow of the first, or the first an illuminated reflection. The boy just looked a bit of a dick.

Gideon rubbernecked until a white-robed priest with another parti-coloured belt hurried over from the trio to them, tapping on Teacher's shoulder and murmuring in worried half-heard snatches: "—were inflexible—the household's backing—born at the exact— both the adept—"

Teacher waved it off with an indulgent hand and a wheezing laugh: "What can we do, what can we do?"

"But it's impossible—"

"Only trouble at the end of the line," he said, "and a trouble confined to them."

Once the other priest had gone, Harrowhark said repressively: "Twins are an ill omen."

Teacher seemed tickled. "How delightful to hear someone say an ill omen could come from the Mouth of the Emperor!"

From the shuttle that carried the Seventh House came consternation. The skeletons had pried the hatch open, and someone tottered out. In what felt like painful slow-motion—like time had decided to slow to a gruesome crawl to show itself off—they had fainted dead away into the arms of the waiting priest, an old man who was singularly unprepared for it. His legs and arms were buckling. The figure was dragging on the ground, threatening to spill entirely. There was red blood on the priest's front. He cried out.

Gideon never ran unless she had to, and Gideon ran now. Her legs moved as swiftly as her awful judgement, and all of a sudden she was scooping the crumpled, drooping figure out of the priest's buckling arms, lowering his cargo to the ground as he murmured in amazement. In response, the ice-cold point of a blade bit gently through her hood to the back of her neck, right up to the base of her skull.

"Yo," said Gideon, her head absolutely still. "Step off."

The sword did not step off.

"This isn't a warning," she said. "I'm just saying. Give her some air."

For the person folded up in Gideon's arms seemed a *her*. It was a slender young thing whose mouth was a brilliant red with blood. Her dress was a frivolous concoction of seafoam green frills, the blood on it startling against such a backdrop. Her skin seemed transparent—horribly transparent, with the veins at her hands and the sides of her temples a visible cluster of mauve branches and stems. Her eyes fluttered open: they were huge and blue, with velvety brown lashes. The girl coughed up a clot, which ruined the tableau, and those big blue eyes widened in dismay.

"Protesilaus," said the girl: "stand down." When the sword didn't move an inch, she coughed again and said unhappily: "Stand down, you goof. You're going to get us in trouble."

Gideon felt the pressure and the edge remove itself from her neck, and she let out a breath. Not for long, though; it was replaced with a gloved hand pressing over the place where the blade had been, a hand which was pressing down as though its owner would quite like to punch her occipital bone into crumbs. That hand could belong to only one person. Gideon braced to be dropped headfirst into the shitter, and Harrowhark's voice emerged as though it had been dredged up from the bottom of a charnel house.

"Your cavalier," said the Lady of the Ninth quietly, "drew on my cavalier."

As Gideon died gently of shock, buoyed back to this life only by the weird bruises forming at the top of her spine, the other girl broke out into miserable coughs. "I'm so sorry!" she said. "He's just over-protective— He never would have meant— Oh my God, you're black vestals— Oh my God, you're the Ninth cav!"

The girl in Gideon's lap covered her face and seemed to break into sobs, but it became apparent that they were gurgles of mirth. "You've done it now, Pro!" she gasped. "They could demand satisfaction, and you'd end up a mausoleum centrepiece! Lady or Lord of the Ninth, please accept my heartfelt apologies. He was hasty, and I was a fool."

"Come on," said Gideon, "you fainted."

"I *do* do that," she admitted, and gave another wicked chuckle of delight. This appeared to be the greatest thing that had ever happened to her. She fluttered her hands like she was having the vapours. "Oh, God, I was rescued by a shadow cultist! I'm so sorry! Thank you! This is one for the history books."

Now that the threat of violence had passed, the priest, with difficulty, had dropped to his knees. He unwound the exquisite prismatic scarf at his waist and hesitated before her. The girl gave an imperious little nod and he began wiping the blood away from her mouth, reverential, seeming far less worried about the entire mess than—Gideon didn't know. Discouraged? Disconcerted?

"Ah, Duchess Septimus," he said, in a tweedling old voice, "and is it so advanced as all that?"

"Yes, indeed."

"Oh, Lady," he said sadly, "you should not have come."

She gave a flashing, sudden smile, the edges of her teeth scarlet. "But isn't it beautiful that I did?" she said, and looked up at Gideon, and strained past her to look at Harrow, and clasped her hands together. "Protesilaus, help me up so that we can apologise. I can't believe I get to look real tomb maidens in the face."

Great, rugged arms thrust past Gideon's vision, and the girl in her lap was lifted up by a six-foot collection of sinews. The man who'd put the sword to her neck was uncomfortably buff. He had upsetting biceps. He didn't look healthy; he looked like a collection of lemons in a sack. He was a dour, bulky person whose skin had something of the girl's strange, translucent tinge. He was waxen looking in the sunlight, probably with sweat, and he wore the girl half-draped over his shoulder as though she were a baby or a rug. Gideon sized him up. He was dressed richly, but with clothes that looked as though they'd seen practical wear: a long cape of washed-out green, and a belted kilt and boots. There was a shining length of etched chain rolled up and over his arm, and a big swept-hilt rapier hung at his hip. He was staring at Gideon emptily. *You're gigantic*, she thought, *but you move awkwardly, and I bet I could take you.*

The hand at the back of her neck relaxed a fraction. Gideon didn't even get a hard flick to the skull, which boded ill. Whatever punishment Harrow was going to mete out would be meted out later, in private, and viciously. She'd screwed up but couldn't quite regret it; as Gideon brushed herself off and picked herself up to stand, the Lady of the Seventh House was smiling. Her babyish face made it difficult to give her a timestamp. She might've been seventeen, or thirty-seven.

"What must I do to gain forgiveness?" she said. "If my House blasphemes against the House of the Ninth in the first five minutes, I'm going to feel like a boor."

"Keep your sword off my cavalier," said Harrow, in tones of the sepulchre.

"You heard her, Pro," said the girl. "You can't just get your rapier out willy-nilly."

Protesilaus did not deign to reply, his gaze fixed on Gideon. In the awkward silence that resulted, the girl added: "But now I can thank you for your aid. I'm Lady Dulcinea Septimus, duchess of Castle Rhodes; and this is my cavalier primary, Protesilaus the Seventh. The Seventh House thanks you for your gracious assistance."

Despite this pretty, even coaxing introduction, Gideon's lady merely bowed her hooded head, her bound eyes giving away nothing. It was with glacial disregard that she said, "The Ninth House wishes health to the Lady Septimus, and prudence to Protesilaus the Seventh," turned on her heel, and left in an abrupt swish of black cloth.

Gideon was obliged to turn heel and move after her. She wasn't such a fool as to stay. But before she left, she caught the Lady Dulcinea's eye. Rather than being missish or horrified, she looked as though giving offence to the House of the Ninth might prove the highlight of her life. Gideon swore that she was even favoured with a coy wink. They left the priest of the First House there to worry, brow furrowed, folding his scarf now encrusted with blood.

They'd caused a general ruckus. The curious eyes of the other adepts and their cavaliers rested upon the black-robed Ninth. Gideon was discomfited to find the gaze of the bloodless Third twin on her and Harrowhark both, her pale eyes like sniper sights, her mouth exquisitely chill. There was something in her stare that Gideon disliked on impact, and she held that gaze until the pale head was dropped. As for Teacher's expression—well, that one was hard to fathom. In the end, it was something like melancholy and something like resignation, and he did not say a word about what Gideon had done. "A blood flaw runs through the ruling House of the Seventh," was all he said, "sparing most who carry the gene . . . but fatal to a few."

Harrowhark asked, "Teacher, was the Lady Septimus so diagnosed?"

"Dulcinea Septimus was not meant to live to twenty-five," said the little priest. "Come along, come along . . . We are all here now, and we've had ample excitement. What a day, what a day! We will have something to talk about, won't we?"

Twenty-five, thought Gideon, distantly ignoring the ugly twist beneath Harrow's veil that promised that there would be much to talk about later and that it would not go well for Gideon. Twenty-five years, and Harrowhark was probably going to live forever. They billowed obediently into the priest's wake, and Gideon remembered the coy wink, and felt terribly sad.

THEY WERE BIDDEN TO SIT IN A VAST ATRIUM—a cavern of a room; a Ninth House mausoleum of a room, except that through the glorious wreck of the smeared and vaulted ceiling light streamed down in such quantities it made Gideon halfway blind again. There were deep couches and seating benches, with cracked covers and the stuffing coming out, with broken armguards and backs. Embroidered throws that clung to the seats like the skins of mummies, piebald where the light had touched them and dank where it hadn't.

Everything in that room was beautiful, and all had gone to seed. It wasn't like back in the Ninth where unbeautiful things were now old and ruined to boot—the Ninth must have always been a corpse, and corpses putrefied. The House of the First had been abandoned, and breathlessly waited to be used by someone other than time. The floors were of *wood*—where they weren't of gold-shot marble, or a rainbow mosaic of tiles gone leprous with age and disrepair—and enormous twin staircases jutted up to the floor above, spread with narrow, moth-eaten rugs. Vines peeked through in number where the glass of the ceiling had cracked, spreading tendrils that had since gone grey and dry. The pillars that reached up to support the shining glass were carpeted thickly with moss, still alive, still radiant, all orange and green and brown. It obscured old portraits on the walls in spatters of black and tan. It hung atop an old, dry fountain made of marble and glass, three tiers deep, a little bit of standing water still skulking in the bottom bowl.

Harrowhark refused to sit. Gideon stood next to her, feeling the hot, wet air glue the black folds of her robe to her skin. The cavalier of the Seventh, Protesilaus, didn't sit either, she noticed, not until his mistress patted the chair next to her own, and then he folded down with unhesitating obedience. The white-garbed skeletons circulated trays filled with cups of astringent tea, steaming green— funny little cups with no handles, hot and smooth to the touch, like stone but smoother and thinner. The Seventh cavalier held his but did not drink it. His adept tried to drink but had a minor coughing fit that lasted until she gestured for her cavalier to thump her on the back. As the other necromancers and cavaliers drank with varied enjoyment, Harrowhark held her cup as though it were a live slug. Gideon, who had never drunk a drink hot in all her days, knocked back half in one gulp. It burned all the way down her throat, more smell than flavour, and left a grassy tang on her cauterised taste buds. Some of her lip paint stayed on the rim. She choked discreetly: the Reverend Daughter gave her a look that withered the bowels.

All three priests sat at the lip of the fountain, holding their teacups unsipped in their hands. Unless they were hiding a bunch more in some cupboard, it seemed terrifically lonely to Gideon. The second was the tottery priest, his frail shoulders bowing as he fretted with his bloodstained belt; the third was mild of face and sported a long salt-and-pepper plait. They might have been a woman and might have been a man and might have been neither. All three wore the same clothes, which gave them the look of white birds on rainbow leashes, but somehow Teacher was the only one of the three who seemed real. He was eager, interested, vital, alive. The penitent calm of his fellows made them seem more like the robed skeletons arrayed at the sides of the room: silent and immovable, with a red speck of light dancing in each socket.

Once everyone was awkwardly perched on the exquisite wrecks of furniture, finishing their tea, clutching their cups with the gaucherie of people who didn't know where to put them, making zero conversation, salt-and-pepper plait raised their pale voice and said:

"Now let us pray for the lord of that which was destroyed, remembering the abundance of his pity, his power, and his love."

Gideon and Harrowhark were silent during the ensuing chant: *"Let the King Undying, ransomer of death, scourge of death, vindicator of death, look upon the Nine Houses and hear their thanks. Let the whole of everywhere entrust themselves to him. Let those across the river pledge beyond the tomb to the adept divine, the first among necromancers. Thanks be to the Ninefold Resurrection. Thanks be to the Lyctor divinely ordained. He is Emperor and he became God: he is God, and he became Emperor."*

Gideon had never heard this one. There was only one prayer on the Ninth. All other services were call-and-speaks or knucklebone orison. Most of the crowd rattled it off as though they'd been saying it from the cradle, but not all. The hulking mass of man-meat, Protesilaus, stared straight ahead without even mouthing the words, his lips as still as the pale Third twin's. The others joined in without hesitation, though with varying fervour. Once the last word had sunk into silence, Teacher said: "And perhaps the devout of the Locked Tomb will favour us with their intercession?"

Everyone's heads twisted their way. Gideon froze. It was the Reverend Daughter who maintained complete equanimity as she dropped her cup into Gideon's hands and, before a sea of faces—some curious, some bored, and one (Dulcinea's) enthusiastic—Harrow began: *"I pray the tomb is shut forever. I pray the rock is never rolled away . . ."*

Gideon had known on some basic level that the religion practised in the dark depths of Drearburh was not quite the religion practised by the other Houses. It was still a shock to the system to have it confirmed. By the expressions on some of the faces—bewildered or blank or long-suffering or, in at least one case, openly hostile—the others hadn't been confronted with it either. By the time Harrow had finished the three priests looked softly delighted.

"Just as it always was," sighed the little bent priest in ecstasy, despite the wretched dirge.

"Continuity is a marvellous thing," said salt-and-pepper plait, proving themself insanely tedious.

Teacher said: "Now I'll welcome you to Canaan House. Will someone bring me the box?"

The gangling silence focused on a robed skeleton who carried over a small chest made entirely of wood. It was no wider than a book and no deeper than two books stacked on top of each other, estimated Gideon, who thought of all books as being basically the same size. Teacher threw it open with aplomb, and announced: "Marta the Second!"

An intensely dark girl snapped to attention. Her salute was as crisp as her flawless Cohort uniform, and when Teacher beckoned, she marched forward with a gait as starched as her officer's scarlets and snowy white necktie. As though bestowing a jewel upon her, he gave her a dull iron ring from the box, about as big around as the circle made by a thumb and forefinger. To her credit, she did not gawk or hesitate. She simply took it, saluted, and sat back down.

Teacher called out, "Naberius the Third!" and thus followed a rather tiresome parade of rapier-swinging cavaliers in varying attitudes coming up to receive their mysterious iron circles. Some of them took the Second's cue in saluting. Others, including the man-hulk Protesilaus, bothered not at all.

Gideon's tension grew with each name. When at last in this roll-call Teacher said, "Gideon the Ninth," she ended up disappointed by the banality of the thing. It was not a perfect iron loop, as she had thought, but a twist that overlapped itself. It locked shut by means of a hole bored into one end and a ninety-degree bend at the other, so that you could prise it open simply by fiddling the bend back through the hole. The metal in her hand felt granular, heavy. When she returned to her place she knew Harrow was sweating to snatch it off her, but she clutched it childishly tight.

Nobody asked what it was, which Gideon thought was fairly frigging dumb. She was near to asking herself when Teacher said: "Now the tenets of the First House, and the grief of the King Undying."

Everyone got very focused again.

"I will not tell you what you already know," said the little priest. "I seek only to add context. The Lyctors were not born immortal. They were given eternal life, which is not at all the same thing. Sixteen of them came here a myriad ago, eight adepts and the eight who would later be known as the first cavaliers, and it was here that they ascended. Those eight necromancers were first after the Lord of Resurrection; they have spread his assumption across the blackness of space, to those places where others could never reach. Each of them alone is more powerful than nine Cohorts acting as one. But even the divine Lyctors can pass away, despite their power and despite their swords . . . and they have done so, slowly, over these ten thousand years. The Emperor's grief has waxed with time. It is only now, in the twilight of the original eight, that he has listened to his last Lyctors, who beg for reinforcement."

He took his cup of tea and swirled the liquid with a twitch of his wrist. "You have been nominated to attempt the terrible challenge of replacing them," he said, "and it is not at all a sure thing. If you ascend to Lyctor, or if you try and fail—the Kindly Lord knows what is being asked of you is titanic. You are the honoured heirs and guardians of the eight Houses. Great duties await you. If you do not find yourself a galaxy, it is not so bad to find yourself a star, nor to have the Emperor know that the both of you attempted this great ordeal.

"Or the *all* of you," added the little priest brightly, nodding at the twins and their sullen-ass cavalier with a flash of amusement, "as the case may be. Cavaliers, if your adept is found wanting, you have failed! If you are found wanting, your adept has failed! And if one or both is wanting, then we will not ask you to wreck your lives against this impossible task. You will not be forced if you cannot continue onward—through single or mutual failure—or make the decision not to go on."

He looked searchingly over the assembled faces, somewhat vague, as though seeing them for the first time. Gideon could hear Harrowhark chewing the inside of her cheek, fingers tightly knuckled over her prayer bones.

Teacher said: "This is not a pilgrimage where your safety is assured. You will undergo trials, possibly dangerous ones. You will work hard, you will suffer. I must speak candidly—you may even die . . . But I see no reason not to hope that I may behold eight new Lyctors by the end of this, joined together with their cavaliers, heir to a joy and power that has sung through ten thousand years."

This sank into the room like water into sand. Even Gideon got a minute chill down the back of her neck.

He said, "To practical matters.

"Your every need will be met here. You will be given your own rooms, and will be waited on by the servants. There is space in abundance. Any chambers not given to others may be used as you will for your studies and your sitting-rooms, and you have the run of all open spaces and the use of all books. We live as penitents do—simple food, no letters, no visits. You shall never use a communication network. It is not allowed in this place. Now that you are here, you must understand that you are here until we send you home or until you succeed. We hope you will be too busy to be lonely or bored.

"As for your instruction here, this is what the First House asks of you."

The room drew breath together—or at least, all the necromancers did, alongside a goodly proportion of their cavaliers. Harrow's knuckles whitened. Gideon wished that she could flop into a seat or take a sly nap. Everybody was poised in readiness for the outlined syllabus, and scholarship made her want to die. There would be some litany of how breakfast would take place every morning at this time, and then there'd be study with the priests for an hour, and then *Skeleton Analysis*, and *History of Some Blood*, and *Tomb Studies*, and, like, lunchtime, and finally *Double Bones with Doctor Skelebone*. The most she could hope for was *Swords, Swords II*, and maybe *Swords III*.

"We ask," began Teacher, "that you never open a locked door unless you have permission."

Everyone waited. Nothing happened. They looked at the little priest and he looked back, completely at his ease, his hands resting on his white-clad thighs, smiling vaguely. A nail went *ping* out of a rotting picture frame somewhere in the corner.

"That's it," said Teacher helpfully.

Gideon saw lights dull in every eye that had gleamed for Double Bones with Doctor Skelebone. Someone ventured a bit timidly, "So what is the training, then—how to attain Lyctorhood?"

The little priest looked at them again. "Well, *I* don't know," he said.

His words went through them all like lightning. The very air chilled. Anticipation for Double Bones with Doctor Skelebone not only died, but was buried deep down in some forgotten catacomb. It only took one look at Teacher's kind, open-hearted countenance to confirm that he was not, in fact, screwing with them. They were stupefied with confusion and outrage.

"You're the ones who will ascend to Lyctor," he said, "not me. I am certain the way will become clear to you without any input from us. Why, who are we to teach the first after the King Undying?"

Then he added smilingly, "Welcome to Canaan House!"

* * *

A skeleton took Gideon and Harrow to the wing that had been set aside for the Ninth. They were led deep into the fortress of the First, past ruined statuary within the gorgeous wreck of Canaan House, the wraithlike, mansionlike hulk lying sprawled and chipped around them. They passed rooms with vaulted ceilings, full of green light where the sun shone through thick algae on the glass. They passed broken windows and windows wrecked with salt and wind, and open shadowed arches where reeked rooms too musty to be believed. They said absolutely jack to each other.

Except when they were taken down flights of stairs to their rooms, and Gideon looked out the windows now into the featureless lumps of blackness and said thoughtlessly: "The lights are broken."

Harrow turned to her for the first time since they left the shuttle, eyes glittering like beetles beneath the veil, mouth puckered up like a cat's asshole.

"Griddle," she said, "this planet spins much faster than ours." At Gideon's continued blank expression: "It's *night*, you tool."

They did not speak again.

The removal of the light, strangely, made Gideon feel very tired. She couldn't escape its having been there, even though Drearburh's brightest was darker than the darkest shadows of the First. Their wing turned out to be low on the level, right beneath the dock; there were a few lights here outside the huge windows, making big blue shadows out of the iron struts that held up the landing platform above them. Far below the sea roared invisibly. There was a bed for Harrow—an enormous platform with feathery, tattered drapes—and a bed for Gideon, except that it was placed at the foot of Harrowhark's bed, which she could not have noped at harder. She set herself up with a mass of musty bedding and pillows in front of a huge window in the next room, and left Harrow back in the bedroom with a black expression and probably blacker thoughts. Gideon was too tired even to wash her face or undress properly. Exhaustion had spread upward through her toes, spiking up her calves, freezing the bottom of her spine.

As she stared out the window into the bluish blackness of night after a day, she heard a huge, overhead grinding sound: a big velvety pull of metal on metal, a rhythmic scrape. Gideon watched, paralysed, as one of the very expensive shuttles fell hugely and silently over the landing platform: it dropped like a suicide and seemed to hang, grey and shining, in the air. Then it fell from sight. To its left, another; farther left, another. The scraping ceased. Skeletal feet pattered away.

Gideon fell asleep.

ACT TWO

9

GIDEON WOKE TO AN unfamiliar ceiling, a fuzzy taste on her tongue, and the exciting smell of mould. The light blazed in red slashes even through her eyelids, and it made her come to all at once. For long moments she just lay back in her nest of old bedding and looked around.

The Ninth quarters had low ceilings and wide, sweeping rooms, decaying away in magnificence before enormous floor-to-ceiling windows. The dock above their quarters cast a long shadow outside, cooling and dimming the light, which gleamed quietly off the chandeliers of festooned black crystals on wire. It would have been muted and peaceful to someone used to it, but to Gideon, on her first First morning, it was like looking at a headache. Someone had, a very long time ago, dressed these apartments lavishly in dead jewel colours: dark ruby, dark sapphire, dark emerald. The doors were set above the main level and reached by sloping stone ramps. There was not a great deal of furniture that wasn't sighing apart. The meanest stick of it still outclassed the most exquisite Ninth heirlooms back home. Gideon took a particular fancy to the long, low table in the centre of their living room, inset with black glass.

The first thing she did was roll away and reach for her sword. Aiglamene had spent half of training simply convincing Gideon to reach for her rapier hilt rather than her two-hander, to the point where she'd been sleeping with her fingers on the thing to try to get used to it. There was a note crumpled between her hand and the basket—

*Don't talk to **anybody***.

"Guess I won't talk to . . . any *body*," said Gideon, but then read on:

I have taken the ring.

"Harrow," Gideon bellowed, impotently, and slapped her hands down into her pockets. The ring was gone. There was no mistake greater or stupider than to let Harrowhark Nonagesimus at you when you were in any way vulnerable; she should have booby-trapped the threshold. It wasn't like she even cared about the ring: it was just the cut, again and again, of Harrow considering all of Gideon's property her property in common. She tried to cheer herself up with the thought that this at least meant Harrow wasn't around, a thought that would have cheered up anyone.

Gideon shrugged off her robe and wrestled out of her trousers and shirt, all of which had hot and damp insides from her sweat. She opened doors until she found the largest bathroom she had ever seen. It was so big she could walk around in it. She stretched out her arms on either side and still couldn't touch the walls, which were of slippery stone, glowing like coals where they were whole and scored and dull where they weren't. Maybe this pretending to be a cavalier gig wasn't so bad after all. The floor was marble tile, sheen marred by only a few spots of black mould. There was a bowl with taps that Gideon knew to be a sink only because she'd read a lot of comics, and an enormous person-sized recess in the ground that she didn't know what to do with at all. The sonic cleaner was set, gleaming gently, at either side of a rectangular chamber with a weird nozzle.

Gideon pulled a lever next to the tap. Water gushed from the nozzle, and she yelped and skittered away before she got over the sight and turned it off. Her survey identified a chubby cake of soap next to the sink (but Ninth soap had been made of human fat so no thanks) and a tub of antibac gel. She decided eventually to take a sonic and to use the gel to scrape the blurred paint off her face.

Newly clean, with fresh clothes and her robe shaken out in the sonic, she was feeling good about herself until she espied another note stuck tersely on the autodoor:

Fix your face, idiot.

There was another note atop the paint box, which some skeletal servant had helpfully placed on one of the less precarious sideboards:

Do __not__ try to find me. I am working. Keep your head down and stay out of trouble. I reiterate the order that you do not talk to __anybody__.

Another note was stuck beneath, belatedly:

To clarify, anybody is a word that refers to any __person__ alive or dead.

Inside the box, yet another:

Paint your face __adequately__.

Gideon said aloud, "Your parents must have been so relieved to die."

Back in the bathroom, she smeared cold wads of alabaster on her face. The nun's-paint went on in pale greys and blacks, swabbed over the lips and the hollows of her eyes and cheeks. Gideon comforted herself by recoiling at her reflection in the cracked mirror: a grinning death's-head with a crop of incongruously red hair and a couple of zits. She pulled her sunglasses out of the pocket of her robe and eased them on, which completed the effect, if the effect you wanted was "horrible."

Feeling slightly more at ease with life, rapier bobbing at her hip, it was the cavalier of the Ninth who stalked down the dilapidated corridors of Canaan House. It was pleasantly quiet. She heard the far-off sounds of a lived-in place—footsteps, blurry moans from the autocooler, the unmistakable pitter-pat of foot bones on tattered rugs—and she retraced her steps to the original atrium. From there, she followed her nose.

Her nose led her to a hot, glass-topped hall, modern conveniences haphazardly pasted atop ancient riches, out of place among the tapestries and gone-black filigree. There was netting spread all over the rafters to keep out the birds, because the glass-topped roof had holes in it that you could jump through. A fountain of fresh water burbled at the wall, ringed in old concrete, with a filtration tank snuggled beside. And there were many long, worn tables—wooden slabs that had been freshened up with antibac and had legs that must have come from eight table sacrifices. The place could have seated fifty. The early light flooded down in electric yellow blasts, green where it touched the living plants and brown where it touched the dead ones, and she was grateful that she'd worn her glasses.

The room was nearly empty, but a couple of the others were there, finishing their meals. Gideon sat down three tables away and spied on them shamelessly. There was a man sitting close to a pair of ghastly teens: younger than Gideon, still in the midst of losing their fight with puberty. The boy wore trim navy robes and the girl had a jewelled scabbard on her back, and when Gideon entered they had looked up at the cultist of the Ninth with unabashed interest close to awe. The man close to this horrible pair had a kind, jovial face and curly hair, with clothes of excellent cut and a gorgeously wrought rapier at his side. Gideon reckoned him well into his thirties. He had the guts to raise his hand to her in a tentative greeting. Before she could do anything in return, a skeleton placed a steaming bowl of sour green soup and a massive hunk of lardy yeast bread on the table, and she got busy eating.

These were sophisticated skeletons. Hers returned with a cup of hot tea on a tray and waited until she took it to retreat. Gideon had noticed that their fine motor control would have been the envy of any necromancer, that they moved with perfect concert and awareness. She was in a position of some expertise here. You couldn't spend any time in the Ninth House without coming away with an unwholesome knowledge of skeletons. She could've easily filled in for Doctor Skelebone without practising a single theorem. The sheer amount of complex programming each skeleton followed would have taken all of the oldest and most gnarled necromancers of the Locked Tomb months and months to put together. Gideon would have been impressed, but she was too hungry.

The awful teens were muttering to each other, giving Gideon looks, giving each other looks, then muttering again. The wholesome older man leaned over and gave them some bracing rebuke. They subsided reluctantly, only casting the occasional dark glance her way over their soup and bread, not knowing that she was physically immune. Back in the Ninth she had endured each meal under Crux's fantastically dismal stare, which had turned gruel into ash in her mouth.

A waiting white-robed bone servant relieved her of her bowl and her plate almost sooner than she was done. She was quietly sucking tea through her teeth, trying not to drink half a pint of face paint with it, when a hand was stuck out in front of her.

It was the hand of the kind-faced older man. Up close he had a strong jaw, the expression of the terminally jolly, and nice eyes. Gideon was genuinely surprised to find that she was shy, and more still to find she was relieved by Harrow's diktat against talking. Gideon Nav, absolutely goddamn starved of any contact with people who didn't have dark missals and advanced osteoporosis, should've yearned to talk. But she found that she couldn't imagine a single thing to say.

"Magnus the Fifth," he said. "Sir Magnus Quinn, cavalier primary and seneschal of Koniortos Court."

From three tables over, the loathsome teens greeted his audacity with low moans: they lost all appearance of restrained respectability and instead chorused his name in slow, hurt-animal noises, lowing "Magnus! *Maaaaagnus,*" which he ignored. Gideon had hesitated too long in taking his hand, and with the very soul of manners he mistook her reluctance for refusal, and rapped his knuckles on the table instead.

"Do forgive us," he said. "We're a bit short on black priests in the Fourth and the Fifth, and my valiant Fourth companions are, er, a bit overcome."

("Nooooo, Magnus, don't say we're overcome," moaned the nasty girl, sotto voce.

"Don't mention us, Magnus," moaned the other.)

Gideon clattered her chair back to stand. Magnus Quinn, Magnus of the Fifth, was too old and too well schooled to do anything so stupid as flinch, but some reputation of the Ninth House that Gideon had only barely begun to comprehend widened his eyes, just a bit. His clothes were so restrained and so beautifully made; he looked trim and tasteful without being intimidating. She hated herself for hearing Harrow's voice, low and urgent, in her hindbrain: *We are* not *becoming an appendix of the Third or Fifth Houses!*

She nodded to him, somewhat awkwardly, and he was so relieved that he pumped his chin up and down twice in response before he caught himself. "Health to the Ninth," he said firmly, and then jerked his head in what was so transparently a *Come on! Clear off!* motion that even the bad teens couldn't ignore it. They pushed their bowls away to two waiting, hunched skeletons, and tiptoed out in the older man's wake, leaving Gideon amused and alone.

She stood there until their voices died away ("Really, chaps," she caught Magnus saying repressively, "anyone would think you'd both been raised in a barn—") before she twitched her sunglasses up her nose and left, sticking her hands in the pockets of her robes and heading out in the opposite direction from where Magnus and the crap Fourth House youths had gone, down a short flight of stairs. Gideon had nowhere to go and nothing to be, and no orders and no goals: her black robe flapping at her ankles and the light getting stronger all the time, she decided to wander.

Canaan House was a nest of rooms and corridors, of sudden courtyards and staircases that dripped down into lightless gloom and terminated in big, rusting doors beneath overhangs, ones that looked as though they would go *clang* no matter how quietly you tried to shut them. More than once Gideon turned a corner and found she was back at some landing she thought she had travelled miles and miles away from. Once she paused on a blasted terrace outside, gazing at the rusting, hulking pillars that stuck up in a ring around the tower. The sea on one side was broken up with flat concrete landings like stepping-stones, set wet and geometric in the water, mummified in seaweed: the sea had covered up more structures long, long ago, and they looked like square heads with long, sticky hair, peering up suspiciously through the waves. Being outside made her feel dizzy, so she headed back inside.

There were doors—a multiplicity of doors—a veritable warehouse of doors: cupboard doors, metal autodoors, barred doors to dimly lit passageways beyond, doors half her height with no handles, doors half-rotted so you could voyeuristically look through their nakedness to the rooms they didn't hide. All these doors must have been beautiful, even the ones that led only to broom cupboards. Whoever had lived in the First House had lived in beauty once. The ceilings were still high and gracious, the plaster mouldings still graceful ornaments; but the whole thing creaked and at one point Gideon's boot went clean through a particularly soft bit of floorboard to empty space below. It was a death trap.

She went down a short flight of cramped metal stairs. The house often seemed to split its level without letting her travel very far, but this was farther down and darker than any steps had taken her before. They led to a tiled vestibule where the lights fizzed disconsolately and refused to come on all the way; she pushed open two enormous, groaning doors, which led into an echoing chamber that made her nostrils flare. It smelled badly of chemicals, and most of the smell came from the huge, filthy, perfectly rectangular pit that dominated the centre of the room. The pit was lined with dull tile, and it gave the filthiest and oldest parts of the Ninth House a run for their money. There were metal ladders going down into the pit, but why would you though.

Gideon abandoned the pit and peered through a set of grubby glass double doors. From the other side of the room beyond, a hunched, cloaked figure peered back at her, and she reflexively went for her rapier: the hunched figure swiftly—identically—went for its own.

Good going, dickhead! thought Gideon, straightening up. *It's a mirror.*

It was a mirror, an enormous one that covered the far wall. She pressed her face closer to the glass door. The room beyond had a flagstone floor, stones worn smooth from years and years of feet. There was a rusting basin and tap, where one love-abandoned towel had sat for God only knew how long, decayed to a waterfall of spiderous threads. Corroded swords were bolted to corroded panels on the wall. Through a window somewhere high up, the sunbeams poured down dust in golden torrents. Gideon would have dearly loved this training room in its prime, but she wouldn't touch those rusted blades now if you paid her.

Going back to the vestibule with the spitting lights, she noticed another door, set close to the staircase. She hadn't seen it before because a tapestry covered it almost entirely, but one of the corners had slipped and hinted at the frame beneath. She pushed the mouldering old tapestry aside to find a dark wooden door; she tried its handle, pulled it open, and stared. A long tiled corridor stared back, windowless, a succession of square lights in the ceiling whirring to life with a *clunk . . . clunk . . . clunk . . .* and tracing a path to an enormous door at the other end, totally out of place. Bracketed by heavy pillars, set with forbidding stone supports, the overall effect was not exactly welcoming. The door itself was a crossbar of black stone set in a bevelled frame of the same. A weird relief was carved above the lintel, set within a moulded panel. Gideon's boots echoed down the shiny stone tiles as she came closer to see. The relief was five little circles joined with lines, in no pattern that Gideon recognised. Below this sat a solid stone beam with carved leaves swagged horizontally from one end to the other. At the apex of each swag was carved an animal's skull with long horns, which curved inward into wicked points that almost met. Slim columns reached up to support this weird stone bunting, and wound around each column was something carved to seem writhing and alive—a fat, slithering thing, bulging and animal. Gideon reached out to touch the intricately carved marble and felt tiny overlapping scales, touched the seam where its ridged underbelly met its back. It was very cold.

There was no handle, no knocker, no knob: just a dark keyhole, for teeth that would have been as long as Gideon's thumb. She peered through the keyhole and saw—jack shit. Suffice to say, all pushing, gripping, finger-inserting and pressing was in vain. It was locked as damn.

Curious, thought Gideon.

She went back to the claustrophobic little vestibule and, out of a complete sense of perversity, tacked the tapestry back up so that the door was totally covered. In the shadows, the effect was very good. Nobody'd be finding that one any time soon. It was a stupid, secretive Ninth thing to do, done out of habit, and Gideon hated how comforting it felt.

Voices were fading into the edge of her hearing from the top of the landing that led to the stairs. Another Ninth instinct had Gideon flatten herself back into the bottom of the stairwell: done a million times before to avoid the Marshal of Drearburh, or Harrowhark, or one of the godawful great-aunts or members of the Locked Tomb cloister. Gideon had no idea whom she was avoiding, but she avoided them anyway because it was such an easy thing to do. A conversation, conducted in low, rich, peevish tones, drifted down.

"—mystical, oblique claptrap," someone was saying, "and I have half a mind to write to your father and complain—"

"—what," drawled another, "that the *First House* isn't treating us fairly—"

"—a lateral puzzle isn't a trial, and, now that I think about it, the idea that the old fogey doesn't know a thing about it is beyond belief! Some geriatric playing mind games, or worse, and this is my theory, wanting to see who breaks—"

"Ever the conspiracy theorist," said the second voice.

The first voice was aggrieved. "Why're the shuttles gone? Why is this place such a tip? Why the secrecy? Why is the food so bad? QED, it's a conspiracy."

There was a thoughtful pause.

"I didn't think the food was that bad," said a third voice.

"I'll tell you what it is," continued the first voice. "It's a cheap, Cohort-style enlisted man's hazing. They're waiting to see who's stupid enough to take the bait. Who falls for it, you see. Well, *I* shan't."

"Unless," said the second voice—which now that Gideon was hearing it, was very like the third voice in pitch and tone, differentiated only by affect—"the challenge is one of protocol: *we* have to provide a valid response to a necessarily vague question in order to authenticate ourselves. Making meaning from the meaningless. Et cetera."

The first voice had taken on a tinge of whine when it said, "Oh, for God's sake."

Scuffle. Movement. The stairs echoed with footsteps: they were coming down.

"I do wonder where that funny old man hid the shuttles," mused the third voice.

The second: "Dropped them off the side of the dock, I expect."

"Don't be mad," said the first, "those things cost a fortune."

At the bottom of the stairs, deep in the shadows, Gideon got her first good glimpse of the speakers. The strange twin-scions of the Third House were looking around, attended to by their sulky, slightly bouffant cavalier. Up close, Gideon was more impressed than ever. The golden Third twin was probably the best-looking person she'd ever seen in her life. She was tall and regal, with some radiant, butterfly quality—her shirt was haphazardly tucked into her trousers, which were haphazardly tucked into her boots, but she was all topaz and shine and lustre. Necromancers affected robes in the same way cavaliers affected swords, but she hadn't tucked her arms into hers, and it was a gauzy, gold-shot, transparent thing floating out around her like wings. There were about five rings on each hand and her earrings would've put chandeliers to shame, but she had an air of wild and innocent overdecoration, of having put on the prettiest things in her jewellery box and then forgotten to take them off. Her buttery hair was stuck to her forehead with sweat, and she kept tangling a curl of it in one finger and artlessly letting it go.

The second twin was as though the first had been taken to pieces and put back together without any genius. She wore a robe of the same cloth and colour, but on her it was a beautiful shroud on a mummy. The cavalier had lots of hair, an aquiline face, and a self-satisfied little jacket.

"*I* think," the bright twin was saying, "that it's a hell of a lot better than sticking us in a room and playing *who's the best necromancer?* Or worse—loading us up with old scrolls and having us translate rituals for hours and hours on end."

"Yes, it would have been unfortunate," agreed her sister placidly, "considering it would have demonstrated within the first five minutes that you're completely thick."

A curl was wound about one finger. "Oh, shut it, Ianthe."

"We should be celebrating, if we're being honest with ourselves," the pallid girl continued, warming to her subject, "since the already poorly hidden fact of you being a great big bimbo would have come to light so quickly that it would have broken the sound barrier."

The curl was let go with a visual *sproing.* "Ianthe, don't make me cross."

"Please don't be cross," said her sister. "You know your brain can only deal with one emotion at a time."

Their cavalier's expression got ugly.

"You're sore, Ianthe," he said sharply. "You can't show off with books ad infinitum, and so you're invisible, isn't that it?"

Both girls rounded on him at once. The pallid twin simply stared, eyes closed to pale-lashed slits, but the lovely twin took one of his ears between a thumb and forefinger and tweaked it unmercifully. He was not a short young man, but she had half a head on him, and a whole head if you counted her hair. Her sister watched from the side, impassive—though Gideon swore that she was smiling, very slightly.

"If you talk like that to her again, Babs," said the golden twin, "I'll destroy you. Beg her forgiveness."

He was shocked and defensive. "C'mon, you know I didn't—it was for *you*—I was meeting the insult for you—"

"She can insult me as she likes. You're insubordinate. Say you're sorry."

"Princess, I live to serve—"

"Naberius!" she said, and pulled his ear forward so that he had to come with it, like an animal being led by a bit. Two bright red spots of outrage had formed in his cheeks. The lovely twin waggled his ear gently, so that his head shook with it. "Grovel, Babs. As soon as possible, please."

"Leave it, Corona," said the other girl, suddenly. "This isn't the time to horse around. Drop him and let's keep going."

The bright twin—Corona—hesitated, but then dropped the ear of the unfortunate cavalier. He rubbed it fretfully. Gideon could only see the back of his head, but he kept looking at the girl who'd basically clouted him like a whipped dog, the arrogant line of his head and shoulders drooping. Suddenly, impetuously, Corona slung one arm around him and perambulated forward, giving his other ear a tweak—he jerked sullenly away—before wheeling him through the doors to the pit room. The pale twin held the door open for them both.

As they went through, exclaiming at the smell, the pale twin paused. She did not follow them. She looked straight into the darkness instead, the deep shadows around the stairwell. Gideon knew that she was completely hidden—hooded—invisible, but she felt herself pressing backward anyway: away from that pale, washed-out gaze, which was staring with discomfiting accuracy straight at her.

"This is not a clever path to start down," she said softly. "I would not attract attention from the necromancer of the Third House."

The pale twin stepped through and closed the door behind her. Gideon was left alone.

10

HARROWHARK DID NOT APPEAR for a midday meal. Gideon, still unused to the concept of *midday meal* or honestly *midday*, appeared a good hour earlier than anyone else would have. Either everyone had an appropriate circadian pattern of hunger or they were being too Housely and well bred not to follow one. Gideon sat in the hot, scrubbed room where she had eaten breakfast, and was given a meal of pallid white meat and a bunch of leaves. It was good that she was alone. She had no clue what to do with it. She ate the meat with a fork—you didn't need a knife; it was so tender that it flaked away if you touched it—and ate the leaves one by one with her fingers. She realised partway through that it was probably a salad. Raw vegetables in the Ninth came in the form of pitiable cairns of grated snow leek, stained through with as much salty black sauce as it would absorb. She filled up on the bread, which was really very good, and stuck a piece in her robe for later.

A skeleton had brought her food; a skeleton had taken it away, with the same pinpoint accuracy the others had shown. There were no cheap tricks with them, she noticed—nobody had jammed pins through the joints so that they'd stick together easier, or slabbed on big gobs of tendon. No, whoever had raised them had been extraordinarily talented. She suspected it was Teacher. Harrow wouldn't like that. The House of the Ninth was meant to have cornered the market on perfect reconstruction, and here were a whole bunch of them probably made by a little man who clapped his hands together unironically.

Just as Gideon had shaken the crumbs off her lap and was rising to leave, two more novitiates entered. When they saw Gideon, both they and she stopped dead.

One of the pair was a wan, knife-faced kid dressed in antiseptic whites and chain mail you could cut with a fork, it was so delicate. He was draped in it even down to a kilt, which was strange: necromancers didn't normally wear that type of armour, and he was definitely the necromancer. He had a necromancer build. Pale silk fluttered from his slim shoulders. He gave the impression of being the guy fun sought out for death. He was prim and ascetic-looking, and his companion—who was older, a fair bit older than Gideon herself—had the air of the perpetually disgruntled. He was rather more robust, nuggety, and dressed in chipped bleached leathers that looked as though they'd seen genuine use. At least one finger on his left hand was a gross-looking stump, which she admired.

The reason why *they* had stopped dead was unclear. She had stopped dead because the necromancer was staring at her with an expression of naked hostility. He looked at her as though he had finally come face-to-face with the murderer of a beloved family pet.

Gideon had spent too long in the depths of Drearburh not to know when to, put scientifically, *get outie.* It was not the first time she had received that look. Sister Lachrimorta had looked at her that way almost exclusively, and Sister Lachrimorta was blind. The only difference in the way that Crux had looked at her was that Crux had managed also to encapsulate a complete lack of surprise, as though she already had managed to disappoint his lowest expectations. And a very long time ago—painfully folded in the back of her amygdala— the Reverend Mother and the Reverend Father had *also* looked at her like that, though in their case, their diffidence had been cut through with a phobic flinch: the way you'd look at an unexpected maggot.

"Please deal with the shadow cultist," said the whey-faced boy, who had the deepest, weariest, most repressive voice she had ever heard in her life.

"Yes, Uncle," said the bigger man.

Gideon was raw for a fight. She wanted nothing more than for the cross-faced man in boiled leather to draw on her. He was strong-boned and weathered, deeply creased, yellow-brown and yellow-coarse all over. Next to his almost daintily dressed necromancer in white, he looked dusty and ferocious. He looked tough. Thank God. She wanted to fight bloody. She wanted to fight until bone adepts had to be called to put people's feet back on. She knew the price—waking up mummified in aggressive notes, or maybe dying—but didn't care anymore. Gideon was measuring, in her mind's eye, the length of her rapier to the collarbones of the cavalier opposite.

He disappointed her viscerally by standing a few steps away, putting his hands together, and bowing over them to her. It was polite, though not apologetic. He had a lighter, rougher voice than his necromancer, somewhat hoarse, like he suffered from a lifelong cold or a smoker's cough.

"My uncle can't eat with your kind around," he said. "Please leave."

Gideon had a million questions. Like: *Your kind?* And: *Why do you have such a baby uncle, one the colour of mayonnaise?* And: *Is "your kind" people who aren't nephews and who have middle fingers?* But she said nothing. She stared him down for a few seconds; he stared back—his face did not hold the same brand of hate, but it held a bullish, deadened expression that seemed to go right through her. If it had been Crux she would have given him the finger. As it was, she nodded and pushed past with her mind an indignant whirl.

Gideon felt awfully suckered by the whole thing. She had longed for the Cohort, in part, due to being heartily sick of her time alone in the dark; she'd wanted to be a part of something bigger than encroaching dementia and snow-leek husbandry. What was she now? An unwelcome spectre roaming the halls without a necro to pursue— the stinging slap in the face that she didn't even have *Harrow*—still alone, just in better lighting. She had cherished the tiny delusion that the Lyctor trials would see her being useful for more than spying on conversations and spoiling breakfasts. Even *Swords II* would have been a sweet reprieve from idleness. It was in this frame of mind, reckless with disappointment, that she pushed her way at random through a collection of dark, empty antechambers and up a flight of damp brick steps; and then suddenly she found herself outside, in a terraced garden.

The sun blazed down through a canopy of glass or some thick, transparent plex. It was admittedly a garden only in a very sad sense of the word. Wherever the First House grew its food leaves, they didn't grow them here. The salt was thick on each metal strut. The planters were full of shrubby, stunted green things, with long stems and drooping blossoms, bleached from the thick white light overhead. Weird fragrances rose like heat above them, heavy smells, strange smells. Nothing that grew on the Ninth had a real scent: not the moss and spores in its caves, and not the dried-out vegetables cultivated in its fields. The plex ended in a genuinely open area where the wind ruffled the wrinkled leaves of some wrinkled old trees, and there—under an awning in the undulating sun, looking like a long-stemmed, drooping blossom herself—was Dulcinea.

She was entirely alone. Her man-hulk was nowhere to be seen. Lying in a chair, she looked flimsy and tired: fine lines marked the corners of the eyes and the mouth, and she was wearing a fashionable and inane hat. She was dressed in something light and clingy that she had not yet hawked blood upon. It looked as though she were sleeping, and Gideon, not for the first time, felt a spike of pity; she tried to backtrack, but it was too late.

"Don't go," said the figure, her eyes fluttering open. "Thought so. Hello, Gideon the Ninth! Can you come and put this chair's back up straight for me? I'd do it myself, but you know by now that I'm not well and some days I don't feel entirely up to it. Can I beg you that favour?"

There was a fine sheen of sweat on the translucent brow under the frivolous hat, and a certain shortness of breath. Gideon went to the chair and fiddled with the fastening, immediately emasculated by the difficulty of working out a simple chair-latch. The Lady Septimus waited passively for Gideon to pull it flush, smiling at her with those big gentian eyes.

"Thank you," she said, once she had been propped up. She took the silly hat off her damp, fawn-coloured curls and set it in her lap, and her expression was somewhat conspiratorial. "I know that you're doing penance and can't talk, so you don't have to figure out how to tell me through charades."

Gideon's eyebrows shot up over her sunglasses' rims before she could stop them. "Oh, yes," said the girl, dimpling. "You're not the first Ninth nun I've ever met. I've often thought it must be so hard being a brother or sister of the Locked Tomb. I actually dreamed of being one . . . when I was young. It seemed such a romantic way to die. I must have been about thirteen . . . You see, I knew I was going to die then. I didn't want anyone to look at me, and the Ninth House was so far away. I thought I could just have some time to myself and then expire very beautifully, alone, in a black robe, with everyone praying over me and being solemn. But then I found out about the face paint you all have to wear," she added fretfully, "and that wasn't my aesthetic. You can't drape yourself over your cell and fade away beautifully in face paint— Does this count as a conversation? Am I breaking your penance? Shake for *no* and nod for *yes*."

"Good!" she said, when Gideon mutely shook her head *no*, sucked completely under this mad, bubbling riptide. "I love a captive listener. I know you're only doing this because you feel bad for me. And you do look like a nice kid. Sorry," she added hastily, "you're not a child. But I feel so old right now. Did you see the pair from the Fourth House? Babies. They have contributed to me feeling ancient. Tomorrow I might feel youthful, but today's a bad day . . . and I feel like a gimp. Take off your glasses, please, Gideon the Ninth. I'd like to see your eyes."

At the juxtaposition of *Gideon* with *obedient* many people would have rocked with laughter and gone on chuckling and gurgling for quite some time. But she was helpless now in the face of this extraordinary request; she was helpless at the thin arms and rosebud smile of the woman-girl in front of her; she was utterly helpless at the word *gimp*. She slid her sunglasses off her nose and obligingly presented her face for inspection.

And she was inspected, thoroughly and immediately. The eyes narrowed with intent, and for a moment the face was all business.

There was something swift and cool in the blueness of those eyes, some deep intelligence, some sheer shameless depth and breadth of looking. It made Gideon's cheeks flare, despite her mental reproach to *Slow down, Nav, slow down.*

"Oh, singular," said Dulcinea quietly, more to herself than to Gideon. "Lipochrome ... recessive. I like looking at people's eyes," she explained suddenly, smiling now. "They tell you such a lot. I couldn't tell you much about your Reverend Daughter ... but you have eyes like gold coins. Am I embarrassing you? Am I being a creep?"

At the head-shake *no*, she settled back more into her chair, tilting her head to the seat back and fanning herself with the frivolous hat. "Good," she said, with satisfaction. "It's bad enough that we're stuck in this burnt-out old hovel without me scaring you. Isn't it fantastically abandoned? Imagine all the ghosts of everyone who must have lived here ... worked here ... still waiting to be called, if we could figure out how. The Seventh doesn't do well with ghosts, you know. We offend them. We're worrisome. The old division between body and spirit. We deal too much with the body ... crystallising it in time ... trapping it unnaturally. The opposite of your House, don't you think, Gideon the Ninth? You take empty things and build with them ... We press down the hand of a clock, to try to stop it from ticking the last second."

This was all so far over Gideon's head that it sat somewhere out in space, but there was something soothing about it anyway. Gideon had only ever been clotheslined this way with Harrowhark, who explained herself seldom and as you would only to a very stupid child. Dulcinea had the dreamy, confiding manner of someone who, despite spouting grade-A horseshit, was confident you would understand everything she was saying. Also, as she talked she smiled widely and prettily, and moved her lashes up and down.

Thus hypnotised, Gideon could only watch with a mouth full of teeth as the blue-eyed necromancer laid one slight, narrow hand on her arm; her skin stretched thin over very marked metacarpals, and wrist bones like knots in a rope. "Stand up for me," said Dulcinea. "Indulge me. Lots of people do . . . but I want *you* to."

Gideon pulled away and stood. The sunlight dappled over the hem of her robe in rusty splotches. Dulcinea said, "Draw your sword, Gideon of the Ninth."

Grasping the smooth black grip beneath the black nest of the knuckle bow, Gideon drew. It seemed as though she had drawn this damn thing a thousand times—that Aiglamene's voice had taken permanent residence in her head now, just to keep up the charade. *Draw. Lean on the right foot. Arm bent, not collapsed, naked blade angled at your opponent's face or chest. You're guarding the outer side of your body, Nav, you're on your right foot, and you're not weighting forward like a goddamned piece of freight—you're centred, you can move backward or forward at will.* The rapier blade, away from its black home in Drearburh, burned a lightless, opaque metal colour, a long slender absence of hue. Gideon acknowledged its beauty, grudgingly—how it looked like a needle, an ebon ribbon. *Offhand up and high.* She relaxed into position, triumphant in the new body memory that her teacher had beaten into her, and wanted to fight again.

"Oh, very good!" said Dulcinea, and she clapped like a child seeing a firework. "Perfect . . . just like a picture of Nonius. People say that all Ninth cavaliers are good for is pulling around baskets of bones. Before I met you I imagined that you might be some wizened thing with a yoke and panniers of cartilage . . . half skeleton already."

This was bigoted, assumptive, and completely true. Gideon relaxed her sword and her stance, at her ease—and saw that the fragile girl engulfed by her chair had stopped playing with her frivolous hat. Her mouth was quirked in a quizzical little smile, and her eyes said that she had calculated two plus two and ended up with a very final four.

"Gideon the Ninth," said Dulcinea, slowly, "are you used to a heavier sword?"

Gideon looked down. She looked at her rapier, pointed skyward like a black arrow, her off hand cupped and supporting what should have been more grip but now was the long knob of pommel, the way you'd hold—*a fucking longsword.*

She sheathed it immediately, sliding it home to its scabbard in a tight iron whisper. A cold sweat had broken out beneath her clothes. The expression on Dulcinea's face was simply bright-eyed, mischievous interest, but to Gideon it was the Secundarius Bell chiding a child already ten minutes late for prayer. For a moment a lot of stupid stuff felt very ready to happen. She nearly confessed everything to Dulcinea's mild and denim-coloured gaze: she nearly opened her mouth and begged wholeheartedly for the woman's mercy.

It was in this moment of charged stupidity that Protesilaus turned up, saving her bacon by dint of being very large and ignoring her. He stood with his muddy hair and bleary skin and blocked the shaft of sunlight that was pattering over his adept's hands, and he said to her in his dreary, rumbling voice: "It's shut."

No time to figure out that one. As Dulcinea's eyes flickered between her cavalier and the cavalier of the Ninth, Gideon took the opportunity to turn tail and—not run, but slope extremely fast in the direction of anywhere but there. There were cracks in the plex and the wind was coming in hot and salty, rippling her robes and her hood, and she had nearly escaped when Dulcinea called— "Gideon the Ninth!"

She half-turned her head back to them, dark glasses crooking down over her eyebrows. Protesilaus the Seventh stared at her with the empty eyes of someone who would watch with equal heavy disinterest if part of the wall were kicked out and she were punted down into the sea, but his adept was looking at her—wistfully. Gideon hesitated by the door for that look, in the shadows of the archway, buffeted by the wind from the water.

Dulcinea said: "I hope we talk again soon."

Hell! thought Gideon, taking the stairs blindly two at a time. *She* didn't. She had said too much already, and all without speaking a single word.

11

THOSE EARLY DAYS AT Canaan House spaced themselves out like beads on a prayer string, dilated. They consisted of big, empty hours, of eating meals in unoccupied rooms, of being alone amid very strange strangers. Gideon couldn't even rely on the familiarity of the dead. The skeletons of the First were too good, too capable, too watchful—and Gideon didn't feel truly at her ease anywhere except shut up in the dim rooms that the Ninth had been given, doing drills.

After nearly giving everything away she spent two days almost entirely cloistered, working with her rapier until the sweat had smeared her face paint to a leering, staved-in mask. She stacked a rusting stool on top of the sagging ebon dresser and did chin-ups into the iron wedge that ran across the rafters. She did press-ups in front of the windows until Dominicus limned her with bloody light, completing its sprint around the watery planet.

Both nights she went to bed sore and furious with loneliness. Crux always had said that she was at her most unbearable after confinement. She fell into a deep, black sleep and woke up only once, the second night, when—in the very early morning when the night outside seemed more like the lightless Ninth—Harrowhark Nonagesimus shut the door behind herself, very nearly silently. She kept her eyes mostly closed as the Reverend Daughter paused before the makeshift bed, and as she watched the robed black figure drifted over to the bedroom. Then there was no more noise; and Harrow was gone again, in the morning, when Gideon awoke. She didn't even leave rude notes.

It was in this abandoned state that the cavalier of the Ninth House ate two breakfasts, starved of both protein and attention, dark glasses slipping on her nose as she drank another bowl of soup. She would have killed to see a couple of haggard nuns tottering around the place, and was therefore 100 percent vulnerable when she looked up to see a Third House twin stride into the room like a lion. It was the lovely one; she had the sleeves of her gauzy robe haphazardly rolled up to each golden shoulder and her hair tied back in a tawny cloud, and she looked at Gideon with an expression like an artillery shell midflight.

"The Ninth!" she said.

She sauntered over. Gideon had risen to stand, remembering the pale eyes of her pissed-off twin, but instead found a beringed hand proffered in her direction: "Lady Coronabeth Tridentarius," she was told, "Princess of Ida, heir of the Third House."

Gideon did not know what to do with the hand, which was offered to her fingers out, palm upward. She touched her fingers to it in the hope that she could grip it briefly and get out that way, but Coronabeth Tridentarius, Princess of Ida, took her hand and roguishly kissed the backs of Gideon's knuckles. Her smile was sparklingly pleased with her own gall; her eyes were a deep, liquid violet, and she spoke with the casual effrontery of someone who expected her every command of *jump!* to be followed by a rave.

"I've organised sparring matches for the cavaliers of all the Houses," she said. "It's my hope that even the Ninth will accept my invitation. Will it?"

If Gideon had not been so lonely; if Gideon had not been so used to having a fighting partner, even one more used these days to battling rheumatism; if Coronabeth Tridentarius had not been so astonishingly hot. All these *ifs* she contemplated wearily, led by the Third House necromancer down the poky, confined little staircase immediately familiar to her as the one she'd explored before; down to the dark, tiled vestibule with the flickering lights, and through to the room with the foul-smelling chemical pit.

This room was now alive with activity. There were three skeletons down in the pit with hairy mops and buckets, cleaning the slime out of it; a fourth was wiping down the streaked glass double doors through to the mirror room beyond. The fug of rot was overlaid with the equally pervasive fug of surfactants and wood polish. Old age still had the place in a chokehold, but in the hot light of the early morning, two figures danced around each other on the outspread flagstone dais of the mirror room. The urgent metal scrape of sword on sword filled the space up to the rafters.

A skeleton in the corner wound a long pole into a network of cobwebs, displacing showers of dust; a couple of others sat about, watching the fight. The cavalier of the Third she recognised even without his smug little jacket, which he had hung over a peg as he struck a fatigued attitude to clean his sword. She could not mistake the cavalier of the Second in her intense Cohort officer whites, contrasted with a jacket of blazing red. She was watching the two in the centre: facing each other on the flagstones, swords and long knives throwing up bevelled yellow reflections on the walls, were Magnus and the abominable girl teen, stripped down to their shirtsleeves. Everyone looked up as the Princess of Ida glowed into sight, because you couldn't do anything else.

"Sir Magnus, behold my coup!" she said, and she gestured to Gideon.

This did not produce a susurrus of respectful murmurs, as she had obviously hoped. The dress-uniform cavalier stood to attention, but her gaze was blank and cool. The Fourth girl dropped form and rocked backward on her heels, whistling noisily in fascinated horror. The cavalier of the Third raised his eyebrows and took on an expression of dismay, as though his necromancer had just presented them with a leper. Only Magnus gave her a genial, if slightly bewildered, smile.

"Princess Corona, trust you to nab Gideon the Ninth!" he said, and to his dreadful teen: "See, now you can have a duel with someone else, and not bore everyone by how soundly Jeannemary the Fourth can thrash me."

("*Nooooo, Magnus, don't mention me,*" hissed that dreadful teen.)

"*I'd* be ashamed to admit to that," said the Third cavalier significantly.

The unfortunate Jeannemary the Fourth was going red in the face. She drew herself up to say something obviously unwise, but her sparring partner clapped her on the back with an unsinkable smile.

"Ashamed, Prince Naberius? To lose to a Chatur?" he said heartily. "Goodness me, no. Cavalier family since the time of the Resurrection. Should feel ashamed if she lost to *me*. I've known her since she was a child—she knows I'm absolutely no good. You should have seen her when she was five—"

("*Magnus, do not talk about me being five.*")

"Now, let me tell you this story—"

("*Magnus, do not tell anyone this story.*")

"Challenged me to a duel during a reception, said I'd insulted her—think it was a matter of propping her up with cushions, and to be honest, she would've had me if she hadn't been using a bread knife as her offhand—"

Disgusted beyond all tolerance, the much-tried Jeannemary let out a primal yell and escaped to the benches on the other side of the room, far away from them. Now that she wasn't looking, Magnus gave Naberius a look of frank reproof. The Third's cavalier coloured and looked away.

"I want to see a match," said Princess Corona. "Come—*Gideon* the Ninth, right?—why don't you try Sir Magnus instead? Don't believe him when he says he's rubbish. The Fifth House is meant to turn out very fine cavaliers."

Magnus inclined his head.

"Of course I'm willing, and the princess is gracious," he said, "but I didn't get to be cavalier primary due to being the best with a rapier. I'm cavalier primary only because my adept is also my wife. I suppose you could say that I—ha, ha—cavalier pri*married*!"

From the other side of the room, Jeannemary let out a long noise like a death rattle. Princess Corona laughed outright; Magnus looked extremely pleased with himself. The faces of the other two were patiently blank. Gideon made a mental note to write down the joke so that she could use it herself later.

Corona inclined her bright head in toward Gideon. She smelled nice, like how Gideon imagined soap was meant to smell.

"Will the Ninth honour us?" she murmured prettily.

Stronger women than Gideon could not have said no to an up-close-and-personal Corona Tridentarius. She stepped up to the dais, her boots ringing out on the stone: the older man opposite's eyes widened when he saw that she was not going to take off her robe, nor her hood, nor her glasses. The air in the room thrilled, all except for the dreary *scrape, scrape, scrape* of the skeleton removing cobwebs. Even Jeannemary sat up from her posture of premature death to watch. There was a low murmur of amazement from Corona when Gideon twitched open her robe to reveal the knuckles latched to her belt; they glittered blackly in the sunlight as she slipped them onto her hand.

"Knuckle-knives?" said the Third's cavalier in outright disbelief. "The Ninth uses knuckle-knives?"

"Not traditionally."

That was the cavalier in the Cohort uniform, who had a voice as crisp as her collar. Naberius said with forced languor: "I simply can't remember ever thinking knuckle-knives were a viable option."

"They're tremendously *nasty*." (Gideon admitted to herself that the way Corona said it was kind of hot.)

Naberius sniffed.

"They're a brawler's weapon."

The Cohort cav said, "Well. We'll see."

That was the strange thing about keeping mute, thought Gideon. Everyone seemed to talk at you, rather than to you. Only her erstwhile sparring partner was looking her dead in the eye—as much as he could through dark glasses, anyway.

"Does the Ninth, er—" Magnus was gesturing in a rather general way to Gideon's robes, her glasses, her hood, which she translated to *Are you going to take those off?* When she shook her head *no* he shrugged in wonder: "All right!" and added the slightly bewildering, "Well done."

Corona said, "I'll arbitrate," and they moved into position. Once again Gideon was back down in the half-lit depths of Drearburh, in the cement-poured tomb of a soldier's hall. Cavalier duels worked the same way Aiglamene had taught her they would, which was very much the same way they did back home, just with more folderol. You stood in front of each other and laid your offhand arm across your chest, showing which main-gauche weapon you intended to use: her knuckle-knives were laid, fat and black, against her collarbone. Magnus's sword—a beautiful dagger of ivory-coloured steel, the handle a twist of creamy leather—touched his.

"To the first touch," said their arbiter, badly hiding her rising excitement. "Clavicle to sacrum, arms exception. Call."

First touch? In Drearburh it was *to the floor*, but there was no time to contemplate that one: Magnus was smiling at her with the boyish, teacherly enthusiasm of a man about to play a ball game with a younger sibling. But beneath that excellent mask there was a note of doubt about his eyes, a tugging of his mouth, and something in Gideon rose as well: he was a little afraid of her.

"Magnus the Fifth!" he said, and: "Er—go easy!"

Gideon looked over at Corona and shook her head. The necromancer-princess of Ida was too well bred to query and too quick to mistake, and simply said: "I call for Gideon the Ninth. Seven paces back—turn—begin . . ."

There were four pairs of hungry eyes watching that fight, but they all blurred into the background of a dream: the lines one's brain filled in to abbreviate a place, a time, a memory. Gideon Nav knew in the first half second that Magnus was going to lose: after that she stopped thinking with her brain and started thinking with her arms, which were frankly where the best of her cerebral matter lay.

What happened next was like closing your eyes in a warm and stuffy room. The first feint from the Fifth House was the heavy drowsiness that filled the back of her head, all the way down to her toes; the second the weightless loll of the skull to the chest. Gideon tucked her offhand behind her back, said to herself: *Stop blocking every blow!* and did not even bother to parry. She pivoted away each syrup-slow thrust without meeting it, bent back from the follow-up with the dagger like they had agreed beforehand where it would fall: he pressed his quarter, trying to force her, and she very gently folded his sword to the side with hers, contraparried. The point of her black rapier flickered like paper touched with a flame and came to rest, a quarter-inch away from his heart, making him stutter to a halt. She bumped the tip of her sword into his chest, very gently.

It was over in three moves. A mental haptic jolt bunted Gideon awake, and there she was: rapier held still to Magnus's chest; Magnus with the good-natured but poleaxed expression of a man caught mid–practical joke; four sets of staring, equally blank expressions. Their very good-looking arbiter's mouth was even hanging very slightly open, lips parting over white teeth, gaping dumbly until she caught up—

"Match to the Ninth!"

"Goodness me," said Magnus.

The room let out a collective breath. Jeannemary said: "Oh my *days*," and the Cohort cav of the Second sat up at least two inches taller than before, thumb pressed furiously hard into the soft part under her chin in thought. Gideon was busy sheathing her sword a heartbeat after Magnus had sheathed his, jerky with lag time in returning his bow, turning away. Her sweat had turned to adrenaline; her adrenaline was singing through her as fine, hot fuel, but her brain and heart had not caught up with the result. The only emotion she was feeling was a slow-to-saturate relief. She had won. She had won even though moving in a robe and dark glasses was so stupid. Aiglamene's honour could go another day intact, and Gideon's ass could go spiritually unkicked.

Conversations were happening around her, not to her:

A bit plaintively: "I'm not quite *that* out of form, am I?—"

("Magnus! Maaaaagnus. *Three moves, Magnus.*")

"—Am I getting old? Should Abigail and I divorce?—"

"I didn't even see her move." Corona was breathing hard. "God, she's fast."

Because they were in closest proximity, her first gaze after the fight fell on the overgroomed cavalier of the Third, Naberius: his eyes were taut, and his smile was unnerved. His eyes were blue, but this close she could see that they were stained through in places with a light, insipid brown that made Gideon think of oily water.

"Next match to me," said Naberius.

"Don't be greedy," said his princess, good-naturedly and a trifle distractedly. "The Ninth just fought. Why don't you go toe-to-toe with Jeannemary?"

But it was clear that he did not want to go toe-to-toe with Jeannemary, and judging by the look on her face she was no keener on the idea. Naberius shrugged his shoulders back, rolling up the sleeves of his fine cotton shirt to each elbow. He did not drop his gaze from Gideon. "You didn't even break a sweat, did you?" he said. "No, you're ready to go again. Try *me*."

"Oh, Babs."

"Come on." His voice was much softer, more coaxing and appealing, when he was speaking to Corona. "Let the Third show what it can do, my lady. I know you'd rather watch your own." There was a peculiarly nasal lilt to his voice, a sort of posh elongated vowel that made it *rathah*. "Put me in. Dyas can get another look at me." (Next to him, the Cohort cavalier who was obviously hight *Dyas* raised her eyebrows the exact one-eighth of an inch to indicate how much she wanted to get another look at him.)

"The Ninth?"

Gideon's heart was still ricocheting around her chest. She raised her shoulders in an expression that the brethren of the Locked Tomb would have recognised immediately as the precursor of Gideon about to do something particularly daft, but Corona took it as acceptance, and said mock-indulgently to her cav: "Well, then, my dear, go off and make yourself happy."

He beamed as though he had just been bought a new pair of shoes. Gideon thought: *Shit*.

The Cohort cavalier, Dyas, was saying: "Your Highness. The adept shouldn't officiate for their cavalier."

"Oh, *pff*! Surely just this once can't harm, Lieutenant."

"You can't call yourself a disinterested arbitrator, Princess," Magnus was saying.

"Nonsense: I'm harder on him than anyone else. To the touch; call!"

In a very short space of time she was standing face to face with another cavalier, and there was a juddering in her ears that she recognised as the beating of her own heart. The glass of her knuckle-knives felt black and cold and silky all the way through a layer of robe and her shirt, and her tongue felt thick in her mouth. She hadn't been this overstimulated since that one time when *training* had consisted of Crux, a repeating crossbow, and two skeletons with machetes. The Third's main-gauche dagger was as gorgeously wrought as his hair: chased silver and Imperial violet, the arms of the hilt curved and hugging inward in a way that tugged on her memory but did not grasp the right file. The blade was thin and bright and flared at the top. She was so busy looking at it that she barely heard Naberius say:

"Naberius the Third."

And very, very quietly, just for her:

"Ninth cavs are necro suitcases. Who're *you*?"

It was good that she had already practised how to be quiet, because the traditional Nav response would have been one of any number of pieces of crude backchat. She resented the contempt with which his mouth rounded over *Ninth*; she resented *suitcases*; she resented his hair. But Coronabeth was singing out, "I call for Gideon the Ninth!" and they were marking five paces—six—seven.

She had only a moment to size Naberius up. He was about an inch shorter than her, with a frame that had been whipped within an inch of its life into perfectly sculpted muscle. He was narrow shouldered with long, long arms, and she was beginning to believe that he was not simply a douchebag who used lip balm, but a douchebag who used lip balm and had a very long reach. He stood perfectly:

more perfectly even than her teacher, who had partially fused her spine with standing to attention. His rapier was a froth of silver wire and tracery at the loop of the hilt, and the blade shone notchless, perfect as the line made from his shoulder to its tip: her answering stance felt slouchy and half-assed, and the black knuckle-knives brutish, unsurgical. The hard moue of his mouth told her that he was used to making people feel that way, but also that he definitely used lip balm. Her heart sped up: slowed: renewed, arrhythmic with anticipation.

"Begin!" called Corona.

In the first ten seconds, Gideon had known that the fight with the Fifth House was hers to lose. It took her twenty seconds to come to a very important discovery about the House of the Third: it valued cleanliness. Each twitch of the sword was a masterpiece of technique. He fought like clockwork: inevitable, bloodless, perfect, with absolute economy of movement. The first time the black sword of the Ninth flicked into action, the line of his rapier slicing hers to the side—a simple semicircle arc with the blade, bored, contemptuous, exact—would have brought an expert to tears. His advance and retreat were like lines from a manual, fed directly into his feet.

Stop blocking every blow, her brain told her. Her arm ignored her brain, and sparks glittered as Naberius's sword clanked against the obsidian glass of her defending knuckle-knives; the force of the blow reverberated up Gideon's arm and shuddered into her spine. Her sword sang forward in what she knew to be a perfect thrust, aimed true and hard at his side; she heard an oily *shnk!*, and then another blow quaked its way into her elbow and up to the base of her skull. The blade she had taken for a dagger had separated into three, trapping hers neatly: a trident knife, which was so hopelessly obvious that she probably had to offer to save time and kick her own ass for him. Naberius smiled at her, blandly.

It was the most irritating fight she'd ever had. He wasn't as fast as she was, but he wasn't wearing robes, and anyway he didn't have to be as fast as she was. He just had to keep her at arm's length, and he was a master at it. This *to the touch* nonsense was pissing her off. If she had been wielding her longsword she would have simply smashed through him like a brick through a windowpane. But she had a needle in one hand and a handful of black glass in the other, and had to skip and hop around like he was wielding poison; and he had been a cavalier probably since the day he was born. At some points he could stand there completely still, completely bored, his sword held in perfect form as though he were doing dressage. The light beat down on her robes and her head. She couldn't believe she was being held at bay by someone who had eaten every cavalier manual and chewed dutifully twenty-five times.

Naberius toyed with her languidly—he had a trick where his sword licked out like a cat's claw, immediate, before pulling back again with a measured half step—and he kept her at sword's length, never letting her enter his space. He kept up his litany of *parry; quick attack for space; pressure the sword with the offhand* until she was sick to death of it.

Gideon ran her rapier down the length of his—lightless black on silver—with a shrill squeal, but he circled it deftly down and away. She thrust again, high, and found that the upper breadth of her blade was caught neatly within the fork of that goddamned trident knife: he used the leverage to push her down. . . . down . . . and she found that his rapier was sliding forward, over her arm, through the tuck of her elbow. Aiglamene had taught her to anticipate a death blow. She flinched to the side immediately, letting it press tight against her, swearing mentally all the way: in a real fight he'd be able to slice a hot ribbon over her chest and shoulder, but couldn't kill her either way. And he couldn't touch her with the point, just the edge. She was still in the duel.

But then he did something perfect. It was probably recorded in some shitty Seventh-style swordplay book as *TWO CROWS DRINKING WATER* or *THE BOY STRANGLES THE GOOSE*. He pivoted her sword downward with his three-bladed knife, jerked the wrist of his rapier-hand forward, and flicked the black blade of the Ninth from her grip. It clattered to the worn-out flagstones and was still. Jeannemary gulped off a yelp in the background. Her heart trickled like prayer beads sliding down a string.

Naberius stepped out of his lunge and smiled that irritating smile again.

"You cut too much," he said.

He did not smile when Gideon unwound her sword-arm from his rapier in a swift wheel of movement, ducked forward, and punched him in the solar plexus. The breath wheezed from his lungs like he was an open airlock. Naberius crumpled backward, and she kicked her robes aside to touch one booted foot to the place beneath his knee: he staggered, spat, and fell. She dropped for her sword and backpedalled for space, as he thrashed like a fallen animal trying to rise. Gideon fell into stance, raised her sword, and let it come to rest at his collarbone.

"Match to the Third," said Coronabeth, which startled her.

Her sword was shrugged away; Naberius, furious and wobbly, was finally up on both feet.

"Babs," his princess said hurriedly, "are you all right?"

He was coughing throatily. His face was a dark, velvety red as he sheathed his sword and squeezed down on his knife, causing some mechanism to *snockt* the side blades back into place. When he bowed to her, it was amazingly scornful. Gideon slid her own sword back into her scabbard, somewhat discombobulated, and bowed in return; he tossed his head back haughtily and coughed again, which somewhat ruined the effect.

"She's not some Nonius come-again, she's just a brawler," he said in throaty disgust. "Look, *idiot*, when I disarm you, match is over, you bow, all right? You don't keep going."

The sharply dressed Cohort cavalier said: "You let your guard down, Tern."

"The match was over the moment I got her sword!"

"Yes," she said, "technically."

"*Technically?*" He was getting even redder-faced now. "Everything's the technicals! And that's *Prince* Tern to you, Lieutenant!

What are you playing at, Dyas? I held her at bay the whole time, I won, and the cultist fouled the match. Admit it."

"Yes," said Dyas, who had relaxed into an arms-behind-the-back *at ease* position. It looked more at home in a military parade line-up than at an informal fitness match. She had a neat, mellifluous voice. "You won the bout. The Ninth is the less able duellist. I say she is the better fighter: she fought to win. But, Ninth," she said, "he's right. You cut too much."

The cavalier from the Third looked like he was very close to violence: this, for some reason, had made his eyes bulge with sheer resentment. He looked as though he were about to unsheathe his sword and demand a rematch, and backed down only when one golden arm was slung about his shoulders and he was pulled into a half embrace from his necromancer. He submitted to a hair ruffle. Corona said, "The Third showed its stuff, Babs—that's all I care about."

"It was a convincing win." He sounded like a huffy child.

"You were brilliant. I wish Ianthe had seen you."

Jeannemary had risen to stand. She was a brown, bricklike young thing, Gideon had noticed, seemingly all corners: her eyes were alight, and her voice was piercing when she said:

"That's how I want to fight. I don't want to spend all my time in show bouts. *I* want to fight like a real cavalier, as though my life's on the line."

Naberius's expression shuttered over again. His gaze met Gideon's briefly, and it was somewhere beyond hostile: it was contempt for an animal that had crapped indelicately in the corner. But before any more could be said, Magnus coughed lightly into his hand.

"Perhaps," he said, "we should fall to exercises, or paired work, or—something that will make me feel like I'm practising to be fighting fit. How about it? Sparring may be the meat of a fighter's training, but you've got to have some—well—vegetables and potatoes?"

("Magnus. Potatoes are a vegetable, Magnus.")

Gideon stepped from the dais, unbuckling the knuckle-knives from her wrist, easing her fingers out of the grips. She wondered what Aiglamene would have thought of the fight; she almost wanted to see that disarm again. If Naberius hadn't looked at her like she had personally taken a whiz on his nicest jacket, she would have asked him about it. It was sleight of hand rather than brute force, and she had to admit that she'd never even thought about a defence, which was stupid—

Some sixth sense made her look upward, beyond the skeleton still swabbing industriously at the glass door, out past the pit where centuries of old chemicals were being wiped away. In the aperture before the tiled room, a cloaked figure stood: skull-painted, a veil pushed down to the neck, a hood obscuring the face. Gideon stood in the centre of the training room, and for a second that emasculated minutes, she and Harrowhark looked at each other. Then the Reverend Daughter turned in a dramatic swish of black and disappeared into the flickering vestibule.

12

"EXCELLENT TO HAVE YOU with us," said Teacher one morning, "excellent to see the Ninth fitting in so well! How beautiful to have all the Houses commingled!"

Teacher was a fucking comedian. He often sat with Gideon if he caught her at table for later meals—he never showed up to breakfast; she suspected he had his much earlier than anyone else at Canaan House—with the jovial, *I find vows of silence very restful!* Constant questions were still being asked of Teacher and the Canaan House priests, some coaxing, some curt, all in varying stages of desperation. He was implacably ignorant.

"I do enjoy all this bustle," Teacher said. (Only he and Gideon were in the room.)

By the end of that week, Gideon had met nearly all of the adepts and their cavaliers. This did not break down barriers and form new friendships. They nearly all gave her wide berths in the dim Canaan House corridors—only Coronabeth would greet her breezily according to Coronabeth's whims, which were capricious, and Magnus was always good for a cordial *Good morning! Er, excellent weather! Or Good evening! Weather still excellent!* He tried pathetically hard. But most of them still looked at her as though she were something that could only be killed with a stake through the heart at midnight, a half-tame monster on a dubious leash. Naberius Tern often sneered at her so hard that he was due a lip injury.

But you got a lot of information by being silent and watching. The Second House acted like soldiers on unwilling leave. The Third revolved around Corona like two chunks of ice about a golden star. The Fourth clustered by the Fifth's skirts like ducklings—the Fifth necromancer turned out to be a fresh-faced woman in her mid-thirties with thick glasses and a mild smile, who looked about as much the part as a farmer's wife. The Sixth and Seventh were perennially absent, ghosts. The Eighth's creepy uncle–creepy nephew duo she saw seldom, but even seldom was more than enough: the Eighth necromancer prayed intensely and fervidly before each meal, and if they passed in the corridor both flattened themselves to the furthest wall as though she were contagious.

Small wonder. The way to the Ninth's living quarters—the corridor that led to their front door, and all about their front door, like ghoulish wreaths—was now draped in bones. Spinal cords bracketed the door frame; finger bones hung down attached to thin, nearly-invisible wires, and they clinked together cheerlessly in the wind when you passed. She had left Harrowhark a note on her vastly underused pillow—

WHATS WITH THE SKULLS?

and received only a terse—

Ambiance.

Well, *ambiance* meant that even Magnus the Fifth hesitated before saying *Good morning,* so fuck ambiance in the ear.

As far as Gideon could tell, Dulcinea Septimus spent 100 percent of the time on the terraces, reading romance novels, being perfectly happy. If she was trying to psych out the competition, she was doing so with flair. It was also very difficult to avoid her. The Ninth's cavalier elect would walk past an open doorway, and a light voice would call out *Gideon—Gideon!* And then she would go, and no mention of her sword would be made: just a pillow to be moved, or the plot of a romance novel to be related, or—once—a woman seemingly lighter than a rapier to be picked up and very carefully transferred to another seat, out of the sun. Gideon did not resent this. She had the sinking feeling that Dulcinea was doing her a favour. Lady Septimus was, delicately, showing she did not care that Gideon was Gideon *the Ninth*, a paint-faced shadow cultist, a Locked Tomb nun apparent: or at least, if she cared, she viewed it as the delight of her days.

"Do you ever think it's funny, you being here with me?" she asked once, when Gideon sat, black-hooded, holding a ball of wool for Dulcinea's crocheting. When Gideon shook her head, she said: "No . . . and I like it. I send Protesilaus away a good deal. I give him things to do: that's what suits him best. But I like to see you and make you pick up my blankets and be my scullion. I think I'm the only person in eternity to make a Ninth House cavalier slave away for me . . . who's not their adept. And I'd like to hear your voice again . . . one day."

Fat chance. The one half-glimpsed vision of Harrow Nonagesimus was all that Gideon had seen, after that first spar. She didn't appear again, in the training room or at the Ninth quarters. Her pillow was rumpled in a different way each morning, and black clothes heaped themselves untidily in the laundry basket that the skeletons took away at intervals, but she did not darken Gideon's door.

Gideon went back to the training room regularly—and so did the cavaliers of Fourth and Fifth, and Second and Third—but the Sixth and Seventh cavaliers avoided it, even now that it was laminated to a high shine and smelled of seed oils. The skeletons had moved their efforts to cleaning the floors now. The burly Eighth cavalier had come in once when she was there, but on seeing Gideon, bowed politely and left posthaste.

Gideon still preferred to train by herself. It was her habit of long years to wake and wedge her feet under some piece of furniture, and do sit-ups until she had counted them out in their hundreds, and then press-ups: a hundred normal, a hundred clapping. Standing upside down, on her arms with her feet in the air. Sitting on the heels of her hands with her legs extended, testing to what degree she could stretch her toes. You didn't need half of what she'd done to gain medical entry to the Cohort, but she had fed her entire life into the meat grinder of hope that, one day, she'd blitz through Trentham and get sent to the front attached to a necromancer's legion. Not for Gideon a security detail on one of the holding planets, either on a lonely outpost on an empty world or in some foreign city babysitting some Third governor. Gideon wanted a drop ship—first on the ground—a fat shiny medal saying INVASION FORCE ON WHATEVER, securing the initial bloom of thanergy without which the finest necromancer of the Nine Houses could not fight worth a damn. The front line of the Cohort facilitated glory. In her comic books, necromancers kissed the gloved palms of their front-liner comrades in blessed thanks for all that they did. In the comic books none of these adepts had heart disease, and a lot of them had necromantically uncharacteristic cleavage.

This had all played out in Gideon's imagination on many solitary nights, and often she had indulged in a wilder flight of fancy where Harrowhark would open an envelope galaxies and galaxies away, and read the news that Gideon Nav had won a bunch of medals and a huge percentage of prize money for her role in the initial strike, a battle in which she was both outstanding and very hot. Harrow's lip would curl, and she would drawl something like, *Turns out Griddle could swing a sword after all.* This fantasy often got her through a hundred reps.

Back in the Ninth she would have ended the day with a jog around the planting fields, as the photochemical lamps dimmed for the end of their cycle, running through the fine moisture mist spritzed out at even times to wet the soil. The mist was recyc water and smelled ureal. It was a before-bedtime smell to her. Now the scent was old wood, and the sulfide reek of the sea, and water on stone.

But not even Gideon could train all the time. She amused herself by exploring the huge, sinuous complex of Canaan House, often getting profoundly lost. That you could only explore so far was her first discovery. There must have been floors beneath floors all the way down, many hundreds of feet of building, but as you descended the prevalence of *** CAUTION *** printed on yellow plastic tape and crosses spray-painted onto big iron blast doors only grew. You could only get about fifty metres below the dock layer before all ways were closed. You could only go up so far too, about an equivalent hundred metres up: there was a broken lift you could walk into, and there was a staircase up the tower that branched off in two directions. To the left was where Teacher and the other two priests of Canaan House slept, in a whitewashed network of corridors where potted succulent plants grew lasciviously in long tendrils. She had not yet tried the right.

After two silent, ironed-out days of exploring and squats, Gideon did not exactly get bored. It took a hell of a lot more to *bore* a denizen of the House of the Ninth. It was a lack of change at the microscopic level that made her suspicious: one morning she realised that the rumples on Harrow's bed and the top layer of black clothes in the laundry hamper had not changed for over twenty-four hours. Two nights had passed without Harrow sleeping in the Ninth quarters, or changing out of dirty clothes, or refreshing her paint. Gideon cogitated:

1. Harrow had been prevented from coming home
   for reasons, e.g., that
   (i)   She was dead;
   (ii) She was too impaired;
   (iii) She was busy.
2. Harrow had chosen to live elsewhere, leaving
   Gideon free to put her shoes on Harrow's bed
   and indiscriminately rifle through all her things.
3. Harrow had run away.

#3 could be discounted. If Harrow were the type, Gideon's childhood would have been a hell of a lot smoother. #2 was an exciting prospect in that Gideon longed to put her shoes on Harrow's bed and to indiscriminately rifle through all Harrow's things, but given that those things were still there, this seemed unlikely. Given twenty-four hours to break a bone ward, Gideon would have immediately made plans to get into Harrow's wardrobe and do up all the buttons on her shirts, making sure that each button went into the hole above the one it was meant to go into. It was an inevitability that the Reverend Daughter never would have allowed for.

This left #1. (iii) relied on Harrow being so busy doing whatever she was doing that she'd forgotten to come back, though given previous reasoning and the sheer availability of buttons to be tampered with this was a nonstarter. (i) was contingent on either the world's happiest accident or murder, and if it *was* murder, what if the murderer was, like, *weird*, which would make their subsequent marriage to Gideon pretty awkward? Maybe they could just swap friendship bracelets.

In the end, (ii) had the most traction. The paint supplies were all here. She had never seen Harrowhark Nonagesimus's naked face. With a deep resentment of heart and weariness of soul, Gideon threw on her robe and embarked upon a long, disconsolate day of searching.

Harrow was not in the central atrium, or in the dining room, or in the increasingly clean pit full of industriously scrubbing skeletons. Magnus the Fifth was standing watch over them with a furrowed expression of good-natured bewilderment, right next to his trig and glossy-haired adept, and he managed an "Er—Ninth! Hope you're enjoying the . . . room!" before she bolted out of it.

Harrow was not on the long and sun-swept docking bay, its concrete an eye-sizzling white in the sweltering light of morning. Gideon tracked all across it—standing next to the weathered magnetic locks, listening to the churning water far below where the shuttles rested somewhere. Harrow was not on the terrace where Dulcinea Septimus often read, and neither was Dulcinea Septimus, though a few novels sat abandoned beneath a chair. It was lunchtime by the time she had walked the whole eastern wing leading up from a glorious, rotten old staircase to the left of the atrium, terminating in a door with a freshly chiselled plaque marked EIGHTH HOUSE that she backed away from in record time. Gideon went back to the dining hall and brooded over her cheese and bread and decided to give up.

Leave Harrow to her two broken legs and shattered pelvis. Finding her was an impossibly futile task, in an impossibly large and complex area where you could search all day every day for weeks and not exhaust the *floor*. It was stupid and it made her feel stupid. And it was Nonagesimus's own fault for being controlling and secretive about every aspect of her whole ghastly little life. She would not thank Gideon even if she had sat her flat ass in a puddle of molten lava, especially not as Gideon would religiously mark each anniversary of the day Harrow destroyed her butt with magma. She washed her hands of the entire scenario.

After she had choked down food and drunk half a jug of water in quick succession, Gideon gave up and resumed the search. She decided on a whim to go bang on the doors of the lift that didn't work, and then found that the neighbouring water-swollen door could be opened if you applied force. This revealed a cramped staircase, which she followed down until she burst out into a corridor she'd only once explored. It was a broad, low-ceilinged shaft with *** CAUTION *** tape hollering from every door and surface, but there was one door at the end where people had obviously passed: the tape had snapped and fell in limp ribbons to both sides. The door led to another corridor that was cut off midway by a huge old tarpaulin, which someone had tacked to the rafters to serve as a half-hearted barrier. Gideon ducked under the tarpaulin, turned right, and opened a narrow iron door out to a terrace.

She'd been here once before. Fully half of this terrace had crumbled off into the sea. The first time Gideon had seen it, the whole looked so precarious she had consequently gone down with a fit of acrophobia and beat hasty retreat to somewhere less insane. The sky had seemed too wide; the horizon too open; the terrace too much like a total death trap. The landing dock loomed overhead, and so did the opaque, sweeping windows where the Ninth was housed. Looking up was fine. Looking down, still hundreds and hundreds of metres above the sea, made her want to lose her lunch.

Fuelled by the reminder that the only difference between the drillshaft of Drearburh and the broken terrace was that one was fenced and one wasn't, she ventured up there again. The wind screamed her into the side of the tower. It was crumbled only at the far end, and the part closest to the trunk of Canaan House seemed intact. Stone windbreakers and dry-soiled, extinct gardens trailed off as far as the eye could see around to the other side, rugged with long stretches of empty planter bed and trellis. Gideon took this path. It was not at all clear—some of the big boxy stone structures had collapsed and the rubble never cleared, and there was really not enough structure still left to distract the eye from the bitten-off terrace that had fallen away to its death—but if you travelled around enough, there was a spiralling staircase of wrought iron and brick clasped to the tower's bosom.

This was also a bitch to travel up, as the more you climbed, the more of the dead terrace you saw—the sea creaked below, changeful in its colour, a deep grey-blue today and whitecapped with wind—but Gideon readjusted her sunglasses, took a deep breath through her nose, and climbed. The first autodoor she saw, she took, and had to hammer five full times before it silently slid open and gave her entry. Gideon ducked in and pressed against the wall as it slid reproachfully shut, and had to take a minute to collect herself.

It was dark here. She found herself in a long hall that terminated in a left-hand corner. It was very quiet, and very cool. The floor was of pale, cream-and-black tile, set in a starry pattern that repeated itself all the way down the corridor; the paler tiles seemed to float, luminous, as the darker melted into the shadows. Great panes of smoked glass had been set into the walls, lit by dark yellow lamps: sconces held dribbles of mummified candle. It was a wide, shady space, and had something of the inner sanctum of Drearburh about it, just with fewer bones. In fact, there was almost no decoration here. The hall seemed strangely closed in, smaller than the space ought to have been, shrugging inward. The floor was beautiful, and so were the doors—they were wood-inlaid with tiny squares of smoked glass, set smoothly in metal frames. There was a single statue at the end of the corridor where it turned left. It must have once been a person, but the head and arms had been lopped off, leaving only a torso with beseeching stumps. It took her a while to realise that she was in a lobby, and that the doors were elevator lifts: each had a dead screen overhead that must have once shown the floor number.

Gideon folded her sunglasses into a pocket of her robe. Quiet echoes caromed off the walls, up and down, then clarified. Voices floating upward. The stairs at the corner of the hallway led down two short flights, the landing visible below, and Gideon crept down them with careful and noiseless steps.

The indeterminate murmurs thinned into sound—

"—s impossible, Warden."

"Nonsense."

"*Improbable*, Warden."

"Granted. But still—relative to what, exactly?"

There was some shuffling. Two voices: the first probably female, the second probably male. Gideon risked another step down.

"Six readings," the second voice continued. "Oldest is nine thou. Youngest is, well, fiftyish. Emphasis *ish.* But the old stuff here is really very old."

"The upper bound for scrying is ten thousand, Warden." Yes, it was a woman's voice, and not one Gideon had heard: low and calm, stating the obvious.

"The point is here, and you are far over there. Nine thousand. Fiftyish. *Building.*"

"Ah."

"*Fiat lux!* If you want to talk improbable, let's talk about this"—a scrape of stone on stone—"being three thousand and some years older than *this.*" A heavy *clunk.*

"Inexplicable, Warden."

"Certainly not. Like everything else in this ridiculous con-glomeration of cooling gas, it's perfectly explicable, I just need to explic-it."

"Indubitable, Warden."

"Stop that. I need you listening, not racking your brain for rare negatives. Either this entire building was scavenged from a garbage hopper, or I am being systematically lied to on a molecular level."

"Maybe the building's shy."

"That is just tough shit for the building. No; there's a wrong thing here. There's a trick. Remember my fourth circle exams?"

"When the Masters shut down the entire core?"

"No, that was third circle. Fourth circle they seeded the core with a couple of thousand fake records. Beautiful stuff, exquisite, even the timestamps, and all of it obviously wrong. Drivel. No one could have believed a word of it. So why bother?"

"I recall you said they were 'being a pack of assholes.'"

"W—yes. Well, in substance, yes. They were teaching us a particularly annoying lesson, which is that you cannot rely on anything, because anything can lie to you."

"Swords," said the woman with a trace of satisfaction, "don't lie."

The necromancer—because Gideon had never been so sure in her life that she was listening to a damn necromancer—snorted. "No. But they don't tell the truth either."

By now she was almost at the foot of the stairs, and she could see into the room below. The only light came from its centre; the walls were splashed with long shadows, but seemed to be generic concrete, split in places by peeling lines of caution tape. In the centre, lit by a flashlight, was an enormous shut-up metal hatch, the kind Gideon associated with hazard shafts and accident shelters.

Crouching in front of the hatch was a rangy, underfed young man: he was wrapped in a grey cloak and the light glinted on the spectacles slipping down his nose. Standing next to him holding a big wedge of broken sculpture and the flashlight was a tall, equally grey-wrapped figure with a scabbard outlined at her hip. She had hair of an indeterminate darkness, cut blunt at her chin. She was restless as a bird, stepping from one foot to the other, quirking her elbows, rocking from the balls of her feet to the heel. The boy had one hand pressed to the heavy corner of the hatch, brooding over it like a seer with a piece of ritual intestine, lineated weirdly by the half-light. He was using his own tiny pocket torch to investigate the place where the seam of the floor met the metal of the hatch frame.

Both were filthy. Dust caked their hems. There were odd, still-wet smears on their clothes and hands. It looked as though they'd both been wrestling in some long-forgotten Ninth catacomb.

Gideon had moved too close: even in the darkness, hooded and cloaked, they were both nervy. The young man in glasses jerked up his chin, staring blindly back to the stairwell: at his sudden switch in focus, the young woman with the sword whirled around and saw Gideon on the stairs.

It was probably not a comforting sight to see a penitent of the Locked Tomb in the half dark, swathed in black, skull-painted. The cavalier narrowed her hooded eyes, fidgets gone and absolutely still; then she exploded into action. She dropped the wedge of sculpture with a *clonk*, drew her sword from its shabby scabbard before the wedge had bounced once, and advanced. Gideon, neurons blaring, drew her own. She slid her hand into her ebon gauntlet—the grey-cloaked girl let the flashlight fall, drew a knife with a liquid whisper from a holder across one shoulder—and their blades met high above their heads as the cavalier leapt, metal on metal ringing all around the chamber.

Holy shit. Here was a warrior, not just a cavalier. Gideon was suddenly fighting for her life and exhilarated by it. Blow after lightning blow rattled her defences, each one coming down like an industrial crush press, the short offhand knife targeting the guard of Gideon's blade. Even with the advantage of higher ground she was forced to mount the steps backward. They were fighting in close, cramped quarters, and Gideon was getting pinned. She smashed the other girl's offhand out of the way and into the wall, scattering loose glass tiles in its wake as it fell: her opponent dropped as though shot, crouched, *kicked* her dagger up into her hand, and *did a handspring backward down the stairs.* Gideon descended like an avenging necrosaint as she rose—slicing down in a winging cut that would have destroyed the blade given a longsword and the right footing, just for the pleasure of seeing her partner duck, huff between her teeth with exertion. Her sword met the other cavalier's dagger and she pressed, both leaning hard into the blow. The cav in grey's eyes were only mildly surprised.

"*Camilla!*" She only distantly registered the call. Gideon was stronger; the girl's arm was buckling—she brought up her rapier to harass Gideon's blocking arm, stabbing at the ebon cuff of the knuckle-knife, the tiny torch spotlight wavering drunkenly from face to face, turning their pupils into big black wells—"*Camilla the Sixth*, disengage!"

"Camilla" brought her elbow forward, sliding her sword down Gideon's, jabbing it away with the hilt. Momentarily discombobulated, Gideon backed into the stairs and reset her stance; by then the cavalier in grey was already backing off, sword held high, off-hand held low. The necromancer in matching grey was standing; the darkness in the small room was banded with hot shimmers, as though with heat. She thrust her arm forward—

—and stumbled back. Her heart was panicking in her chest, seized as though in the midst of a cardiac arrest, and her hand seemed to wither around the hilt of her sword—the flesh melting before her eyes, the fingernails going black and curling close to the skin as though burnt. She snatched her fist back and found that, clutched close, it was whole and unaffected again, but she did not press onward. She wasn't a total goon. She backed away from the necromantic seal and sheathed her sword instead, hands held out in the universal *ceasefire!* gesture. The necromancer in grey, torch hand outstretched, exhaled: he wiped faintly pinkish sweat from his face.

"It's the other one," he said tersely, not sounding at all as though he'd just raised a massive thanergetic barrier and broken out in minor blood sweat. She was amazed it was only minor: the whole space before her shimmered like the oily surface of a bubble, fully three bodies high and three wide. "We don't want an interhouse incident—not that it wouldn't give our policy wonks back on the Sixth something to think about. You too"—this was to Gideon, a little more formally—"I offer apology that my cavalier engaged you in an unscheduled bout, Niner, but I don't apologise for her drawing on someone sneaking around dressed all in black. Be reasonable."

Gideon peeled the knuckle-knife off her hand and latched it back to her belt, and she surveyed the scene before her. Both cavalier and necromancer stood before the black hulk of the trapdoor, robes charcoal in the dimness, both of their eyes and hair mellowed to no colour in the thin light from the hallway. The little torch was quickly flicked off, plunging the whole into further gloom. She yearned to talk, beginning with: *How did you do a little flip like that?* but the necro brought her up short with:

"You're here about Nonagesimus, aren't you?"

The stupefied blankness on Gideon's face must have been mistaken for something else. Face paint was good for masking. The necromancer scrubbed his hands together in sudden, fretful activity, wringing his fingers together hard. "Assumed she'd just—well. Have you seen her since the night before last?"

Gideon shook her head so emphatically *no* that she was surprised her hood didn't fall off. The cavalier's face was turned toward him, expressionless, waiting. The young man strummed his fingers together before coming to some unknown decision.

"Well, you're cutting it fine," he said abruptly. He pulled his thick, nerdy spectacles off his long nose and shook them as though wicking them free of something. "She was down there last night too and, if I'm correct, never surfaced. Her blood's on the floor down there." Because necromancers lived bad lives, he added: "To clarify. Her *intravenous* blood. *Her* intravenous blood."

At this clarification, a very strange thing happened to Gideon Nav. She had already exhausted neurons, cortisol, and adrenaline, and now her body started moving before her head or her heart did; she strode past the boy and yanked so hard on the top of the hatch that it damn near broke her wrists. It was shut tighter than Crux's ass. At this embarrassing heaving, the boy sighed explosively and threw his zipped-up bag to Camilla, who caught it out of midair.

"Cavaliers," he said.

Camilla said, "I wouldn't have left you alone for twenty-seven hours."

"Of course not. I'd be dead. Look, you simpleton, it's not going to open," he told Gideon, swinging his sights on her like a man levelling a blade. "She's got your key."

Up close, he was gaunt and ordinary looking, except for the eyes. His spectacles were set with lenses of spaceflight-grade thickness, and through these his eyes were a perfectly lambent grey: unflecked, unmurked, even and clear. He had the eyes of a very beautiful person, trapped in resting bitch face.

Gideon hauled again at the hatch, as though offering up the universe's most useless act might endear her to the physics of a locked door. His sigh grew sadder and more explosive as he watched her. "You're winners, you and Nonagesimus both. Hang on—Cam, do a perimeter, please—Ninth, *listen*. It's well above freezing down there. That means blood stays wet for an hour, let's say an hour and a half. Hers hadn't skeletonised altogether. You with me? She might have spilt it deliberately—although, she's an osseo, she's not going to do blood ritual on herself—right, you're not even pretending to pay attention."

Gideon had stopped paying attention somewhere around *wet* and was now bracing both feet to pull: she was pressing down the frame with a foot, distantly taking in every fifth word. *Blood. Skeletonised. Osseo.* The necro called out, "Camilla, any sign she left while—"

Camilla was on the stairs.

"No, Warden."

He said to Gideon, gruffly: "Odds are she's still down there."

"Then get off your ass and *help me*," said Gideon Nav.

This did not surprise or alarm him. In fact, his tightly-wound shoulders relaxed a fraction from *black-hole stress fracture* to *pressure at the bottom of the ocean.* He sounded almost relieved when he said, "Sure."

A jangling object sailed through the air, visible more as sound and movement than as thing. The necromancer failed to catch it: it banged him hard on his long, scrabbling hands. Gideon recognised it as the iron loop that she had been given on the very first day in Canaan House. As he squatted beside her, smelling like dust and mould, she could see that a long key had been put through the loop and was clanking there untidily. There was another, smaller key dangling off to one side, gleaming golden, with an elaborately carved shank and deep pockmarks instead of cuts in the shaft. A key ring? They'd all been given key rings?

Inserted into the keyhole, the first key opened the trap door with a low, hard snap, and together the boy and Gideon threw it open. It revealed a ladder of metal staples down a long, unbelievably dark hole: light shaded in at the bottom, throwing into relief the fact that one slip meant a broken neck along with your broken ass-bones.

A pointing finger appeared in front of her like a spear tip: Camilla's. The Sixth cavalier had reclaimed the flashlight, and by its glow she could see that Camilla's eyes were much darker than her necromancer's: his were like clear stone or water, and hers were the unreflective, fathomless colour of overturned Ninth House sod, neither grey nor brown. "You go first, Ninth," she said. "Palamedes follows. I bring up the rear."

It took a full minute to descend that long, claustrophobic tube, staring at the rungs of the ladder with her robes tucked between her knees, sword clanking on metal all the way down—and at the bottom, Gideon was utterly nonplussed.

What lay beneath the trapdoor was a retro installation. A six-sided tunnel lined with dusty, perforated panels stretched out before them. The ceiling was merely a grille that air coolers pumped through and the floor a grille with visible pressure pumps beneath, and the lights were electric bulbs beneath luminous white plastic. There were exposed pipes. The supporting archways contained bulky, square autodoor sidings. This rhapsody of greys and sterile blacks was interrupted over the nearest arch, where, twisting in the dry breeze of the climate cooler, hung a bundle of old bones. Ancient prayer wrappers were ringed around it, and it was the only human, normal touch.

"Follow me," said the young man called Palamedes.

He strode forward, filthy hem whispering on the dusty-ass tiles. This place ate sound. There were no echoes: they were squashed and absorbed into the panelling. The three of them clanked unmusically down the tunnel until it opened into a big nonagonal room, with passageways radiating out like bronchiae. Letters of brushed steel were set beside each passage:

LABORATORY ONE–THREE

LABORATORY FOUR–SIX

LABORATORY SEVEN–TEN

PRESSURE ROOM

PRESERVATION

MORTUARY

WORK ROOMS

SANITISER

Light wells above made the panelling white; lights from below— little blinking lights attached to huge machines that went down metres beneath the grille, a huge deep way beneath their feet—made the floors softly green. The walls were unadorned, except for an enormous old whiteboard rimmed in metal, printed with lines for a timetable that had not been used in a very, very, *very* long time. The lines had blurred; the board was stained. Here and there meaningless bits of letters survived: the loop of what might be *O* or *C*; the arch of an *M*; a line-suffixed curve that could be *G* or *Q*. But in one bottom corner lingered the ghost of a message, drawn thickly in black ink once, now faded but still quite clear:

It is finished!

The atmosphere down here was oppressive. The air was so dry it made her eyes and mouth prickle. Camilla had one hand on her sword, and Palamedes kept wringing his together, rocking from foot to foot as he moved in a long, slow, 360-degree sweep of the room. At some stimulus, or lack of stimulus, he took a sharp turn toward Sanitiser. Gideon followed.

The short hallway to Sanitiser was floored with panels rather than grille, covered in a powdery build-up like salt, scuffed underfoot and heaped in little drifts. These dunes dissolved like an exhaled breath if kicked.

Quite abruptly there was blood. Palamedes thumbed his tiny flashlight out of his pocket and the liquid gleamed redly beneath the beam. Blood had been spilt, in some quantity, and then smeared heavily away down the hall, leaving a long dark scrape of drying gore. Smaller splatters had dried on the surrounding walls.

The door at the end of the hallway—a huge blast door, metal, with a glass panel set in its centre that was so grimy you could no longer see through it—opened with a touchpad that was also smudged with curls of dried blood. Dried, and drying. Gideon pressed it so hard that the doors twanged open like they were startled.

The first room of Sanitiser stretched before them as a huge, low-ceilinged, white-panelled maze of cubicles: long steel tables beneath the upside-down metal mushrooms of spray heads, and narrow boxes a human could stand upright in. It was fully as big as the grand, destroyed hall of Canaan House. The lights whirred overhead. A panel on the wall blinked furiously as some mechanism in it tried to wake up—it looked like a screen—but eventually it decided better, went blank, and the room was resubmerged in shadow. Gideon was hunting with a dog's mindless, preternatural panic for a scent, trying to find—

Spatters of blood led her to a big ridged lump in one of the cubicles. This cocoon-looking thing was about the size of a person, if that person wasn't particularly tall. Before Palamedes and Camilla could stop her, Gideon strode up to it and gave it an enormous kick. Osseous matter showered one side of the cubicle, tinkling away as the spell broke into the oily grey ash of cremains. Curled up inside—hands bloodied, paint smeared, the skin beneath it the same oily grey as the cremains—was Harrowhark Nonagesimus.

Gideon, who had spent the morning planning the wild, abandoned dance of joy with which she would greet Harrow's dead body, turned back to Camilla and Palamedes.

"I can take it from here," she said.

Ignoring her, Palamedes pushed past to the broken-bone chrysalis and fished around in its awful contents. He pulled a bit of Harrow's black robe aside, then the collar of her shirt, past three necklaces of bone chips strung on thread, revealing a startling patch of bare skin—yikes—and pressed two fingers to her neck; he held a hand over her mouth; he said sharply, "Cam," and she dropped to her knees beside him. She pulled a wallet from somewhere inside her shirt and removed, of all things, a wire. The outer insulation had been stripped from each end, revealing sharp metal tips, and one of these he jabbed into the fleshy part between his thumb and forefinger. It drew blood. The other end he pressed to Harrow's neck where his fingers had been.

There followed a rapid conversation, high-speed, totally obtuse:

"High dilation rate. Blood loss not from outside injury. Hypovolemia. Breathing's okay. Honestly—dehydration more than anything."

"Saline?"

"Nah. She can refill herself when she's awake."

Gideon couldn't help herself. She could understand finding Harrow with her legs on backward and an exploded skull, but she was only following about half of this. "What are you *talking* about?" she demanded.

Palamedes rocked back on his haunches. He was pinching the edge of the bone cocoon, testing it, flexing it this way and that. "She hasn't eaten or taken water for a while," he said. "That's all. She would have pushed too hard and experienced a rapid drop in blood pressure and heart rate. Likely fainted, woke up, made this—this is incredible, I can't even . . . then she fell asleep. It's all one piece, no wonder she's out. Is this normal for her?"

"You can tell all that with Sixth necromancy?"

Shockingly, both he and Camilla laughed. They had gruff, barking little laughs, and Camilla took this opportunity to roll the wire back up into its wallet, pinching Harrow's blood off one end. "Medical necromancy," said her adept drily, "there's an oxymoron for you. No. Being a necromancer helps, but no. It's curative science. Don't you have that on the Ninth? Don't answer, I was joking. You can move her now."

The Reverend Daughter was very light as Gideon folded her (both Palamedes and Camilla winced) into an over-shoulder lift. Air wheezed out of Harrow's lungs, and the bone cocoon dissolved into a shower of chips and pebbles pattering onto the floor like hail. This seemed to be the one thing to really unnerve the Sixth House necromancer. He swore under his breath and then *actually whipped a ruler out of his pocket*, measuring one of the chips on the floor.

Gideon shifted, so that the weight and heft of Harrow was more evenly distributed. Her brain had not come back online enough to register that weight, or to save it for later detail in her fantasies where she dropped the Ninth House scion off the side of the docking bay. Her necromancer smelled like sweat and blood and old, burnt bone; her corselet of ribs poked painfully into Gideon's shoulders. Ascending a staple-wall ladder with a body in tow was a hell of a lot more difficult than descending without one. Palamedes ascended first, then she did, each rung a fight with her awkward load; Camilla followed, and by the time they got to the top Gideon's jaw hurt from clenching.

The cavalier of the Sixth took Harrow's shoulders when she reached the top so that Gideon could get out, which was decent of her. Maybe it was just so they could hurry up and close the huge metal trapdoor, turning the key in the lock with a satisfying *click*. She sat down next to the unconscious figure and rolled one shoulder in its socket, then the other.

Palamedes was shouldering the zip-up bag and saying, "Give her water and food when she wakes up. She'll take care of the rest. Probably. She needs eight hours of sleep—in a bed, not a library. When she asks how I knew she was in the library, tell her Cam says she clinks when she walks."

Gideon reached down to take her burden up again, slinging Harrow's limp and speechless body to occupy her other shoulder. She paused at the foot of the stairs, measuring in her mind's eye the distance back down the corridor, to the terrace, down the zigzag flights of steps and back through to the Ninth House quarters. Plenty of corners to concuss Harrow with, on the way.

"I owe you one," she said.

It was Camilla who said, in her quiet, curiously deep voice, "He did it for free." It was the first time she had looked at Gideon without the flat, stony aggression of a retaining wall, which was nice.

Palamedes said, "What Cam said. Just—look, take a word of advice, here."

As she waited, he pressed the pads of his fingertips together. His cavalier was looking at him dead on, tense, waiting. In the end, he said: "It's unbelievably dangerous down there, Ninth. Stop splitting your forces."

"Dangerous *how*?"

"If I knew," said Palamedes, "it'd be a hell of a lot less dangerous."

Gideon was impatient with vagaries. She wasn't in Drearburh now. "How do you figure?"

The Sixth House necromancer walked forward and paused before her in the stairwell. He was washed in dilute light from above and behind Gideon, and it showed that he really *was* thin—the kind of thin made thinner by his grey, shapeless robe, the thinness of trousers cinched too tight to hips. Camilla hovered a perfect half step behind—the half step Aiglamene had trepanned into Gideon—as though suspicious even of the steps.

He said coolly: "Because I'm the greatest necromancer of my generation."

The unconscious figure sacked across Gideon's shoulder muttered, "Like hell you are."

"Thought that would wake her up," said Palamedes, with no small amount of satisfaction. "Well—I'm off. Like I said, liquids and rest. Good luck."

EITHER HARROWHARK FELL BACK unconscious, having used her last remaining energy to spite Palamedes, or she was just already such a dick she could spite him in her sleep. Or maybe she was playing dead. Gideon didn't care. Her necromancer remained heavy and unmoving all the way back to their rooms. Nobody saw them on the way, for which she was grateful, and she was heartily glad by the end of it to dump her prone and black-wrapped burden on the bed.

Nonagesimus had looked like crap in the darkness of the weird facility. In the comfortable gloom of their quarters she looked worse. Unwrapping her hood and veil revealed torn lips and cracked face paint, flaking off in big brown-glazed smears at one temple. The veil had slipped down with the trip up the ladder. Gideon could see that her nostrils were ringed with a thick black rime of blood, and her hairline was also smeared with thin, crusty traces of it. There were no other signs of blood on the rest of her clothes or her robes, just sweat patches. Gideon had checked for injuries and been traumatised by the experience.

She went to the bathroom and filled up a glass of water from the tap, and she left it next to Harrow, then hesitated hard. How to rehydrate? Was she meant to—wash her mouth, or something? Did she need to clean off the tusks of dried blood at each nostril? Gideon popped each shoulder twice in indecision, grabbed the water glass, and reached toward Harrow.

"Touch me again and I'll kill you," said Harrow, scratch-throated, without opening her eyes. "I really will."

Gideon pulled her fingers back as though from a flame, and exhaled.

"Good luck with that, bucko," she said. "You look all mummification and no meat."

Harrow did not move. There was a bruise peeking out behind her ear, already deep purple. "I'm not saying it wouldn't *hurt* me, Griddle," she murmured. "I am just saying you'd be dead."

Gideon leant back heavily against the bedside table and took a long, malicious pull from Harrow's glass of water. She felt tight and jangly, and the sweat had cooled to both an itch and a shiver inside her robes. She threw back the hood and shrugged herself out of the robe, feeling like a sleep-deprived child. "'Thanks, Gideon,'" she said aloud. "'I *was* in a pickle and you saved me, which I had no reasonable expectation of, since I'm an asshole who got stuck in a bone in a basement.' Is that what you've been doing without me, all this time? Dicking around in a basement?"

The adept's lips curled back, showing little slashes of swollen pink through the grey. "Yes," she said. "Yes, I was dicking around in the basement. You didn't need to get involved. You did *just* what I was afraid you would do, which was to remove me from a situation that I didn't need to be removed from."

"Didn't *need*—? What, you were having a nap of your own free will?"

"I was recuperating—"

"Balls you were."

Harrow opened her eyes. Her voice rose, cracking with tension: "The *Sixth House*, Griddle! Do you know how difficult it is to stay ahead of Palamedes Sextus? Didn't I tell you to keep your pneumatic mouth *shut*? I would have been fine; I'd fainted; I was resting."

"And how I'm meant to know that," said Gideon heavily, "I've got no idea. I want answers, and I want them yesterday."

The whites around Harrow's eyes were pink and inflamed, probably from too little rest and too much fainting. She closed them again and her head came down, heavy, back to the bed. Her dead black hair fell in lank and tangled hanks on the pillow. She looked flat and tired.

"I'm not having this conversation with you," she said finally.

"Yeah, you are," said Gideon. "I took my key ring back, so if you ever want to dick around in that basement again you'll have a hell of a time getting back in there."

The necromancer's lips pursed in a sour, thin line that was obviously meant to show iron resolve but simply showed a bunch of mouth scabs. "That's easily contrived. You can't stay awake forever."

"Quit bluffing, Nonagesimus! Quit acting like I was the one who messed up here! You haven't spoken more than twenty words to me since we arrived, you've kept me totally in the dark, and yet I've done every single thing you ever goddamned asked of me no matter what it was—okay, I did come to find you, nearly every single thing—but I kept my head down and I didn't start shit. So if you could see your way to being even *ten percent* less salty with me, that'd be just terrific."

Silence spread between them. The iron resolve on that scabrous mouth seemed to waver, just a little bit. Gideon added, "And don't push me. The places where I can and would stick this thing for safekeeping would astonish you."

"Puke," murmured Harrow. And: "Give me the water, Griddle."

She could barely drink it. She lifted her head for a few spluttering sips, then lay back down, eyelashes brushing eyelids again. For a couple of moments Gideon thought she had gone back to sleep: but then Harrow stirred and said colourlessly: "I'd hardly call suckerpunching the Third cavalier keeping your head down."

"You disapprove?"

"What? Hardly," said Harrow, unexpectedly. "You should have finished the job. On the other hand, dallying with the Seventh House is the act of the naif or the fool, or both. What part of *Don't talk to anybody* did you not register—"

"Dulcinea Septimus is dying," said Gideon. "Give me a break."

Harrow said, "She picked an interesting place to die."

"What are you doing, where are you doing it, why are you doing it? Start talking, Reverend Daughter."

They stared each other down, both similarly mulish. Harrow had taken another swig of water and was slowly swilling it around in her cheeks, apparently thinking hard. Gideon dropped back to sit on the gently sagging dresser, and she waited. Her necromancer's mouth was still puckered up with a sourness that would've impressed a lemon, but she asked abruptly:

"What did the priest specify was the only rule, the first day we were here?"

"You're not very good at *I'm Asking the Questions Now, Bitch,* are you," said Gideon.

"This is going somewhere. Answer me."

Gideon resented the *answer me,* but she begrudgingly cast her mind back through a montage of rotting furniture, assholes, and astringent tea. "Teacher?" she said. "Uh—the door thing. We weren't to go through any locked door."

"More specifically, we weren't to go through a locked door without permission. The old man's a pain in the neck, but he was giving us a clue—take a look at this."

Harrow appeared to be thawing to her subject. She thrashed feebly trying to sit up, but before this could soften Gideon's concrete heart she got cross and snapped two bone chips out of her sleeve. Harrow pressed them against the dank arm of the four-poster bed, and out sprung bony arms that hauled her up into a sitting position. They dragged her flush with the headboard, and a shower of dust trickled down from the enormous cloth drapes. Harrow sneezed fretfully, half of it blood.

She searched about in her robes and came up with a thick little book bound in cracked, blackened stuff, with the awful orange tone of tanned human leather. The book was a thousand pages thick, maybe a million. "Light," she demanded, and Gideon nudged the lamp forward. "Good. Look here."

Harrow flicked through pages with scabby fingers until she had opened the squat book midway, showing three sets of angular diagrams. They appeared to be numerous overlapping squares, with lines coming out at odd angles and a scrawl of notes or numbers bumping up against the lines. The writing was minute and spidery: the squares mazelike and innumerable. Gideon realised after a moment that she was looking at an architectural drawing, and that it was an architectural drawing of Canaan House. It was scribbled thickly with cross marks.

"I've divided Canaan House into its three most significant levels, but that's not quite accurate. The central floor is more of a mezzanine providing access to the top and bottom floors. The terraces are sections in and of themselves, but they're not important for what I'm identifying here. Each X denotes a door. Current count is seven hundred and seventy-five, and Griddle—only six are locked. The first two hundred doors I identified—"

"You spent this whole time counting doors?"

"This calls for rigor, Nav."

"Maybe rigor . . . *mortis,*" said Gideon, who assumed that puns were funny automatically.

"The first two hundred doors I identified," Harrow repeated, through gritted teeth, "included the access hatch to the lower area of Canaan House. My method was to start at the bottom and go up as far as I could from a static starting point. There are two lockpoints here, at X-22 and X-155. X-155 is the hatch, X-22 is another door. I went to Teacher and asked permission to enter both. He agreed to let me through the hatch if I could provide a safe place for the key, but said that X-22 didn't belong to him and that he couldn't in good conscience give permission. All the while he was winking at me so hard that I thought he had suffered a stroke."

Despite everything, Gideon was starting to get interested. "Okay. Then what?"

"Then in the morning I retrieved the key ring," said Harrow.

"Hold up, hold up. *My* key ring, more correctly, but let's be clear here, you'd counted *two hundred doors* before the first morning?"

"A head start," said her necromancer, "is the only advantage one can claim by choice. My other advantage is in workforce. In this case

I'm fairly sure that Sextus started a mere two hours after me, and that Eighth House zealot not long after."

All of this said a lot about the psyche of Harrowhark Nonagesimus, something about Palamedes Sextus, and a little about the mayonnaise uncle, but Gideon was given no time to interrupt. Harrow was continuing, "And I'm not at all sure about the Third. Never mind. Anyway, I've spent the majority of my time down the access hatch in the facility. Here."

Another dry, crackly page was turned. This one was stained with unmentionable fluids and brown patches, which could have been tea and could have been blood. The diagram was much less detailed than the three for the upper levels. In a fat-leaded pencil Harrow had drawn a network of question marks, and some of the rooms were vague sketches rather than the perfectly ruled mazes of the first maps.

Here there were familiar labels: LABORATORY ONE through to LABORATORY TEN. PRESSURE ROOM. PRESERVATION. MORT. WORK ROOM ONE through to WORK ROOM FIVE. And SANITISER, though also: CONTROL ROOM?, CONSOLE? and DUMP ROOM?. It was set out neatly, with corridors all the same width and doors in expected places. It reminded Gideon of some of the oldest parts of the Ninth House, the bits secluded deep below the more modern twisty little hallways and crooked walls with squints.

"It's very old," Harrow said, quietly, more to herself than to Gideon. "Considerably older than the rest of Canaan House. It's pre-Resurrection—or made to look pre-Resurrection, which is just as curious. I know Sextus is obsessed with dating the structure, but as usual, he's getting caught up in the details. What's important is the function."

"So what was it for?"

Harrow said, "If I knew that, I'd be a Lyctor already."

"Do you know who used it?"

"That's a much better question, Nav."

"And why," said Gideon, "were you down there with your ass kicked to hell, hiding in a bone?"

The Reverend Daughter sighed heavily, then had a fit of coughing, which served her right. "Whoever left the facility also left the majority of their work behind and intact. No theorems or tomes, unless they've been removed—and I doubt Teacher removed them—but, as I've discovered, it's possible to trigger . . . tests. Theorem models that they would have used. Most of the chambers down there were used to prepare for something, and they were left in a state where anyone who comes across it can re-enact the setup. Someone left—challenges—down there for any necromancer talented enough to understand what they were doing."

"Stop being opaque, Nonagesimus. What do you mean by *challenges*?"

"I mean," said Harrowhark, "that I have lost one hundred and sixty-three skeletons to a single laboratory construct."

"*What.*"

"I'm prevented from seeing whatever destroys the skeletons I raise," came the terse answer. "I haven't worked out how to properly outfit them yet. If the priests have managed to engineer a scaffolded skeleton of the type they use as servants—my God, Nav, have you *seen* the bonework on them?—then I surely can, but I haven't worked out how to disassemble one of the First House corpus yet and I can't do enough just by looking. Don't get me wrong; I will. I get closer every day. You found me when I'd exhausted myself, that's all."

"But what the hell's it all for?"

"As I have repeated to excess, Griddle, I'm still working on the theory. Nonetheless—look back at the maps."

The necromancer fell to brooding, staring through swollen eyelids down at the journal. Somewhat astonished still, Gideon leaned over and, ignoring her adept's dumb mystic despond, flipped the pages back to the three-level plan for Canaan House. A few of the X-marked doors were circled with scratchy black ink and marked with crabbed symbols that she did not recognise. These seemed to be distantly distributed throughout the First House building, tucked away or secreted.

Gideon flipped another page. There was a pencil sketch of an animal's skull with long horns. The horns curved inward into points that almost touched but not quite, and the sockets were deep holes of black pencil lead. An electric thrill of recognition ran through her.

"I've seen this before," she said.

Harrow bestirred herself. Her eyes narrowed. "Where?"

"Hang on. Let me look at the map again." Gideon flipped back and found the atrium; she traced with her finger the twisty route from there to the corridor and stairs that led to the cavalier's dais. She found the staircase, and jabbed with her thumbnail: "You haven't got it—*way* ahead of you, Nonagesimus. There's a hidden hallway here, with a locked door."

"Are you certain?" Now Harrow was well and truly awake. At the answering nod she rummaged in her robes for a long iron needle and jabbed it inside her mouth—Gideon winced—before the bones at the bedhead unceremoniously shoved her up to a ninety-degree angle, weapon held ready, end shining with red blood. She said, "Show me, Nav."

Thoroughly satisfied with herself, Gideon placed her finger next to the enormous door of black stone she'd hidden behind the tapestry. Harrow marked the place with a bloody red cross and blew on the ink: it skeletonised immediately into a tarry, dry brown. *X-203.* The necromancer could not hide a triumphant smile. It stretched her mouth and made her split lips bleed. The sight was incomparably creepy. "If you're correct," she said, "and if *I'm* correct—well."

Exhausted by all the effort, Harrow closed the journal and tucked it back inside her robe. She sank back down into the dusty embrace of the bones, wrist joints clacking as they lowered her onto the dark slippery material of the duvet. She groped blindly for the water and spilled half of the remnants down her front as she took gulping, greedy sips. She dropped the empty glass onto the bed next to her, and then she closed her eyes. Gideon found herself gripping the slender rapier at her hip and feeling the heft of its basket hilt.

"You could've died today," she said conversationally.

For a long time the girl on the bed was supine and silent. Her chest rose and fell slightly, evenly, as though in sleep. Then Harrow said without opening her eyes, "You could attempt to finish me right now, if you liked. You might even win."

"Shut up," said Gideon, flat and grim. "I mean that you're making me look like a disloyal buffoon. I *mean* it's your fault that I can't take being your bodyguard seriously. I mean that all this *sacred duty do exactly as I say blah blah blah* shit does not matter in the least if you die of dehydration in a bone."

"I wasn't about to—"

"Baseline standard of a cavalier," said Gideon, "is you not dying in a bone."

"There was no—"

"No. It's Gideon Nav Talking Time. I want to get out of here and you want to be a Lyctor," she said. "We need to get in formation if that's going to happen. If you don't want me to ditch the paint, this sword, and the cover story, you're taking me down there with you."

"Griddle—"

"*Gideon Nav Talking Time.* The Sixth must think we're absolutely full of horseshit. I'm going down there with you because I am sick of doing nothing. If I have to wander around faking a vow of silence and scowling for one more day I will just open all my veins on top of Teacher. Don't go down there solo. Don't die in a bone. *I am your creature*, gloom mistress. *I serve you with fidelity as big as a mountain*, penumbral lady."

Harrow's eyes flickered open. "Stop."

"*I am your sworn sword*, night boss."

"Fine," said Harrow heavily.

Gideon's mouth was about to round out the words "bone empress" before she realised what had been said. The expression on the other girl's face was now all resignation: resignation and exhaustion and also something else, but mostly resignation. "I acknowledge your argument," she said. "I disagree with it, but I see the margin of error. Fine."

It would have been pushing her luck to point out that there was no real way Harrowhark could have denied her; she had the key, the upper hand, and significantly more blood. So all she said was, "Okay. Great. Fine."

"And you had better stop it with all this *twilit princess* garbage," said Harrow, "because I may start to enjoy it. Helping me will be achingly dull, Nav. I need patience. I need obedience. I *need* to know that you are going to act as though giving me devotion is your new favourite pastime, even though it galls us both senseless."

Gideon, dizzy with success, crossed one leg around the other and leant back on the dresser in a posture of triumph. "Come on. How bad could it be?"

Harrow's lips curled. They showed her teeth, stained slightly pink with blood. She smiled again—slower than before, just as terrible, just as strange.

"Down there resides the sum of all necromantic transgression," she said, in the singsong way of a child repeating a poem. "The unperceivable howl of ten thousand million unfed ghosts who will hear each echoed footstep as defilement. They would not even be satisfied if they tore you apart. The space beyond that door is profoundly haunted in ways I cannot say, and by means you won't understand; and you may die by violence, or you may simply lose your soul."

Gideon rolled her eyes so hard that she felt in danger of twisting the optic nerve.

"Knock it off. We're not in chapel now."

But Harrow said: "It's not one of mine, Griddle. I'm repeating exactly—to the *word*—what Teacher said to me."

"Teacher said that the facility was chocka with ghosts and you might die?"

"Correct."

"Surprise, my tenebrous overlord!" said Gideon. "*Ghosts and you might die* is my middle name."

14

THIS LAPSE OF HARROWHARK'S did not make her one bit nicer to live with. Very early next morning, despite all logic and sense, she forced Gideon to put on the robe and paint on the paint like every morning since they'd arrived at Canaan House: she was impatient with what Gideon saw as the necessities of life, i.e., eating breakfast and stealing lunch. Gideon won the breakfast argument, but lost the right not to stare wretchedly at the mirror as she stippled black paint over her cheekbones.

At Harrow's behest, the Ninth House moved through the silent grey corridors like spies. There were many times when the necromancer would stop in the shadow of a doorway and wait there for fully five minutes before she would allow them both to carry on, to creep noiselessly down the shabby staircases and down to the bowels of the First. They only met one person on the way: in the light before sunrise, Harrow and Gideon pressed themselves up into the shadow of an archway and watched a figure with a book clenched in one hand cross a dusty hall, silent and shadowed, littered with sagging chairs. Because she had spent her whole life in the darkest hole of the darkest planet in the darkest part of the system, Gideon could make out the etiolated profile of the repellent Third twin, Ianthe. She disappeared out of sight and Harrow remained, silently waiting, far longer than Gideon thought necessary before she gestured for them to move.

They made it to the dismal hole with the access hatch without incident, though it was dark enough *there* that Gideon had to pocket her glasses and Harrow had to tug down her veil. Harrow was breathing impatiently through her nose as Gideon slid the key into the lock, and flung herself down the hole as though being chased. They descended the long, frigid ladder, and Harrow brushed herself off at the bottom.

"Good," was the first thing she said since they'd left the room. "I'm relatively sure we're alone. Follow me."

Dogging her adept's rapid steps, rapier bumping against her hip, Gideon was interested to see that they did not traverse the mazelike corridors to Sanitiser. They instead passed down a long, broad hallway, buzzing quietly with the sound of electric light, until after a few corners they reached a door marked LABORATORY TWO. Harrow pushed this open.

The little foyer beyond was cupboard sized. There were hooks on the walls, and on one what Gideon took to be some ugly, partly dissolved tapestry, until she realised it was the remains of somebody's abandoned coat. On the door ahead was a dilapidated folder behind a piece of plex, with a scribbled and pale title in a faded, haphazard hand: #1–2. TRANSFERENCE/WINNOWING. DATACENTER.

Above the sterile metal door was the more familiar sight of a mounted skull, probably once painted red but now tarry brown. It had lost its jaw at some point and seemed all front teeth. Harrow fussily crammed minuscule chips of phalange in and around the entryway. It was an unusual experience to be crossing, rather than barred from, a Nonagesimus bone ward, but Gideon didn't get the time to enjoy it: Harrow pushed through the door and led Gideon through to another room.

This room—more spacious, more elongated—gave the distinct impression of having been ransacked. It was ringed with broad metal desks, and the walls were pockmarked with empty electrical sockets. There were shelves and shelves that must once have contained books and files and folders, but now only contained a lot of dust; there were discoloured places on the walls where things must have been tacked up and had since been taken down. It was a naked and empty room. One wall was windowed all along its length to let you see into the chamber ahead, and that wall had a door in it marked with two things: one, a sign on the front saying RESPONSE, and two, a little plaque on the top marked OCCUPIED. This had a bleary glow of a green light next to it, indicating that Response was probably *not* occupied. Looking through to Response—a bleak, featureless chamber, characterised only by a couple of vents on the far side of the square—the floor was an absolute shitshow of bits of broken bone.

The other wall—filled with brackets to prop up books that had long since been removed—had a door too, and this one was labelled: IMAGING. The Imaging door had the same plaque as Response, but with a little red light instead. Imaging also had a little plex window whose outside was smeared with old bloody handprints.

"Someone's been having fun in here," said Gideon.

Harrow shot her a look but did not enforce the vow of silence. "Yes," she said. "Me."

Her cavalier tried the door marked Response, but it wouldn't move and there didn't seem to be a conventional touchpad. Harrow said, "It won't open like that, Nav. Come with me, and don't touch anything."

Gideon went with Harrow and did not touch anything. The autodoor to Imaging obligingly opened at their approach, revealing a dismal cupboard of a room with a huge array of old mechanical equipment, lightless and dead. A single ceiling panel fuzzed its way to life, white and pallid and not revealing much but more shadow. The long desk still had what she realised was a rusted old clipboard, to which a thin, nearly transparent piece of paper was attached. Gideon at last gave in to the urge to touch something, and the paper dissolved as though it were ash. It left a grey stain on her fingertips.

"Fucking yuck," she said, wiping them on her front.

Harrow said curtly, "Have some care, you dolt, everything here is impossibly old."

In the centre of the room was a tall metal pedestal. Atop the pedestal was a strange, flat panel of weirdly reflective glass—beautiful, with a dichromatic black fleck. The black-robed necromancer, painted brow furrowed with concentration, passed her hand over the top of the glass: it buzzed at her proximity, sending shivering green sparks jumping over the pedestal. Harrow peeled off her glove and placed one long-fingered hand directly on the glass. Two things happened: the glass folded over her hand like a cage, and the Imaging door shut with a heavy *whunk*. Gideon pressed into it, but it did not open again.

"What happens now?"

Harrow said, "Look through the window."

Through the smeary little window Gideon could see that Response had opened up. Harrow continued, joylessly: "The door shuts in response to—as far as I can tell—weight and motion. I didn't test precisely how much weight, but it's around thirty moving kilograms. I have, at this point, sent around ninety kilos' worth of bone matter into that room."

The things Harrow could pull off with the tip of someone's toe bone were astonishing. Three kilos of osseo for Harrow could have been anything. A thousand skeletons, crammed and interlocked within Response. Seas of spines. An edifice of cranium and coccyx. Gideon just said, "*Why?*"

Harrow said, stiffly: "Every single construct I've put into that room has been pulverised."

"By what?"

"I don't know," she said. "If I take my hand off the pedestal, the door unlocks and the room reverts. I can't see it. I only hear it."

At *hear it* the hairs on the back of Gideon's neck rose, and she shook off her hood. Harrow jerked her wrist away from the pedestal and the glass neatly unfolded itself from her hand. The Imaging door opened with another automatic *whunk*, spilling light in from the anterior room.

Harrow worked each finger gently within its socket, and said, this time more brightly: "So, Griddle, this is where you are to be my shining star. You're going out there to be my eyes."

"What?"

"My skeletons don't have photoreceptors, Nav," the necromancer said calmly. "I know they're being destroyed with blunt force. I have no idea what by, and I need to keep my hand on the thanergetic lock. You have perfectly functional eye jelly; you have a dubious but capable brain; you're going to stand out there and look through the window. Got it?"

There was nothing objectionable to this role, which was why Gideon was automatically suspicious of it. But she said, "As you wish, my lamentable queen," and ducked out the Imaging door. Her adept followed close behind her, rummaging in her pockets. She brought out a whole knuckle, which was telling. Harrow threw it down and, with an awful grinding sound, it sprang into a burly skeleton: she flicked her wrist at it impatiently and it lumbered toward Response, standing, waiting. Then Harrow ducked back inside Imaging.

This is dumb, thought Gideon. The Imaging door wheezed shut, presumably as Harrow placed her hand upon the pedestal, and the Response door ground open: the skeleton stepped forward, bone feet crunching on a carpet of other bones. As it stepped through, the door plunged shut behind it, and the little light next to Occupied turned red.

Whatever happened next happened pretty goddamn fast. The lights in Response flared as the vents started choking out cloudy puffs, obscuring the far wall: she pressed herself so close to the glass that her breath made it misty and wet. There was no sound from within, and there should have been (it must have all been sound-proofed) which simply made it all the more absurd when something enormous and misshapen came raging out of the fog.

It was a bone construct, she could tell that much. Grey tendons strapped a dozen weirdly malformed humeri to horribly abbreviated forearms. The rib cage was banded straps of thick, knobbly bone, spurred all around with sharp points, the skull—was it a skull?—a huge knobble of brainpan. Two great green lights foamed within the darkness there, like eyes. It had way too many legs and a spine like a load-bearing pillar, and it had to crouch forward on two of its heavyset arms, fledged all over with tibial spines. The exterior arms were thrust back high, and she could see now that they did not have hands: just long slender blades, each formed from a sharpened radius, held at the ready like a scorpion's tail. It rampaged forward; Harrow's skeleton patiently waited; the construct fell on it like a hot meal, and it disintegrated under the second blow.

The construct turned its awful head toward the window, fixed its burning green gaze on Gideon, and got very still. It lumbered toward her, gaining speed, when the red light for Occupied turned green: there was a low and doleful *parp* from some klaxon, and then the construct dissolved. It became soup, not bones, and it moved as though sucked into some small grating toward the centre of the room. It was totally gone, along with all the fog, when Imaging sprang open and Harrow found her cavalier with her jaw dropped open.

It took a few moments of explanation. Harrow cross-questioned the measurements and looked disgusted with all her answers. Before Gideon had finished, Harrow was pacing back and forth, robes swishing around her ankles like black foam.

"Why can't I *see* it?" she raged. "Is it testing the skeleton's autonomy, or is it testing my control? How much multidexterity does it want?"

"Put me in there," said Gideon.

That brought Harrow up short, and her eyebrows shot to the top of her hairline. She fretted at the veil around her neck, and she said slowly: "Why?"

Gideon knew at this point that some really intelligent answer was the way to go; something that would have impressed the Reverend Daughter with her mechanical insight and cunning. A necromantic answer, with some shadowy magical interpretation of what she had just seen. But her brain had only seen the one thing, and her palms were damp with the sweat that came when you were both scared and dying of anticipation. So she said, "The arms kind of looked like swords. I want to fight it."

"You want to fight it."

"Yep."

"Because it looked . . . a little like swords."

"*Yop.*"

Harrow massaged her temples with one hand and said, "I'm not yet so desperate for a new cavalier that I'm willing to recycle you. No. I'll send in three this time, and *you're* to tell me how it handles that—exactly how it responds; I'm not yet convinced that this isn't testing my multidexterity . . ."

The next time she sent a skeleton in, it was clutching a crinkly bundle of phalanges in each bony fist. Gideon watched dutifully as the light turned green, and as Harrow sightlessly raised two identical skeletons next to her first. They were models of their kind: beautifully made, built to spec, animated and responsive. Harrow's skeletons looked almost like First House servants now. When the construct flailed out of the mist, they moved with admirable poise and fluency, and got demolished in three moves. The last skeleton ran around in a sad little sprint before the monstrous construct raised one bladed arm and shattered it from sacrum to shoulder.

The second time Harrow emerged to get the blow-by-blow, one nostril was bleeding. The third time, both nostrils. The fifth time—the floor of Response carpeted with the remains of twenty skeletons—she was wiping blood off her eyelashes and her shoulders were drooping. She had listened to each playback with numb, blank-eyed thoughtfulness, too distracted even to needle Gideon, but this time she balled her hands into fists and pressed them into her skull.

"My mother and my father and my grandmother together could not do what I do," she said softly, not speaking to Gideon. "My mother *and* my father *and* my grandmother together . . . and I've advanced so far beyond them. One construct or fifty—and it simply slows it down . . . for all of half an hour."

She shook away frustration like an animal with a wet pelt, shivering all over before fixing dead black eyes on Gideon. "Right," she said. "Right. Again. Keep watching, Nav."

She staggered back, door whipping shut behind her. Gideon Nav could only put up with so much. She took off her robe, folded it up, and put it on a hook in the foyer. She stood next to a skeleton whose arms were so full with bits of bone and lengths of tibia that it trailed chips like breadcrumbs. It was easy enough to stand beside it politely until the door opened, then to trip it up, then to step over it. She unsheathed her rapier with a silver whisper, slipping the knuckles of her left hand through the obsidian bands. The Response door breathed shut behind her.

"Harrow," she said, "if you wanted a cavalier you could replace with skeletons, you should've kept Ortus."

From whining speakers set in each corner, Harrow cried out. It wasn't a noise of annoyance, or even really a noise of surprise—it was more like pain; Gideon found her legs buckling a little bit and she had to stagger, shift herself upright, shake her head to clear the brief bout of dizziness away. She held her rapier in a perfect line and waited.

"What?" The necromancer sounded dazed, almost. "What, seriously?"

The vents breathed out huge sighs of fog. Now that she was in the room, Gideon could see that they were blasting moisture and liquid into the air, stale-smelling stuff; from within *this* cloud the construct was rising—leg to horrifying leg, to broad plates of pelvis, to thick trunk of spine—to the green motes of light that swung around, searching, settling on Gideon. Her stance shifted. From Imaging Harrow grunted explosively, which nearly got her cavalier knocked ass-over-tits.

Air was displaced. The construct rushed her, and it was only *just* in time that she deflected two heavy overhand blows onto the naked black blade of her sword. Harrow let out a yelp as though she had touched her hand to a flame.

"Nonagesimus!"

Gideon considered the good news and the bad news. The good news: the blows that rained down on her were not as heavy as she had expected from something so enormous. They came down hard and fast, but no harder than the hand of Naberius Tern; lighter, for the lack of muscle. Osseous matter never weighed as much as blood and flesh, which was one of the problems with pure construct magic.

The bad news: she couldn't do jack shit to it. Her light sword could barely deflect the blows. She had some small hope with her obsidian knuckle-knives—one good strong backhand bash and she had knocked out part of one arm, snapping the blade off near the tip—but then watched with a sickening weight in her gut as the blade reformed.

"Nonagesimus," she hollered again between attacks, "this shit is regenerating!"

There was nothing from the speakers. Gideon wondered if Harrow could hear her. She leapt to the side as the construct fell forward, slashing heavily—it slammed into a pile of bone that had built up from Harrow's previous failures, and a chip careered out like a bullet and nicked Gideon's arm. From the speakers, the girl cried out again.

"Nonagesimus!" she said, alarmed now. The construct wallowed in its nest of victims, then reared up again. "Hey—*Harrow*!"

The speakers crackled. "Stop thinking!"

"What?"

"I can't—it's too—damn it!"

She was about to tell Harrow to take her hand off the damn pedestal, but she was charged again in a lurching flurry of blades. The construct bounded forward on its hands and feet like a lopsided predatory animal. Gideon charged too, and she sliced her sword straight through the interosseous membrane on the arm coming down to spear her. Arm and construct flailed independently, and with her offhand she punched it hard in the pelvis. Bone splintered out explosively as half the ilium came away. The monster fell and thrashed, trying to rise, as the pelvis and the top of one femur knit themselves back together with unsavoury speed. Gideon fell back in a hurry, pulling her sword free and wiping bone matter off her face.

The speakers sizzled with heavy breathing. "Nav. Close one eye."

She would question later why she did it, but she did it. Depth perception fled as she squinted an eye shut, backing away from the construct as it slithered around in useless circles, crippled. For a moment her gaze drunkenly slid into place, and she could see—something—at the very corners of her vision: some kind of peripheral mirage, a susurrus of light that moved in a way she'd never seen before. It was like a gel overlay across real life. It balled around various bits of the construct as though attracted to it, like iron filings to a magnet. She blinked hard. There was fresh panting over the speakers.

"All right," came Harrow's voice, "all right, all right—"

The construct reared up, centre of gravity restored. Gideon's heart hammered. The speakers hissed again. Harrow said, "What's on top of it?"

"What—the arms?"

"I can't see," said Harrow, "blurry—"

Gideon had to open both eyes again. She couldn't not. She parried the first uppercut thrust from the construct as it bounded toward her, but it cracked her in the shoulder with another. She got it with her knives on the backswing—the sharpened arm cracked, bounced away, and hit the wall—but she had to fall back into a crouch and seethe with pain, worrying that her shoulder had popped out entirely. The speakers bellowed. The construct reared up, other blades at the ready, and—disassembled.

It turned to liquid and trickled toward the grate in the centre of the room as Gideon stared. The Response door slid open, and after a moment's testing of her shoulder, she pulled herself to stand. She was working the muscles as she went through the doorway—it locked shut, Imaging opened—and she found herself face-to-face with Harrow, who was taut as death and trembling.

"The hell," said Gideon, "was *that*?"

"It's the test." Harrow's lips were pink where she had bitten off the paint. She seemed to be having trouble swallowing, and she was staring right through her cavalier. She said unsteadily, "You're the test."

"Um—"

"Frontal, parietal, temporal, occipital, hippocampus—I fought with them all inside you," she said. "I'm not equipped to deal with a living spirit still attached to a nervous system. You're so noisy. It took me five minutes to peel away the volume just to see. And the pain is so much worse than skeleton feedback—your spirit rendered me deaf! Your whole body makes noise when you fight! Your temporal lobe—God—I have *such* a headache!"

This entire speech was incoherent, but the bottom-line realisation was humiliating. Heat rose rapidly up Gideon's neck. "You can control my body," she said. "You can read my *thoughts*."

"No. Not remotely." That was a relief, until it was followed up with: "If only I could. The moment I get a handle on even one of your senses, I'm overwhelmed by another."

"You are banned from squatting in my lobes and my hippocampus. I don't want you pushing all the furniture around in there."

Perhaps there was some tiny grain of sympathy in Harrow. She did not respond with a horrid laugh or a dark Ninth saying: she just flapped her hand. "Don't have an aneurysm, Nav. I cannot and will not read your thoughts, control your body, or look at your most intimate memories. I don't have the ability and I certainly don't have the desire."

"It's for your protection, not mine," said Gideon. "I imagined Crux's butt once when I was twelve."

Harrow ignored her. "*Winnowing*," she said. "I'm a fool. It wants the wheat from among the chaff—or the signal from the noise, if you like. But why? Why can't I just do it myself?"

She swayed lightly, and swabbed a pink line across her face with one sleeve. Her cultist paint was looking distinctly sepia, but she looked elated, grimly satisfied somehow.

"I now know how to complete this trial," she said meditatively. "And we'll do it—if I work out the connection and rethink what I know about possession theory, I can do it. Knowing what to work on was the battle, and now I know. But first, Griddle, I'm afraid I have to pass out."

And she crumpled neatly back onto the floor. Pure sentiment found Gideon kicking out one leg to catch her. She ended up lightly punting her necromancer on the shoulder but assumed that it was the thought that counted.

15

"I'D DO A HELL of a lot better with a longsword," Gideon said.

A few hours after, Harrowhark had woken up from her floor nap and accompanied her cavalier back to their quarters. She'd been all for trying again then and there, but it took Gideon one look at her slightly crossing eyes and shaky hands to nix that plan. Now they were back in their main, dark-panelled room, the noonday light filtering through the blinds in hot slats of white, with Gideon galumphing down bread and Harrow picking at crusts. The necromancer had woken up just as sour as ever, which gave Gideon some hope that everything back there had been a passing fit of insanity.

"Insinuation denied," said Harrowhark. "You don't have one"— sweet, that meant Harrow hadn't successfully been through all her stuff—"and more importantly, you should do without. I never liked that cursed thing anyway; I always felt like it was judging me. If you require a two-handed sword every time the chips are down you're worth nothing as my cavalier."

"I still don't get how this whole test is meant to work."

The Reverend Daughter gave this consideration, for once. "All right. Let me—hmm. You know that a bone construct is animated by a necromantic theorem."

"No way! I assumed you just thought super hard about bones until they happened."

Ignoring this, Harrow continued: "This particular construct is animated by *multiple* theorems, all—woven together, in a sense. That enables it to do things normal constructs can't possibly."

"Like regenerate."

"Yes. The way to destroy it is to unpick that tapestry, Nav, to pull on each thread in turn—in order—until the web gives way. Which would take me ten seconds, if I only had it at arm's length."

"Huh," said Gideon, unwillingly starting to get it. "So I unpick it for you."

"Only with my assistance. You are not a necromancer. You cannot see thanergetic signatures. I have to find the weak points, but I have to do it *through your eyes,* which is made infinitely more difficult by you waving a sword around the whole time while your brain—yells at me."

Gideon opened her mouth to say *My brain is always yelling at you,* but was interrupted by a sharp rap on the door. The necromancer froze as though she were under attack, but this knock was followed by guttural hysterics of the kind that Gideon had heard before. The sound drifted off down the corridor accompanied by the hurried footsteps of two semiterrified teenagers. Jeannemary and what's-his-face had shoved something underneath the door, and left.

She went to see what it was. It was a plain, heavy envelope—real paper, creamy brown. *"Reverend Daughter Harrowhark Nonagesimus,"* she read out loud. *"Gideon the Ninth.* Fan mail."

"Give it to me. It might be a trap."

Gideon ignored this, as it was quite likely Harrow would toss the thing out the window rather than give it a chance. She also ignored Harrow's lemon-pucker scowl as she withdrew a piece of flimsy—less impressive than the envelope, but who barring the Emperor would use real paper for a letter—and read aloud its contents.

LADY ABIGAIL PENT AND SIR MAGNUS QUINN

IN CELEBRATION OF THEIR ELEVENTH
WEDDING ANNIVERSARY

PRESENT THEIR COMPLIMENTS TO THE HEIR AND
CAVALIER PRIMARY OF THE NINTH HOUSE

AND REQUEST THE HONOUR OF THEIR
COMPANY THIS EVENING.

DINNER TO BE SERVED AT SEVEN O'CLOCK.

Underneath in hasty but still beautifully-formed handwriting was another note:

> *Don't be affrighted by the wording, Abigail can't resist a formal invitation, at home am practically issued one for breakfast. Not at all a serious function & would be deeply pleased if you could both see fit to come. I will make dessert, can reassure you I cook better than I duel.—M.*

Harrow said, "No."

"I want to go," said Gideon.

"This sounds impossibly vapid."

"I want to eat a dessert."

"It occurs to me," said Harrow, drumming her fingers, "that during a single dinner the deaths of multiple House scions could be assured by one clever pair, a bottle of poison, and then—suddenly, the Fifth House's primacy is assured. And all because *you* wanted a sweet."

"This is a formal invitation to the Ninth House, not just you and me," said Gideon, more cunningly, "and being dyed-in-the-wool traditionalists, shouldn't we make a *teeny weeny appearance*? It'll look rude if we don't go. We can extrapolate heaps from whoever doesn't come, and everyone will, to be polite. Politics. Diplomacy. I'll eat yours if you don't want it."

The necromancer lapsed into brooding. "But this delays finishing the trial," she complained finally, "and wastes an evening in which Sextus can get ahead of us at his leisure."

"Bet you Palamedes will be there. We can do the trial afterward. And I'll be so good. I'll be silent and Ninth and melancholy. The sight will astound and stimulate you."

"Nav, you are a hog."

But that meant they were going to go. Gideon reflected on her unexpected victory as she stared in the mirror, idly counting the pimples cropping up as the result of repeated slathers of cult paint. The atmosphere was—relaxed, in this strange and waiting way, like the time she'd got a sedative and knew a nun was coming to whip out her tonsils. She and Nonagesimus were both waiting for the knife. She had never known Harrow to be so malleable, nor to go such a long time without raking her claws across Gideon's internal tender spots. Maybe the Lyctor trials were having a mellowing effect on her.

No, that was too much to hope for. Harrowhark was pleased because everything was coming up Harrowhark—she was glutted on getting her own way, and the moment that glow wore off the knives would come out again. Gideon couldn't trust Harrow. There was always some angle. There was always some shackle closing on you before you could even see it, and you'd only know when she turned the key. But then—

That evening, it was funny to see Harrow fuss. She put on her best and most senescent Ninth robes, and became a skinny black stick swallowed by night-coloured layers of Locked Tomb lace. She fiddled with long earrings of bone in front of the mirror and repainted her face twice. Gideon realised with no small amount of amusement and curiosity that Harrowhark was very frightened. She got more snappish as the evening wore on, and moved from languid postures of affected boredom with a book to a tense, rolled-up curl with hunched shoulders and knees. Harrow kept staring at the clock and wanted to go a full twenty minutes early. Gideon had just thrown on a clean robe and her tinted glasses, and noted that the necromancer was too tetchy even to veto those.

Why on earth was she scared? She had headed up function after dreary, overembroidered Ninth function, ornate in its rules and strict in its regulations, since she was a kid. Now she was all jitters.

Maybe it was about being denied her dark necromantic needs down past the access hatch. In any case, both she and Harrowhark turned up, gorgeously gowned in their Locked Tomb vestments, painted like living skulls, looking like douchebags. Harrow clinked when she walked with the sheer multiplicity of bonely accoutrement.

"You came!" said Magnus Quinn when he saw them; he was too well bred to double-take at two horrible examples of Drearburh clergy on the loose. "I'm so pleased you're wearing your, ah, glad rags; I was convinced I'd be the only one dressed up, and would have to sit resplendently among you all, feeling a bit of an idiot. Reverend Daughter," he said, and he bowed very deeply to Harrow. "Thank you for coming."

He himself was immensely trim in a pale brown, long-coated suit that had probably cost more than the Ninth House had in its coffers. The Ninth was high on ancient, shitty treasures but low on liquid assets. In a lower and chillier voice than Harrow usually ever affected, she said: "Blessings on the cavalier of the Fifth. Congratulations on the eleventh year of your espousal."

Espousal. But Magnus said, "Indeed! Yes! Thank you! It was actually yesterday. By happy accident I remembered and Abigail forgot, so in her resulting angst she wanted to make me dinner. I suggested we all benefit. Come in, please—let me introduce you."

The dining room off the atrium looked as it ever did, but with certain festive additions. The napkins had all been folded very carefully and some mildly yellowing tablecloth had come out of deep storage. There were correctly articulated place cards by each bright white plate. They were both led to the little kitchen and introduced to the slightly stressed Fifth necromancer whom Gideon had only ever seen in passing: she proved to have more or less the same easy, unaffected manner as Magnus, the type you only got when you came from a house like the Fifth. She looked Gideon very straight in the eye and shook her hand very firmly. Unlike Magnus, she also had the manner some necromancers and librarians developed when they had been working on dead spells for the last fifteen years and no longer worried too much about the living: her stare was far too intense. But she was wearing an apron and it was hard to feel intimidated by her. Her very correct pleasantries with a po-faced Harrow were interrupted with the appearance in the doorway of the wretched teens, who were wearing around a million earrings each. The Ninth moved back to the hall.

It was a strange evening. Harrow nearly vibrated with tension. Teacher, perennially pleased to see them for no reason Gideon ever knew, cornered them immediately. He and the other priests were there already and each had a birthday expression of glee: for his part, Teacher was twinkling with a magnitude usually reserved for dying stars.

"What do you think of Lady Abigail?" he said. "They do say she's an extraordinarily clever necromancer—not so much in your line, Reverend Daughter, but a gifted summoner and spirit-talker. I have fielded many questions from her about Canaan House. I hope she and Magnus the Fifth are good cooks! We First have all hyped the occasion, I'm afraid, but priests who live plainly *must* get excited over food. Of course, the sombre Ninth must be similar."

The sombre Ninth, in the form of its adept, said: "We prefer to live simply."

"Of course, of course," said Teacher, whose attention had already wandered to trashy gossip. His bright blue eyes had searched the room for other objects of interest, and finding them, leaned in confidingly. "Yes, and there's young Jeannemary the Fourth and Isaac Tettares. Looking very pretty, the both of them. Isaac looks as though he has been studying too much." (Isaac, the necromancer teen with brushed-up hair bleached orange, looked more like he was suffering an abundance of pituitary gland.) "Naturally he is Pent's protégé. I hear the Fifth takes special pains with the Fourth . . . hegemonic pains, some may say. It must be difficult when they are both so young. But they all seem to get on well . . ."

"How do you know?"

"Reverend Daughter," the priest said, smiling, "you miss out on important things spending *all* your time so usefully down in the dark. Now, Gideon the Ninth—she could tell you a great deal if she were not bound to her admirable vow of silence. Your penitence shames me."

At this, Teacher gave Gideon a roguish wink, which was also the worst.

Movement in the doorway. The Third and Sixth Houses had arrived all at once, the drab moth of Palamedes making the golden butterfly of Coronabeth Tridentarius all the more aureate and fair. They were sizing each other up like prize fighters. Teacher said, "Now, the main event!"

It turned out that the Fifth's idea of a rollicking good time was a seating arrangement. This realisation caused Harrow's carefully controlled mask to take on a distinct veer to the tragic. They were separated, and Gideon found herself elbow to elbow between Palamedes and the dreadful teen cavalier of the Fourth, who looked as though she regretted everything that had ever led up to this moment. Dulcinea, opposite, kissed her hand to Gideon twice before Gideon had even sat down.

At least Harrow wasn't faring any better. She had been placed at the other end of the table diagonal to the mayonnaise uncle, who looked even more appalled than Jeannemary the Fourth. Opposite was Ianthe and to the other diagonal was Protesilaus, completing one of the worst tableaus in history; Naberius Tern was to Harrow's left and was carrying on some long communication with Ianthe conducted entirely in arch eyebrow quirks. As Harrow smouldered with hatred, Gideon began to enjoy herself.

Magnus clinked his spoon against his water glass. The conversation, which was terminal to start with, convulsed to a halt.

"Before we begin," he said, "a short speech."

The three priests looked as though they had never wanted anything so much in their lives as a short speech. One of the teens, slumped out of Magnus's sight, mimed putting their neck in a noose.

"I thought I'd, er," he began, "say a few words to bring us all together. This must be the first time in—a very long time that the Houses have been together like this. We were reborn together but remain so remote. So I thought I'd point out our similarities, rather than our differences.

"What do Marta the Second, Naberius the Third, Jeannemary the Fourth, Magnus the Fifth, Camilla the Sixth, Protesilaus the Seventh, Colum the Eighth, and Gideon the Ninth all have in common?"

You could have heard a hair flutter to the floor. Everyone stared, poker-faced, in the thick ensuing silence.

Magnus looked pleased with himself.

"The same middle name," he said.

Coronabeth laughed so hard that she had to honk her beautiful nose into a napkin. Someone was explaining the joke to the salt-and-pepper priest, who, when they got it, said "Oh, '*the*'!" which started Corona off again. The Second, entombed in dress uniforms so starched you could fold them like paper, wore the tiny smiles of two people who'd had to put up with Cohort formal dinners before.

The appearance of two skeletons bearing an enormous tureen of food broke the last tension. Under Abigail's direction, they filled everyone's bowl with good-smelling grain, white and fluffy, boiled in onion broth. Little drifts of chopped nuts or tiny tart red fruits were scattered throughout, and it was hot and spicy and good, which had completed Gideon's requirements for a meal at *hot*. She put her head down and ate, insensible, until one of the white-robed skeletons stepped forward to give her seconds.

At that point she could tune in to the conversations around her, which had survived their first faltering encounters with the enemy and were now in full swing:

"—the juicy part is the sarcotesta. Good, aren't they? There's a red seed apple growing in the greenhouse. Have you seen the greenhouses?—"

"—in keeping with Ottavian custom for a necromancer's fast until evening, which includes—"

"—which failed to fix the drive, which failed to get her back to the system in time, which meant I spent the first nine months wrapped in house dirt—"

"—interesting question," Palamedes was saying at Gideon's right.

"You might say that *Scholar* recognises the specialist, and *Warden* recognises the duty, which is why Master Warden is the higher rank. Taken in the sense of the supervisor and, if you think about it another way, the sense of the prison. D'you know what we call the internal jaws of a lock?—"

Opposite, Dulcinea murmured to Abigail: "I think that is a perfect shame."

"Thank you. We're over it; it simply wasn't in our cards," the necromancer said, a bit bracingly. "My younger brother's the next in line. He'll do well. It gives me more time to collate the manuscript, which I've been married to longer than I have to Magnus."

"So keep in mind I'm the kind of pity case you bring out at parties to make other people feel better about themselves," the other woman said smilingly, ignoring the Fifth's polite protests to the contrary, "but I would love you to explain your work, just so long as you pretend I am five and go from there."

"If I can't explain this clearly, then the fault is mine, not yours. It's not so complex. We have so little that survived from the period post-Resurrection, pre-sovereignty and pre-Cohort, except in secondhand records. We have transcripts of those from the Sixth, though they're keeping the originals."

"They're kept in a box full of helium so they'll outlast the heat death of Dominicus, Lady Pent," said Palamedes.

"Your Masters won't even let me look at them through the glass."

"Light is the paper-killer," he said. "Sorry. It's nothing against you. It's not in our particular interest to hoard Lyctoral records."

"They're good copies, at least—and I spend my time studying those. Writing commentary, naturally. But being here meant almost more to me than the idea of serving the Emperor. Canaan House is a holy grail! What we know about the Lyctors is tremendously antiseptic. I've actually found what I think are unencrypted communiqués between—"

Even with Dulcinea Septimus making the intense eyelash bat of *What you are doing and saying is so fascinating to me, Dulcinea Septimus*, Gideon knew a boring conversation when she heard one.

She took cautious sips of the purple, slightly chewy wine and was trying not to cough as she swung her attention over to her own shadowy marchioness of bones: Harrow was picking at the food, sandwiched between the stony cavaliers of the Seventh and Second. Every so often she would say something terse to Protesilaus, who would take sixty seconds to think about it before making replies so uninflected and curt that they made Harrow sparkle by comparison.

The mayonnaise uncle was talking to the anaemic twin, his probable future bride. "I was removed by . . . surgical means," Ianthe was saying calmly, her long fingers toying with the stem of her glass. "My sister is a few minutes older."

The white-kirtled young uncle was not eating. He had taken a few priggish sips of wine, but spent most of his time with his hands folded quietly over each other and staring. He had the posture of a metre ruler. "Your parents," he said, in his unexpectedly deep and sonorous voice, "risked intervention?"

"Yes. Corona, you see, had removed my source of oxygen."

"A wasted opportunity, I'd think."

"I don't live alternate histories. Corona's birth put my survivability somewhere around *definite nil.*"

"It wasn't on *purpose*, mark you," drawled her cavalier from across the table. His hair was so perfect that Gideon kept staring at it, mesmerised, hoping some specific bit of the ceiling would break down and squash it flat.

Ianthe affected shock. "Why, Babs, are you part of this conversation?"

"I'm just saying, Princess, you don't have to be so down on her like that—"

"You don't have to contradict me in public, and yet—and yet."

Naberius flicked his eyes very obviously over to the other end of the table, but Coronabeth was busy with Magnus: probably swapping new jokes, Gideon thought. He said, "Stop being a pill."

"I repeat, Babs, *are* you part of this conversation?"

"Thank God, no," said the hapless Babs sourly, and turned back to his previous conversation partner: the thickset nephew cavalier, stolidly refilling his bowl. He did not look thrilled to repossess the Third's undivided attention. Next to the spruce Naberius Tern, he looked shabbier and more worn-out than ever. "Now, look, Eighth, *here's* why you're wrong about the buckler . . ."

Gideon would have liked to know what was wrong about the buckler; but as she reached over for her glass again, she felt a tug on her sleeve. It was the disagreeable teen who was sitting on her other side, looking at her with a particularly fierce expression, emphasised with near-Ninth quantities of black eye makeup. Jeannemary the Fourth screwed up her mouth as though expecting an injection, all the little corners of her face more angular in ferociousness, her jillion earrings jingling.

"This is going to be a weird question," said Jeannemary.

Gideon dropped her arm and tilted her head quizzically. A little bit of blood drained from the teen's face, and Gideon almost felt sorry for her: hood and paint and robes on the priesthood around her had put her off dinners at the same age. But the teen stuck her awful courage to its sticking place, breathed out hard through her teeth, and blurted very quietly:

"Ninth . . . how big *are* your biceps?"

It seemed to be long after Gideon was forced to supinate and flex at the whim of a teenage girl that their bowls were replaced with new ones, these filled with confections of cream and fruit, and mostly sugar; the Fifth had obviously been busy. Gideon ate three helpings and Magnus, not bothering to hide his amusement, pushed a fourth her way. Magnus was inarguably a much better cook than a duellist. Before she had come to Canaan House, Gideon had considered getting full a grim process of gruel and spoon and mouth that had to be done in order to maximise chances of not having her ass later kicked by Aiglamene in some dim room. It was one of the first times that she had felt full and fat and honestly happy about it.

Afterward there was a tray of the hot, grassy tea to clear the mouth, and the various Houses stood around with warm cups in their hands to watch the skeletons clear up.

Gideon looked around for Harrow. Her necromancer was ensconced in a corner with, of all people, Teacher: she was talking to him in low tones as he alternately nodded or shook his head, looking more thoughtful than giddy for once, his thumbs stuck in his gorgeous rainbow sash.

Someone touched Gideon's hand, very lightly, as though afraid of startling her. It was Dulcinea, who had taken refuge in a chair; she was shifting her hips a little awkwardly in the hard wooden seat with the tiny, restless motions Gideon suspected she made when she was sore. She looked tired, and older than usual; but her pink mouth was still very pink, and her eyes alight with illicit amusement.

"Are your biceps huge," she said, "or are they just *enormous*? Ninth, please tick the correct box."

Gideon made sure her necromancer couldn't see her, and then made a rude gesture. Dulcinea laughed her silvery laugh, but it was sleepy somehow, quiet. She pointed serenely to a spot next to her seat and Gideon obligingly squatted there on her haunches. Dulcinea was breathing a little harder. She was wearing a filmy, foam-coloured dress and Gideon could see her ribs expand beneath it, like a shocked animal's. Her silky, chestnut-coloured ringlets, painstakingly curled, spread out over her shoulders.

"I liked that dinner," said Lady Septimus, with deep satisfaction. "It was useful. Look at the children."

Gideon looked. Isaac and Jeannemary were standing close to the table, Jeannemary's sleeves pulled down to reveal her biceps. They were the muscles of an athletic and determined fourteen-year-old, which was to say, unripped but full of potential; her floppy-haired teen-in-crime was wearily measuring them with his hands as they carried on a conversation in whispers—

("I *told* you so."

"Yours are fine?"

"Isaac."

"It's not like this is a bicep competition?"

"Dumbest thing you ever said?")

Their hisses carried. Abigail, who was standing nearby deep in conversation with one of the Second, reached out a hand to touch Isaac lightly on the shoulder in reproof. She did not even turn around or break off talking. The Fourth adept winced: his cavalier had a hard, resentful, told-off expression on her face.

Dulcinea murmured, "Oh, Gideon the Ninth, the Houses are arranged so badly . . . full of suspicion after a whole myriad of peaceable years. What do they compete for? The Emperor's *favour*? What does *that* look like? What can they want? It's not as though they haven't all gotten fat off our Cohort prizes . . . mostly. I have been thinking about all that, lately, and the only conclusion I can come to is . . ."

She trailed off. They were both silent in that pause's pregnant wake, listening to the polite and impolite after-dinner chatter all around them, the clatter of skeletons with used-up knives and forks. Into that white noise came Palamedes, who was, weirdly enough, bearing a full teacup on a tray: he proffered it to the weary lady of the Seventh, who looked at him with frank interest.

"Thank you awfully, Master Warden," she said.

If she had looked at him with interest, he looked at her with— well. He looked at her thin and filmy dress and her swell-jointed fingers, and at her curls and the crest of her jaw, until Gideon felt hell of embarrassed being anywhere near that expression. It was a very intense and focused curiosity—there wasn't a hint of smoulder in it, not really, but it was a look that peeled skin and looked through flesh. His eyes were like lustrous grey stone; Gideon didn't know if she could be as completely composed as Dulcinea under that same look.

Palamedes said lightly: "I'm ever at your service, Lady Septimus."

Then he gave a small trim bow like a waiter, adjusted his spectacles, and abruptly turned tail. Well! thought Gideon, watching him slide back into the crowd. Hell! Then she remembered that the Sixth had a weirdo fascination with medical science and probably found chronic illness as appealing as a pair of tight shorts, and then she thought: Well, hell!

Dulcinea was placidly sipping her tea. Gideon stared at her, waiting for the conclusion that had never come. Eventually the Seventh tore her gaze away from the small crowd of House scions and their cavalier primaries, and she said: "My conclusion? It's— Oh, there's your necromancer!"

Harrow had broken off from Teacher and was homing in on Gideon like iron to a lodestone. She offered Dulcinea only the most cursory glance; Dulcinea herself was smiling with what she obviously thought was infinite sweetness and what Gideon knew to be an expression of animal cunning; for Gideon not even a word, but a thrust of the pointy chin upward. Gideon propelled herself to stand and tried to ignore the Seventh's eyebrows waggling in their direction, which thankfully her necromancer didn't notice. Harrowhark was too busy storming out of the room with her robe billowing out behind her in the way Gideon suspected she had secretly practised. She heard Magnus the Fifth call out a gentle, "I am glad you came, Ninth!" but Harrow took no time to say goodbye, which hurt her feelings a little because Magnus was nice.

"Slow down, numbnuts," she hissed, when she thought they were out of earshot of anyone. "Where's the fire?"

"Nowhere—yet." Harrow sounded breathless.

"I've eaten my own body weight. Don't make me hurl."

"As mentioned before, you're a hog. Hurry up. We don't have much time."

"What?" There was a moment's respite as Harrow hauled open one of the little escape-route staircase doors. The sun had set and the generator lights glowed a sad and disheartened green: the skeletons, busy with dinner, had apparently not lit the candles. "What do you *mean*?"

"I mean we need to make up time."

"Hey, repeatedly, on what *grounds*?"

Harrow propped open the door with a bony hand. The expression on her face was resolute. "Because Abigail Pent asked that faithless Eighth prig if he knew about access down to the lower floors," she said, "and he said yes. Pent is not stupid, and that's another confirmed competitor on our hands. For God's sake hurry up, Griddle, I give us five hours before she's in the chamber herself."

16

GIDEON NAV HELD HER sword parallel to her body, the grease-black glass of her knuckle-knives close to her chest, and bit her tongue bloody. As most bitten tongues did, it hurt like an absolute bitch. Over the speakers, Harrow heaved. In front of her, still wet with the hot reek of powdered bone, the construct opened its mouth in a soundless shriek. They were back in Response, and they'd failed once already.

It wasn't as though Harrow's necromantic inability to chisel her skull open was from some reluctance of Gideon's (which would have been *completely fucking understandable*); she was trying as hard as she could. She was sleepy from the food and she was sore from earlier that morning, and being sleepy and sore meant there was so much more for Harrowhark to wade through. Gideon was forced to give her necromancer the first particle of credit in her life: Harrow did not yell at her. Harrow simply sank deeper and deeper into a morass of frustration and self-hatred, her fury at herself rising like bile.

The construct charged forward like a battering ram, and she leapt out the way and left half the skin of one knee on the ground for her pains. She still had a mouthful of blood as she began to holler, "*Har—*"

"Nearly," crackled the speaker.

"—*row,* just let me take a whack at it—"

"Not yet. Nearly. The bitten tongue was good. Hold it off for a second, Nav! You could do this asleep!"

Not with a *rapier.* She might as well have chucked both knuckle and sword to the ground and started jogging for all the good her weapons were doing. Gideon wasn't equipped for defence, and her head hurt. Her focus kept twitching in a migraine blur, dots and sparks coruscating in and out of her vision. A titanic blow from the construct bent her parry almost all the way back around to her head, and she moved *with* the blow rather than *against* as more of an afterthought.

"Three seconds. Two." It almost sounded like begging.

Gideon was feeling more and more nauseous: there was an oily, warm feeling in the back of her throat and her tongue was running wet with spit. When she looked at the construct now it was through a hazy overlay, as though she were seeing double. There was a sharp pain between her eyes as it hauled back its centre of gravity, lurched—

"I can see it."

Later on Gideon would think about how little triumph there was in Harrow's voice: more awe. Her vision blurred, then spiked back abruptly into twenty-twenty colour. Everything was brighter and crisper and cleaner, the lights harder, the shadows colder. When she looked at the construct it smoked in the air like hot metal—pale, nearly transparent coronas wreathed its malformed body. They simmered in different colours, visible if you squinted this way or that, and in admiring them Gideon nearly got her leg broken.

"*Nav,*" hollered the speakers.

Gideon took a hard dive out of the way of a low stab, and then rolled away as the construct followed up by stomping hard where her foot *had* been. She hollered back: "Tell me what to *do!*"

"Hit these in order! Left lateral radius!"

Gideon focused on the nubbly, too-thick joint of the high left arm, and was surprised to find one of those mirage-like lights there: she sliced down and fell nearly off balance as her blade went through like a hot knife through fat. The long blade of the mutant arm clattered to the floor forlornly.

"Bottom-right tibia, lower quadrant, near the notch," said Harrow.

Now her triumph was barely held at bay. "Don't make any other hits."

Easier said than done. Gideon had to play grab-ass, snaking out of the construct's remaining blades, before she disdained the rapier and slammed her booted foot down instead. It wasn't hard: that part, just like the radius, was glowing like a flare. She got a square hit in and the construct's leg shattered—it rocked to the side, trying to compensate, and the leg did not start regenerating.

The next was easy. Side of the mandible. The eighteenth rib. She peeled the construct apart, removing the unseen strut mechanisms that turned it from monster into pathetic, jaw-clattering fuckup, some kid's first attempt at bone magic without ever having taken a look at an anatomy chart. When at last the Reverend Daughter said, "Sternum," Gideon was already there—raising one gauntleted fist up where a slice of sternum glowed like a candleflame, and punching it into dust. The construct collapsed. Gideon felt dizzy for just a second, and then it left her. The whole world brightened and sharpened.

The only thing left of the monster was a big chunk of pelvis, atomizing slowly into sand. There was a pleasing overhead *beep* and the door to Response whooshed open—and remained open, letting through a Harrow so wet with sweat that her hood was stuck to her forehead. Gideon was distracted by the pelvis as the sand crumbled and parted to reveal a gleaming black box. Its lead-coloured screen ticked up—15 percent; 26 percent; 80 percent—until it swung open with a soft *click* to reveal nothing more interesting than—a key.

Harrow uttered a soft cry and swooped, but Gideon was quicker. She took it up and unsnapped the key ring she now kept down her shirt, and she looped it through one of the ornate clover-shaped holes on the handle. Two keys now dangled there in triumph: the upper hatch key, and their new prize. They both admired them for a long moment. The new key was chunky and solid, and dyed a deep, juicy scarlet.

Gideon found herself saying, "I saw—lights, when I was fighting it. Overlay. Bright spots, where you told me to hit, a glowing halo. Is that what you meant by *thanergetic signature*?"

She expected some dismissive *You could not have comprehended the dark mysteries only my mascara'd eye doth espy,* and was not prepared for Harrow's open astonishment. Beneath the thick rivulets of blood and the smeared paint, she looked completely taken aback. "Do you mean," her adept said slowly, "that there were things *in* the skeleton framework—mechanical lights, perhaps? Dyed segments?"

"No, they were just—googly areas of light. I couldn't really see them properly," she said. "I only saw them toward the end, when you were messing around."

"That's not possible."

"I'm not lying."

"No, I'm just saying—that shouldn't have been possible," Harrow said. Her dark brows were furrowed so deeply that they looked like they were on a collision course. "I thought I knew what the experiment was doing, but—well. I cannot assume."

Gideon, tucking the keys safely back into her bandeau and, wincing at the chill, readied a flip comment; but as she looked up Harrowhark was looking at *her,* dead in the eye. Her chin was set. Harrow always *looked* so aggressively. Her face was moist from the effort and there were starbursts of broken red capillaries tucked into the white of each eye, but she turned those pitch-black irises right on her cavalier. The expression on her face was completely alien. Harrowhark Nonagesimus was looking at her with unalloyed admiration.

"But for the love of the Emperor, Griddle," she said gruffly, "you are something else with that sword."

The blood all drained away from Gideon's cheeks for some reason. The world spun off its axis. Bright spots sparked in her vision. She found herself saying, intelligently, "Mmf."

"I was in the privileged position of *feeling* you fight," Harrow continued, fingers nervously flexing. "And it took me a while to work out what you were doing. Longer still to appreciate it. But I don't think I'd ever really watched you, not in context . . . Well, all I can say is thank the Tomb that nobody knows you're not really one of ours. If *I* didn't know that, I'd be saying that you were Matthias Nonius come again or something equally saccharine."

"Harrow," said Gideon, finding her tongue, "don't say these things to me. I still have a million reasons to be mad at you. It's hard to do that *and* worry that you got brain injured."

"I'm merely saying you're an incredible swordswoman," said the necromancer briskly. "You're still a dreadful human being."

"Okay, cool, thanks," said Gideon. "Damage done though. What now?"

Harrowhark smiled. This smile was unusual too: it betokened conspiracy, which was normal, except that this one invited Gideon to be part of it. Her eyes glowed like coals with sheer collusion. Gideon didn't know if she could handle all these new expressions on Harrow: she needed a lie down.

"We have a key, Griddle," she said exultantly. "Now for the *door*."

* * *

Gideon was thinking about nothing in particular when they left #1–2. TRANSFERENCE/WINNOWING. DATACENTER., except that she was happy; buzzed with adrenaline and anticipation. She'd eaten a good meal. She'd won the game. The world seemed less maliciously unfriendly. She and Harrow left in companionable silence, both swaggering a little, though newly conscious of the cold and the dark. They hurried along the corridors, Harrowhark leading, Gideon following half a step behind.

There was nobody but them to trigger the motion sensors, and the lamps popped to life in rhythmic *whumpk—whumpk—whumpk*. They lit the way through the central room with the bronchial passages, and then down the short corridor to the access hatch ladder. At the beginning of that hall, Harrowhark stopped so abruptly that Gideon bumped into her in a flurry of robes and sword. She had gone absolutely still, and did not push back against her cavalier's stumble.

For the first moment, following Harrow's line of sight to the foot of the ladder, Gideon disbelieved her eyes. Her brain in an instant supplied all the information that her guts didn't want to conceive, and then it was her, stuck, frozen, as Harrow sprinted to kneel alongside the tangle of wet laundry at the bottom of the ladder.

It wasn't wet laundry. It was two people, so gruesomely entangled in each other's broken limbs that they looked like they had died embracing. They hadn't, of course: it was just the way their back-to-front limbs had arranged themselves in untidy death.

Hot bile rose in her mouth and made her tongue sticky. Her gaze drew away from the blood and exposed bone and fixed, inanely, on the empty wet scabbard by one busted wet hip: nearby was the sword, fallen point down in the flooring grille. The green lighting underfoot made its ivory steel glow a sickly lime. Gideon's necromancer stonily flopped the top corpse to the side, exposing what remained of both faces, before rising to stand.

She'd known before Harrow had rolled him over that before them lay the sad, crumpled corpse of Magnus Quinn, jumbled up with the sad, crumpled corpse of Abigail Pent.

ACT THREE

17

IN THE EARLY MORNING, after hours and hours of trying, even Palamedes admitted defeat. He didn't say so in as many words, but eventually his hand stilled on the fat marker pen that he had used to draw twenty different overlapping diagrams around the bodies of the Fifth, and he didn't try to call them back anymore.

Six necromancers had tried to raise them, singly or in concert, simultaneously or sequentially. Gideon had squatted in a corner and watched the parade. In the beginning a group of them had opened their own veins in a bid to tempt the early hunger of the ghosts. That period ended only when the teens, mad with rage at the inadequacy of only Isaac's blood, both started stabbing at Jeannemary's arm. They stood screaming at each other wordlessly, corseting belts above each other's elbows to make the veins stand out, until Camilla took the knives from their hands and began dispensing rubber bandages. Then they held each other, knelt, and wept.

Harrow did not open herself up. She walked the perimeter like a wraith, measuring her steps for Palamedes to draw by, swaying minutely with what Gideon knew was exhaustion. Nor did Coronabeth spill her blood: she only drew close to the work to pull Ianthe's hair away from her face, or to take a tiny knife from the twins' bags to replace the one her sister was using. They had both come from their beds without bothering to dress, and hence were wearing *astonishingly* flimsy nightgowns, the only solace of the night. The air was full of chalk and ink and blood and strong light from the electric torches that the Sixth had rigged up.

The Sixth had been painfully useful. Palamedes, wearing a scruffy bedrobe, had put up lights and marked the ladder with bits of tape at obscure places. He had stained the fluff on his dowdy old slippers pink as he walked quietly among the bodies, saying *excuse me* once when he stepped too close to Abigail's arm. He held the light up for Camilla as she sketched the whole unlovely scene on a big sheet of white flimsy, from the side, from the top, from their feet. He shed his scruffy bedrobe to reveal button-up pyjamas when Dulcinea drifted in wearing only a short shirt and trousers too big for her, and wrapped the robe around her shoulders without prompting. Then he went back to work.

A tableau of magicians and their guardians revolved around the corpses. Books were hauled out of pockets or the insides of coats, read, abandoned. People would go in, work, leave, be replaced, return, stay, leave as more of the inhabitants of Canaan House arrived. Harrowhark worked for nearly two hours before fainting abruptly into a puddle of congealing blood, at which point Gideon had removed her from the scene: upon waking she shadowed the Sixth instead, much to the ill-concealed annoyance of Camilla, who seemed to regard all incursions on Palamedes's personal space as probable assassination attempts. For his part, Palamedes talked quietly and briskly to Harrow as though to a colleague he had known all his life.

The Third princesses worked like musicians who couldn't help but return for the encore: a spell, retirement, another, another. They knelt side by side, holding hands, and for all that Ianthe had made fun of her sister's intellect Corona never broke a sweat. It was Ianthe who ran wet with blood and perspiration. At one point she beckoned Naberius forward and, in a feat that nearly brought up Gideon's dinner (again), *ate him*: she bit off a hunk of his hair, she chewed off a nail, she brought her incisors down on the heel of his hand. He submitted to all this without noise. Then she lowered her head and got back to work, sparks skittering off her hands like fire off a newly beaten sword, every so often spitting out a stray hair. Gideon had to stare pretty hard at skimpy nighties to get over that one.

The horrid Isaac worked, but Gideon didn't like to look at him. He was sobbing with his entire sad teen face, mouth, eyes, nose. Dulcinea reached out as though to join the fray until Protesilaus drew her back with a hand as inexorable as it was meaty. The revolving parade of necromancer after necromancer went on, until just Palamedes was left; then he slumped as though his strings had been cut, blindly reaching for the bottle of water Camilla held out, pulling long gasps of liquid.

"Coming down," said a voice from the top of the ladder.

Down the ladder came the jaundiced, faded cavalier of the Eighth House, dressed in his leathers with his sword at his hip; he helped his uncle, who was white and silver and alight with distaste, to the bottom. The Eighth adept primly rolled up his alabaster sleeves and skirted the corpses, considering, licking two fingers as though to turn a page.

"I will try to find them," he said, in his strangely deep and sorrowful voice.

Harrow said, "Don't waste your time, Octakiseron. They're gone."

The Eighth necromancer inclined his head. The hair that fell over his shoulders was the funny, ashy white you got when a fire burned away; a headband kept it scraped back and away from his sharp and spiritual face.

"You will pardon me," he said, "if I do not take advice on spirits from a bone magician."

Harrow's face slammed shut. "I pardon you," she said.

"Good. Now we need not speak again," said the Eighth necromancer. "Brother Colum."

"Ready, Brother Silas," said the scarred nephew immediately, and stepped in closer to the younger man, so that they were near enough to touch.

For a moment Gideon thought they were going to pray in front of the corpses. Or they might share an emotional moment. They were close enough to hug it out. But they did neither: the necromancer laid his hand on one of Colum's brawny shoulders, having to stretch up somewhat, and closed his eyes.

For a moment nothing seemed to happen. Then Gideon saw the colour begin draining from Colum the Eighth as though he were covered with cheap dye: leaching as shadow leached hue in the nighttime, more horrible and more obvious in the unforgiving light of the electric torches and underfloor lamps. As *he* faded, the pale Silas incandesced. He glowed with an irradiated shimmer, iridescent white, and the air began to taste of lightning.

Someone close by said softly, "So it's real," just as someone else said, "What is he *doing*?"

It was Harrow who said, without rancour but also without joy: "Silas Octakiseron is a soul siphoner."

By this point Colum the Eighth looked greyscale. He was still standing, but he was breathing more shallowly. By contrast the adept of the Eighth was putting on a light show, but not much else happened. The furrow deepened in the ghostly boy's brow; he wrung his hands together, and his lips soundlessly began to move.

Gideon felt an internal tug, like a blanket being pulled off in the cold. It was a little bit like the sensation back in Response (which was, what, a thousand years ago?)—something deep inside her being prodded in its tender spot. But it also wasn't, because it hurt like hell. It was like having a headache inside her teeth. The torchlights gave an asthmatic *gurk* and dimmed as though their batteries were being sucked dry, and when Gideon looked at her hands through bleary eyes they were deepening grey.

There was something pale blue sparking within the corpse of Abigail Pent, and suddenly and horribly the body shuddered. The world grew heavy and black around the edges, and Gideon felt cold all the way to her marrow. Someone screamed, and she recognised the voice as Dulcinea's.

Abigail's body shivered once. It shivered again. Silas opened his mouth and let out a guttural sound like a man who had eaten hot iron—one of the torches exploded—and out of the corners of her eyes Gideon saw him stretch out his arms. Gideon moved thickly through the grey-lipped crowd, watching Dulcinea collapse in what felt like slow motion, reaching out to the rumpled figure in the big dressing gown. Gideon slung Dulcinea's arm over her shoulder and pulled her limp body upright, teeth chattering so hard she was worried about biting the insides of her cheeks. Protesilaus stalked forward, and he did not even bother to draw his sword: he simply punched Silas in the face.

Dulcinea wailed out from Gideon's arms, weak and shrill: "*Pro!*" but it was too late. The Eighth necromancer went down like a sack of dropped potatoes and twitched on the floor. Now Protesilaus drew his rapier with an oily click of metal on scabbard: the lights crackled, then blazed back to life. The cold receded as though someone had closed a door against a howling wind. Strangely enough, Colum the Eighth did not even react. He just waited greyly next to Protesilaus like concrete, as Protesilaus stood over Colum's floored uncle, sword held at the ready. They both looked like crude sculptures of men.

"Children!" cried a voice high from the hatch: "Children, stop!"

It was Teacher. He had descended the first few staples of the ladder, but this was all he could apparently bear. For the first time since Gideon had met him, he seemed real and old and frail: the serene and frankly impenetrable good cheer had been replaced by wild terror. His eyes were bulging, and he was huddled against the top of the ladder like it was a life raft. "You mustn't!" he said. "He cannot empty anybody here, lest they become a nest for something else! Bring Abigail and Magnus the Fifth upstairs—do it quickly—"

Palamedes said, "Teacher, we should leave the bodies where they are if we want to know anything about what happened."

"I dare not," he called back. "And I daren't come down there to remove them. You must bring them up. Use stretchers—or magic, Reverend Daughter, use skeletons—use anything. But you must get them out of there immediately, and come up with them."

Maybe they were all still slothful from what had just gone on; maybe it was just the fact that it was the very small hours of the morning, and they were all very tired. The numb hesitation was palpable. It was a surprise when Camilla raised her voice to say: "Teacher. This is an active investigation. We're safe down here."

"You are absolutely wrong," said Teacher. "Poor Abigail and Magnus are dead already. I cannot guarantee the safety of any of you who remain down there another minute."

18

"Bring them up" was easier said than done. It took nearly an hour to remove the bodies and to store them safely—there was a freezer room, and Palamedes reluctantly allowed them to be interred there—and to get the Houses up and crowded into the dining hall. Harrowhark's skeletons could climb a ladder, even bearing wrapped corpses, but Colum the Eighth did not respond to pleas, threats, or physical stimulus. He was slightly less grey than previous, but he had to be hauled up bodily by Corona and Gideon. The moment he saw Colum, Teacher cried out in horror. Getting him up had been the hardest part. He now rested at the end of the table with a bowl of unidentifiable herbs burning under his chin, the smoke curling around his face and eyelashes. Currently everyone not stretched out on the floor of the dining room, lying in state in the freezer room, or huffing herbs was sitting around miserably clutching cups of tea. It was weirdly like their first day in Canaan House, in both suspicion and dullness, just with a bigger body count.

The only ones who seemed even vaguely compos mentis were the Second House. As it turned out, they had been the ones to call Teacher to the access hatch, and now they sat ramrod-straight and resplendent in their Second-styled Cohort uniforms, all scarlet and white. They both affected the same tightly braided hairstyle and abundance of gilt braid, and also the same serious-business expression. They were only distinct because one wore a rapier and the other quite a lot of pips at her collar. Teacher sat a little way away from them, his naked fear replaced by a deep and weary sadness. He sat close to the wheezy little heater taking off the morning chill, and the other two Canaan House priests shrouded themselves in their robes and refilled everybody's cups.

The necromancer of the Second House cleared her throat.

"Teacher," she said, in a cultured and resonant voice, "I would like to repeat that the best course of action is to inform the Cohort and bring military enforcers."

"I will repeat, Captain Deuteros," he said sadly, "that we cannot. It is the sacred rule."

"You must understand that this is nonnegotiable. The Fifth House must be informed. They of all houses would want an investigation carried out immediately."

"A *murder* investigation," added Jeannemary, who had not touched her tea.

"Murder," said Teacher, "oh, *murder* . . . we cannot assume that it was murder."

Whispers began to cross the room. The Second cavalier said, rather more heatedly: "Are you suggesting that it was an accident?"

"I would be very surprised if it were, Lieutenant Dyas," said Teacher. "Not Magnus and Lady Abigail. A seasoned necromancer and her cavalier, and sensible adults in their own right. I do not think it was an unhappy misadventure. I think they were killed."

"Then—"

"Murder is done by the living," said Teacher. "They were found entering the facility . . . I cannot begin to explain how grave a threat that is to anyone's safety. I will not bother trying to keep it secret now. I told each of you who asked my permission to enter that place that it would mean your death. I did not say that figuratively. I told all of you that you were walking into the most dangerous place in the system of Dominicus, and I meant it. There are monsters here."

Naberius said, "So why aren't they coming for *you*? You've lived here years."

Teacher said, "Years and years . . . and years. They are not coming for the guardians of Canaan House . . . yet. But I live in fear of the day they do. I believe Abigail and Magnus have run tragically afoul of them . . . I cannot countenance the idea that whatever grief they came to was orchestrated by someone in this room."

Silence rippled outward to the four corners of the dining hall. Captain Deuteros broke it by saying repressively: "This is still a case for the proper authorities."

Teacher said, "I cannot and will not call them. Lines of communication off-planet are forbidden here. For pity's sake, Captain Deuteros, where is the motive? Who would harm the Fifth House? A good man and a good woman."

The necromancer steepled her gloved fingers together and leaned forward. "I cannot speculate about motive or intent," she said. "I hardly *want* it to be murder. But if you don't comply with me, I have reasonable grounds to stop this trial. I will take command if you cannot."

Someone thumped their tea mug down on the table, hard. It was Coronabeth, who even with her violet eyes full of sleep and her hair in burnished tangles around her face would still have caused tourist traffic to wherever she was standing. "Don't be silly, Judith," she said impatiently. "You don't *have* that kind of authority."

"Where no other authority exists to ensure the safety of a House, the Cohort is authorized to take command—"

"In a *combat zone*—"

"The Fifth are dead. I take authority for the Fifth. I say we need military intervention, and we need it right now. As the highest-ranked Cohort officer present, that decision falls to me."

"A Cohort captain," said Naberius, "don't rank higher than a Third official."

"I'm very much afraid that it does, Tern."

"*Prince* Tern, if you please," said Ianthe.

"Judith!" said Corona, more coaxingly, before an interhousal war kicked off. "This is us. You've come to all our birthday parties. Teacher's right. Who would have killed Magnus and Abigail? Neither of them would have ever hurt a fly. Isn't it possible that the hatch was left up, and something happened, and it's *such* a long fall . . . Who was in there? Ninth, wasn't it you?"

With marked frostiness, Harrow said: "We locked the hatch before continuing in."

"You're sure?"

Gideon, who had been the one to turn the key, was oddly grateful that Harrowhark did not even bother looking in her direction: she simply said, "I am certain."

"How many people had these hatch keys other than the Ninth?" said Corona. "We had no idea the basement was even *there*."

"The Sixth," said Camilla and Palamedes as one.

Dulcinea said, small and tired: "Pro and I have one," which made Gideon's eyebrows raise right to her hairline.

"Colum has the copy given to the Eighth House," said a voice from the floor.

It was Silas. He had sat up and was now mopping his face with a very white piece of cambric. His eye was red and shiny and swollen, and he dabbed carefully around it: Corona gallantly offered him her arm but he refused, pulling himself to stand heavily against a chair. "He has the key," he said. "And I told Lady Pent of the existence of a facility beneath this floor, after the party."

It was Harrow who said, "*Why?*"

"Because she asked," he said, "and because I do not lie. And because I'm not interested in the Ninth House ascending to Lyctorhood alone . . . simply because they guessed a childish riddle."

Harrowhark closed herself up like a folding chair, and her voice was like cinders: "Your hatred of us is superstition, Octakiseron."

"Is it?" He folded the dirty handkerchief neatly and tucked it inside his chain mail. "Who was in the facility when Lady Pent and Sir Magnus died? Who was conveniently first on the scene to discover them—"

"You have one black eye already, courtesy of the Seventh House," said Harrow, "and you seem to yearn for symmetry."

"That was the Seventh, then?" The Eighth necromancer did not seem particularly displeased. "I see . . . it happened so swiftly I wasn't sure."

Gideon had thought Dulcinea asleep again, she was so limp and prone in Protesilaus's arms, but she opened her big blue eyes and struggled to raise her head. "Master Silas," she said thickly, "the Seventh House begs forgiveness of the merciful Eighth. Please grant it . . . this would be such an embarrassment to the House. Pro reacts quicker than I do. You wouldn't duel *me*, would you?"

"Never," said Silas gently. "That would be heartless. Colum will face the cavalier of the Seventh."

Gideon felt her fingers clench into fists as Dulcinea took a deep, wobbly breath and said quietly, "Oh, but *please*—"

"Stop this now," said Coronabeth. "This is madness."

The laughing golden butterfly was gone. She stood now, hands on her hips, chilly amber. Her voice rang out like a trumpet. "We must make a pact," she said. "We can't leave this room suspecting one another. We're meant to be working for a higher power. We knew it was dangerous—we agreed—and I can't believe that any of us here would have meant harm to Magnus and Abigail. We need to trust one another, or this'll devolve into madness."

The Captain of the Second rose too. Her intensely dark eyes settled on each of them in turn before ending on Teacher.

"Then what must we logically assume?" she said. "That, as Teacher has said, there is a malevolent or obstructive force within the First House? Vengeful ghosts, or monsters born of some necromantic act?"

The awful necromantic teen rose to stand now. His eyes were raw and red, and his fists were dirty with blood. The numb agony on his face was like an animal in pain: when he spoke one expected only tortured baying.

But he said, "If there is a monster—it's got to be hunted. If there's a haunting—it's got to be banished. Whatever was strong enough to kill Abigail and Magnus, it can't be left alone." Then, more wildly: "I *can't go home* until whatever killed Abigail and Magnus is dead."

Jeannemary said instantly, "I'm with Isaac. I say we hunt it."

"No," said Palamedes.

He had taken off his glasses to polish them, huffing once on one lens, then on the other. Everyone's eyes were on him by the time he put his spectacles back on his beaky nose. Camilla perched on the table behind him like a grey-coated crow, haunting his shoulder. "No," he repeated. "We'll proceed scientifically. Nothing can be assumed until we have a better sense of how they both died. With everyone's permission, I'll examine the bodies; anyone who wants to join me can do so. Once we ascertain the facts we may plan a course of action, but until then, no conclusions. No monsters, no murder, no accidents."

Coronabeth said warmly, "Hear, hear."

"Obliged, Princess. We now all know about the existence of the facility," he continued. "I imagine this will lead to it being explored freely. We should all keep an eye out for—*unusual* danger, and agree that information is the best gift we can give one another."

Harrowhark said, "I have no intention of collaborating."

"You won't be forced to, Reverend Daughter. But it's not orthogonal to the Lyctor experiment to warn your colleagues if you think there's something out of place," said Palamedes, leaning his chair back. "Exempli gratia, a horde of vengeful ghosts."

"There is one final matter of keys," said Teacher.

Everyone, now probably getting neck strain, looked back to him. They waited for a punchline, but there was none. Then they followed his line of sight: he was looking straight at Princess Ianthe in her clinging nightgown, pallid hair falling in two smooth braids down to bloodless shoulders, staring back with eyes like violets on dialysis.

"I am also in possession of one," she said, unruffled.

"*What?*"

She did not lose composure. "Don't act the jilted lover, Babs."

"You never said a damned word!"

"You didn't keep your eyes on your key ring."

"Ianthe Tridentarius," said her cavalier, "you are—you're—Corona, why didn't *you* tell me?"

Corona stopped him, one slender hand on his shoulder. She was looking at her twin, who calmly avoided her gaze. "Because I didn't know," she said lightly, chair scraping as she rose to stand. "I didn't know either, Babs. I'm going to bed now—I think—I'm somewhat overwrought."

Courteously, Palamedes stood too: "Cam and I want a look at the bodies," he said. "If Captain Deuteros and Lieutenant Dyas would like to accompany us—as I assume you're going to?"

"Yes," said Judith. "I'd like a closer look."

"Cam, you go on ahead," Palamedes said. "I want a quick word."

The scene broke up after that. The salt-and-pepper priest was talking to Isaac very quietly, and Isaac's shoulders were shaking as he tucked himself into his seat. The Third left with dislocated proximity and the clenched jaws of three people on their way to have an enormous tiff. Dulcinea was whispering quietly to her cavalier, and they surprised Gideon by following the mob to the freezer. Maybe not that surprising. Dulcinea Septimus could out-morbid the Ninth.

The word Palamedes wanted turned out to be with Harrow; he plucked her sleeve and beckoned her off to the corner of the room, and she went without a cavil. Gideon was left alone, watching Teacher join the whey-faced Silas as he knelt before his cavalier. His lips moved in silent prayer. Colum was now greyish all over, and his eyes had the thousand-yard stare of a man in a stupor. Silas did not appear to be worried. He had clasped one of those big hard-bitten hands between his own and murmured to him, and Gideon caught some of the words: *I bid you return.*

Teacher was saying: "He'll have a hard fight to come back, Master Octakiseron . . . harder than he may have anticipated. Is he used to the journey?"

"Brother Colum has fought harder and in colder climes," said Silas calmly. "He has come back to me through stranger ghosts. He has never once let his body become corrupted, and he never shall." Then he went back to the mantra: *I bid . . . I bid . . .*

For some reason that image stayed with her: the mayonnaise magician and his thickset nephew, older than him by far, staring out of empty eyes as Teacher watched with the air of a man with front-row seats to back-alley dental surgery. Gideon watched too, fascinated by an act she couldn't understand, when a hand closed around her wrist.

It was Jeannemary Chatur, her eyes red-rimmed, sticky and stained, her hair in a frizz. There was no sign of pluck in her now, except maybe a wild hardness around the eyes as she looked at Gideon.

"Ninth," she said hoarsely, "if you know anything, tell me now. If you—if you know anything, I've got to— They meant too much to us, so if you know—"

Gideon felt very sad. She put her hand on the bad teen's shoulder, and Jeannemary flinched away. She shook her head *no*, and when Jeannemary's big eyes—lashes clumped with last night's makeup, irises an inky brown—filled with tears she tried to furiously blink away, Gideon stopped being able to even slightly deal. She put her hand on top of the other cavalier's head, which was damp and curly like a sad puppy's, and said: "I'm sorry. I'm really sorry."

"I believe you," said Jeannemary thickly, not seeming to register the fact that the Ninth had spoken. "Magnus likes you . . . liked . . . He wouldn't have let anything happen to Abigail," she added all in a rush. "She hated heights. She never would've risked falling. And she was a spirit magician. If it was *ghosts*, why couldn't she—"

From before them, Colum gave such a racking and explosive cough that it made both Jeannemary and Gideon jump. His eyes rolled back in his head as he choked, staccato gasps, pulling in reeking smoke, while his adept said merely: "Fifteen minutes. You're getting tardy," and nothing more.

* * *

Gideon would have liked Jeannemary to finish her sentence, but Harrow was limping over with an expression like trouble. She had the distant, brow-puckered frown of a woman untying gruesomely knotted shoelaces. Gideon watched the cavalier of the Fourth walk away with hunched shoulders and a hand clasped around the grip of her rapier, and she fell into Harrow's wake, a half step behind her.

"You okay?"

"I'm sick of these people," said Harrowhark, ducking down a passageway and away from the central atrium. "I am sick of their slowness . . . sick to death. I can't wait here for one of them to grasp the implications of everything they have been told"—Gideon couldn't wait to grasp those implications either, but it didn't seem likely anytime soon—"because we will be *far* ahead of them by then. We have a door to open."

"Yes, tomorrow morning after at least eight hours' sleep," Gideon suggested without hope.

"An admirable attempt at comedy in these trying times," said Harrowhark. "Let's go."

19

THE KEY THEY HAD purchased so dearly from the construct gave very little away, other than its unusual colour. It was big; the shaft was as long as Gideon's middle finger, and the clover head satisfactorily heavy to hold, but it had no helpful tag saying, e.g., FIRST FLOOR. This did not seem to give Harrowhark pause. She whipped out her stained journal and brooded over her maps, hiding in a dark alcove and making her cavalier keep watch. Considering that there were exactly zero people around, this seemed stupid.

Then again, the idea that there might *not* be zero people around— that there was something horrible infesting Canaan House, something that had killed Abigail and Magnus for a perceived slight—well, Gideon did not stand there as easily as she might have yesterday. The First House was no longer a beautiful and empty shell, buffeted by the erosion of time. Now it seemed more like the blocked-up labyrinths beneath the Ninth House, kept sealed in case something became restless. When she was young she used to have nightmares about being on the wrong side of the door of the Locked Tomb. Especially after what Harrow had done.

"Look," said Harrowhark.

No murder, sorrow, or fear could ever touch Harrow Nonagesimus. Her tired eyes were alight. A lot of her paint had peeled away or been sweated off down in the facility, and the whole left side of her jaw was just grey-tinted skin. A hint of her humanity peeked through. She had such a peculiarly pointed little face, high browed and tippy everywhere, and a slanted and vicious mouth. She said irascibly, "At the *key*, moron, not at me."

The moron looked at the key, but did give her the middle finger. Harrow was holding the thing upside down for inspection. At the butt end, where the teeth terminated, a tiny carving had been made in the metal. It was a collection of dots joined together with a line and two half circles.

"It's the sign on my door," said Gideon.

"You mean—X-203?"

"Yeah, I mean that, if you're talking in moonspeak," said Gideon. "It's definitely the symbol on my door."

Harrow nearly trembled with eagerness. It took them a while to sneak down the curling route from the atrium to the corridor to the foyer leading to the pit; she was paranoid, and her paranoia had infected Gideon. They kept waiting before turning corners and then stopping to hear if they were being followed. By the time they reached the airless little vestibule, and had slipped the tapestry aside from the door frame and ducked through, Gideon's stomach wanted breakfast.

Nonetheless, her palms were slick with anticipation as they stood in front of the enormous black door. The animal skulls were as eerie and unwelcoming as they had been the first time; the writhing fat figure curled around each column as creepy and as cold. Harrowhark set her hands on the black stone crossbar of the door almost reverently, and pressed her ear to the rock as though she could hear what was going on inside. She stroked her thumbpad over the deep-set keyhole and pulled her hood over her head.

"Unlock it," she said.

"Don't you want the honours?"

"It's your key ring," said Harrow unexpectedly, and: "We will do this by the book. If Teacher's correct, there is something around here that is fairly hot on etiquette, and etiquette is cheap. The key ring is yours . . . I have to admit it. So you must admit us." She held out the key to Gideon. "Put it in the hole, Griddle."

"That's what she said," said Gideon, and she took the ring from

Harrow's gloved fingers. She did not put her own hood up, but she slipped her glasses back on to her nose: now that she'd adjusted she really only needed them for the midday light, but they'd become something of a comfort. She drummed her fingers on the bevelled frame of lightless stone, and then she slid the red Response key into the lock.

It fit. The lock clicked open as easily as if it had been kept oiled for the last ten thousand years. Without the slightest creak or groan of hinge, the door swung inward at a push. Gideon slipped her rapier from her belt and her knuckle-knives onto her left hand, and she walked into the darkness.

It *was* dark. She did not dare go farther into the quiet and shadowy stillness, thrown into deeper quiet by her necromancer slipping in behind and pushing the massive door shut. They stood in the room and smelled the age of it: the dust, the chemicals hanging in the air. You could almost smell the darkness.

Harrow's voice, almost a whisper: "A light, Nav."

"What?"

"You *did* bring a torch."

"This is a service I was unaware I was meant to provide," said Gideon.

There followed soft cursing. She felt Harrow turn back toward the door, measure its width with her hands, grope blindly along the doorframe in order to find a lantern: she found *something*, and from the wall there came a loud *click*. Electric lights blared to life overhead, throwing the dark and lonely room into knife-sharp relief.

Gideon didn't know what she'd expected. She stood, rooted to the ground, and so did Harrow; and for long moments they just got their fill of looking.

It was a study, left crystallised by someone who had one day stood up and never come back to the place where they must have worked for years. It was a long, square, spacious apartment, windowless, but beautifully lit. A long rail of electric lamps threw spotlights on important points in the room's geography. One end of the room was occupied by a laboratory: stained, scoured-laminate benches, and shelves and shelves of notes in leather-bound books or ring binders. The big metal sink and the scrubbing-up brush looked strange against the walls, which were inlaid with bones. A pot was still full of fat chalk sticks to draw diagrams, and the flasks of preserved blood were still full and very red. Tacked up over one bench were thick sheaves of flimsy, dark with graphs and models: one of the flimsies was a rough drawing of a familiar chimera, many armed, armour ribbed, squat skulled. There were jewelled tools. There were epoxy spatulas that had been melted in some experiment. There was a blown-up picture on the wall—a lithograph, or a polymer photograph—of a group of people clustered around a table. Their faces had all been scribbled out with a thick black marker pen.

Harrowhark had already drifted to the laboratory. She hadn't drawn breath yet. She was going to have to, Gideon thought distantly, or she'd be out on the floor. The room had been split into three main parts—there was the laboratory, and then a broad space where the furniture had been moved out of the way for an empty stone floor. The wall had a sword rack, and the sword rack still held two lonely rapiers, gleaming as though they'd been filed and whetted an hour before. A training floor. Leant up against the wall was a hideous collection of oblong metal shapes and stocks. It took Gideon a long time to realise that she was looking at something goddamn *ancient*: it was a blowback carbine *gun*. She'd only ever seen pictures.

The third part of the room was a raised platform with polished wooden stairs. The wood here was not so degraded as in the rest of Canaan House—this lightless, shut-off room must have preserved it, or otherwise somehow been stopped in time. The hairs on the back of Gideon's neck had risen when the lights came on, and they hadn't gone back down, as if her intrusion might well tempt time back to claim its grave goods. She found herself climbing the stairs and staring at a sweetly banal and domestic sight: a bookcase, a low table, a squashy armchair, and two beds. On the table was a teapot and two cups that lay abandoned forever.

The two beds were close to each other—if you lay in one, you could stretch out and touch whoever was sleeping in the other, provided you had a long arm—separated only by a nightstand. Much like the grotesque cradle tacked to the end of the enormous four-poster back in Harrow's bedroom, the two people here would have been in proximity to wake if the other one sneezed. On the nightstand was another lamp, and debris that people had never cleared up. A very old watch. An empty glass. A filament-fine silver bracelet with no clasp. A shallow, greasy glass dish full of grey stuff like ashes. Gideon could tell they weren't cremains, and when she touched them a strong scent clung to her fingers. The pillows had been smoothed out on the carved wooden cots, and the beds had been made. Someone had left a pair of extremely worn slippers beneath one, a crumpled piece of flimsy next to the nightstand. Gideon picked up the latter.

Harrow let out a cry of triumph. Gideon turned away from the beds and put the flimsy in her pocket, then stretched over the stair railing to see what her necromancer was delighted about. She was by the workbench staring at two great stone tablets that had been fused to the stone, shot through with pale green filaments glowing beneath Harrow's touch. The writing was small and cramped and the diagrams totally impenetrable in their obtuseness. Harrow was already pulling out her journal.

"It's the theorem from the trial room," she called out. "It's the completed methodology for transference—for the utilisation of a living soul. It's the *whole experiment.*"

"Is this an exciting necromancer thing?"

"*Yes,* Nav, it is an exciting necromancer thing. I need to copy this down, I can't lift the stone. Whoever did this was a genius—"

Gideon let Harrow have at it, and opened the first drawer of the nightstand. Sitting there, offensively ordinary, were three pencils, a finger bone, a coarse sharpening stone—bones and whetstones were beginning to feed her growing suspicion about who'd lived there—and an old, worn-down seal. She stared at the seal awhile: it was the crimson-and-white emblem of the Second House.

She sat down carefully on one of the beds, and the sprung mattress squeaked. She took the piece of crumpled-up flimsy out of her pocket and began trying to uncrumple it. It was part of a note that had—at some long-ago point—been ripped up, and this was just one scrunched corner.

"I'm done," said Harrow, from below. "Tell me anything of import."

Gideon stuffed the piece of flimsy back into her pocket and had a quick scan through the other drawers. A lost sock. A scalpel. Oilcloth. A tin with nothing in it but the vague waft of peppermints. This was all the stuff you'd find in anyone's bedside drawers—though then again, not quite anyone's; a particular pair of people. She descended the stairs and tipped her dark glasses high on her head. "A cav and their necro lived here," she said.

"I drew the same conclusion," said Harrowhark, shuffling her papers. She put one of her diagrams close to the one inscribed on the stone tablet to compare them for accuracy. "Here. Come and take a look at this."

Harrow's cramped handwriting was just as bad as the etching on the tablet. At the very end of a long list of exquisitely boring notes was a line on its own:

> *In the hope of attaining Lyctoral understanding. All glory and love to the Necrolord Prime.*

The Ninth necromancer said, "Now *there's* a helpful postscript if ever I saw one."

"Yeah, and the fact that there are two beds upstairs and a bunch of swords also help," said Gideon. "They were living in each other's pockets. They studied weird Lyctoral theorems. There's a seriously old Second House sign in one of the top drawers."

They both took the time to roam around the room. Harrow flicked through notebooks and narrowed her eyes over the contents. Gideon picked up another book and squinted at the faded message on the flyleaf, written in black ink forever ago and frozen in time:

208 / TAMSYN MUIR

ONE FLESH, ONE END.
G. & P.

They combed over the detritus of two strangers' lives; inside a forgotten tin Gideon found two expired toothbrushes. They were electronic ones, with revolving heads and push buttons.

"These aren't just seriously old, they're super unbelievably seriously old," she said.

"Yes," said Harrow. "Sextus could tell us how old, but I've no desire to ask him. Something has been done to preserve this room. It has not wasted away into a natural death. We're probably the first people to step inside since its previous occupants left."

It didn't seem to be a proper bedroom; more like a place to stay overnight while doing something else. More lab than living space. Gideon ended up staring at the photo-lithograph, elbows pressed into the countertop, studying faceless bodies gathered primly in their chairs. A rainbow of arms and robes; low-resolution hands clasping low-resolution knees. The hands without faces seemed solemnly posed, almost anxious.

"All I know," said Harrowhark eventually, "is that they created the theorem, and were responsible for the experiment downstairs. I wish I knew more. I yearn to know more . . . But I don't. I'm going to study this spell, Griddle, and learn it, and *then* I will be one step closer to knowing. We cannot suffer the same fate as Quinn and Pent."

Gideon was amazed at how badly it hurt, all of a sudden.

"He's really dead," she said aloud.

"Yes. I will be more upset if he suddenly changes condition," said Harrow. "He was a stranger, Nav. Why does it affect you so much?"

"He was nice to me," she found herself saying. She was very tired. She tried to wake herself up by stretching, dropping down to touch her toes and feeling the blood rush into her head. "Because he was a stranger, I think . . . He didn't have to bother with me, to make time for me or remember my name, but he did. Hell, you treat me more like a stranger than Magnus Quinn did and I've known you all my *life*. Anyway, I don't want to talk about it."

Harrow's hand, peeled and naked without a glove and stained with ink all the way up to her cuticles, appeared in front of her. Gideon found her shoulder drawn back so that she had to look Harrow square in the face. The necromancer regarded her with a strangely fierce eye: mouth a worn-down line of indecision, forehead puckered as though she was thinking her entire face into a wrinkle. There was still blood flaking out of her eyebrows, which was gross.

"I must no longer accept," she said slowly, "being a stranger to you."

"Whoa, whoa, whoa," said Gideon, sudden sweat prickling the back of her neck, "yes you can, you once told me to dig myself an ice grave. Stop before this gets weird."

"Quinn's death proves that this is not a game," said Harrow, moistening her ashy lips with her tongue. "The trials are meant to winnow out the wheat from the chaff, and it is going to be exceptionally dangerous. We are all the sons and daughters that the House of the Ninth possesses, Nav."

"I'm not anybody's son or daughter," said Gideon firmly, now in no small panic.

"I need you to trust me."

"I need you to be *trustworthy*."

In the thick dimness of the room she watched the black-garbed girl in front of her struggle around a thing that had settled over them like a net; a thing that had fused between them like a badly broken limb, shattered numerous times, healing gnarled and awful. Gideon recognised these strictures all of a sudden: the rope tying her to Harrow and back to the bars of the House of the Ninth. They stared at each other with shared panic.

Harrow said finally, "In what way can I earn your trust?"

"Let us sleep for eight bloody hours and never talk like this again," said Gideon, and her necromancer relaxed, very minutely. Her eyes were so lightlessly black that it was hard to see the pupil; her mouth was thin and waspish and unsure. She remembered when Harrow was nine, when she had walked in at just the wrong moment. She remembered that nine-year-old Harrow's mouth falling slightly slack. There was something curious about Harrow's face when it was not fixed into the bland church mask of the Reverend Daughter: something thin and desperate and quite young about it, something not totally removed from Jeannemary's desperation.

"Eight and a half," Harrow said, "if we start again immediately in the morning."

"Done."

"Done."

Several hours later, Gideon turned over in her bed, chilled by the realisation that Harrow had *not* promised to never talk like that again. Too much of this shit, and they'd end up friends.

As they walked back, the halls were as lonely as they ever had been—emptier, somehow, as though with the Fifth's untimely end Canaan House had managed to expunge what little self it had. There was only one exception. A quiet pattering of steps drew both of them pressed flat into an alcove, staring out at the thin grey pre-morning light: on very nearly silent feet, the Fourth teens passed before them, rapidly crossing an empty and dilapidated hall on some mission. Jeannemary led with her rapier drawn, and her necromancer stumbled behind, head bent, blue hood over his hair, looking like a penitent. Another second and they were gone. Gideon found herself thinking: poor little buggers.

* * *

In her nest of blankets, the light coming in yellow and unwelcome from the cracks around the curtains, Gideon was too tired to take off her clothes and almost too tired to sleep. She kept rustling when she turned over, trying to find a comfortable spot, and then she remembered the crinkled note in her pocket. In the dim light she smoothed it open and stared at it, blearily, pillow still sticky with bits of the cold cream she used to take off her paint.

> *ut we all know the sad + trying realit*
> *is that this will remain incomplete t*
> *the last. He can't fix my deficiencies her*
> *ease give Gideon my congratulations, howev*

20

AN INAUSPICIOUS NINE HOURS later Gideon and Harrow were making their way down the long, cold staples of the facility ladder, the air thick with last night's blood. Having been woken up just thirty-five minutes previous (Harrow always lied), Gideon climbed down into the dark with the distinct sensation that she was still asleep: somewhere in a dream, a dream she'd had a long time ago and suddenly remembered. She had mechanically downed the mug of cooling tea and the bowl of congealing porridge that Harrow had brought her that morning—Harrow arranging her breakfast was a concept so disagreeable there was no space left in her head for it—and now it sat leadenly in her stomach. The crumpled note lay hastily interred at the very bottom of Gideon's pocket.

Everything felt dark and strange and incorrect, right down to the still-drying paint her adept had applied to her face. Gideon had not even murmured dissent at this incursion, just got on with spooning porridge into her mouth. It was testament to Harrow being Harrow that none of Gideon's wooden submission had even *perturbed* her, seemingly.

"What the hell are we meant to be doing down there?" she'd asked plaintively, as Harrow led the way back to the dim lobby and the stairs to the hatch. Her voice sounded odd in her mouth. "More bone men?"

"I doubt it," Harrow had said briskly, without looking around. "That was one challenge. There'd be no point doing the same thing for the next one."

"The next one?"

"For God's sake pay *attention,* Griddle. The hatch key is the first step—the warm-up challenge, if you like."

"That wasn't a challenge," Gideon had objected, stepping over a taut strand of yellow tape. "You just asked Teacher for it."

"Yes, and as we discovered, some of our so-called rivals hadn't even cleared that pitiable hurdle. The hatch key grants *access* to the facility complex, which contains a number of testing rooms set up to replicate particular necromantic experiments. Anyone who can accurately carry out an experiment to its intended conclusion—as we did by dismantling that construct—gets the reward."

"A key."

"One assumes."

"And then the key—what, lets you into a room where you can rub your face all over *ye olde necro's olde notebooks*?"

Harrow still didn't turn round, but Gideon knew innately that her eyes were rolling. "The Second House study contained a full and perfect explanation of the theorem which had been used to articulate the construct. Having studied that theorem, any halfway competent necromancer would be able to reproduce its effects. I now possess the competencies required to ride another living soul. I'm perhaps even more interested in what I've learned from the theorem behind the construct."

"Making big shitty bone hunks." Gideon preferred not to think about *riding another living soul.*

At that, Harrow had stopped—almost at the head of the staircase—and finally looked around. "Nav," she'd said. "I could *already* make bone hunks. But now I can make them regenerate."

The outcome literally nobody wanted.

Now here they both were at the bottom of the ladder, staring at the angular outlines on the floor. Someone had immortalised Abigail and Magnus's descent with tape, carefully laid: it looked particularly weird given that none of the blood had been cleaned up. Accusatory splotches of it lay skeletonised on the floor.

"Sextus," said Harrow, having dropped lightly down next to her. "The Sixth is always too enamoured of the body."

Gideon said nothing. Harrow continued: "Investigating the scene of death is barely useful, compared to discovering the motives of the living. Compared to *why*, the question of who killed Pent and Quinn is almost an aside."

"'Who,'" said a voice, "or '*what*.' I love the idea of *what*."

Limned by the greenish light from the grille, Dulcinea Septimus limped into view. In the sulphide lamps she looked transparent, and she was leaning heavily on crutches; her heavy curls had been tied up on top of her head, revealing a neck that looked ready to snap in a strong wind. Behind her hulked Protesilaus, who in the darkness looked like a mannequin with abs.

Next to Gideon, Harrowhark stiffened, very slightly.

"Ghosts and monsters," the lady of the Seventh continued enthusiastically, "remnants and the dead . . . the disturbed dead. The idea that someone is still here and furious . . . or that something has been lurking here forever. Maybe it's that I find the idea comforting . . . that thousands of years after you're gone . . . is when you really live. That your echo is louder than your voice."

Harrow said, "A spirit comes at invitation. It cannot sustain itself."

"But what if one *could*?" cried Dulcinea. "That's so much more interesting than plain murder."

This time neither of the Ninth answered. Dulcinea moved forward, pressing her forearms into the clutches of her two metal poles, and blinked soft brown lashes at them. Gideon noticed that she looked tired, still: that the veins at her temples stood out, that her hands shook just a little bit on each crutch. She was wrapped up in a robe of some pale blue stuff, embroidered with flowers, but still shivered with the chill.

"Greetings, Ninth! You're brave to come down here after what Teacher said."

"One might," said Harrow, "say the same of you."

"Oh, by all rights I ought to have been the first one to die," said Dulcinea, giggling a bit fretfully, "but once one accepts that, one stops worrying quite so much. It would be so *predictable* to bump me off. Hullo, Gideon! It's nice to see you again. I mean, I saw you last night . . . but you know what I mean. Oh no, now I sound like a dope. Still vowing silence?"

Before *that* line of conversation could be pursued, the dark-hooded necromancer of the Ninth said in her most sepulchrous and forbidding tones: "We have business down here, Lady Septimus. Excuse us."

"But that's just what I came to talk to you about," said the other necromancer earnestly. "I think we four should team up."

Gideon could not hide an explosive snort of disbelief. There were *maybe* less likely targets for Harrow to team up with—Silas Octaki-seron, maybe, or Teacher, or the dead body of Magnus Quinn. In fact, Teacher would be a far better candidate. But Dulcinea's dreamy blue eyes were turned on Harrow, and she said:

"I've already completed one of the theorem labs. I think I'm on the path to cracking another. If we both worked together—why, then, there's the key in half the time with just a few hours' work."

"This is not intended to be collaborative."

Dulcinea said, smilingly: "Why does everybody think that?"

The women sized each other up. Dulcinea, leaning into her metal braces, looked like a brittle doll: Harrow, hooded and swathed in miles of black fabric, like a wraith. When she pulled away the hood the older necromancer did not flinch, even though it was a deliber-ately chilling sight; the dark-cropped head, the stark paint on the face, the bone studs punched halfway up each ear. Harrow said coolly: "What would be in it for the Ninth House?"

"All my knowledge of the theory and the demonstration—and first use of the key," said Dulcinea, eagerly.

"Generous. What would be in it for the Seventh?"

"The key once you're done. You see, I don't think I can physically *do* this one."

"Stupidity, then, not generosity. You just told me you can't complete it. Nothing would stop my House from completing it without you."

"It took me a long time to work out the theoretical parameters," said Dulcinea, "so I wish you the best of luck. Because even though I'm dying—there's nothing wrong with my *brain*."

Harrow pulled the hood back over her head, returning her to a wraith, a piece of smoke. She swept past the frail necromancer of the Seventh, who followed her with the wistful, somewhat hungry expression that Dulcinea reserved for the shadowy nuns of the Ninth—for the black robes whispering on the metal floor, the green light reflecting off dark fabric.

Harrowhark turned around and said, curtly: "Well? Are we doing this or *not*, Lady Septimus?"

"Oh, thank you—*thank* you," Dulcinea said.

Gideon was stupefied. Too many shocks in twenty-four hours shut down her thought processes. As Dulcinea stumped along the corridor, crutches clanging unharmoniously on the grille, and as Protesilaus hovered behind her a half step away as though desperate to just scoop her up and carry her, Gideon strode to catch up with her necromancer.

Only to find her swearing under her breath. Harrow whispered a lot of fuck-words before muttering: "Thank God *we* got to her first."

"I never thought you'd actually help out," said Gideon, grudgingly admiring.

"Are you *dim*," hissed Harrow. "If we didn't agree, that bleeding heart Sextus would, and he'd have the key."

"Oh, whoops, my bad," said Gideon. "For a moment I thought you weren't a huge bitch."

They followed the mismatched pair from the Seventh House to the dusty facility hub, filled with its dusty panelling and its whiteboard gleaming sadly beneath big white lights. Dulcinea turned abruptly down the passageway marked LABORATORY SEVEN–TEN, a tunnel identical to the one they had taken to LABORATORY ONE–THREE. This time the creaks and ancient moans of the building seemed very loud, their footsteps a huge addition to the cacophony.

In the middle of a passage past the first laboratory rooms the grille on the floor had been staved in, cracked right down the middle to come to rest on hissing pipes. Protesilaus picked up his adept and stepped her over this pit as lightly as thistledown. Gideon jumped the gap, and turned back to see her necromancer hesitating on the edge, stranded. Why she did it Gideon didn't know—Harrow could have built herself a bridge of bones any second—but she grasped a railing, leaned over, and proffered her hand. Why Harrow *took* it was an even bigger mystery. After being helped across, Harrow spent a few moments officiously dusting herself off and muttering inarticulately. Then she strode off to catch up with—of all people—Protesilaus, apparently with the aim of engaging him in conversation. Dulcinea, who had taken a moment to fit herself back into her crutches, slipped one arm into Gideon's instead. She nodded at the broad span of her cavalier's back.

"Colum the Eighth is fixing to fight him tomorrow," she said to Gideon, beneath her breath. "I wish Master Silas had just fought me. Not much can hurt me anymore . . . it would be an interesting sensation, is what I mean."

In response Gideon's grip tightened around the languid arm tucked in her own. Dulcinea sighed, which sounded like air being pushed through whistly sponges. (Up this close her hair was very soft, Gideon noted dimly.) "I know. I was an idiot to let it happen. But the Eighth are so touchy in their own way . . . and Pro *was* unpardonably bad. They couldn't let the insult pass. I just let my worst instincts get the better of me . . . and yelped."

The curly-haired necromancer paused to cough, as though simply remembering how she'd yelped was enough to send her into spasms. Gideon instinctively put an arm around her shoulders, steadying her so that the crutches did not give way, and found herself looking down where the edge of Dulcinea's shirt met her bulging collarbones. A fine chain around her neck supported a rather less delicate bundle hanging tucked into her camisole: Gideon only saw them for a second, but she knew immediately what they were. The key ring was snapped around the chain, and on the key ring were two keys: the saw-toothed hatch key, and a thick grey key with un-pretentious teeth, the kind you'd lock a cabinet with.

She made herself look anywhere else. By now they had reached the very end of the corridor, which terminated in a single door marked LABORATORY EIGHT. Wriggling free of Gideon's arm, Dulcinea opened it onto a little foyer alike in indignity to LABORATORY TWO. There were hooks on the walls here, and a bunch of old, crumpled boxes made of thin metal, the type you might carry files in; these were dented and empty. Someone had taken the time and effort to affix a beautiful swirl of human teeth above the door in a widening spiral of size: in the centre, the neat little shovels of incisors, tessellated with arched canines and ringed all around with the long, racine tusks of molars. In neat print the label on the door read: #14–8 DIVERSION. PROCEDURAL CHAMBER.

Beneath the neat print, a more elaborate hand had written in fainter ink: AVULSION!

"Here we are," said Dulcinea. "Before we go through, please give me a little bit of your blood. I have warded the place up *and* down and I'm dreadfully afraid you won't be able to go through the door without giving me a shock."

This little nod to paranoia made Harrow's shoulders relax minutely. Gideon looked to her, and Harrowhark nodded. In the dim and dusty foyer both offered up their hands to be pricked: the necromancer of the Seventh tilted her head, beautiful brown ringlets spilling over her shoulders, and took blood from their thumbs and their ring fingers. Then she pressed the blood into her palm and spat delicately with what Gideon noticed was pink-tinged spittle; she pressed her thin hand to the door.

"It's not a hold ward," Dulcinea explained, "but it's not just physical. The ward will alert me if the immaterial try to pass . . . if they've instantiated, I mean, if they've crossed over. I don't want to stop them," she added, when Harrowhark started fidgeting with a bone fragment from her pocket. "I want to *see* whatever would try to sneak in on us . . . I want to know what it looks like. Let's go."

Rather than the neatly sectional space that had constituted

Laboratory Two, with its Imaging and Response chambers and orderly empty shelves, Laboratory Eight opened up on an enormous grate. A lattice of thick black steel barred the first part of the room from the second, which—espied through the holes—proved to be a long space with a claustrophobic ceiling. It was like stepping into a pipe. The door led to a metal platform on struts and a short flight of stairs leading down into the space, barred by the huge grate. The Seventh necromancer went to the wall and flicked a switch, and with a low vibrating moan, the grate slowly began to tuck itself up into the ceiling.

With the removal of the grate, the room seemed enormously grey and empty. Only two things broke up the vast monotony of grey metal and white light: far off at the other end of the chamber was a metal plinth, boxed on top with what looked like clear glass or plex; and at the bottom of the stairs, about a metre away from its base, was a yellow-and-black-striped line that had been painted horizontally from wall to wall.

It was easily a hundred metres from the stripe to the plinth: a long way to walk. It looked simple enough, which was how Gideon knew it was probably a huge pain in the ass.

And yet her adept was already gliding down the stairs, standing before the yellow-and-black-emblazoned line as though at the edge of a fire. Dulcinea came after, leaning more heavily on her crutches as she swung herself down the stairs. Protesilaus came last.

"If you put your hand through," she said, "you'll see—there." Harrow had bitten off a cry of pain. She had stuck her gloved fingers tentatively over the line, and now she was yanking off her glove to see the damage. Gideon had been the victim of this once before, through Palamedes Sextus, but it was still a disquieting sight. Harrow's fingertips had shrivelled: the nails had split horribly, and the moisture looked as though it had been siphoned forcibly out, wrinkling the skin like paper. Her adept shook her hand in the air like you would with a burn; the wrinkles smoothed out, slowly, and the nails knit themselves back together.

"Hardly insurmountable," said Harrow, having regained her composure.

"Very hopeful! What would you use?"

"A corporeal ward; skin-bound, tight focus."

"Try it."

Harrowhark flexed her fingers slowly. Gideon watched as she narrowed her eyes into obsidian slits, fringed thickly with blunt black lashes, and then extended her hand beyond the line again. There was a brief shower of blue sparks; Harrow snatched her hand back, amazed and furious. The fingers had withered into puckered twigs; her little nail had fallen off entirely. The edges of her sleeve had holed and frayed as though assaulted by moths. Gideon lunged out of a sheer desire to do *something,* but Harrow held her back with her healthy hand, staring fixedly at the hurt one as it slowly mended. Dulcinea watched with eager eyes: Protesilaus hulked next to the stairs.

Harrow shook a bracelet over her hurt hand, and bands of spongy osseous matter wrapped around her knuckles before forming thick plaques of bone. Gauntleted, she reached her hand out again—

"It won't work," said Dulcinea, dimpling.

—The gauntlet exploded into fragments of bone. Those that passed the yellow line fragmented further, and those bits degraded into dust and that into powder. The glove fell away in hunks, dwindling into fine sand before it even hit the ground, and Harrow yanked her hand back to stare at its sad puckered appearance a third time. She sat heavily on the stairs, and a bead of blood sweat trickled down one temple as, away from the barrier, her hand relaxed back into wholeness. Gideon longed to say: *What the fuck?*

"It's two spells, overlaying each other," said Dulcinea.

"You can't have two spells with coterminous bounds. It's impossible."

"But true. They're really coterminous—not just interwoven or spliced. It's truly delicious work. The people who set it in place were geniuses."

"Then one half is senescence—"

"And the other half is an entropy field," said Dulcinea simply.

Gideon followed Harrow's gaze over the long, dully gleaming field of corrugated metal, and the plinth shining at the end like a beacon. She saw Harrow suck in and bite the inside of one cheek, always a sign of furious thinking, flexing her fingers all the while as though still worried about their integrity. She took an old, ivory-coloured knuckle from her pocket, and she passed it to Gideon. "Throw," she commanded.

Gideon obligingly threw. It was a good toss—the knuckle hit the field high and travelled for about half a metre before fragmenting into a rain of grey particles. Harrow's gaze fixed on the crumbling shards: more tiny spikes and spurs of bone burst out of them and shrivelled, stillborn—another burst as Harrow curled her fist into a ball—then nothing. There was no more bone left.

Dulcinea breathed in admiration: "It's *awful* quick."

"Then," said the adept of the House of the Ninth, "it is—and I don't say this lightly—impossible. This is the most efficient death trap I've ever seen. The senescence decays anything before it can cross, and the entropy field—God knows how it's holding—disperses any magical attempt to control the rate of decay. But why hasn't the whole room collapsed? The walls should be so much dust."

"The field and the flooring are a few micrometres apart—maybe the Ninth could make a very *very* weeny construct to go through that gap," said the Seventh helpfully.

Harrow said, in bottom-of-the-ocean tones: "The Ninth House has not practised its art on—weeny—constructs."

"Before you ask, it's not a lateral puzzle either," said Dulcinea. "You can't go through the floor because it's solid steel, and you can't go through the ceiling because that's also solid steel, and there's no other access. And Palamedes Sextus estimated you could walk for probably three seconds before you died."

Harrow got very focused very suddenly. "Sextus has seen this?"

"I asked him first," said Dulcinea, "and when I told him the method, he said he'd never do it. I thought that was fascinating. I'd love to get to know him better."

That got every particle of Harrowhark Nonagesimus's attention. Dulcinea absently tossed her crutches to Protesilaus one by one, and he caught them out of the air as though he didn't even have to think about it, which Gideon had to admit was cool. She sat down heavily on the stairs quite close to Harrow, and she said: "There *is* one way of doing it . . . and he wouldn't. I'm sorry that I didn't admit it . . . but you were my second choice. If black vestals won't cross this line, I don't think anyone will. And I can't, because I physically can't walk the whole way unassisted. If I faint or go funny halfway there it will mean my timely death."

"And what is it," said Harrow, in a voice that meant trouble, "that even Palamedes Sextus won't do?"

"He won't siphon," said Dulcinea.

The shutters on Harrow's face were pulled shut. "And nor will I," she said.

"I don't mean soul siphoning . . . not quite. When Master Octakiseron siphons his cavalier, he sends the soul elsewhere and then exploits the space it leaves behind. The power that rushes in to fill that space will keep refilling, for as long as either of them can survive. You wouldn't have to *send* anyone anywhere. But the entropy field will drain your own reserves of thanergy as soon as you cross the line, so you need to draw on a power source on this side of the line, where the field can't touch it. Do you understand?"

"Don't patronize me, Lady Septimus. Of course I understand. Understanding a problem is nowhere near the same as implementing a solution. You should have asked Octakiseron and his human vein."

"I probably would have," said Dulcinea candidly, "if Pro hadn't blacked his eye for him."

"So technically," said Harrow, acid as a battery, "we're your third choice."

"Well, Abigail Pent was a very talented spirit magician," said Dulcinea, and relented when she saw Harrow's expression. "I'm sorry! I'm teasing! No, I don't think I would have asked the Eighth House, Reverend Daughter. There is something cold and white and inflexible about the Eighth. They could have done this with ease . . . maybe that's why. And now Abigail Pent is dead. What am I to do? If you were to ask Sextus for me, do you think he'd do it? You seem to know him better than *me*."

Harrow pushed herself up from the stairs. She had not seemed to notice that Dulcinea was leaning with her flowerlike face in her hands and drinking in her every movement, nor her expression of carefully studied innocence. Gideon was undergoing complicated feelings about not being the centre of the Seventh's attention.

With a flourish of inky skirts, Harrowhark turned back to the stairs, staring through Dulcinea rather than at her. "Let's say I agree with your theory," she said. "To maintain enough thanergy for my wards inside the field, I'd need to fix a siphon point outside it. The most reasonable source of thanergy would be—you."

"You can't move thanergy from place to place like that," said the Seventh, with very careful gentleness. "It has to be life to death. . . . or death to a *sort* of life, like the Second do. You'd have to take my thalergy." She raised a wasted hand, and then let it flutter back to her face like a drifting paper plane. "Me? I could get you maybe— ten metres."

"We adjourn," said Harrowhark.

Harrow grasped Gideon hard around the arm and practically dragged her back up the stairs, out past the foyer and into the hallway. The noise of the door slamming behind them echoed around the corridor. Gideon found herself staring straight down the barrel of a loaded Harrowhark Nonagesimus, hood shaken back to reveal blazing black eyes in a painted white face.

"'Avulsion'," she said bitterly. "Of course. Nav, I'm going to bear down hard on your trust again."

"Why are you so into this?" asked Gideon. "I know you're not doing it for Dulcinea."

"Let me make my business plain. I have no interest in Septimus's woes," Harrow said. "The Seventh House is not our friend. You're making yourself an utter fool over *Dulcinea*. And I dislike her cavalier even more—" ("Massive slam on Protesilaus out of nowhere," said Gideon.) "—but I would finish the challenge that sickened

Sextus. Not for the high ground. But because he must learn to stare these things in the face. Do you know what I'd have to do?"

"Yeah," said Gideon. "You're going to suck out my life energy in order to get to the box on the other side."

"A ham-fisted summary, but yes. How did you come to that conclusion?"

"Because it's something Palamedes wouldn't do," she said, "and he's a perfect moron over Camilla the Sixth. Okay."

"What do you mean, 'okay'—"

"I mean *okay*, I'll do it," said Gideon, although most of her brain was trying to give the part of her brain saying that a nipple-gripple. She chewed at a damp fleck of lip paint and took off her dark glasses, then popped them into her pocket. Now she could look Harrow dead in the eye. "I'd rather be your battery than feel you rummaging around in my head. You want my juice? I'll give you juice."

"Under no circumstances will I ever desire *your juice*," said her necromancer, mouth getting more desperate. "Nav, you don't know precisely what this is asking. I will be draining you dry in order to get to the other side. If at any point you throw me off—if you fail to submit—I die. I have never done this before. The process will be imperfect. You will be in . . . pain."

"How do you know?"

Harrowhark said, "The Second House is famed for something similar, in reverse. The Second necromancer's gift is to drain her dying foes to strengthen and augment her cavalier—"

"Rad—"

"It's said they all die screaming," said Harrow.

"Nice to know that the other Houses are also creeps," said Gideon. "*Nav.*"

She said, "I'll still do it."

Harrowhark chewed on the insides of her cheeks so hard that they looked close to staving in. She steepled her fingers together, squeezed her eyelids shut. When she spoke again, she made her voice quite calm and normal: "Why?"

"Probably because you asked."

The heavy eyelids shuttered open, revealing baleful black irises. "That's all it takes, Griddle? That's all you demand? This is the complex mystery that lies in the pit of your psyche?"

Gideon slid her glasses back onto her face, obscuring feelings with tint. She found herself saying, "That's all I *ever* demanded," and to maintain face suffixed it with, "you asswipe."

When they returned, Dulcinea was still sitting on the stairs and talking very quietly to her big cavalier, who had dropped to his haunches and was listening to her as silently as a microphone might listen to its speaker. When she saw that the Ninth House pair were back in the room, she staggered to rise—Protesilaus rose with her, silently offering her an arm of support—as Harrowhark said, "We'll make our attempt."

"You could practise, if you wanted," said Dulcinea. "This won't be easy for you."

"I wonder why you make that assumption?" said Harrowhark.

Dulcinea dimpled. "I oughtn't to, ought I?" she said. "Well, I can at least look after Gideon the Ninth while you're over there."

Gideon still saw no reason why she would need looking after. She stood in front of the stairs feeling like a useless appendage, hand gripping the hilt of her sword as though through sheer effort she could still use it. It seemed dumb to be a cavalier primary with no more use than a big battery. Her necromancer stood in front of her with much the same nonplussedness, hands working over each other as though wondering what to do with them. Then she swept one gloved hand over the side of Gideon's neck, fingers resting on her pulse, and breathed an impatient breath.

It felt like nothing, at first. Besides Harrow touching her neck, which was a one-way trip to No Town. But it was just Harrow, touching her neck. She felt the blood pump through the artery. She felt herself swallow, and that swallow go down past the flat of Harrow's hand. Maybe there was a little twinge—a shudder around the skull, a tactual twitch—but it was not the pressure and the jolt she remembered from Response and Imaging. Her adept took a step back, thoughtful, fingers curling in and out of her palms.

Then she turned and plunged through the barrier, and *there* was the jolt. It started in Gideon's jaw: starbursts of pain rattling all the way from mandible to molars, electricity blasting over her scalp. She was Harrow, walking into no-man's-land; she was Gideon, skull juddering behind the line. She sat down on the stairs very abruptly and did not pay attention to Dulcinea, reaching out for her before drawing back. It was like Harrow had tied a rope to all her pain receptors and was rappelling down a very long drop. She dimly watched her necromancer take step after painstakingly slow step across the empty metal expanse. There was a strange fogging around her. It took Gideon a moment to realise that the spell was eating through Harrow's black robes of office, grinding them into dust around her body.

Another lightning flash went through her head. Her immediate instinct was to reject it, to push against awareness of Harrow—the sense of crushing pressure—the blood-transfusion feel of *loss*. Bright lights danced in her vision. She fell to the side and became disjointedly aware of Dulcinea, her head on Dulcinea's thin thigh, the glasses slipping off her nose and rattling down onto the next step. She watched Harrow walk as though against a wind, blurred with particles of black—then she found herself snorting out big hideous fountains of blood. Her vision blurred again greyly, and her breath stuttered in her throat.

"No," said Dulcinea. "Oh, no no no. Stay awake."

Gideon couldn't say anything but *blearrghhh*, mainly because blood was coming enthusiastically out of every hole in her face. Then all of a sudden it *wasn't*—drying up, parching, leaving her with a waterless and arid tongue. The pain moved down to her heart and massaged it, electrifying her left arm and her left fingers, her left leg and her left toes. It was beyond pain. It was as though her insides were being sucked out through a gigantic straw. In her dimming vision she saw Harrowhark, walking away; no longer haloed by fragments but limned with a great yellow light that flickered and ate at her heels and her shoulders. Tears filled Gideon's eyes unbidden, and then they gummed away. It all blurred grey and gold, then just grey.

"Oh, Gideon," someone was saying, "you poor baby."

The pain went down her right leg, and to her right toes, and then up her spine in zigzags. She dry-heaved. There was still that pressure—the pressure of Harrow—and the sense that if she pushed at it, if she just went and fucking knocked at it, it would go away. She was sorely tempted. Gideon was in the type of pain where consciousness disappeared and only the animal remained: bucking, yelping an idiot yelp, butting and bleating. Throw Harrowhark off, or slip into sleep, anything for release. If there had been any sense that she had to try to *hold* the connection, she would have lost it already; Gideon was just overwhelmed with how badly she wanted to shove against it, not huddle in a corner and scream. Was she screaming? Oh, shit, she was screaming.

"It's all right," someone was saying, over the noise. "You're all right. Gideon, Gideon . . . you're so *young*. Don't give yourself away. Do you know, it's not worth it . . . none of this is worth it, at all. It's cruel. It's so cruel. You are so young—and vital—and alive. Gideon, you're all right . . . remember this, and don't let anyone do it to you ever again. I'm sorry. We take so much. I'm so sorry."

She would remember each word later, loud and clear.

Her forehead and face were being mopped. Touch did not register. She had lost control of her limbs, and each was flailing independently of the others, a roiling mass of nerves and panic. Her hair was being stroked—softly—and she did not want to be touched, but she was terribly afraid that if it stopped she would roll away into the field and dissolve just to get away. She held on to the sound of talking, so that she didn't go mad.

"She's all the way across," said the voice. "She's made it to the box . . . can you see the trick of it, Reverend Daughter? There *is* a trick, isn't there? Gideon, I am going to put my hand over your mouth. She needs to think." A hand went over her mouth, and Gideon bit it. "Ow, you feral. There she goes . . . perhaps they thought that if it was easy to obtain, someone could finish the demonstration some other way. It's got to be foolproof, Gideon . . . I know that. I wish it were me. I wish I were up there. She's got the box open . . .

I wonder . . . yes, she's worked it out! I was afraid she'd break the key . . ."

Clutched in the thin lap, Gideon could make no response that was not retching, gurgling or clamouring, silenced only by one rather skinny hand. "Good girl," the voice was saying. "Oh, good girl. She's got it, Gideon! And I've got you . . . Gideon of the golden eyes. I'm so sorry. This is all my fault . . . I'm so sorry. Stay with me," the voice said more urgently, "stay with me."

Gideon was suddenly aware that she was very cold. Something had changed. It was getting harder to suck in each breath. "She's stumbled," said the voice, detached, and Gideon *heaved*: not against the connection, but into it. The consequent pain was so intense that she was afraid she might wet herself, but the spike of cold faded. "She's up . . . Gideon, Gideon, she's up. Just a little bit more. Darling, you're fine. Poor baby . . ."

Now Gideon was scared. Her body had the soft, drunken feeling you got just before fainting away, and it was very hard to stay conscious. *Three seconds before you die,* Palamedes had calculated. Anything less than Harrow crossing the threshold would make the struggle meaningless. The hand touched her face, her mouth, her eyebrows, smoothed her temples. As if knowing her thoughts by her face, the voice whispered: "Don't. It's very easy to die, Gideon the Ninth . . . you just let it happen. It's so much worse when it doesn't. But come on, chicken. Not right now, and not yet."

It felt like all the pressure in her ears was popping loose. The voice said, musical and distant: "Gideon, you magnificent creature, keep going . . . feed it to her . . . she's nearly made it. Gideon? Gideon, eyes open. Stay put. Stay with me."

It took an infinity amount of seconds for her to stay put: for her to crack her eyes open. When her eyes opened Gideon was distantly worried to discover that she was blind. Colours swam in front of her vision in a melange of muted hues. Something black moved—it took her a moment to realise that it was moving very quickly: it was *sprinting*. Mildly startled, Gideon realised that she was starting to die. The colours wobbled before her face. The world revolved, then revolved the other way, aimlessly spinning. The air stopped coming. It would have been peaceful, only it sucked.

A new voice said: "Gideon? . . . *Gideon!*"

When she opened her eyes again there was a dazzling moment of clarity and sharpness. Harrow Nonagesimus was kneeling by her side, naked as the day she was spawned. Her hair was shorn a full inch shorter, the tips of her eyelashes were gone, and—most horrifyingly—she was absolutely nude of face paint. It was as though someone had taken a hot washcloth to her. Without paint she was a point-chinned, narrow-jawed, ferrety person, with high hard cheekbones and a tall forehead. There was a little divot in her top lip at the philtrum, which gave a bowlike aspect to her otherwise hard and fearless mouth. The world rocked, but it was mainly because Harrow was shaking her shoulders.

"Ha-ha," said Gideon, "first time you didn't call me *Griddle*," and died.

* * *

Well, passed out. But it *felt* a hell of a lot like dying. Waking up had an air of resurrection, of having spent a winter as a dried-out shell and coming back to the world as a new green shoot. A new green shoot with problems. Her whole body felt like one traumatised nerve. She was lying within the cradle of thin and wasted arms; she looked up into the soft and weary face of Dulcinea, whose eyes were still the dusty blue of blueberries. When she saw that Gideon was awake, she sparkled to life.

"You big baby," she said, and shamelessly kissed her on the forehead.

Harrowhark was sitting on the cold ground opposite. She was wrapped in chilly dignity and Gideon's overcloak. Even the bone studs in her ears had disappeared, leaving little pockmarks where they ought to have been. "Lady Septimus," she said, "unhand my cavalier. Nav, are you able to stand?"

"Oh, Reverend Daughter, no . . . give her a minute," Dulcinea begged. "Pro, help her . . . don't let her stand alone."

"I do not want you or your cavalier to touch her," said Harrow. Gideon wanted to say, *Nonagesimus, quit the sacred-bat-black-vestal act,* but found she couldn't say *anything.* Her mouth felt like a dried-out sponge. Her adept rummaged around in her overcloak pockets and emerged with a few bone chips, which gave rise to the horrible idea that she had *stashed* them there. "Again . . . unhand her."

Dulcinea ignored Harrow totally. "You were incredible," she told Gideon, "astonishing."

"Lady Septimus," the other necromancer repeated, "I will not ask thrice."

Gideon could not manage anything better than a very feeble thumbs-up in Dulcinea's direction. Dulcinea unwound herself, which was a shame; she was warm, and the room was colder than ten witches' tits. She reached out one last time to skim a hand over Gideon's forehead. She whispered archly: "Nice *hair.*"

Harrow said, "Septimus."

Dulcinea scooted herself back to the stairs. Gideon watched with dim interest as Harrow cracked her knuckles and sucked in a breath: nothing loath, her necromancer leant down and heaved one of Gideon's arms around her skinny shoulders. Before Gideon could even think *Oh shit,* she had been pulled to stand as Harrowhark's knees buckled beneath her. There was a bad moment when she wanted to puke, a good moment when she didn't, and a bad moment again when she realised that she only hadn't because she couldn't.

The lady of the Seventh was saying, "Reverend Daughter . . . I'm terribly grateful for what you just did. I'm sorry for the cost."

"Don't. It was a business decision. You'll get your key when I'm done."

"But Gideon—"

"Is not your business."

Dulcinea's hands came to rest in her lap, and she tilted her head. "I see," she said, smiling and somewhat crestfallen.

A barefoot Harrow grunted under her breath as she continued to try to haul Gideon up the short flight of stairs, panting for breath by the top step. Gideon could only watch, willing herself to come to full consciousness, astonished by the unreceptivity of her body. It was all she could do to not deliquesce out of Harrow's grip. At the top of the stairs they stopped, and the Reverend Daughter looked back searchingly.

She said abruptly, "Why did you want to be a Lyctor?"

Gideon mumbled, "Harrow, you can't just ask someone why they want to be a Lyctor," but was roundly ignored.

The older woman was leaning against Protesilaus's arm. She looked extraordinarily sad, even regretful; when she caught Gideon's eye, a tiny smile tugged on the corners of her mouth, then drooped again. Eventually, she said: "I didn't want to die."

Walking back through the chilly foyer out to the corridor was bad: Gideon had to break away from Harrow and rest her cheek on the cold metal panelling next to the door. Her necromancer waited with uncharacteristic patience for her to regain some semblance of consciousness, and they stumbled onward—Gideon drunken, Harrow flinching her bare feet away from the grille.

"You didn't have to be a dick," she found herself saying, thickly. "I like her."

"*I* don't like her," said Harrowhark. "I don't like her cavalier."

"I still don't get why you're all up in arms against what is a very basic man hulk. Did you get the key?"

The key appeared in Harrow's other hand, shining silvery white, austerely plain with a single loop for a head and three simple teeth on the shaft. "Nice," said Gideon. She rummaged in an inner pocket and removed the ring; the key slid next to the hatch key and red Response key with an untidy musical tinkle. Then she said: "Sorry your clothes melted."

"Nav," said Harrow, with the slow deliberation of someone close to screaming, "stay quiet. You're not—you're not . . . entirely well. I underestimated how long it would take me. The field was *vicious*, much more so than Septimus communicated. It had started to strip the moisture from my eyeballs before I refined on the fly."

"By which point it had eaten your underwear," said Gideon.

"*Nav.*"

"I just had a near-death experience," she said, "let me have my little moment."

How they got all the way up the ladder, Gideon later had no idea; it was with strange, dreamlike precision that Harrowhark bullied and bolstered her down the long, winding halls of Canaan House and back to the quarters that the Ninth House occupied, without a flicker of magic, Harrow wearing nothing but a big black overcloak. Every so often she wondered if she *had,* in fact, kicked the bucket and this was her afterlife: wandering empty halls with a half-naked, chastened Harrowhark Nonagesimus who had no recourse but to be gentle with her, handling her as though at any moment she would explode into wet confetti giblets.

She even let Harrow steer her toward the blankets that constituted her bed. Gideon was too exhausted to do anything but lie down and sneeze three times in quick succession, each sneeze a migraine gong through sinus and skull bone.

"Quit looking at me like that," she eventually commanded Harrow, wiping bloody muck onto her hanky. "I'm alive."

"You nearly weren't," said Harrow soberly, "and you're not even aggrieved about it. Don't price your life so cheaply, Griddle. I have absolutely no interest in you losing your sense of self-preservation. What are these theorems *for*?" she suddenly exploded. "What did we gain from that? What was the point? I should have walked away, like Sextus—but I don't have the luxury! I need to become Lyctor *now*, before—"

She bit off her words like meat from a bone. Gideon waited to know before *what,* but no more was forthcoming. She closed her eyes and waited, but opened them when she panicked and realised that she had forgotten how long it had been since she had shut them. Harrowhark was sitting there with that same curious expression on her paintless face, looking thoroughly unlike herself.

"Get some rest," she said imperiously.

For the first time, Gideon obeyed her without compunction.

21

WHEN GIDEON WOKE UP later, Dominicus had made the room wet and orange with evening light. She was cramped from hunger. When she rolled over, she was assaulted with a series of increasingly aggressive notes.

> *I have taken the keys and gone to examine the new laboratory.*
> *DO NOT come and find me.*

This was plainly unfair, even if the delights locked behind a Lyctoral door could only really be enjoyed by someone who gurgled over necromantic theorems, but anyway–

> *DO NOT leave the quarters. I will ask Sextus to look at you.*

Willingly go to Palamedes? Harrow must have had a hell of a fright. Gideon reflexively checked her pulse in case she was still dead.

> *DO NOT go anywhere. I have left some bread for you*
> *in a drawer.*

Yum.

> *"Go anywhere" in this case is defined as leaving the quarters to*
> *go to any other location in Canaan House, which you are*
> *banned from doing.*

"I'm not eating your nasty drawer food," said Gideon, and rolled out of bed.

She felt terrible—like she hadn't slept for days and days—then remembered that she hadn't, really, excepting last night. She felt feeble as a kitten. It took all her strength just to get to the bathroom, wash her scabrously painted face, and lap at the tap like an animal. The mirror reflected a haggard girl whose blood probably resembled fruit juice, with anaemia all the way up to her ears. She combed through her hair with her fingers, and thought of Dulcinea, and for some reason blushed deeply.

The water was fortifying. The bread in the drawer—which she ate, ravenously, like a wraith—was not. Gideon searched around in her pockets just in case she had left something there—an apple, or some nuts—and found herself startled when she found the note, and then wondered why she was startled. Her memory caught up a laggard step behind her comprehension: the piece of flimsy was still there, though the piece of flimsy had been there *all the time,* so there was a horrible possibility inherent.

There was a knock on the door. Nonplussed, unpainted, and hungry, she opened it. Nonplussed, much-tried, and impatient, Camilla the Sixth stared back.

She sighed, obviously tired of Gideon's bullshit already, and raised a hand with three digits bent. "How many fingers?" she demanded.

Gideon blinked. "How many bent, or how many you're showing, and do I count the thumb?"

"Vision's fine," said Camilla to herself, and retracted the hand. She elbowed into the room as though she had licence, and let a heavy bag drop to the floor with a thud, kneeling down to riffle through it. "Language is fine. Where are we? What did we come here for? What's your name?"

"What's your *mum's* name," said Gideon. "Why are you here?"

The compact, grey-clad cav of the Sixth did not even look up at this question. It was interesting to see her in the light: her fine sheets of slate-brown hair were cut sharply below her chin, giving a general air of scissor blades. She glanced up at Gideon without seeming very perturbed. "Your necromancer talked to my necromancer," she said. "My necromancer said you should be a corpse. You breathing?"

"Yes?"

"Passing blood? In your piss?"

"Look, this conversation is all I've ever dreamed about," said Gideon, "but I'm fine. H— My necromancer overreacted." (This, at least, seemed to strike a chord with Camilla, whose glance softened with the understanding of someone whose necromancer was also prone to gross overreaction.) "I'm just hungry. Do I or do I not seem totally fine to you?"

"You do," said Camilla, who had pulled a frankly upsetting bulbous glass object out of her bag. "That's what I'm worried about. Warden said you'd be in a coma. Put this in."

The bulb, thankfully, went in the mouth. Another one tucked up into her armpit. Gideon submitted to this treatment because she had gone a round with Camilla the Sixth before and had a healthy fear of her. The other cavalier looked at her toes and fingertips, and inside her ears. Whatever she found—plus her pulse, which the other cavalier took carefully—was noted down in a fat notebook with a stub of lead pencil. These numbers were scanned with due diligence, and then Camilla shook her head.

"You're fine," she said. "Shouldn't be. But you're fine."

Gideon said bluntly, "Why didn't Sextus want to do the spell?"

The tools were wiped and put back in the bag. For a moment, the other cavalier didn't answer. Then she pushed a strand of hair away from her grim, oval painting of a face, and said: "Warden did the calculations. He and I could have—completed it, but. With caveats."

"Caveats like?"

"My permanent brain damage," said Camilla shortly, "if he didn't get it right immediately."

"But I'm healthy."

"Didn't say your brain was."

"I'm taking that as a very witty joke and want it to be known that

I laughed," said Gideon. "Hey—Septimus said the Eighth could have done it easily."

"The Eighth doesn't train cavaliers," said Camilla, even more shortly than before. "The Eighth breeds batteries. Genetic match for the necromancer. He's been accessing his cavalier since he was a child. The Eighth probably *does* have brain damage. It's not his brain they need. And Lady Septimus . . . is too willing to believe in fairy stories. Same as always."

This was probably the longest speech she had ever heard Camilla give, and Gideon was deeply interested. "Are you two friends?"

The look in response wasn't quite withering, but it *would* suck all the moisture out of anyone it was aimed at. Camilla said, "Lady Septimus and I have never met. Look, you should eat."

This turned out to be an invitation. Camilla—obviously used to being someone's cav-of-all-work—helped her sling on her rapier, and waited as she applied a very cursory amount of face paint. She wouldn't have passed muster with a glaucomic nun in a room with the lights shot out, but it was enough to get on with. She didn't quite have to lean on Camilla's arm, but every so often was the recipient of a brusque shoulder press to get her standing straight. They kept mutual and pleasant silence, and the sunset bled through all the windows and gaps of the House of the First and made puddles of red and orange before them.

Every so often a white-belted skeleton crossed their path with an easy, arm-swinging gait. Each time a bonely figure appeared from a corner or clattered through a doorway, Gideon noticed Camilla's fingers close on her rapier out of pure reflex. When they stopped at the threshold of the dining hall, the cavalier of the Sixth was poised like a waiting shrike: there were voices within.

"—Princess *Ianthe* has one. It's not at all the same thing," someone was saying.

A tall and golden figure was standing before the tables, her saffron hair unbrushed and sleep in her eyes. Her clothes looked as though she had slept in them. Coronabeth was still magnificent.

She was talking to Teacher, who was sitting at one of the long polished tables—there was Palamedes next to him with an uneaten meal and a piece of paper scribbled almost to holes, and some of the sizzling tautness surrounding Camilla went off the boil. Her shoulders relaxed, just a fragment.

Teacher said gently: "Ah, ah, that is also not correct. The owner is Naberius the Third. If it is being held for him by Princess Ianthe— it's still his. One key for the Third House and one only, I am afraid."

"Then the Fifth's key should be given to me. Magnus wouldn't mind—wouldn't have minded."

"Magnus the Fifth had asked for his own facility key, and I do not know where it is," said Teacher.

Scalded by the bright orange light of the setting sun coming down through the great ceiling windows, Corona looked like a grief-stricken king: her lovely chin and shoulders were thrust out defiantly, and her mouth was hard and remorseless as glass. Her violet eyes looked as though she had been crying, though perhaps from anger.

Palamedes's chair clattered as he rose, saying courteously to this vision: "Princess, if you wish it, I'll escort you down to the facility right now."

Gideon caught Camilla's low "The hell you will."

More chairs scraped on the tiled floor. Gideon hadn't noticed the duo from the Second House at the table farthest away, drinking hot coffee and looking, as they ever did, as though they had just trimly stepped from the pages of a military magazine. Captain Deuteros said: "I am surprised that the Warden of the Sixth House would break compact like this. You've said yourself that this can't be solved communally."

"And I was right, Captain," said Palamedes, "but this is harmless."

Coronabeth had crossed the floor to Palamedes, and though he was tall she towered a full half a head over him if you included the hair. Camilla had edged around the room to stand half a step behind her necromancer, Gideon sloping helplessly behind, but war was not on the Third's mind. Corona was not smiling, but her mouth was fine and frank and eager, and she rested her hand on his shoulder: "Do this for me," she said, "and the Third House will owe the Sixth House a favour. Help me get the same keys as my sister—and the Third House will go down on its knees for the Sixth House."

Captain Deuteros said, icily: "'Harmless.'"

"Princess," said Palamedes, who had had to blink his extremely lambent grey eyes under this assault, "I can't. What you're asking is impossible."

"I mean it. Wealth—military prizes—*research* materials," she said, intent on encroaching into Palamedes's personal space. Gideon was in awe of the Sixth at this point, as under the same treatment she would have breathed so hard that she fainted. "The Third's thanks will be as gracious as you need them to be."

"Corona. This is rank bribery. The Second won't stand for it, and the Sixth is too wise to buy into it."

"Oh, shut *up*, Judith," she said. "Your House would give bribes in a heartbeat if you had any money."

Judith said slowly, "You insult the Second."

"Don't toss the gauntlet at me," said Corona, "Naberius would just treat it as an early birthday present— Sixth, believe me, I'm good for it."

"It's not that I don't want what you're offering. It's that you're asking for the impossible," said Palamedes, with a touch more impatience in his voice. "You *can't* get the keys your sister has. Each key is unique. Frankly, there are only one or two left in all Canaan House that haven't been claimed already."

The room fell silent. The Second's carefully placid faces were frozen. Corona had gone still. Gideon's own face must have been doing something, because the rangy necromancer of the Sixth looked at her, and then looked at the Second, and said: "You must have realised this."

Gideon wondered why she hadn't realised this: she wondered why she had assumed that—that maybe there were infinity keys, or enough for a full set each. She sat down hard on the closest chair at the closest table, counting the keys mentally—the red and white keys that she and Harrow had won, the second of them half Dulcinea's by right. At another look at everyone's faces, Palamedes said, more irascibly: "You *must* have realised this."

The golden hand had not dropped from his shoulder, but instead fisted in his shirt. "But that means—that means the challenge *must* be communal," said Corona, with an exquisite furrow of her brow. "If we're all only given pieces of this puzzle, refusing to share the knowledge means that nobody can solve it. We need to pool everything, or none of us will be ever be Lyctor. That has to be it, hasn't it, Teacher?"

Teacher had sat with his hands around his cup of tea as though enjoying the heat, breathing in its curls of fragrant steam. "There is no law," he said.

"Against teaming up?"

"No," said Teacher. "What I mean is, there is no law. You could join forces. You could tell each other anything. You could tell each other nothing. You could hold all keys and knowledge in common. I have given you your rule, and there are no others. Some things may take you swiftly down the road to Lyctorhood. Some things may make the row harder to plough."

"We still come under Imperial law," said Marta the Second.

"All of us come under the sway of Imperial law," agreed her necromancer, whose expression was now a shade doubtful. "Rules exist. Like I've said before, the First House falls under Cohort jurisdiction."

"Where you got *that* idea from," said Teacher tartly, and it was the first time Gideon had heard him give even a little reproof, "I do not know. We are in a sacred space. Imperial law is based on the writ of the Emperor, and here the Emperor is the only law. No writ, no interpretation. I gave you his rule. There is no other."

"But natural law—the laws against murder and theft. What prevents us from stealing one another's keys through intimidation, blackmail, or deception? What would stop someone from waiting for another necromancer and their cavalier to gather a sufficient number of keys, then taking them by force?"

Teacher said, "Nothing."

Coronabeth had finally dropped her hand from Palamedes's shoulder. She looked over at the Second House—a sombre understanding was dawning on Captain Deuteros's face, and Lieutenant Dyas's was as inscrutable as ever—and then she looked at Palamedes, whose expression was that of a soldier who had just heard the call to the front. There was a shields-up twist to his mouth and eyes.

Corona breathed, "Ianthe has to know," and fled from the room. Her leaving was a little like an eclipse: the evening sun seemed to cool with her, and the duller electric lights vibrated to life with her passing.

In an almost inexcusably banal act, a white-belted skeleton appeared from the kitchen with two steaming plates of the poached pale meat and root vegetables. One of these was put in front of Gideon, and she remembered that she was ravenous. She ignored the knife and fork that the skeleton carefully laid at either side of the plate, as nicely as anyone with a soul would have, and started cramming food into her mouth with her hands.

Teacher was still bracing his hands around his cup, his expression more final than troubled: too serene to be worried, but still somehow thoughtful, a little woebegone.

"Teacher," said Palamedes, "when did Magnus the Fifth ask you for a facility key?"

"Why, the night he died," said Teacher, "he and little Jeannemary. After the dinner. But she didn't take hers. Magnus asked me to hold on to it . . . for safekeeping. She was not happy. I thought perhaps the Fourth would come and ask for it today. Then again—if I could prevent either of those two children from going down to that place, I would."

He looked up through the skylight at the deepening dusk, the curls of steam from his mug slowly thinning away.

"Oh, Emperor of the Nine Houses," he said to the night, "Necrolord Prime, God who became man and man who became God—we have loved you these long days. The sixteen gave themselves freely to you. Lord, let nothing happen that you did not anticipate."

There came the noisy clatter of bowls. It was the Second, who—instead of sitting back down—were collating their cutlery and pushing in their chairs. They left in taut silence, single file, without a glance back at anyone remaining. Camilla sat down opposite Gideon as the skeleton put the second plate in front of her, and she used her knife and fork, though not with any great elegance.

The necromancer of the Sixth was rubbing at his temples. His cavalier looked at him, and he offhandedly took a few bites of his meat and his vegetables, but then he stopped pretending and put down his fork.

"Cam," he said. "Ninth. When you're finished, come with me."

It didn't take long for Gideon to finish, as in any case she hadn't much bothered to chew. She stared with glassy eyes at Camilla the Sixth's plate—Camilla, who had finished most of hers, rolled her eyes and pushed her leftovers to Gideon. This was an act for which she was fond of Camilla forever after. Then they both followed a stoop-shouldered Palamedes as he pushed through the door that the Second had left from—down a corridor and a short flight of steps—turning a wheel on an iron door, its glass window rimed thickly with frost.

This appeared to be where the priests stored anything perishable. Strings of startle-eyed, frozen fish with their scales and tails intact hung like laundry on lines above steel countertops, bewildering Gideon with the reality of what she had been eating. Other, even weirder meats were stacked in alcoves to one side of the room, expiration dates labelled with spidery handwriting. A fan blasted the area with toe-curlingly cold air as Gideon wrapped her cloak more thickly around her. Barrels lined some of the other walls: fresh vegetables, obviously just picked for tonight's chopping, lay on a granite board. A skeleton was packing linen-wrapped wheels of some waxy white substance into a box. A door led away from this fridge—it opened, and the Second emerged. They did not look happy to see the newcomers.

Captain Deuteros said heavily, "You're a fool, Sextus."

"I don't deserve that," said Palamedes. "You're the one who just found nothing for the second time."

"The Sixth House is welcome to succeed where the Second has failed." She tugged her already perfect gloves into even glassier unwrinkled smoothness, and flakes of ice settled on her braided head. "The community needs this over and done with," she said. "It needs someone who can take command, end this, and send everyone back in one piece. Will you consider working with me?"

"No," said Palamedes.

"I'm not bribing you with goods and services. I'm asking you to choose stability."

"I can't be bribed with goods and services," said Palamedes, "but I can't be bribed with moral platitudes, either. My conscience doesn't permit me to help anyone do what we have all embarked upon."

"You don't understand—"

Palamedes said savagely, "Captain, God help you when you understand. My only consolation is that you won't be able to put any responsibility on my head."

The Cohort necromancer closed her eyes and seemed to count slowly to five. Then she said: "I'm not interested in veiled threats or vagaries. Will you answer honestly, if I ask you how many keys you have?"

"I would be a fool to answer," he said, "but I can tell you that I have fewer than you think. I am not the only one who came here wanting to be a Lyctor, Captain. You've just been too damned slow on the uptake."

Lieutenant Dyas's fingers closed slowly and deliberately around the hilt of her functional rapier. Camilla's fingers were already on hers; her other hand was on the hilt she kept at her left hip, the unembossed grip of her dagger. Gideon, who had just eaten one and a quarter dinners, felt unbelievably unready for whatever was about to go down. She was relieved when the necromancer of the Second said, "Leave it. The die is cast," and both women pushed past them.

Palamedes led the other two cavaliers through the nondescript door to another nondescript room past the cooling larder. This room held big shelves at one end, stacked one atop the other; a few tables with wheels from which the rubber was peeling off in big strips were parked in a corner. These tables were high and long enough to hold a whole person, lying flat. It was the morgue, though a more impersonal and featureless morgue Gideon could not imagine.

Gideon said, "How long have you known about the keys?"

"Long enough," said Palamedes, hooking his fingers underneath the lid of a morgue shelf. "Your Nonagesimus confirmed it with me after the Fifth were killed. Yes, I know you've known the whole time."

Oh, exquisite! Harrowhark had kept *Palamedes Sextus* in a loop that didn't include Gideon. She felt angry; then she felt bereft; then she felt angry again. This felt like being hot and cold at once. Totally heedless of her, the Sixth necromancer continued: "I meant what I said though. There are precious few keys left. The faeces hits the fan starting now. Cam, did you bring the box?"

Gideon said, "What do you *mean*?"

Camilla had dropped her heavy bag next to her necromancer, and he was riffling through it with one hand, pulling the shelf out with the other. Well-greased struts smoothly produced a body covered with a thin white sheet, murmuring into view feetfirst. Palamedes pulled the sheet up from the feet all the way to the abdomen and started carefully feeling the legs through the clothes. It was Magnus, and he had not improved since Gideon had last seen him. She regretted again eating one and a quarter dinners.

"Put it this way," he said eventually, palpating a hip. "Up till now I'd assumed everyone was being remarkably civil. If the initial method of obtaining keys was cleverness and hard work, the way forward from here will be either what you just saw—heavy-handed alliance attempts—or worse. Why do you think the Eighth picked a fight with the Seventh?"

"Because he's a prig and a nasty weirdo," said Gideon.

"Intriguingly put," said Palamedes, "but although he *is* a prig and a nasty weirdo, Dulcinea Septimus has two keys. Silas has made her a target."

This was all getting unreal: a weird mathematics that she hadn't even been counting. But she was still Ninth enough to hold her tongue. She said instead: "No offense, but what the hell are you doing?"

He had taken a fingerful of jelly out of a little tub Camilla had proffered. He was rubbing it over, bizarrely enough, the dull gold hoop of Magnus Quinn's wedding ring. With a stick of grease he made two marks above and below the band of metal, and then held his hand over it like someone cupping a flame. Palamedes closed his eyes, and—after a pregnant pause—steam began to curl above his knuckles.

All at once, he muttered crossly to himself and took his hand away. This time the grease went beneath the ring, and he started to ease it off the sad dead finger.

"I need more contact," he said to his cavalier. "This touched the key ring, but there's too much jumble." And to Gideon: "Our reputation doesn't precede us, I see. Thanergy attaches to more than just the body, Ninth. Psychometry can track the thanergy lingering in objects—when you get to it early and when there's a strong association. Give me the scissors, I'm going to take some of his pockets."

"What are you—"

"Quinn's *key ring*, Ninth," said Palamedes, as though her question was really hopelessly obvious. "There was nothing on the bodies yesterday. The Second came to look, but they haven't got my resources."

"That or they took the evidence," said his cavalier gloomily, but her adept countered: "Not their style. Anyway, if I couldn't find anything after yesterday's examination, they wouldn't."

"Don't get cocky, Warden."

"I won't. But I'm fairly sure, here."

Gideon said, "But—hold up. Magnus had only just picked up his facility key the night—you know. He hadn't reached any challenge labs. The facility key was all he had. Who'd take that?"

"That's precisely what I want to know," said Palamedes. He dropped the wedding ring into a small bleached pouch that Camilla was holding open, and then took a tiny pair of scissors and started clipping at the dead man's trousers. "Your vow of silence is conveniently variable, Ninth, I'm very grateful."

"Turns out I'm variably penitent. Hey, you should be talking to Nonagesimus."

"If I wanted to talk to Nonagesimus, I'd talk to Nonagesimus," he said, "or I'd talk to a brick wall, because honestly, your necromancer is a walking Ninth House cliché. You're at least only half as a bad."

Palamedes glanced up at her. His eyes really were extraordinary: like cut grey rock, or deep weather atmosphere. He cleared his throat, and he said: "How much would you do for the Lady Septimus?"

Gideon was glad of the paint; she was thrown off balance, unsure of her footing. She said, "Uh—she's been kind to me. What's your interest in Lady Septimus?"

"She's—been kind to me," said Palamedes. They stared at each other with a kind of commingled weariness and embarrassed suspicion, skirting around something juvenile and terrible. "The Eighth is both determined and dangerous."

"Protesilaus the Seventh is uncomfortably hench, though. She's not alone."

Camilla spoke up: "The man's a glorified orderly. His hand's never on his rapier. First instinct's to punch, and he moves like a sleepwalker."

"Just bear witness," said Palamedes. "Just—keep her in mind."

The scissors went *snip, snip* and tiny squares of fabric were added to a new linen bag. With more reverence than she'd given him credit for—he had just given a corpse an invasive massage and stolen its jewellery—Palamedes softly pulled the sheet back over the abdomen and legs of Magnus the Fifth. He said, quite gently: "We'll get to the bottom of this one, if you give us a little time," and Gideon realised he was speaking to the body.

Gideon suddenly ached to hear one of the Fifth's terrible jokes, if only because it would be a refreshing trip back to the status quo.

She had to leave—her hand was on the door—but something in her made her look back and say: "What happened to them, Sextus?"

"Violent head and body trauma," he said. For a moment he seemed to hesitate, and then he turned his laser-sharp gaze on her. "What I do know is—it wasn't just a fall."

His cavalier said lowly, warningly: "Warden."

"What good is silence now?" he said to her. And then, to Gideon: "Their wounds contained extraordinarily tiny bone fragments. The fragments weren't homogenous—they were samples from many different osseous sources, which is indicative of—"

What it was indicative of was interrupted by a small sound from beyond the door. The noise of skeletons packing things away had disappeared a long time ago: this was the noise of the door wheel being quietly spun. Gideon threw open the door to the cooling room, which Camilla burst into with her sidearm drawn: a hemline was escaping through the wheel-operated portal to the cooler, which had been left open in haste. Gideon and Palamedes stood, watching the door creak forlornly in the cold air. The hemline had been blue embroidery, and the pattering feet around the size of a crappy teen's.

"Poor dumb kids," Gideon said, all of four years their elder.

"Do you think so?" said Palamedes, surprising her. "I don't. I often find myself wondering how dangerous they really are."

22

THAT EVENING, HARROWHARK HAD still not re-
turned. Gideon busied herself with catching up on her training exercises, frustrated by her sore muscles, which wanted to pack it in
after the first hundred push-ups. She spent a long time doing her
solo drills—the automatic litany of grip and guard, flexing into hand
positions while staring out the window into the drooping black
night—and then, pretty certain that Harrow wasn't returning, she
got out her longsword and did it all again. Having two hands on the
grip was precisely the thing that Aiglamene had told her not to do,
but it felt so good that by the end she was happy as a child.

Harrow never came back. Gideon was used to this by now. Seized
with sudden experimental courage, she filled up the uncanny tub
in the bathroom from the hot-liquid tap. When nothing jumped out
at her, Gideon sat there in it with water all the way up to her chin.
It was incredible—the strangest thing she'd ever felt in her life; like
being buoyed on a warm current, like being slowly boiled—and she
worried, irrationally, whether water could get inside you and make
you sick. All her paint came off and floated in long, dirty flecks in
the water. When she put soap in the water oily rainbow slicks shone
across the top. In the end—suspicious of how clean it really got
you—she went and stood in the sonic for twenty seconds, but she
smelled incredible. When her hair dried it stood up on end, and it
took a lot of effort to get it flat again.

The bath was soporific. For the first time since she'd come to
Canaan House, Gideon was truly content to lie down in her nest,

get out a magazine and do absolutely nothing for half an hour. Nine dreamless hours later she woke up with the pages stuck to her face via a thin sealant of drool.

"*Ffppppp*," she said, peeling it off her face, and: "Harrow?"

As it turned out, in the next room Harrow was curled up in bed with the pillows over her head and her arms sticking out. Haphazardly flung laundry was piled next to the wardrobe door. The sight filled Gideon with a sensation that she had to admit was relief.

She said, "Wake up, assmunch, I want to yell at you about keys," but this imperative did not have the desired effect.

"The white key is now with your precious Septimus, as per the agreement," snapped Harrow, then pulled the covers over her head. "Now go away and shrivel."

"This does not satisfy me. *Nonagesimus*."

Harrow slithered more deeply underneath the covers like a bad black snake, and refused to get up. It was hopeless pushing further. This freed Gideon to dress in relative peace and quiet, paint without critique, and leave their quarters feeling unusual amounts of peace with the world.

She realised she was being followed somewhere down the long, sweeping staircase that led to the atrium. A peripheral blur huddled in doorways, still when she was still, making tiny movements when she was in motion. The mouldering floorboards creaked wetly underfoot. At last, Gideon spun around, her rapier drawn in one long fluid line forward and her gauntlet already half-snapped onto her fingers, and was presented with the wild young face of Isaac.

"Stop," he said. "Jeanne wants you."

He looked ghastly. His hands were sooty, the metallic thread on his embroidered robe soiled, and somewhere along the way he'd lost at least three earrings. Previously he had contrived to brush his hair up in that bleached avian crest on the top of his head, but now everything was crumpled flat. His mouth and eyes seemed emptied out, and his pupils were dilated with an amount of cortisol that said: *I've been on edge for three days.* The sweet puppy fat at his cheeks only served to make him a more awful sight.

Gideon cocked her head. "Jeanne wants you," he repeated. "Someone's dead. You've got to come with me."

For a moment Gideon hoped that this was a terrifically misplaced cry for attention, but Isaac had already turned away from her, dark eyes like stones. She had no choice but to follow in his wake.

Isaac led her down through the dilapidated great hall, and then down the stairs to the vestibule that led through to the sparring room, and he flinched at the sight of every white-belted skeleton that crossed their path. The tapestry was still securely in place, the door still hidden. He shouldered through the other door—it must have given his elbow a hell of a bang—and pushed into the room where electric lights poured down on what had previously been a filthy, reeking pit. It was now a square of glimmering water. Gideon had seen skeletons unrolling great tracts of rubber hose into the pit room and even beheld them slowly glurking sea-smelling liquid into the cavity, but the end result was extraordinary. The tiles gleamed with spray as Naberius the Third and Coronabeth—both wearing light singlets and trunks—did laps up and down the pool.

If she'd thought the bath was mad, this blew her mind. Gideon had never seen anyone swim before. Both bodies cut through the liquid with efficient, practised strokes: she focused on the long golden arms of Corona Tridentarius as she sliced through water, propelling her as she hit the wall and pushed off hard with her feet. Beyond the glass doors in the sparring room, Colum the Eighth sat on a bench, polishing his targe with a soft cloth while Lieutenant Dyas knelt into a perfect lunge, over and over.

Isaac made a beeline for the water. He stood in front of where the Crown Princess of Ida was churning her way through the water. She slowed her pace and bobbed up to the edge of the pool, shaking water out of her ears quizzically, hair a wet and leaden amber.

"Princess Corona," he said, "someone's dead."

The lovely face of the Princess of Ida made the exact same expression Gideon's had wanted to, which was: *What??* "What??" she said.

"Jeanne wants you," he said dully, "specifically."

Naberius had finished his length of the pool, too, and had struck through the water to come and see them. His swimming shirt was a lot tighter than Coronabeth's, and his fifty-seven abdominal muscles rippled under it importantly. He gave a long and rather obvious stretch, but stopped when he realised nobody was looking. "What's the holdup?" he said, rather pettishly.

"You'd better hurry up," Isaac said. "I promised I'd only leave her for five minutes. She's with the remains."

"Isaac, slow down!" Corona had vaulted herself out of the water in a flash of warm golden skin and her exceedingly long legs, and Gideon made her first and only devout prayer to the Locked Tomb of thankfulness and joy. Corona wrapped herself in a white towel, still dripping feverishly. "Who's dead? Isaac Tettares, what does this mean?"

"It means someone's dead," Isaac said curtly. "If you're not coming, I'm out of here in the next ten seconds. I'm not leaving Jeanne by herself."

Corona dashed over to the training room, sticking her dripping head through the door. Her cavalier was wrapping his body and head in his own white towels, sticking wet feet in his shoes. Coronabeth bothered with neither of these. By now she was being followed by Lieutenant Dyas, whose only nod to *training kit* involved undoing the top button of her military jacket, and by the scuffed wiriness of Colum the Eighth close behind.

This baffled gaggle was led outside to another broad terrace, though this one had not been built with beauty in mind. They weren't far from the edge of the dock terrace. This place had possibly shared that function, once—there was room for maybe one shuttle—but it was now focused on a huge steel chimney, metal flue standing up like a flagpole. It was bricked and supported all about with big stone tiles, and there were buckets of old vegetation and filthy cloths. The latter looked as though they'd been used to clean out the pool: they were emerald with verdigris and black where they weren't green. The chimney had a huge metal grate, about two metres tall, where you could shovel in rubbish. This grate was open, and the contents inside were still lightly smoking.

Isaac came to rest in front of the incinerator, beside Jeannemary the Fourth. He had looked stolid and dead, as though what was going on inside him had built up a thick crust, like a volcano; Jeannemary looked like a malfunctioning electric wire. You could practically see the sparks. Her rapier was naked, and she was pacing between the incinerator and the edge, every so often whirling around in a fit as though someone might attack her from behind. Gideon was beginning to admire her sheer animal readiness. When she saw the gang of idiots that her necromancer had brought her, she was intensely displeased.

"I wanted the *Ninth* and *Princess Coronabeth*," she said. Her voice cracked.

"Everyone tagged along," said Isaac. "I didn't want to leave you—I didn't want to leave you alone."

Careless of her bare feet and her sodden clothes, Corona marched over to the first maladjusted teen. "Sword at ease, Sir Chatur," she said kindly. "You're fine." (It was testament to Corona that the sword was lowered and slid away into the scabbard, though Jeannemary did not take her hand off the pommel.) "What's happened? What have you found?"

The Fourth said bitterly: "The body."

Everyone clustered around. With a piece of old flagstone, Jeannemary knocked the still-smoking grate aside so that they could all peer through: down a short shunt, embers still glowing sooty red, there was a heap of ashes.

The cavalier of the Second picked up an iron poker from beside the incinerator and nudged the pile. The ashes were all soft and even, crumbling to a powdery white, the red lumps breaking up under pressure. There was an expectant pause as she stuck the poker into the far corners of the big expanse, and then drew it away.

"It's just ashes," said Lieutenant Dyas.

"A body was burnt in there," said Jeannemary.

Colum the Eighth had gotten hold of a worn rake and was using that to pull some of the stuff closer. He stuck his hand into the boiling air and scooped out hot ashes, which showed that he either cared very little for his own pain or had a supremely good poker face. He held them out for inspection: whatever had burnt, had burnt down to a sandy grey-white stuff that left grease marks on the Eighth's yellowed palms.

The necromancer teen was saying listlessly: "I can tell fresh human cremains. Can't you, Princess?"

Corona hesitated. The Second butted in: "What if they were burning bones? One of the servants may have fallen apart."

"Someone could . . . just go ask," rumbled Colum the Eighth, shocking Gideon with an inherently sensible suggestion.

Isaac didn't hear: "That's rendered fat and flesh, not dry bone."

"They didn't— Are the Fifth still—"

"Magnus and Abigail are still where they ought to be," said Jeannemary fiercely, "in the mortuary. *Someone's been killed and burnt up in the incinerator.*"

There were long scratches down her face. She was even smudgier than her counterpart teen, if that was possible, and in that moment she looked feral. Her curls had frizzed up into a dark brown halo—one liberally streaked with blood and something else disreputable—and her eyes were welling up from the acrid smoke. She did not look like a stable witness to anyone.

Especially not to Naberius. He crossed his arms, shivered in the morning sun, and drawled: "These are ghost stories, doll. You're both cracking up."

"Shut it—"

"I'm not your doll, dickhead—"

"Princess, tell him—tell him those are remains—"

"Babs, shut your mouth and fix your hair," said Corona. "Don't discount this straight off the bat."

As per usual, he looked wounded, and scruffed the towel around his damp hair. "Who's discounting?" he said. "I'm not discounting. I'm just saying there's no point. No need for all this Fourth House sound and fury. Anyone goes missing, we assume they're having a nap in the incinerator."

"You are being," said the Second cavalier, "surprisingly blasé."

"I hope you end up in the incinerator," said Jeannemary. "I hope whatever killed Magnus and Abigail—and whoever we just found— comes after you. I'd love to see your face then. How will you look when we find you, *Prince* Naberius?"

Gideon pushed between them before Naberius could round on the ash-streaked, wet-eyed teenager. She stared into the incinerator. The cavalier of the Eighth was still poking around, and to her eye she had to admit there was nothing to find: whatever had been burnt here had been burnt down to greasy, bad-smelling smithereens. Particles of ash floated up from the grate like crumbling confetti, making smuts on their faces.

"Needs a bone magician," said Colum, and dropped the rake. "I'm heading back."

Naberius, who had been staring down Jeannemary, was distracted by this. He was more eager and jovial when he said: "You gearing up for your duel with the Seventh? The princess and I'll ref you, naturally."

"Yes," said the other man without much enthusiasm.

"I'll come with. Should be interesting to see the cav; he's not remotely like his rep, is he? Ain't ever matched him in a tournament, myself—"

At the exit of the Third and the Eighth cavaliers, the Eighth looking like he wished he were deaf, the Second went too: more silently, and wiping her hands on her scarlet neckerchief. Only the teens, Gideon, and Corona were left. Coronabeth was staring into the steaming ashes, brief singlet and shorts whipping in the wind, fine dry curls of gold escaping from the wet mass of her hair. She looked troubled, which made Gideon sad, but she was also soaked right through to the skin, which made Gideon need a lie-down.

"I keep seeing things," said the necromantic teen, emptily. They turned to look at him. "Out of the corners of my eyes . . . when it's nighttime. I keep waking up and hearing something moving . . . or someone standing outside our door."

He trailed off. Jeannemary put her arm around his shoulder and pressed her sweat-streaked brown forehead to his, and both sighed defeated sighs in concert. The solace they were taking in each other was the bruising, private solace between necromancer and cavalier, and Gideon was embarrassed to be audience to it. It was only then that they seemed at all grown-up to her. They looked worn down to stubs, like ground-down teeth, greyed out of their obnoxious vitality and youth.

The cavalier of the Fourth House looked up at Gideon and Corona.

"I wanted you two because Magnus liked you both," she said. "So you get the warning. *Don't say I didn't tell you.*"

Then she led Isaac away, him looking like an expectant prey animal, her like dynamite, ushering him back through the salt-warped door. Gideon was left alone with Coronabeth. The princess was closing the huge grate to the incinerator and sliding the handle down to lock it. They both beheld it silently: it did seem big enough to heave a person through, down into what—when set—would have been roaring flames. Clouds passed overhead, plunging what had been dazzling brightness into relative gloom. The clouds were fat and bluish, which Gideon had learned meant that they would soon explode into rain. She could taste it on the air, washing the prickle of smoke off her tongue. When the storm broke, it would break hard.

"This isn't just Fourth House theatrics," said Corona. "I don't think they're being reckless here. I think we're actually in trouble . . . a lot of trouble."

In the newfound dimness Gideon took off her glasses and nodded. Her hood fell back, sliding down in heavy folds of black to her shoulders. The exquisite eyes of the necromancer of the Third were upon her, and the doleful expression turned into a radiant smile, violet eyes crinkling up at the corners with the hugeness of the grin.

"Why, Gideon the Ninth!" she exclaimed, mourning banished. "You're a *ginger*!"

* * *

The clouds broke later that afternoon. The rain beat at the windows like pellets, and the skeleton servants scurried around with buckets, catching the worst of the sleeting drips, putting matting down for the puddles. Apparently Canaan House was so used to this that their response was automatic. Gideon was familiar with rain by now, but the first time she couldn't get over it. The constant pattering drove her mad all night, and she'd had no idea how anyone who lived in atmospheric weather could ever put up with it. Now it was only a murmurous distraction.

To the noise of the storm she had gone back to check on Harrowhark, suddenly paranoid—convinced that she had dreamt up the arms flapping out of the duvet, the short spikes of dark hair visible from under the pillow, that maybe the Reverend Daughter had made Gideon's youthful dreams come true by spending all night in an incinerator—but Harrow hadn't even woken up. Gideon ate lunch next to a skeleton servant carefully balancing a bucket on the table, into which fat drips fell from the windows, *ploing . . . ploing . . . ploing.*

The numinous dread hadn't really left her since that morning. It was almost a relief to see the shadow of Camilla Hect fall over her bowl of soup and bread-and-butter. Camilla's grey hood was wet with rain.

"Duel's off," she said, by way of hello. "Seventh never turned up, and they're not in their quarters. Let's move."

They moved. Gideon's heart hammered in her ears. Her rapier swung against her leg as persistently as the rain peppering the walls of Canaan House. By instinct Gideon led them through a row of dark, dismal antechambers, door handles slippery with rain, and out into the storm itself: the conservatory where Dulcinea liked to sit. It was stultifyingly hot and muggy in there: like walking into the jaws of a panting animal. Rain sleeted off the plex in sky-obscuring sheets. Beyond the conservatory door—under an awning that had long since tipped into the rain—was Dulcinea.

She was sprawled across the wet flagstones. Her crutches lay on either side of her, as though they had slipped from her grasp. Gideon's insides interlaced, lungs into kidneys into bowels, then rubber-banded back with a *twang*. It was Camilla who first dropped to her knees beside her and rolled her over on her back. A bruise popped on her temple, and her clothes had soaked right through, as though she had been lying there for hours. There was a terrible bluish tinge to her face.

Dulcinea gave an enormous, tearing, terrible cough, pink spittle foaming from her mouth. Her chest jerked, staccato. It was not a pretty sight, but Gideon welcomed it with open arms.

"He never came back," she said hopelessly, and fainted.

PROTESILAUS THE SEVENTH WAS MISSING. Dulcinea Septimus was critically ill. Left stranded when her cavalier failed to return, then threatened by the rain, she had tried to walk by herself and slipped: now she was confined to bed with hot cloths on her chest and no good to anybody. Teacher moved her to one of the tiny rooms in the priest wing, and she had to be laid on her side so that whatever was choking her lungs could drain out of her mouth and into a basin. Teacher's two nameless colleagues sat with her, replacing the basin and boiling noisy kettles.

Everyone else—the Second House with their brass buttons; the twins of the Third and their now-bouffant cavalier; the Fourth teenagers, gimlet eyed; and the Fifth asleep forever in the mortuary; the Sixth in grey and the mismatched Eighth; and the Ninth, with Harrow roused and tight lipped in her spare habit—was accounted for.

The ashes in the incinerator had been raked out and combed over, and the confirmation that they were human remains was not illuminating. The surviving necromancers had gathered around a bowl of them, and they had all pounced on it like a bowl of peanuts at a party. Only Coronabeth disdained fingering a bunch of smuts and crumblings.

"They're much older than they ought to be," said Ianthe Tridentarius, cool as a cucumber, which was the first sign of hope for Protesilaus. "I would have said these belonged to a corpse three months dead."

"You're out by about eight weeks," said Palamedes, brow furrowed. "Which would still predate us significantly."

"Well, in either case it's not him. Has anyone else died? Teacher?"

"We have not held a funeral in a very long time," said Teacher, a bit prissily. "And at any rate, we certainly would not have consigned them to the waste incinerator."

"Interesting you should say *them.*"

Ianthe had two small fragments on her palms. One of them was recognisably part of a tooth. For some reason, this dental fact had Harrow looking at Ianthe's palms, then Ianthe, then Ianthe's palms again as though both were suddenly the most fascinating things in the world. Gideon recognised this sudden diamond focus: Harrowhark was reestimating a threat.

Ianthe said, idly: "You see? There's at least two people in there."

"But the time signature's consistent throughout the remains—"

She tipped both fragments into the palms of Palamedes. "Happy birthday," she said. "They must have died at the same time."

Captain Deuteros said tersely: "The incinerator is a snare. I'm as curious as anyone to know what's in there, but the fact remains that Protesilaus is evidently not, so where is he?"

"I have set the servants to find him," said the First House priest. "They will search every nook and cranny, apart from your rooms . . . which I ask you to search yourselves, on the bizarre chance that Protesilaus the Seventh is there. I will not breach the facility, nor will my servants. If you want to go down there, you must go down there yourselves. And then there is the outside of the tower . . . but if he left the tower, the water is very deep."

Corona turned her chair around and straddled the seat, crossing her slim ankles at the front. Gideon noticed that she and Ianthe had not entirely made up in the wake of whatever fight they must have had; their chairs were close together but their bodies were angled away from each other. Corona shook her head again, as though to clear it of cobwebs. "He must be alive. There's no motive. He was— I mean, any time I met him, I thought—"

"*I* thought he was, perhaps, the most boring man alive," supplied her twin, languidly, wiping her hands. Corona flinched. "And not even a classic Seventh House bore; he hasn't subjected us to even one minimalist poem about cloud formations."

"Consider this: maybe there's no motive," said Jeannemary Chatur, who refused to sheathe her rapier. She had positioned herself and Isaac nearly back-to-back, as though united they could take all comers. "Consider this: they went through the hatch, just like Magnus and Abigail, and now he's dead and *she's* about to kick the bucket."

"Would the Fourth drop this insane monster theory—"

"Not insane," said Teacher to Naberius, "oh, no, not insane."

Captain Deuteros, who had been scribbling in her notepad, leant back in her chair and tossed down her pencil. "I'd like to supply a more human mens rea. Yes, the Duchess Septimus and her cavalier had accessed the facility. Did they have any keys?"

"Yes," said a voice at the door.

Gideon hadn't noticed the chain mail–skirted, whitewashed figure of Silas Octakiseron leave, but she noticed him come back in. He entered the eating-atrium from the kitchen side looking pallid and unruffled, his bladed face as pitiless as ever, free from a normal human emotion. "Yes, she does," he repeated, "or rather, she did."

"What the hell did you just do," said Palamedes quietly.

"Your aggression is unseemly and unwarranted," said Silas. "I went to see her. I felt a certain responsibility. I was the one who asked for satisfaction, and Brother Asht had been ready to duel her missing cavalier. I did not want bad blood between us. I feel nothing but pity for the Seventh House, Warden Sextus."

"You haven't answered my question."

Silas felt about in his pocket and raised his hand to display its contents. It was one of the iron key rings, and on it were two keys, one grey, one a familiar white.

"If foul play has befallen her cavalier," he said, in his curiously deep voice, "then the culprit will get no joy of it. I found her conscious, keeping hold of this. She's surrendered it to me for safekeeping."

"That's dubious in the extreme," said Captain Deuteros. "Surrender them to *me* now in a show of good faith, Master Silas. If you please."

"I cannot in good conscience, until I know the fate of Protesilaus the Seventh. Anyone here could be guilty. Brother Asht. Here." The chain mail–kirtled boy tossed the ring to his cavalier, who caught it out of the air and fished his own heavy key ring out of his pocket. Gideon noticed that their ring held a facility key and one other, in black wrought iron with curlicues. Colum the Eighth locked the two rings together with a very final *click*. "I'll keep these until such a time as she wants them. Judging by our conversation, that may well be never."

This was received with a brief silence.

"You callous bastard," shouted Naberius, "you just went and heavied a nearly dead girl for her keys."

Jeannemary said, "You're just sorry you didn't think of it first."

"Chatur, if you say one more bloody word I'll make sure you never get through puberty—"

"Hold your tongue, Prince Tern," said Captain Deuteros. "I have bigger fish to fry than listening to you abuse a child."

She stood. She took them all in, with the face of a woman who had come to a final conclusion.

"This is where the tendon meets the bone. This—key hoarding—cannot continue. I told you before that the Second House would take responsibility if nobody else had the stomach for it. That begins now."

The slender necromancer in his pure Eighth whites had slid into a chair proffered by his nephew, and he sat straight-backed and thoughtful.

"Is that a challenge to me, then, Captain?" he said sorrowfully.

"You'll keep." The Second adept thrust her chin toward *Palamedes*, who had been sitting with fingers steepled beneath his jaw, staring through the walls as though discord was so intensely distasteful that he could only distance himself from it. "Warden, the Sixth is the Emperor's Reason. I asked you earlier, and I'm telling you now: hand over what keys you've won for my safekeeping."

The Sixth, the Emperor's Reason, blinked.

"With all respect," he said, "piss off."

"Let the record state that I was forced into a challenge," said Lieutenant Dyas, and she peeled off one white glove. She threw it down on the table, looking Palamedes dead in the eye. "We duel. I name the time, you name the place. The time is now."

"Duel the Sixth?" squawked Jeannemary. "That's not fair!"

A perfect babel broke out. Teacher rose with a curious, resigned expression on his face: "I will not be party to this," he said, as though that was going to stop anyone, and he left the room. In the vacuum of his exit, Corona slapped both of her hands down on the table: "Judith, you coward, pick on someone your own size—"

"This is what happens, isn't it?" The bad necromancer teen was in a stupor, still: he sounded wondering, not angry. "This is what happens with Magnus and Abigail gone."

"Yes, I'm sure Magnus the Fifth would have issued us a strongly worded memorandum—"

"Ianthe! Not helping!—Sixth, you mustn't accept—the Third will represent the Sixth in this, if they'll consent. At arms, Babs."

Her twin sister's voice was thin and soft as silk: "Don't unsheathe that sword, Naberius."

"Ianthe, what—are—you—*doing*."

"I want to see how this plays out," she said with a pallid shrug, heedless of the growing ire in her twin's voice. "Alas. I have a bad personality and a stupefying deficit of attention."

"Well, Babs, thank God, has much better sense than to listen to you—Babs?"

Naberius's hand was hesitating hard on the hilt. He had not sprung into action as proposed, nor had he flanked the commanding twin. He was staring at her pale shadow, knuckles white, hand still, with a resentment very near hate. Corona's smile flickered. "*Babs?*"

Through all this, Palamedes had slopped the weight of his head into one hand, then into the other, scrubbing his fingers down his long face. He had taken his glasses off and was tapping the thick frames against the table. His nail-grey stare had not left Judith Deuteros, whose own gaze was as resolute as concrete.

"Default, Warden," said the captain. "You are a good man. Don't put your cavalier through this."

Palamedes seemed to snap out of it all at once, squeaking his chair legs horribly on the tiled floor as he scooted it backward and away from the table's edge.

"No, we're doing this," he said abruptly. "I pick here."

The captain said, "Sextus, you're mad. Give her some dignity."

He did not even stand; just crooked his fingers at his cavalier. Rather than tensing up in anticipation, as Gideon might have, Camilla had relaxed. She shook her dark fringe off her forehead, shivered out of her hood and her cloak, swung her neck back and forth like someone limbering up to dance.

"Oh, I am," he said. "Cam?"

Camilla Hect stepped on to the wooden table with one long, lean movement. She wore a long grey shirt and grey slacks beneath her cloak, and she looked less like a cavalier than an off-duty librarian. Still, this startled her audience except for Lieutenant Dyas, who vaulted up to the opposite side of the table, which creaked crossly beneath the strain. Dyas had not bothered to take off her jacket. She slid her utilitarian and bone-sharp knife out of its cross-hip sheath and laid it there for display. With her main hand she drew her rapier, plain-hilted, polished until it hurt.

The Sixth stared at her for a moment as though she had no idea of the protocol—and then she drew both of her weapons at once in a way that nagged at the back of Gideon's brain. The rapier looked, like Gideon's, maybe a million years old. It was the first time she had seen it in a good light, and here it looked as though it had never been designed to take an edge blow; the blade was light and delicate as a cobweb. The offhand looked like Camilla's whole House had gone searching down the back of the sofa for weapons. They had come up with what looked more like a long hunting or hacking knife than a duelling dagger: thick, meaty, cross-guarded, with a single sharpened edge. The whole effect was sadly amateurish.

The lovely and miserable Coronabeth had shouldered forward to stand at the table too, positioned in the space between them. She called to Judith and Palamedes: "Clav to sac—?"

"Hyoid down, disarm legal, necromancer's mercy," said the Second's necromancer calmly. Coronabeth sucked a breath through her teeth. "Sextus. Do you agree to the terms?"

"I have no idea what any of that means," said Palamedes.

Gideon drew forward to them, leaning in to hear Corona saying in an urgent whisper: "Warden—that means she can hit your cavalier anywhere below the neck, and it ends only when you give in. She's being an absolute cad, and I'm not even slightly sorry for pantsing her when we were eight."

"Nor should you be."

"Don't let her make an example of you," said the princess. "She's picking on you because you can't fight back, like a bully kicking a dog. She's given herself leeway to hurt your cavalier very badly, and she will, just to scare Octakiseron and Nonagesimus—no offense, Ninth."

The Warden of the Sixth drummed his feet on the floor percussively. He said, "So you're saying her cavalier can do more or less anything to my cavalier, all in the name of making me cry uncle?"

"Yes!"

From across the table, Captain Deuteros said sternly: "No more waiting. Default or fight. Corona, if you insist on arbitrating, arbitrate."

Those exquisite eyes would have persuaded a stone to roll uphill, but finding no purchase with Palamedes, Corona raised her voice reluctantly: "To the mercy call. Hyoid down. The neck is no exception. Point, blade, ricasso, offhand. Call."

"Marta the Second," called Lieutenant Dyas.

Camilla did not call. She looked down at her necromancer and said, "Warden?"

"You can't hit her in the head," he said. "I think. I choose when you're done."

"Just tell me how to play it." Camilla raised her voice: "Camilla the Sixth."

Gideon had moved back to her necromancer. Everyone else in the room looked grave. For a moment she thought the Fourth were holding hands, but she realised Isaac was holding Jeannemary *back*: his hand around her wrist was a clamp, and her face the picture of outrage. There were bleakly hungry faces—the pale Ianthe, and Naberius licking his lips—and then there were the Eighth, who were filling their own bingo sheet by praying.

Harrowhark looked as taut and distant as a hangman's rope, but something in Gideon's face must have caught her attention: she went from distant to bemused, and from bemused to something even a little bit offended. Gideon couldn't blame her. The general atmosphere was of a disapproving crowd before an execution, but she was trying and failing to smother a grin of savage anticipation.

Corona was saying, "Two paces back—can't turn, damn!—this is so hard to do on a table—"

"Cam," Palamedes said. "Go loud."

"—and begin," said Coronabeth.

Gideon had to give Dyas her due; it took her much less time than it had taken Gideon, fighting Naberius Tern, for the Second to realise she was in trouble. Lieutenant Marta Dyas was in every line of her a smart, efficient fighter: not given to folderol or showboating, at the very peak of her fitness. Unlike the Third, she was a soldier, far more used to fighting people who weren't moving to a playbook of legal duelling moves. She had trained her whole life with the front in mind, with veterans and bloodthirsty recruits. Her sword arm was balanced and light, her posture neat but not starchy. She was incredibly reactive, ready for any gambit her opponent could bring.

Camilla hit her like a hurricane. She exploded forward with her rapier wide and her butcher's knife held close, knocking the lieutenant's hurried parry out the way and sliding away from a belated lunge with the dagger. She sliced a red gouge down Dyas's immaculate white jacket and shirt, bashed her across the knuckles with the hilt of her rapier, and kicked her in the knee for good measure.

The kick was Cam's only mistake. The pain clearly set every neuron in Dyas's body shrieking with adrenaline. Someone like Naberius would have been prone on the table from shock, probably bleating and shitting. But the Second kept her wits about her—she took the pain with a stagger, kept her footing and held her blade, and parried another sweeping blow from Camilla's knife. She moved back for breathing space—Camilla harassing her with strike after strike to get back inside her guard—until she could move no more: she was, after all, fighting on a table. Camilla's foot lashed out to her offhand, and the dagger clattered to the ground. The Second, with an honestly beautiful dodge and a perfect reaction, took her one opportunity and lunged.

Dyas was desperate, and Dyas was of the Second House. Cam fought like a grease fire, but she left herself too many openings. Dyas's thrust would have pierced a lesser fighter right beneath the collarbone and run her through. It caught Camilla Hect low in the right forearm as she *nearly* dodged it—piercing the meat next to the ulna and making her snarl. She dropped her cobweb-light rapier, grabbed Marta's wrist, and yanked. The arm dislocated with a bright *pop.*

Lieutenant Dyas didn't quite scream, but she got most of the way there. She windmilled at the edge of the table. Still holding the wrist, Camilla stepped past her, kicked her legs out almost dismissively, and drove her down facefirst into the wooden boards with a crunch. This left Camilla standing over her opponent, one foot pressed into the back of her neck, the dislocated arm pinned up at an angle that looked seriously uncomfortable. Dyas made a strangled, agonised noise, and Judith Deuteros snapped: "Mercy!"

"Mercy called, match to the Sixth," said Coronabeth, as though saying it faster would make it over sooner.

There was silence, except for Camilla's ragged breathing and the lieutenant's tiny, half-amazed gasps. Then Jeannemary said, "Hot *dog.*"

Both cavaliers were oozing blood. It dripped from Camilla's wound where the sword had stuck her, and it was soaking through

Lieutenant Dyas's shirt and dribbling from her nose, the exact same colour as her neckerchief. She had her eyes screwed up tightly. Palamedes was already standing beside the table, and with another excruciating noise he set Marta's arm back inside its joint. This time she really did scream. Captain Deuteros watched, face absolutely blank.

"Your keys," he said.

"I don't have—"

"Then your facility key. Hand it over."

"You have its exact copy."

Palamedes rounded on her with a sudden fury that made everyone jump, even Gideon. "Then maybe I'll *throw it out the fucking window*," he snarled. "Two good cavs hurt, yours *and* mine, all because the Second tried to beat up the weak kid first." He jabbed a finger at Judith's immaculate waistcoat with intent to impale; she didn't flinch. "You have no idea how many keys we're holding! You have no idea how many keys anybody's holding, because you haven't paid any damn attention since the shuttles landed! You picked on us because the Sixth aren't fighters. You could have fought Gideon the Ninth, or Colum the Eighth. You fought Camilla because you wanted a quick win, and you didn't even watch her first, you just assumed you could take her. And I can't stand people who assume."

"I had cause," said the Second, doggedly.

"I don't care," said Palamedes. "Isn't it funny how it took the Second, of all houses, to blow this whole thing open? You've stuck a target on the back of everyone toting a key. It's a free-for-all now, and it's your fault, and you'll pay for it."

"For God's sake, Warden, you misunderstand my intention—"

"*Give me your key*, Captain!" roared the scion of the Sixth. "Or is the Second faithless, as well as dense?"

"Here," said Lieutenant Dyas. She had mopped most of the blood away from her mouth and nose, although her once-white shirt was drenched with scarlet. She fumbled in her jacket pocket with her unhurt arm and held out a key ring, adorned with a single key. Palamedes gave her a curt nod, plucked it from her fingers, and turned his back on them both. Camilla was sitting on the edge of the table, her hand clapped over her wound, blood seeping freely from between her fingers.

"Missed the bone," she said.

"Remember that you're using a rapier, please."

"I'm not making excuses, but she was quick as hell—"

A voice interrupted: "I challenge the Sixth for their keys. I name the time, and the time is now."

24

EVERYONE'S HEADS FOLLOWED THE SOUND—
except for Ianthe Tridentarius, who was lounging in her chair
with one eyebrow raised, and Naberius Tern, who had issued the
challenge. He vaulted to the table in one lustrous movement, swinging himself up to stand on it, even as Judith Deuteros very carefully
eased her cavalier down into an empty seat. He looked down at
them all with a hard sneer and the one stupid curl that he always
managed to get right in the middle of his forehead.

"No, you don't," said Coronabeth faintly.

"Yes, he does," said Ianthe, rising to stand. "You need a facility
key, don't you? Here's our chance. I suspect we won't be given a
better."

There was an expression of grim alarm rising on Judith Deuteros's
face. She had both hands across the oozing slit on her cavalier's
chest, and she had paused in her work out of sheer annoyance.

"You have no cause," she said.

"Neither did you, if we're all being honest with ourselves. Sextus
was perfectly right."

"If you want to cast me as the villain, do it," said the captain. "I'm
trying to save our lives. You're giving in to chaos. There are rules,
Third."

"On the contrary," Ianthe said, "you've amply demonstrated that
there are no rules whatsoever. There's only the challenge . . . and
how it's answered."

When she looked at her sister's stricken face—Corona was

somewhere beyond fury and shame now, and had lost every atom of her poise—she only said, quite softly: "This is for you, dear, don't be picky. This may be the only chance we have. Don't feel bad, sweetheart—what can you do?"

Corona's face changed—the struggle gave way to exhaustion, but at the same time there was a weird relief in her. Her teeth were gritted, but one of her hands tangled in her sister's long, thin, ivory-blond locks and she drew their heads close. "I can do nothing," she said, and Gideon realised they'd just lost her, somehow.

"Then let's do this together. I need you."

"I need you," echoed her twin, rather piteously.

Camilla hauled herself up to stand. She had taken Palamedes's handkerchief and bound her arm, but the blood was already showing through and she held it in a funny way. Palamedes looked close to vibrating out of his skin from fear or anger. "Right," she said laconically, "second round."

But Gideon was experiencing one powerful emotion: being sick of everyone's shit. She unsheathed her sword. She slid her gauntlet over her hand, and tightened the wrist straps with her teeth. And she looked over her shoulder at Harrowhark, who was apparently breaking out of a blue funk to experience her own dominant emotion of *oh, not again*. Gideon silently willed her necromancer to put her knucklebones where her mouth was and, for the first time in her life—for the first real time—do what Gideon needed her to do.

And Harrowhark rose to the occasion like an evening star.

"The Ninth House will represent the Sixth House," she said, sounding cold and bored, as though this had been her plan all along. Gideon wanted to sing. Gideon wanted to dance her up and down the corridor. She broke out in a broad, unnervingly un-Ninth smile, and Naberius Tern—who had gone from greasy villainy to aggrieved caution—was having to force his smirk.

Ianthe just looked a little amused. "The plot congeals. Since when has the Ninth been bosom with the Sixth?"

"We're not."

"Then—"

Harrowhark said, in the *exact* sepulchral tones of Marshal Crux: "Death first to vultures and scavengers."

Unable to bear it any longer, Jeannemary hopped up on the table too: she held her shining Fourth House rapier before her, the beautiful navy-and-silver fretwork of her dagger gripped in an altogether professional way at her hip. Although her puffy eyes and corrugated, unbrushed hair proved that she had not slept more than a few hours in the last few days, she looked intimidatingly ready. Gideon was coming to the conclusion that despite an overworked pituitary gland, there was really something in the Chatur name after all.

"Once you face her, you face the Fourth House," she said ringingly. "Fidelity, and the Emperor!"

Naberius Tern sheathed his sword and his neat, gleaming knife, rolling his eyes so hard that they ought to have fallen backward into his sinuses. He sighed explosively and swung himself down from the table, wiping that stupid curl off his forehead with an airy head toss.

"I should've stayed home and gotten married," he said resentfully.

"As though anyone was even offering," snapped Ianthe.

"If you have all finished," said Silas Octakiseron with his deep, tyrannically servile politeness, "Brother Asht and I are going to go and look for Protesilaus the Seventh. He is, after all, still missing."

"Which will somehow involve trying those keys you've taken in doors you've never been able to open," said Palamedes. "What a co-incidence."

"I have no interest in talking to you anymore," said Silas. "The Warden of the Sixth House is an unfinished inbred who passed an examination. Your companion is a mad dog, and I doubt her legal claim to the title of cavalier primary. I would not even bother to thrash her. Enjoy the patronage of the shadow cult, while it lasts; I am sorry that it came to this. Brother Asht, we leave."

When they dispersed, it was with the manner of people reluctantly turning their backs on their enemies. The Eighth Master swept out with his cavalier like a legion retreating from a battlefield. The Second—the unsteady cavalier supported by the captain's arm—looked even more so, with something of the tattered refugee thrown in. The three Houses that were left looked at one another.

Palamedes rounded on Harrowhark, his hands bloody and his shining eyes a little wild. He had torn off his spectacles, and there were greasy red thumbprints over the lenses.

"There's only one more key," he said.

Harrow frowned. "One more to claim?"

"No, they've all been claimed. I've been through every challenge except the one I won't play ball with."

Harrow's frown deepened fractionally, but Gideon was putting the pieces together. So too, apparently, was the necromantic teen Isaac. "If there's only one of each key," he said slowly, "what happens when you do a challenge someone else already completed?"

Palamedes shrugged. "Nothing. I mean, you can do the challenge, but you get nothing at the end of it."

Jeannemary said, "So it's just a huge waste of time," and Gideon could not imagine how she'd have felt after the avulsion room if the plinth at the other end had been empty.

"Sort of. The challenge itself is still—instructional. It makes you think about things in a new way. Right, Nonagesimus?"

"The challenges so far," said Harrow carefully, "have encouraged me to consider some . . . striking possibilities."

"Right. But it's like—imagine if someone showed you a new sword move, or whatever, but then you never actually got to sit down and read up on how it worked. It might give you ideas, but you wouldn't really *learn* it. D'you follow?"

Jeannemary, Gideon, and Camilla all stared at him.

"What?" he said.

"The Sixth learns sword-fighting out of a book?" said Jeannemary, horrified.

"No," put in Camilla, "the Warden just hasn't been to Swordsman's Spire since he was five and got lost—"

"Okay, okay!" Palamedes put his hands out. He was still holding the bloodstained spectacles. "That was clearly an inapposite comparison, but—"

"A challenge taken purely as a necromantic exercise," said Harrow calmly, "suggests many things, but reveals none. Only the underlying theorem can lay bare the mystery."

"And the theorems are behind the locked doors," Isaac said meditatively, "aren't they? You need the keys for the doors, or you're screwed."

Everyone's attention was on the two shitty teens. They both looked back, with no small scorn, all grief, uncombed hair, and stud earrings. "We know about the *doors*," said Jeannemary. "We've seen the doors . . . and people go through the doors . . . Well, what else could we do?" she added, somewhat defensively. "If we hadn't been trailing everybody it would have been that creep Ianthe Tridentarius. And she's stalking everyone. Believe me."

("And *trailing* differs from *stalking* how?"

"Because the Fourth doesn't stalk?")

"Nothing was preventing you from getting your facility key," said Palamedes.

Isaac said emptily, "Abigail said—to wait for her."

Gideon did not know how much the Sixth knew about the keys they'd amassed so far, or what they'd learned of the labs and the studies, how much they knew of the theorems. Palamedes was nodding, thoughtful. "Well, you've come to the right conclusion. Behind the doors there are studies, and all eight—there's eight, obviously, one per House—contain notes on the relevant theorem. All eight theorems presumably add up to some kind of, ah . . ."

"Megatheorem," supplied Isaac, who, after all, was like thirteen.

"Megatheorem," he agreed. "The key to the secrets of Lyctorhood."

Jeannemary Chatur's brain had obviously ground forward, struggling past confusion and puberty hormones to some slowly formed conclusion. "Wait. Go back, Sixth House," she demanded. "What did you mean by *one more key*?"

Palamedes drummed his fingers on the table. "Well. Forgive me the explanation, Ninth, I know you've been keeping track of the keys—" (Ha! Ha! Ha! thought Gideon. She hadn't.) "—but I couldn't work out how many keys Lady Septimus had. I knew she had at least one, but when Octakiseron convinced her to hand them over"—he freighted *convinced* with such heavy scorn it ought to have fallen through the floor—"he accidentally showed us her card. She had two. That means there's one left that I haven't accounted for, and we've got to account for it."

"We need to find the Seventh cav," added Camilla.

He nodded. "Yes, and we also have to work out who the hell's in the incinerator. Ianthe Tridentarius was right—a sentence I don't like saying—in that there's more than one person in there."

Isaac said: "I have a duty to find out who killed Magnus and Abigail, first and foremost."

"You're right, Baron Tettares," said Palamedes warmly, "but trust me, I think answering those three questions will help us quite considerably in solving that mystery. Ninth, Protesilaus was still down in the facility as of last night."

Harrow looked at him blankly. "How do you know?"

"We saw him go in," said the Fourth as one. And Isaac added: "After we eavesdropped on you and the Sixth."

"Good for you. But it makes sense, too. Lady Septimus said *He didn't come back,* and when we saw her key ring just now it only had challenge keys—no hatch key. She must have given that to him so he could access the facility by himself—although why, I still don't know. I bet you the whole of my library's physical sciences section that he's still down there. It would be impossible for someone to bring him up without being seen."

"Then we need to go down and look," said Jeannemary, visibly impatient at the lack of action. "Let's go!"

"Don't be so Fourth," said Palamedes. "We should split up. We're fighting a battle on two fronts here. Frankly—I would not leave Lady Septimus unguarded, sans cavalier, with just the First House to guard her."

Harrowhark said, "Her keys are gone. What's the attraction now?"

Camilla said, "Vulnerability."

"Yes. It can't just be a game of keys, Nonagesimus. Why did Magnus Quinn and Abigail Pent die, when they had nothing on them but a facility key and their own good selves? Why has Protesilaus gone missing, when the most he would have had was his facility key? Is he still down there? Who died before this challenge even began? And then there's the issue of the other Houses. I do not know about you, Reverend Daughter, but until Cam's healed up, I plan on wetting myself lavishly."

Isaac gave a rather lame and high-pitched giggle. Camilla said gruffly: "Warden, it's just my right hand—"

"Hark at her! Just your right hand. *My* right hand, more like. God, Cam, I've never been so scared in all my life."

Harrowhark ignored this cavalier-necromancer banter and cleared her throat, pointedly. "Septimus wants guarding. Her cavalier should be found. What do you suggest?"

"The Fourth House stays with the Lady Dulcinea," said Palamedes, slipping his glasses back over his long nose. "Gideon the Ninth stays with them as backup. You, I, and Camilla go down to the facility and see if we can locate Protesilaus."

There was more than one bewildered stare aimed his way: his own cavalier looked at him as though he had taken leave of his senses, and Harrow yanked her hood off her head painfully as though to relieve her feelings. "Sextus," she said, as though to a very stupid child, "your necromancer is wounded. I could kill the both of you and take your keys—or just take your keys, which would be worse. Why would you willingly put yourself in that position?"

"Because I am placing my trust in you," said Palamedes. "Yes, even though you're a black anchorite and loyal only to the numinous forces of the Locked Tomb. If you'd wanted my keys through chicanery you would have challenged me for them a long time ago. I don't trust Silas Octakiseron, and I don't trust Ianthe Tridentarius, but I trust the Reverend Daughter Harrowhark Nonagesimus."

Beneath the paint, Gideon could see that Harrow had changed colours a number of times through this little speech. She went from being a rather ashen skeleton to a skeleton who was improbably green around the gills. To an outsider, it would have just been a blank Ninth House mask twinging from *darque mystery* to *cryptique mystery,* giving nothing away, but to Gideon it was like watching fireworks go off.

Her necromancer said gruffly: "Fine. But we'll watch over the Seventh House. I'm not going down the ladder with your invalid cavalier."

Palamedes said, "Fine. Perhaps that's better use of our talents, anyway. Fourth, are you all right to go with Gideon the Ninth? I realise I am presupposing that our motives all align—but all I can assure you is that they really do. Search the facility, and if you find him—or come up short—come back to us, and we'll move from there. Get in and get out."

The bleary necromantic teen looked to his bleary cavalier. Jeannemary said immediately, "We'll go with the Ninth. She's all right. The stories about the Ninth House seem probably bullshit, anyway."

She's all right? Gideon's heart billowed, despite the fact that she had her own suspicions as to why her necromancer didn't want her sitting with Dulcinea Septimus, and they were all extremely petty. The Sixth House adept adjusted his glasses again and said, "Sorry. Ninth cavalier, I should ask you your thoughts on all of this."

She cracked the joints in the back of her neck as she considered the question, stretching out the ligaments, popping her knuckles. He urged again, "Thoughts?"

Gideon said, "Did you know that if you put the first three letters of your last name with the first three letters of your first name, you get 'Sex Pal'?"

The dreadful teens both stared with eyes so wide you could have marched skeletons straight through them.

"You—do you *talk*?" said Isaac.

"You'll wish she didn't," said Camilla.

Her wound had opened again. Palamedes was searching his pockets and the sleeves of his robe for more handkerchiefs to staunch it. As the Fourth conducted a quick conversation in what they thought were whispers, Harrow came to Gideon and unwillingly passed over the great iron ring that their keys jingled on, bodies almost pressing so that she could keep them out of sight of Palamedes.

"Come back with these or having choked on them," she whispered, "and don't get complacent around the Fourth. Never work with children, Griddle, their prefrontal cortexes aren't developed. Now—"

Gideon put her arms around Harrowhark. She lifted her up off the ground just an inch and squeezed her in an enormous hug before either she or Harrow knew what she was about. Her necromancer felt absurdly light in her grip, like a bag of bird's bones. She had always thought—when she bothered to think—that Harrow would feel cold, as everything in the Ninth felt cold. No, Harrow Nonagesimus was feverishly hot. Well, you couldn't think that amount of ghastly thoughts without generating energy. Hang on, what the *hell was she doing.*

"Thanks for backing me up, my midnight hagette," said Gideon, placing her back down. Harrow had not struggled, but gone limp, like a prey animal feigning death. She had the same glassy thousand-yard stare and stilled breathing. Gideon belatedly wished to be exploded, but reminded herself to act cool. "I appreciate it, my crepuscular queen. It was good. You were good."

Harrow, at a total loss for words, eventually managed the rather pathetic: "Don't make this *weird*, Nav!" and stalked off after Palamedes.

Jeannemary sidled up alongside Gideon, rather shyly. Isaac was parasitically drifting with her: he was in the process of braiding her curly hair safely up with a tatty blue ribbon. She said, "Have you two been paired a very long time?"

("Don't just ask them that," her necromancer hissed. "It's a *weird thing to ask.*"

"Shut up! It was just a *question!*")

Gideon contemplated the growing braid, and the sight of Palamedes squeezing the noxious contents of a blue dropper into Camilla's wound, and Camilla kneeing him with beautiful abruptness in the thigh. Harrowhark lurked next to them, pointedly not looking at Gideon, head hidden deep inside her second-best hood. She still didn't understand what she was meant to do or think or say: what duty really meant, between a cavalier and a necromancer, between a necromancer and a cavalier.

"It feels like forever," she said honestly. Gideon slipped her dark-tinted glasses out of her pocket and slid them on, and she felt better for it. "Come on. Let's go."

25

DESPITE THE FACT THAT they now knew Gideon had a working pair of vocal reeds and the will to use them, the trip down to the facility was spent in silence. Any travel into the depths of the First House put both of the teens on high alert: they were so paranoid that they would have been welcomed into the dark bosom of the suspicious Ninth. Both startled at every shadow and watched the passing-by of creaking skeletons with no little hate and despair. They did not like the open terrace where the waves howled far below, nor the cool marble hallway, nor the marble stairwell that led down to the nondescript room with the hatch to the facility. They only spoke when Gideon slipped her facility key into the hatch and turned it with a sharp *click*. It was Jeannemary, and she was troubled.

"We still don't have a key," she said. "Maybe we—shouldn't be here."

"Abigail died, and she had permission," said her counterpart sombrely. "Who cares?"

"I'm just saying—"

"I've been down without permission," said Gideon, as she used one booted foot to ease the hatch open. Cold air wheezed out like a pent-up ghost. "The Sixth let me in once without a key, and I'm still breathing."

Jeannemary seemed uncomforted and unconvinced. So she added, "Hey, look at it this way: you were down here just the other night, so if that's the sticking point, you're already totally boned."

"You don't talk like—how I thought you might talk," said Isaac.

All three travelled down the cold, dark staple-ladder to the fluorescent lights and dead stillness of the landing. Gideon went first. The other two lagged behind a little, captivated by the increasingly old and bloody gobbets that still decorated the grille at the bottom. She had to herd them forward, down the tunnel that led to the radial room, to the ancient whiteboard and the signs above the warren of corridors.

She turned: Jeannemary and Isaac had not come with her. Jeannemary had stopped in the doorway, pressing herself flat against it, looking around at the strange, anachronistic tunnels of steel and plate metal and LED lighting.

"I thought I heard a noise," she said, eyes darting back and forth.

"Coming from where?"

She didn't answer. Isaac, who had pressed himself into the shadows where the side of the doorway met the wall, said: "Ninth, why were bone fragments found in Magnus's body, and in Abigail's?"

"Don't know. It's a good question."

"At first I thought it meant the skeletons," he said, in a sunken whisper, which made sense from the nonsense of why he and his cavalier had jumped at the creaking approach of each bone servant in the place. "There's something unnatural about the constructs upstairs—like they're listening to you . . ."

Gideon looked back at both of them. They had pressed themselves into either side of the corridor, not daring to come into the open space, pupils very dilated as though with adrenaline. They both looked at her: the young cavalier with her brown eyes muddy in the darkness, the young necromancer with his deep hazel eyes and spiderleggy mascara. Pressurized air from some cooling fan wheezed through a vent, making the ceiling creak.

"Come on, don't just lurk there," said Gideon impatiently. "Let's find this guy. It shouldn't be too hard, he's massive."

Neither wanted to be coaxed out. Their puff had seemed to leave them. They clustered close together, grave-faced and tense. Isaac raised a hand and faint, ghostlike flames appeared at his fingertips—

bluish-greenish, giving off a sickly little light that did not do much to illuminate what was going on around them. He insisted on warding every single radiating doorway—daubing blood and his cavalier's spit around the mouth of each corridor. He was nervous and crabby, and it was slow work applying teen gunge to every single exit. "His enclosures are good," Jeannemary kept saying defensively.

"I thought the Fourth were meant to be all about headfirst dives and getting all crazy," said Gideon, who stared hard into every shadow.

"It's stupid to get killed if it doesn't help," said Isaac, tracing his thumb in curious shapes along the doorjamb. "The Fourth isn't cannon fodder. If we're first on the ground we need to stay alive ... wards were the first thing I learned. When we get shipped out next year, we'll get them scarified onto our backs."

Next year. Gideon was taut with impatience, but still spent a couple of seconds grappling with the notion that the gawky teens in front of her would be facing the Empire's foes at age fifteen-and-whatever. For all that she'd longed to be on the front lines from the age of eight up, it suddenly didn't seem like such a great idea.

"We wanted to go this year," said the cavalier, dolorously, "but Isaac got mumps a week before deployment."

Remembrance of Isaac's mumps threw them both into gloom, but at least that diluted their terror. In the end Gideon found herself leading them down the hallway marked SANITISER, the place where she had first found Harrow. Their three pairs of feet kicked up huge scuffs of white powder, glowing mixed colours under Isaac's necrolight, settling down in silent sprays in the panel grouting, grinding to nothing beneath their footsteps. The doors moaned open to the panelled maze of stainless steel cubicles, and the vents moaned too in sympathy, creaking so much that the teens both gritted their molars.

Harrow's old blood was still here, but Protesilaus wasn't. They all split up to walk the maze of metal tables, checking beneath them to see if he had lain down for a swift nap, or something equally probable; they prowled rows of metal cubicles, all empty. They called out, "Hello!" and "Protesilaus!," their voices reverberating thinly off the walls. As the echoes faded, they heard the scuttling noises of air being blown through the vents' metal teeth. "There's something here," Isaac said.

They all listened. Gideon could hear nothing but the sounds of old machinery running in the same exhausted way it had run for thousands of years, kept alive by perfect mechanism and necromantic time. They were no different from the background noises of the Ninth House. She said, "I can't hear it."

"It's not just hearing," said Isaac, brow furrowing, "it's more—what I'm feeling. There's movement here."

Jeannemary said, "Another House?"

"No."

"Wards?"

"Nothing."

She stalked the facility with her rapier drawn and her dagger clutched in her hand. Gideon, stranger to teamwork, worried that if she startled her by accident she'd end up with the Fourth's offhand in her gut. Isaac said, "Bodies were brought into here—a long time ago. A lot of bone matter. The First feels like a graveyard all over, but this is worse. I'm not faking."

"I believe you," said Gideon. "Some of the stuff I've seen down here would ruin your eyelids. I don't know what the hell they were researching, but I don't like it. Only bright side is that it's all pretty self-contained."

"I'm . . . not super certain," said the adept. Sweat was beading on his brow.

Jeannemary said, "He's not in here. Let's go somewhere else."

They left the bright antiseptic room of Sanitiser. The lights went off with rhythmic *boom, boom, booms* as Gideon pressed down on the touchpad that still held little black whorls of Harrow's blood, and they spilled out into the corridor. Sweat was openly dripping down the sides of Isaac's temples now. His cavalier threw her arm over his shoulder, and he buried his hot wet face in her shoulder. Gideon again found this difficult to look at.

"Let's bounce," said Jeannemary.

As they turned the corner to where the Sanitiser corridor met the main artery, the rhythmic *boom, boom, boom* of lights shutting down caught up with them. The lights in the grille beneath them winked out of existence, and so did the dully glowing panels above, and so did the bright lights ringing the big square room ahead. They were left in total darkness, every nerve in Gideon's body singing with fear. She ripped her glasses off to try to cope.

The necromancer was close to hyperventilating. His cavalier kept saying, with eerie calm: "Your wards aren't tripped. It's just the lights. Don't freak out."

"The wards . . ."

"Aren't tripped. You're good with wards. There's nobody down here."

One of the motion-sensor lights struggled back on behind them, a short way down the passage. A ceiling panel threw the metal siding into sharp white relief. It was daubed with words that had not been there a few seconds before, written in blood so fresh and red that there were little drips:

DEATH TO THE FOURTH HOUSE

The light flickered off. After no sleep—after days of threat and grief and panic that would have floored a man twice his age—Isaac lost it completely. With a strangled cry he flared in a halo of blue and green. Jeannemary yelled, "Isaac, *behind me*—" but he was sizzling with light, too bright to see by, a sun and not a person. Gideon heard him flee into the room ahead of them, blinded by the running aurora.

When her eyes cleared, Gideon was confronted with the biggest skeletal construct she had ever seen. The room was full of it, bluely aflame with Isaac's light, a massed hallucination of bones. It was bigger by far than the one in Response, bigger than anything recorded in a Ninth history textbook. It had assembled itself into the room by no visible means, since it never could have fit through one of the doors. It was just simply, suddenly *there*, like a nightmare—a squatting, vertiginous hulk; a nonsense of bones feathering into long, spidery legs, leaning back on them fearfully and daintily; trailing jellyfish stingers made up of millions and millions of teeth all set into each other like a jigsaw. It shivered its stingers, then stiffened all of them at once with a sound like a cracking whip. There was so much of it.

It was cringing away from Isaac Tettares, who had planted his feet wide in line with his hips and was screaming soundlessly in fear and anger. He had thrown his arms out wide as though in embrace, and there was a sodium explosion in the air between him and the room-cramping construct. It left a suction, like he was trying to drag something out of the unwilling creature. Bright blue points of contact appeared on it, and the mass of bone and energy began to lose form, drifting instead toward Isaac, tiny bones plinking down to the grille like rain.

Gideon woke from her confusion, drew her sword and ran. With a gauntleted hand she picked up the nearest stinger and yanked it, then smashed the back of her heavy glove into another, finding a naked shank of legbone and punching it as hard as she could. One of the tendrils of teeth wrapped around her ankle, but she found purchase and stamped it into a corona of molars. Gideon looked behind her to see Jeannemary whipped off her feet by another tendril, lashing out wildly with her feet and her blades. Everywhere she looked was filled with construct: everywhere Isaac's light touched there was a veritable cancer of bone and tooth.

Gideon bellowed, voice deadened by a thousand million frigging bones:

"Run! Don't fight it, RUN—"

But the enormous thing slapped another couple dozen tendrils down on the grille, sinuous, and flexed into long sharp wires. Isaac's blue-green fire fell upon a giant trunk of bone, a skull terrifically mangled into the thing's only coherent core: a simulacrum of a face with closed eyes and closed lips, as though locked perpetually in prayer. This vast mask loomed down from the ceiling and strained beneath Isaac's pull. One of the tendrils gave in and was sucked into the vortex that the Fourth House was so valiantly creating. The spirit pinned to it was dissolving, the limb pattering into individual bits, one among hundreds.

Isaac did not stop and he did not run. It was one of the bravest and stupidest things Gideon had ever fucking seen. The construct teetered, getting its footing, cocking its great head as though in contemplation. The long straight spars of teeth hovered above the necromancer, bobbing and warping occasionally as though about to be sucked into his fiery gyre. Then at least fifty of them speared him through.

Blue fire and blood sprayed the room. Gideon sheathed her sword, set her shoulders, put one arm up above her eyes, and charged through the field like a rocket. It was like running through a landslide. A thousand fragments of bone ripped her robes to shreds and tore at every inch of exposed skin. She didn't pay them any mind, but crashed into Jeannemary Chatur like the vengeance of the Emperor. Jeannemary had no intention of stopping: she was tearing into her unbeatable foe as though running away had never been in question. She barely seemed to notice that Gideon had grabbed her, her limbs thrashing, her throat one long howl that Gideon only translated later: *Fidelity! Fidelity! Fidelity!*

How she scrambled through that hallway, the other girl clutched to her bosom, long tendrils of bone snaking after them from the central room, she did not know. The fact that she shinnied up the ladder with Jeannemary attached, kicking and screaming, was even more unlikely. She tossed the cavalier down—she would have been surprised if the girl had even felt it—slammed the hatch lid, and turned the key so frantically that it made gouges in the metal.

Jeannemary rolled over on the cold black tiles, and she threw up. She pulled herself up on her bone-whipped, cut-up, bashed-in arms and legs, wobbling, and she began to shake. She sank back to her knees and screamed like a whistle. Gideon caught her up again— the grief-stricken teenager thrashed and bit—and started off on a jog away from the hatch.

Jeannemary kept kicking in her arms. "Put me down," she wept. "Let me go back. He needs me. He could still be alive."

"He's seriously not," said Gideon.

Jeannemary the Fourth screamed again. "I want to die," she said afterward.

"Tough luck."

She did, at least, stop kicking. The myriad cuts over Gideon's hands and face were starting to really sting, but she paid them no mind. It was still a deep black night outside and the wind was howling around the side of Canaan House; she carried Jeannemary inside and down the big rotting staircase, and then she absolutely blanked on what to do next. The Fourth House cavalier couldn't even stand: she was reduced to the small, disbelieving sobs of someone whose heart had broken forever. It was the second time Gideon had listened to Jeannemary really cry, and the second time was a lot worse than the first.

She had to get her to safety. Gideon wanted her longsword and she wanted Harrow. There were the Ninth quarters—but bone wards could be broken, even Harrow's. She could march straight to where the others were guarding Dulcinea—but that was a long way to go with her catatonic cargo. And if she met an avaricious Naberius, or an overobedient Colum—she'd still prefer them to whatever was down there, in the facility, in the dark. Gideon's hand was still gripping the key ring with the facility key she had just now so frantically used, and the red key on it—and lightning struck.

Jeannemary did not ask where they were going. Gideon ran down the soggy Canaan House staircase, and across silent nighttime corridors, and down the sloping little passage that led to the foyer for the training rooms. She pushed aside the tapestry and sprinted down the hall to the great black door that Harrow had called X-203. The door and the lock were so black in the night, and she was so slippery with fear, that for an excruciating minute she couldn't seem to find the keyhole. And then she found it, and slid the red key home, and opened the door to the long-abandoned study.

The rail of spotlights all lit up, illuminating the clean laminate countertops of the laboratory and the still-shining wooden stairs to the living room. She slammed the door shut behind them and locked it so quickly that it ought to have broken the sound barrier. Gideon half-heaved, half-carried Jeannemary up the staircase and put her down on the squashy armchair, which wheezed with the sudden use. The sorrowful teen curled into a foetal position, bleeding and hic-cupping. Gideon barrelled away and started taking stock of the room, wondering if she could haul the big wooden bookcases down as barricades.

"Where are we?" the Fourth eventually said, drearily.

"One of the key rooms. We're safe, here. I'm the only one with a key."

"What if it breaks down the door?"

Gideon said bracingly, "Are you kidding? That thing's three-inch-thick iron."

This neither comforted nor satisfied Jeannemary, who had possibly seen a makeshift blockade in the other girl's eyes, but her crying diminished—every five seconds another sob would rack her, but she had swapped weeping for hysterical sucked-in breaths. Until she said: "It's not fair," and started up again with the great lung-filling fits of tears.

Gideon had moved before the aged gun, frightened into wonder-ing whether or not it worked. Who knew? The swords still all held edges. "No. It's not."

"You d-don't understand." The cavalier was fighting for control, fierce eyes wet with hate and despair. She was shivering so hard that she was vibrating. "Isaac's cautious. Not *reckless*. He's not—he didn't— He was always so careful, he shouldn't have— I hated him when we were little, he wasn't at all what I wanted—"

She gave in to crying again. When she could, she said, "It's not fair! Why did he get stupid now?"

There was absolutely nothing Gideon could say to this. She needed more firepower than bookcases and antiques. What she badly needed was Harrow Nonagesimus, for whom a gigantic con-struction of bones would be more fun opportunity than hellish monstrosity, and she needed her longsword. But she couldn't leave Jeannemary, and right now Jeannemary was a liability.

She mopped her hands over her bleeding face, demolishing her face paint and trying to get her thoughts straight, and settled on: "Look. We'll stay in here until you're fighting fit—don't try to tell me you're fit, you're exhausted, you're in shock, and you look like hot puke. Take half an hour, lie down, and I'll get you some water."

It took an enormous effort to get Jeannemary onto one of the dusty, mattress-squeaking beds, and much more effort to get her to take even tiny sips of the water that came out of the tap at the laboratory—the pipes rattled in shock that they were being used— in a little tin mug that had probably not had anybody's lips near it since the Ninth House was young. The recalcitrant teen drank a little, rested her head on the spongy old pillow, and her shoulders shook for a long time. Gideon settled down in the overstuffed armchair and kept her rapier out over her knees.

"What was that thing?"

Gideon startled; she had been lulled into a fug of reverie, and Jeannemary's voice was thick with weeping and the pillow.

"Dunno," she said. "All I know is that I'm going to kick its ass for it."

Another moment's silence. Then: "This is the first time Isaac and me really left the House . . . I wanted him to sign us up to go out to the front ages ago, but Abigail said no . . . and he wouldn't . . . I mean, he's got three younger brothers and four younger sisters to look after. He had, I mean."

It sounded as though she was going to burst into tears again. Gideon said, "That's—a significant amount?"

"You need spares when you're in the Fourth House," said Jeannemary, sniffling. "I've got five sisters. Do you have a big family?"

"The Ninth doesn't do big families. I think I'm an orphan."

"Well, that's pretty Fourth House too," said the cav. "My mum jumped on a grenade during the Pioneer expedition, even though she wasn't supposed to be out on post-colony planets beyond the rim. Isaac's dad went out on a state visit to a hold planet and got blown up by insurgents."

There was no more after that, not even tears. After a few minutes Gideon was not surprised to see that the poor bloodied girl had cried herself unconscious. She did not wake her. There would be time enough to wake her, and even a short rest would probably do her good. It sucked to be a teen, and it sucked more to be a teen whose best friend had just died in a horrible way, even if you were used to mothers jumping on grenades and fathers getting exploded. At least in the Ninth House, the way you usually went was pneumonia exacerbated by senility.

Gideon rested her head on the fat back of the armchair. She would not have said it was at all possible, but—watching the rise and fall of Jeannemary's breath, a safe up-and-down rhythm, the drying tearstains on the sleeping teen's cheeks—she promptly fell asleep.

* * *

It couldn't have been long. Fifteen minutes at the very most. She startled awake with the sheer unconscious panic of someone realising they couldn't afford to slip into deep REM, a haptic jerk flicking her awake. Her sword rattled off her knees and jangled to the floor. The only sound that could have woken her was a persistent drip she'd thought was coming from the tap.

Gideon did not understand what she was looking at when she awoke, and when she cleared her eyes and looked properly, she still didn't understand.

Jeannemary was still lying prone in the old bed, arms and legs now flung wide, as if she had kicked off the blankets and sheets in a bad dream: this would have been fine, except for the huge shafts of bone spearing each shoulder to the mattress. Two more through the thighs. One straight through the very centre of her ribs. These spears of bone met Jeannemary's body with haloes of red, splotching through her clothes, seeping into the bedspread.

"No," said Gideon meditatively, "no, no, no, no, no."

Jeannemary's eyes were very slightly open. There was blood spattered in her curls, and there was blood spattered over the headboard. Gideon's gaze followed the splatter upward. Written on the wall, in silky wet red, was:

SWEET DREAMS

ACT FOUR

26

SIDE BY SIDE, THE Fourth teens were laid to an uneasy sleep in the morgue, right next to the adults who had failed so terminally to look after them. Somebody had (how? It was a mystery) taken the cooling body from Gideon's arms (who had plucked those spears from those terrible holes and carried Jeannemary back?) and a lot of people had spoken a lot of words to her, none of which had pierced her short-term memory. Teacher was there, in her mind's eye, praying over the broken sieve of Isaac Tettares; and Harrowhark was in there somewhere too, and Palamedes, tweezering a big fragment of something out of the cooling corpse of Jeannemary the Fourth. These images were as jumbled-up and lacking in context as a dream.

She remembered one thing: Harrowhark saying *you* dullard—*you* imbecile—*you* fool, all the old contempt of the Ninth House nursery back and fresh as though she were there again. Harrow the architect, sweeping down the halls of Drearburh. Harrow the nemesis, flanked by Crux. It wasn't clear what in particular Harrow was haranguing her for, but whatever the reason, she deserved it. Gideon had tuned out all the rest of the necromancer's tirade, her head in her hands. And then Harrowhark had balled up her fists—breathed hard once through her nose—and gone away.

The only thing that had made sense was that she had ended up in the whitewashed room where they were keeping Dulcinea, sitting alone in an armchair, and there she had gritted tears out of her eyes for an hour. Someone had washed out all her cuts with reeking

291

vermillion tarry stuff, and it smelled bad and hurt like hell whenever an errant drip of salt water touched the wounds. This made her feel sorry for herself, and feeling sorry for herself made her eyes even wetter.

Dulcinea Septimus was a good person to do this in front of. She did not say "You'll be fine," as Dulcinea lacked the lung capacity to spend on platitudes; she just sat propped up on about fifteen pillows and kept her thin hot hand on Gideon's palm. She waited until Gideon had stopped her hard blinking, and then she said—

"There was nothing you could have done."

"Bullshit there wasn't anything I could have done," said Gideon, "I've thought of everything I should've done. There's about fifty things I could've done and didn't."

Dulcinea gave her a crooked smile. She looked terrible. It was a few hours before morning, and the early light was grey on her biscuit-coloured curls and blanched skin. The fine green veins at her throat and wrists seemed terribly prominent, like most of her epidermis had sloughed off already. When she breathed, it sounded like custard sloshing around an air conditioner. There was high colour in her cheeks, but it had the hectic brilliance of hot slag.

"Oh, could've . . . should've," she said. "You can *could have* and *should have* yourself back into last week . . . back into the womb. I could have kept Pro by my side, or I should have gone with him. I can go back and make things happen perfectly if I just think about what I should have or could have done. But I didn't . . . you didn't . . . that's the way it is."

"I can't bear it," said Gideon honestly. "It's just such crap."

"Life is a tragedy," said Dulcinea. "Left behind by those who pass away, not able to change anything at all. It's the total lack of control . . . Once somebody dies, their spirit's free forever, even if we snatch at it or try to stopper it or use the energy it creates. Oh, I know sometimes they come back . . . or we can call them, in the manner of the Fifth . . . but even that exception to the rule shows their mastery of us. They only come when we beg. Once someone dies, we can't grasp at them anymore, thank God!—except for one person, and he's very far from here, I think. Gideon, don't be sorry for the dead. I think death must be an absolute triumph."

Gideon could not get behind this. Jeannemary had died like a dog while Gideon napped, and Isaac had been made into a big teenage colander; she wanted to be sorry for them forever. But before she could say anything to this effect, a great cough that filled up about two and a half handkerchiefs tore at Dulcinea. The contents of these handkerchiefs made *Gideon* envy the dead, let alone Dulcinea.

"We'll find your cav," she said, trying to sound steady and failing so completely she set a record.

"I just want to know what happened," said Dulcinea drearily. "That's always the worst of it . . . not knowing what happened."

Gideon didn't know whether she could get behind this either. She would've been devoutly grateful to live not knowing exactly the things that had happened, in vivid red-and-purple wobbling intensity. Then again, her mind kept flaying itself over Magnus and Abigail, down there in the dark, alone—over the when, and the how; over whether Magnus had watched his wife be murdered like Jeannemary had watched Isaac. She thought: It is stupid for a cavalier to watch their necromancer die.

Gideon felt hot and empty and eager to fight. She said without real hope, "If you want your keys back from Silas Octakiseron, I'll deck him for you."

The coughing turned into a bubbling laugh. "Don't," said Dulcinea. "I gave them up freely, by my own will. What would I want with them now?"

Gideon asked baldly, "Why were you trying to do this whole thing in the first place?"

"Do you mean, *even though I'm dying*?" Dulcinea gave a friable smile, but one with a dimple in it. "That's not a complete barrier. The Seventh House thinks my condition is an asset. They even wanted me to get married and keep the genes going—me! My genes couldn't be worse—in case they produced poetry down the line."

"I don't understand."

The woman in front of her shifted, raising her hand to brush a few fawn-coloured strands away from her forehead. She didn't answer for a while. Then she said, "When you don't have it too badly—when you can live to maybe fifty years—when your body's dying from the inside out, when your blood cells are eating you alive the whole time . . . it makes for *such* a necromancer, Gideon the Ninth. A walking thanergy generator. If they could figure out some way to stop you when you're mostly cancer and just a little bit woman, they would! But they can't. They say my House loves beauty—they did and they do—and there's a kind of beauty in dying beautifully . . . in wasting away . . . half-alive, half-dead, within the very queenhood of your power."

The wind whistled, thin and lonely, against the window. Dulcinea struggled to raise herself up on her elbows before Gideon could stop her, and she demanded: "Do I *look* like I'm at the queenhood of my power?"

This would've made anyone sweat. "Uh—"

"If you lie I'll mummify you."

"You look like a bucket of ass."

Dulcinea eased herself back down, giggling fretfully. "Gideon," she said, "I told your necromancer I didn't want to die. And it's true . . . but I've been dying for what feels like ten thousand years. I more didn't want to die *alone*. I didn't want them to put me out of sight. It's a horrible thing to fall out of sight . . . The Seventh would have sealed me in a beautiful tomb and not talked about me again. I wouldn't give them the satisfaction. So I came here when the Emperor asked me . . . because I wanted to . . . even though I knew I came here to die."

Gideon said, "But I don't want you to die," and realised a second afterward that she had said it aloud.

The first finger and thumb of the hand ringed around hers. The dark blue eyes were luminous—too luminous; their lustre was wet and hot and bright—and Gideon pressed those fingers between her hands, very carefully. It felt as though even a little bit of pressure would crush Dulcinea to dust between her palms, like the very oldest bones kept in the Ninth House oss. Her heart felt sore and tender; her brain felt sore and dry.

"I don't plan on it, you know," said Dulcinea, though her voice was thinning out now, like water poured into milk. She closed her eyes with a gravelly sigh. "I'll probably live forever . . . worse luck. Whatever happened to *one flesh, one end*?"

"I've seen those words before," said Gideon, thoughtless of where she had seen them. "What do they mean?"

The blue eyes cracked open.

"They're not familiar?"

"Should they be?"

"Well," said Dulcinea calmly, "you *would* have said them to your Reverend Daughter the day you pledged yourself in the service of her cavalier, and she would have said them to you—but you never did that, did you? You weren't trained in the traditions of the House of the Locked Tomb, and you're nothing like a Ninth House nun. And you fight like—I don't know. I'm not even certain you were raised in the Ninth House."

Gideon let her head rest against the bed frame momentarily. When she had thought about this moment, she had expected to feel panic. There was no more panic left in the box. She just felt tired.

"Rumbled," she said. "I'm sick of pretending, so yeah. Right on nearly all those counts. You *know* I'm the fakest-ass cavalier who ever faked. The *actual* cav had chronic hyperthyroid and was a serial limpdick. I've been faking my way through his duties for less than two months. I'm a pretend cavalier. I could not be worse at it."

The smile she got in return had no dimples. It was strangely tender—as Dulcinea was always strangely tender with her—as though they had always shared some delicious secret. "You're wrong there," she said. "If you want to know what I think . . . I think that you're a cavalier worthy of a Lyctor. I want to see that, what you'd become. I wonder if the Reverend Daughter even knows what she has in you?"

They looked at each other, and Gideon knew that she was holding that chemical blue gaze too long. Dulcinea's hand was hot on hers. Now the old panic of confession seemed to rise up—her adrenaline was getting a second wind from deep down in her gut—and in that convenient moment the door opened. Palamedes Sextus walked in with his big black bag of weird shit, adjusted his glasses, and stared two seconds too long at their hands' proximity.

There was something dreadfully tactful and remote and un-Palamedes-y as he said, "I came to check in on the both of you. Bad time?"

"Only in that I am officially out," said Gideon, snatching her hand away. Everyone was mad at her, which was great, albeit they could not possibly be as mad as she was. She stood and rolled her neck until all the joints popped and crackled anxiously, was relieved to find her rapier still on her hip, and squared up to Palamedes feeling—terrifically dusty and guilty. "I'm going back to my quarters. No, I'm fine, quit it. Thanks for the ointment, it smells bewitchingly like piss."

"For God's sake, Ninth," said Palamedes impatiently, "sit back down. You need to rest."

"Cast your mind back to previous rests I have enjoyed. Yeah, nah."

"It's not even ointment, it's drawing salve. Be reminded that Cam pulled twenty bone splinters out of you and said there were still a dozen left—"

"Nonagesimus can get them out—or maybe not," added Gideon, a bit wildly. "Might as well leave them in until I'm through getting people bumped off, am I right?"

"Ninth—"

She indulged herself in storming out past the Warden of the Sixth, and in careering down the hallway like a bomb. It was about the least dignified way to leave a perfectly normal conversation, but it was also really satisfying, and it got her out of there in record time. Gideon staggered down the hallway picking orange goo out of her fingernails, and it was in this scratchy frame of mind that she nearly knocked down Silas Octakiseron in his floaty, bactericidal Eighth

House whites. Colum the Eighth flanked him automatically, looking more like jaundice than ever in the same colour.

"They are dead, then," his uncle said, by way of hello.

The only thing that saved Gideon from howling like an animal was the relief that, finally, she would get the chance to shove one of Octakiseron's feet so deep into his ass he'd be gargling with his calcaneus.

"*They* had names, you lily-livered, tooth-coloured asshole," she said, "and if you want to make a thing about it, I warn you that I'm in the kind of mood that can only be alleviated by walloping you."

Colum blinked. His necromancer did not.

"I had heard that you were speaking now," he said. "It seems a pity. Save your gaucherie for someone else, Gideon Nav. I've no interest in the frightened rantings of a Ninth House thrall."

"What did you call me?"

"Thrall," said Silas. "Serf. Servant."

"I don't want a bunch of synonyms, you smarmy cloud-looking motherfucker," said Gideon. "You said Gideon *Nav*."

"Villein," continued the necromancer of the house of the Eighth, warming to his thesaurus. Colum was staring at Gideon, almost cross-eyed with disbelief. "Foundling. I am not insulting you, I am naming you for what you are. The replacement for Ortus Nigenad, himself a poor representative of a foetid House of betrayers and mystics."

Gideon's brain skidded to a halt: it went back again to Drearburh, sitting with a fat lip and wicked friction burns on her wrists. The cries of the dwindling faithful. Green lights in the powdery dark. The greasy smell of incense. A woman weeping. Someone stealing her getaway shuttle, a million years ago. Two someones. One sad, one sadder, immigrants to the Ninth House themselves.

She still has family back on the Eighth . . .

"You've been listening to Sister Glaurica," she said slowly.

"I talked to Glaurica on her return to the mother house," said Silas. "And now I'd like to talk to you."

"Me. The thrall. The servant. The other five words you said."

"Yes," said the boy, "because you grew up servant to a murderer, in a tribe of murderers. You are, more than anything, a victim of the Ninth House."

That stopped the tiny bone in Gideon's soul snapping; that stopped her from striding forward and balling both hands in the exquisite linen and chill mail of his robes—that and the fact that she hadn't been straight-up shield-bashed yet by Colum the Eighth and wasn't in a hurry to experience this exciting time. She stepped forward. Silas did not step away, but he turned his head a little from her, as though she were a bad breath. He had very brown eyes, startlingly framed by thick, whitish lashes.

"Don't pretend like you know what happened to me there," she said. "Glaurica never remembered I was alive, didn't care about me when she remembered, and she wouldn't have said anything to *you* on the subject. You don't know anything about me and you don't know anything about the House of the Ninth."

"You are wrong on both points," said Silas, to somewhere over her shoulder.

"Prove it."

"You are invited to come and take tea with myself and Brother Asht."

She scrubbed both her dirty fists into her eyes and narrowly avoided gumming one up with the terrible orangey salve, which was so noxious that it apparently caused splinters to leap from her body rather than hang around near it. Her corneas misted up momentarily with the smell. "Sorry, didn't hear you right," she said, "because I thought you said, 'Come and take tea with myself and Brother Asht,' the dumbest thing to say, ever."

"You are invited to come and take tea with myself and Brother Asht," Silas repeated, with the kind of hard patience that indicated a mantra going on inside his pallid head. "You will not bring the daughter of the Locked Tomb, but you'll bring yourself, and you will be ready to listen. No price. No hidden motive. Just an invitation to become more than what you are now."

"Which is—?"

Silas said, "The tool of your oppressors. The lock on your own collar."

She couldn't handle any more, having already lived a long night and suffered a number of emotional torments, among them supernatural murder and petty interpersonal drama. Gideon shrugged her cloak over her shoulders, thrust her free hand into a pocket, and stalked down the corridor away from any uncles and nephews.

The necromancer's voice drifted down after her: "Will you come and listen to what I have to say? Be decisive."

"Eat me, milk man," said Gideon, and staggered around the corner.

She heard Colum's "Means yes, probably," but not the murmured reply.

* * *

From that time on, Gideon could not outfight the nightmares. She willed her subconscious to sink into a pattern of random eye movement that did not involve her waking up in a lather of cold sweat, but like so many things in her life now, it had lost fitness and apt response. She was dumb before the body of her failures, unmanned by the barrage of her brain. Gideon only had to close her eyes to see her own personal, randomly selected shitshow.

Magnus Quinn, still drinking his grassy morning tea, stabbed until his chest was steaming chunks of meat because she could not make her tongue yell *Look behind you*—

—a steaming cauldron filled with fragrant grain and the silent, foetal corpse of Abigail Pent, sinking beneath the surface before Gideon's blistering fingers could dig her clear—

—Isaac Tettares gulping and swallowing from an upturned jug of acid that she was unable to wrench from his febrile, trembling hands—

—Jeannemary Chatur, whose dismembered arms and legs kept turning up while Gideon made a bed that got stickier and wetter and more jumbled with bits of Jeannemary as the covers were turned; and—

—the old dream of her mother. Alive now, overlapping with her life in a way she hadn't in reality, shrieking *Gideon—Gideon—Gideon!* while, as Gideon watched, crones of the Ninth gently levered her skull from the rest of her head with a big crunchy *crack.*

And Harrow, telling her to wake up. That had only happened the once: the Ninth necromancer sitting in the dark, wrapped in a mouldering duvet like a cloak, her face very naked and blank and shorn of its monochrome skull mural. Gideon had fallen back into an uneasy sleep almost immediately. She could never decide if she had dreamed that into being—Harrowhark was not exploding, or having her intestines drip out of her ears like streamers, or sloughing off her skin right down to her subcutaneous fat—but she had been looking at Gideon with a coal-eyed expression of absolute pity. There had been something very weary and soft about the way that Harrow Nonagesimus had looked at her then, something that would have been understanding had it not been so tired and cynical.

"It's just me," she'd said impatiently. "Go back to sleep."

All signs pointed toward hallucination.

At that, Gideon had to sleep, because the consequences of waking were too hideous. But from then on she slept wearing her rapier, her gauntlet on her chest like a heavy obsidian heart.

27

"Let's negotiate," said Palamedes Sextus.

Harrow and Gideon sat in the Sixth House's quarters, which was bizarre as hell as an experience. The Sixth had been housed in high, airy rooms tucked into the curve of the central tower. Their windows opened onto a sweeping view of the sea, or at least, they would've had the Sixth not covered them up with blackout curtains. The whole of the Sixth was huddled on the polar caps of a planet so close to Dominicus that exposure to the light side would melt the House clean away. The great libraries were set in a fat cake tin of a station, designed for the ongoing ordeal of not letting anything get too hot or too cold, which meant no windows at all whatsoever. Palamedes and Camilla had recreated that effect in here to the best of their ability, which meant a room with the airiness and lightness of a closet.

This was not helped by the fact that nearly every square inch was covered by flimsy: Palamedes's scribbles were tacked up like wallpaper across every bare surface. They were taped to tables. They clustered over the mirror. Fat books lay in serried rows on the arms of every chair, stacked haphazardly, as though nobody ever sat down without bringing another one to bear. Gideon had peeked through the open door of the bedroom, into a dark nest where a huge whiteboard stared down at the ancient, wheezing four-poster bed, very neatly made. There was no question about whether or not Camilla inhabited the horrible cot attached to the end, cavalier-style. It sagged beneath assorted weapons and tins of metal polish.

"I'm not moving from my outline," said Harrow. She and Palamedes sat on either side of a table swept hastily clear of books and notes: stray pens rolled across the surface at the least jolt. "I hold the keys. We enter together. You get an hour."

"An hour's not remotely sufficient—"

"You're slow."

"You're paranoid."

"I am—currently—*alive*," said Harrowhark, and Gideon winced. Palamedes had taken off his spectacles ten minutes into the argument, and he was now cleaning them on the front of his robe. This appeared to be more of an aggressive move than a defensive one: his eyes, free of glass plates, were arrestingly grey. It mainly only hurt Gideon, who was trying very badly to avoid his gaze. "So you are. The room in and of itself is of interest to me, and it ought to be of interest to you," he said.

"You're too forensic."

"You lack scope. Give over, Nonagesimus. A key-for-key swap is the most logical and most elegant arrangement here. This refusal is just superstition and paranoia, cooked up with a side of—pure humbuggery."

For a moment Gideon's anger and remorse were overwhelmed by, *Did you legit just say 'pure humbuggery'?*

The necromancers were now mirroring each other's equally bowed postures: bony elbows on the table, hands clasped beneath their chins, staring at each other unblinking. Behind Palamedes's chair, Camilla had the glazed expression of someone who had checked out ten minutes ago. Her arm was bandaged but not kept pinned up, and she appeared to have full range of movement with it. Gideon was lolling behind Harrow, picking at her fingernails and staring at the pieces of paper, which had handwriting that was more like cryptography. Her own necromancer settled back and said, sepulchral: "You are still convinced by your . . . megatheorem idea, then."

"Yes. Aren't you?"

"No. It's sensational."

"But not out of the question. Look. The tasks and challenges—the theories underpinning them—they're really not that disparate. Neural amalgamation. Transferral of energy. As we saw in the entropy field challenge, continuous siphoning. The magical theory's astonishing. Nobody has pushed necromantic power this far: it's unsustainable. If the intent is to show off the sheer breadth of Lyctoral power—well, they did. I've seen the winnowing test, and if the self-replicating bone golem had been the only thing in it I would still be kept up at night. I don't know how the hell they did it."

"I do," said Harrow, "and if my calculations are right I can replicate it. But all this is more than unsustainable, Sextus. The things they've shown us would be powerful—would bespeak impossible depth of necromantic ability—if they were replicable. These experiments all demand a continuous flow of thanergy. They've hidden that source somewhere in the facility, and that's the true prize."

"Ah. Your *secret door* theory. Very Ninth."

She bristled. "It's a simple understanding of area and space. Including the facility, we've got access to maybe thirty percent of this tower. That's what's called hard evidence, Warden. Your megatheorem is based on supposition and your so-called 'instinct.'"

"Thanks! Anyway, I don't like how many of these spells are about sheer control," said Palamedes.

"Don't be feeble. Necromancy is control."

Palamedes slipped his spectacles back on. Phew. "Maybe," he said. "I don't know, some days. Look—Nonagesimus. These theorems are all teaching us something. I believe they're parts of an overarching whole; like the whiteboard in the facility, remember? *It is finished.* You believe they're giving us clues—prompts—toward some deeper occult understanding that's hidden elsewhere, this power source idea. I see puzzle pieces; you see direction signs. Now, maybe you're right and we're meant to follow the crumbs to some master treasure. But if I'm right—if Lyctorhood is nothing more or less than the synthesis of eight individual theorems . . ."

Harrow did not speak. There was a long moment, and Gideon thought that Palamedes had lapsed into thought. But then he said crisply: "Then it's wrong. There's a flaw in the underlying logic. The whole thing is an ugly mistake."

Now her necromancer said, "Leave the cryptic to the Ninth. *What* mistake, Sextus?"

"I'll give you the relevant notes if you help me pick a lock," said Palamedes.

This was enough to give her pause. "Give me your personal notes on all the theorems you've seen. What lock?"

"Throw in a copy of your map—"

"Do I have a map?" Harrowhark remarked, in general, to the air. "My goodness. That is, at the very best, a baseless assertion."

"Not an idiot, Reverend Daughter. A Lyctoral lock—the one that matches the Sixth House key. The grey key. Which Silas Octakiseron currently holds. Hence: picking."

"That's impossible. How?"

"You can't know until we do it. If it works, it gets you every single note on every theorem I've read, in return for yours, your cooperation, and the map. Are you in?"

There was a pregnant pause. As everyone had already known beforehand, Gideon's necromancer was forced to admit that she was in. She rose to stand: the chair behind her teetered dangerously, and Gideon corrected it with her foot. "At least show me the door you told me about," she commanded. "I despise this feeling that the Sixth House is taking my house for all it can get."

"Most people would have looked upon this as a generous deal," remarked Sextus, whose chair was being held back for him by the obliging Camilla, "but I did owe you one—for sticking by us when the Third House made its challenge. Not that we wouldn't have won it—but we would have given more than I'm willing to give. So that's the sticky sentiment part. Come with me for the cold hard facts."

They all traipsed after him for the cold hard facts. When the Sixth House locked their front door, it was grimly amusing to see that as well as Palamedes's wards they had hammered in five deadlocks, and reinforced the door so that it could not be taken off its hinges. Hearing Camilla shove all the bolts home was as good as an orchestra. The two necromancers drifted to the front—their long robes making them look like dreary grey birds—and Gideon and Camilla fell behind them, lingering beyond the mandated half step.

Camilla the Sixth's shoulders were set. Her straight dark fringe fell out of the way as she half-turned her face to Gideon, briefly, expressionlessly, but that was all Gideon needed.

"Ask me how I am and I'll scream," she said.

"How are you," said Camilla, who was a pill.

"I see you calling my bluff and I resent it," said Gideon. "So, hey. What do you really use when you're not pretending the rapier's your main wield? Two short blades of equal length, or one blade and one baton?"

Her keen eyes narrowed into black-lined slits. "How did I mess up?" she asked, eventually.

"You drew your rapier and your dagger at the same time. And you're ambidextrous. You keep cutting like both your blades are curved. Also, there's six swords and a nightstick on your bed."

"Should've tidied my mess," admitted Camilla. "Two blades. Double-edged."

"Why? I mean, that's boss, but why?"

The other cavalier massaged her elbow gingerly, flexing her fingers as though to make sure there was no correlating pain. She seemed to be considering something, and then she came to an abrupt conclusion. "I applied to be the Warden's cavalier primary when I was twelve," she said. "Got accepted. We'd looked at the data on weapons, before. Decided that two short blades had—more general applications. I learnt the rapier,"—that was an understatement—"but I'll be fighting with the blades, when the time comes to really fight."

Before Gideon could get to grips with the disquieting implication this was not yet the time to really fight, Camilla got in an elbow jab: "Why are you acting like you and he are arguing?"

"Nooooo," said Gideon brightly, followed up with a: "thaaaaanks."

"Because you're not arguing." Beat. "You'd know if you were arguing."

"Can you— I don't know! Can you tell him that if he wants me to introduce him to Dulcinea, I can do it? Can you tell him I'm not trying to cramp his friggin' style?"

"The last thing the Warden needs," said Camilla, "is an introduction to Lady Septimus."

"Then can you tell him to maybe stop acting like he read everyone's feelings in a book ages ago? Because that would be completely sweet," said Gideon.

Without another word, Camilla moved to bookend her adept as he paused before a large, gilt-framed picture: the gilt was mostly brown except where it had gone black, and the picture itself was so faded that it looked like a coffee stain. It was a curious image: a dusty expanse of rock, cracked into an enormous canyon running down the centre, a sepia river winding into flaked-off nothingness at the very bottom.

"I documented this one a long time back," said Harrow.

"Let's take another look."

Palamedes and Camilla each shouldered one corner of the portrait, lifting it off some unseen tack. It seemed very light. The great Lyctoral door behind it—with its black pillars and its carved horned skulls, its graven images and grim stone—was not particularly well hidden. In all respects, it was a nearly exact match for the other Lyctoral door Gideon had seen. But Harrow sucked in her breath.

She went to the lock, and then Gideon saw why: it had been filled in with some hard, tarry grey stuff, like putty or cement. Someone had deliberately tampered with the keyhole. Part of the putty had been chipped away at the bottom, with great gouges taken out of it, but otherwise it seemed depressingly solid. There was no getting through that stuff without significant engineering work.

"Sixth," said her necromancer, "it was not in this condition the first night we were in Canaan House."

"I still can't believe you documented every door in this place on the first night," said Palamedes, with one of his slight dry smiles, "and that I didn't. I couldn't tell when the lock was first jammed. I thought I was losing my grip."

Harrow was already easing her gloves off with her teeth, flexing her long nervous fingers like a surgeon. She drew the pad of her thumb over the stuff, furrowed her brow so deeply that it could have held a pencil, and swore under her breath. She tossed the gloves to Gideon—Gideon caught them neatly—and depressed the matter with her thumb and forefinger. "This," she said calmly, "is regenerating ash."

"Perpetual bone, which accounts for it being undateable—"

"Same stuff as the transferral construct."

"In which case—"

"Whoever put this in place would need to have a comparable level of skill to whoever made the construct," said Harrow. "Getting it out again would require more power than most bone specialists hold—in *aggregate*."

"I didn't bring you here to remove it," Sextus said. "I just brought you here to confirm, which you've done nicely, thank you."

"Excuse me. I never said I couldn't remove it."

One eyebrow went up above the thick spectacles. "You don't think . . . ?"

It was the Harrowhark of old who responded, the one who walked down dusty Ninth House halls as though crushing purple silk beneath her feet. "Sextus," she said blandly, "I am embarrassed for you that you can't."

She clapped her hand over the gall of bone matter welted over the lock. Then she drew it back, and—with all the self-affinity of chewing gum or glue—it travelled *back* with her hand, a gummy web of about a finger's length, the point of origin vibrating madly as a bead of sweat appeared at her temple. Palamedes Sextus sucked in a breath—and then the stuff snapped back, like flexible plastic, rubbering together sullenly in an immovable lump. Harrow tried again. Her fingers kept flexing in and out impotently, kneading, and she turned her head away and closed her eyes. She stretched the stuff away a whole hand's length—and then it broke, re-formed, scattered back like a reverse explosion. She tried again. And again; and again after that.

The paint on Harrow's forehead was shiny with blood sweat now. It bubbled up in greyish-pink rivulets. It shone around each nostril. Before she knew what she was doing, Gideon found that she had moved in to flank her: hiding what she was doing from Sextus's impassive gaze, rolling up the long black sleeve of her Ninth cloak, mouth moving before her brain did. "Battery up," she muttered.

It was the first thing Gideon had said to her since Harrow had stalked from the Sixth House quarters, taut with what had seemed to be the world's most dismissive disappointment, a disdainful black crow of a girl. Her adept opened one baleful black eye.

"Pardon?"

"I said *saddle up, sunshine.* Come on. You know what to do."

"I manifestly don't, and never tell me to *saddle up, sunshine* ever again."

"I'm saying to you: siphon me."

"Nav—"

"Sixth are watching," said Gideon, brutally.

At the last remark—which was a sledgehammer of a statement, not a stiletto—Harrowhark fell silent. Her expression was resentful in a way that her cavalier could not understand, except to parse it as grim hatefulness that—once again—the only path open to her was that of using her cavalier, a girl who had screwed up so badly as to provide the universe at large with a new understanding of *screwup.* All she said was, "You don't have to roll up your sleeve, you nincompoop," and then the leaching, squirming feeling of siphoning began.

It was just as bad as the first time, but unquestionably shorter than Harrow's long and awful walk from one side of the avulsion room to the other; and now Gideon knew what to expect. The pain was a familiar brand of terrible. She did not cry out, though that probably would have been more dignified: instead she toned it down to a series of wheezes and grunts as her necromancer took something from her that sandpapered her soul. Her blood boiled in her veins, then froze abruptly and grazed her innards with each pump of her heart.

Harrowhark curved her fingers, and she pulled. At the end of a very long moment she held an inert sphere of compressed ash and bone, grey and pockmarked, tamed to submission. The lock was as clear and as clean as though the obstruction had never existed. The pair from the Sixth stared at them. Eventually, Palamedes leaned down to squint through the newly cleared keyhole.

"Don't get used to using her that way, Nonagesimus," he said, and disapproval had crept into his voice. "It's not good theory and it's not good morals."

It was Gideon who said, "You're sounding more and more like Silas Octakiseron."

"Ouch," said Palamedes, sincerely. Then he straightened up. "Well. It's off, for good or for ill. Maybe we should've left it on, but I want to make it—them—whatever—nervous. Even a supernatural force is vulnerable." He let his finger rest on the lock. "Did you hide the last key too?" he asked it quietly. "Or are we racing you to it? Well, *move faster*, dickhead."

Camilla cleared her throat, maybe because her necromancer was talking to a door. He dropped his hand. "Owe you another one, Ninth," he said to her skull-faced necromancer. "You get a free question."

"It's unattractive to set yourself up as the repository of all knowledge, Sextus."

"'Set up' nothing."

"How many keys are in play now?"

Palamedes suddenly grinned. It was a curious act of alchemy that turned his raw-boned, plain face into something magnetic: very nearly good looking, instead of being the act of three jawbones meeting a chin. "We've got three," he said. "You've got two—or, you did, until you gave one to Lady Septimus, as per the agreement she'd offered me first. You should have haggled for more, by the way— she offered me a look at the keys she already had. But I suspect you didn't need her to sweeten the deal." Harrow didn't react, though Gideon bet she was swearing up a storm in some vile crypt of her brain. "The Eighth had one, and now they've got two more through trickery—Dulcinea's. But that still leaves one spare."

"The Third?" suggested Harrow.

"Nope. Cam heard them talking this morning, they've got nothing. And it's not the Second unless they lied to me after the duel, which, you know, Second. So watch your back. The Second are still looking for a way to shut the whole thing down, the Third don't like coming last, and the Eighth will take anything and justify the cost." He frowned. "It's the Third I'm least certain of. I don't know which twin to watch out for."

"The big one," said Harrow, without hesitation. Gideon was pretty sure both twins were the same size, and was surprised to discover that even the anatomist's gaze of Harrowhark Nonagesimus was not immune to the radiance coming off Princess Corona. "They're both only middling necromancers, but the big one is the dominant. She says *I*; the sister says *we*."

"Honestly a good point. Still not sure. Meet me tomorrow night and we'll start the theorem exchange, Ninth. I've got to think."

"The missing key," said Harrow.

"The missing key."

After the brief goodbyes, both of the Sixth House turned away in their drab greys—until, much to Gideon's acute dislike, Palamedes spun around. He had not met her eye the whole time, maybe out of service to the fact that she was avoiding his, but now he looked her dead in the face. She swallowed down the urge to say: *I'm sorry, I don't hate you, I just kind of hate me right now.* Instead, she coolly looked away, which was the opposite of an apology.

"Keep an eye on her, Nav," said Palamedes quickly. And then he turned to catch up with Camilla.

"He's getting presumptuous," said the Reverend Daughter, watching their retreating backs.

"I think he wasn't—talking about you."

They kept a long and drawn-out silence, as unwillingly stretchy as the ashes and bone shards that had been clumped over the keyhole. "Good point," said Harrow. "That reminds me! I now officially ban you from seeing Lady Septimus."

"Are we having this conversation? Are we *really having this conversation*?"

Harrow's face was pinched into an expression of deliberate patience. "Nav," she said. "Take it from me. Dulcinea Septimus is dangerous."

"You're nuts. Dulcinea Septimus can't even blow her nose. I'm sick of how weird you're getting over this."

"And yet you've never thought about how she still managed to get a key—how am *I* being *weird*?"

"I don't know," said Gideon, heartily fed up with the whole thing. "I don't know! Maybe it's because whenever she's mentioned, you effortlessly tick both boxes for *jealous* and *creep*?"

"If you looked in a dictionary you'd find it's *envious*, and I'm hardly envious of—"

"No, it's one hundred percent jealous," said Gideon recklessly, "on account of how you're always doing this when it looks like she's taking up my time."

There was a horrible pause.

"I have been lax," said her necromancer, steadily ignoring this last statement like it was a dump Gideon had taken in the hallway. She took her gloves from Gideon's awkward hands and slipped them back over her fingers. "I have indulged myself in apathy while you attached yourself to every weirdo in Canaan House." ("You cannot possibly call anyone a weirdo," said Gideon.) "No more. We now have less to hide, but more to lose."

"She's got nobody if that thing comes after her. It's a death sentence."

"Yes. She has no cavalier now," said Harrow. "It's not a question of *if*. It's a question of *when*. Let the dead reclaim the dead. You won't take my word when I've proven my judgement before? Fine. You're still barred from her sickroom."

"No," said Gideon. "Nah. Nope. Denied. That's not me."

"You're not her bodyguard."

"I never pledged to be yours either," said Gideon. "Not really."

"Yes, you did," snapped Harrowhark. "You agreed to act as my cavalier primary. You agreed to devote yourself to the duties of a cavalier. Your misunderstanding of what that entailed does not make you any less beholden to what your duty actually is—"

"I promised to fight for you. You promised me my freedom. There's a hell of a good chance that I'm not going to get it, and I know it. We're all dying here! Something's after us! The only thing I can do is try to keep as many of us as I can alive for as long as I can, and hope that we work something out! You're the ignorant sack of eyeballs who doesn't understand what a cavalier is, Harrow, you just take whatever I give you—"

"Melodrama, Griddle, never became you," said her adept flatly. "You've never complained about any of our previous transactions."

"My ass, *transactions*. What happened to 'I cannot afford to not have you trust me, now I'm going to make awkward eye contact and act like you broke my nose just because you hugged me once'?"

An indrawn breath. "Don't mock my—"

"Mock you? I should kick your ass for you!"

"I'm making a reasonable request," said Harrowhark, who had taken her gloves off and on again three times and was now examining her fingernails as though bored. The only reason Gideon had not already tried to deck her was that her eyelashes were trembling in rage, and also because she'd never hit Harrow before and was tremendously afraid that once she started she wouldn't stop. "I ask you to draw back and reprioritise the Ninth in what—as you've said—is a dangerous time."

"I've got my priorities straight."

"Nothing you have done in the past two days suggests that."

Gideon went cold. "Fuck you. Fuck you, fuck you, fuck you. *I didn't mean to let Jeannemary die.*"

"For God's sake, I didn't mean—"

"Fuck *you*," Gideon added again, for emphasis. She found herself laughing in that awful, high way that was totally devoid of humour. "Fuck. We don't deserve to still be around—have you realised that yet? Have you realised that this whole thing has been about the union of necromancer *and* cavalier from start to finish? We should be toast. If they're measuring this on the strength of that—we're the walking dead. Magnus the Fifth was a better cavalier than I am. Jeannemary the Fourth was ten times the cavalier I am. They should be alive and we should be bacteria food. Two big bags of algor mortis. We're alive through dumb luck and Jeannemary isn't and you're acting like me letting Dulcinea die is all that's standing between you and Lyctorhood—"

"Stop worshipping the sound of your own voice, Nav, and listen to me—"

"Harrow, I hate you," said Gideon. "I never stopped hating you. I will always hate you, and you will always hate me. Don't forget that. It's not like I ever can."

Harrow's mouth twisted so much that it should have been a reef knot. Her eyes closed briefly, and she sheathed her hands inside her gloves. The tension should have deflated then, but it didn't: like a pricked boil, it got full and shiny and hot. Gideon found she had swallowed six times in ten seconds and that the inside of her chest felt dry and bright. Her necromancer said evenly: "Griddle, you're incorrect."

"How—"

"Nothing stands between myself and Lyctorhood," said Harrowhark, "and you are not a part of the equation. Don't get carried away by the Sixth's ideas. The tests are not concerned with some frankly sickening rubric of sentiment and obedience; they're testing me and me alone. By the end, neither I nor the Ninth will need you for this pantomime. You may hate me all you wish; I still don't even remember about you half the time."

She turned away from Gideon. She did not walk away, but stood there for a moment in the simple arrogance of showing the other girl her back—of giving Gideon, with a sword in her scabbard, unfettered access to the back of her rib cage. Harrow said, "You're banned from seeing Septimus. The quicker she shuffles off, the better. If I were in her position . . . I would have already thrown myself out the window."

"Stand in front of a window now and I'll do the hard part," said Gideon.

"Oh, take a nap," snapped Harrowhark.

Gideon very nearly did lay hands on her then, and probably should have.

"If you don't need me, release me to the Seventh House," she said, very slow and very calm, like she was reading at a service. "I'd rather serve—Dulcinea dying—than the living Reverend Daughter."

Harrowhark turned to leave—airily, casually really, as though she and Gideon had finished a conversation about the weather. But then she inclined her head back to Gideon a little, and the fragment of her expression that Gideon saw was as wheezing and airless as a blow to the solar plexus.

"When I release you from my service, Nav," her necromancer said, "you will know about it." And she walked away.

Gideon decided, then and there, her betrayal.

28

HALF AN HOUR LATER, Gideon Nav stood before the doors of the Eighth House quarters, in front of an *extremely* befuddled Colum the Eighth. In the misty red recesses of her mind this traitorous act was the correct thing to do, though she couldn't yet quite decide why.

"Your uncle wanted me," she said. "So. Here I am."

The cavalier looked at her. She had obviously interrupted him in the middle of some domestic housekeeping, which would have been extremely funny at any other time. The flawless white leather and scale mail pauldrons were gone; he was in his white breeches and a slightly dingy undershirt and he was holding a *very* oily cloth. The shabbiness of the cloth and the undershirt looked even dingier against the scintillating Eighth whiteness of the trousers. She had never been alone with Colum the Eighth before. Outside his uncle's shadow he was just as patchy and discoloured, as though he had a liver inflammation; he was still a leathery yellow-brown, and his hair was similar, which made him look the same all over. It was startling to realise that he was maybe a little younger than Magnus. He looked worn-out and secondhand.

"You came alone?" he said, in his perpetually scratchy voice.

"You'd know if my necromancer was here."

"Yes," said Colum. He looked as though he were on the verge of saying something, and then decided against it. Instead he said, "Sword and second, please."

"What? I'm not disarming—"

"Look," he said, "I'd be a fool not to make you. Bear with me."

"That's not part of the deal—"

"There's nothing in here to hurt you," said Colum. "I swear it by my honour. So—give over."

There was nothing likeable about the wiry, rue-eyed man, but there was something sincere about him, and also he had maybe the worst job in the history of the world. Gideon did not trust him. But she handed over her rapier and she handed over her glove, and she trotted after him unwillingly.

The red fog was clearing a little, and now Gideon was regretting the rage that had taken her from Harrow to Teacher and from Teacher's directions to the rooms that housed the Eighth House. They had been put in high-vaulted, squarish rooms with very high windows, airy and gracious; what furniture they had been given would remain a mystery, because they'd gotten rid of it all. The living space had been mopped until it hurt. It was baffling to see such cleanliness in Canaan House; someone had even given them a pot of furniture polish, and the wooden floorboards beneath Gideon's feet smelled oiled and fresh. They had kept a writing desk and chair, and a table and two stools, and that was all. The table was covered with a white cloth. There was a book on the writing desk. The rest was prim and sparse.

The only splash of colour was an enormous portrait of the Emperor as Kindly Master, with an expression of beatific peace. It was placed directly opposite the table, so that anyone sitting there would have him as an unavoidable dinner guest. In one corner was a polished metal box with Colum's targe sitting precariously on a nest of hand weights.

Her sword and glove were both placed carefully next to the door, which she appreciated. Colum disappeared into another room. He reappeared a few minutes later with Silas in tow, kitted out in his perpetual uniform of cornea-white silk and silver-white chain, and his long floating wings of a robe. Gideon must have caught him mid-ablutions, because his chalk-coloured hair was wet and tousled as though it had just been rubbed with a towel. It seemed frivolously long, and she realised she had never seen it except pinned back. He pulled over the chair from the writing desk and sat while his cavalier produced a comb from somewhere, sorting out the still-damp locks of thin white.

Silas looked as though he had not slept well lately. Shadows beneath the eyes made his sharp and relentless chin sharper and even more relentless.

"You must be aware that I would never suffer a shadow cultist in an Eighth sanctuary," he said, "unless I thought it was of huge moral utility."

"Thanks," said Gideon. "Can I sit?"

"You may."

"Give me a moment," said Colum. "I'll finish up, then make the tea."

She squeaked a stool away from the table, wilfully working the back legs into the shining wood. The necromancer shut his eyes as though the sound hurt him. "I was never part of the Locked Tomb congregation," she said, settling herself down. "If you *had* talked to Sister Glaurica, you would have known that."

Having combed the hair to his satisfaction, Colum began separating sections at the back with the teeth of the comb. Silas ignored this treatment as though it happened so often it was not worth attention. Gideon once again thanked her lucky stars that she had not had a traditional cavalier's training.

"A rock does not have to make a vow that it is a rock," said Silas tiredly. "You are what you are. Take your hood off. Please."

The *please* was second cousin to an afterthought. Gideon pulled back her hood a little unwillingly, letting it fall on her shoulders, with the now-strange feeling of a nude head. Silas's eyes were not on her face, now fully exposed, but on her hair, which badly needed a trim.

"I wonder where you come from," he remarked. "Your mother had the same hair phenotype. Unusual . . . perhaps she was Third."

Gideon swallowed.

"Don't," she said. "Don't make cryptic comments about my—my

mother. You don't know the first thing about her, or me, and it's just going to piss me off. When I'm pissed off, I walk out. Are we clear?"

"As crystal," said the necromancer of the Eighth. "But you misunderstand. This isn't an interrogation. I was more interested in the story of your mother than I was in you, when we questioned Glaurica. You were an accidental inclusion. Glaurica confused the erroneous with the useful. But ghosts always do."

"*Ghosts?*"

"Revenants, to be explicit," said Silas. "Those rare and determined spirits who search out the living before they pass, unbidden, by clinging to scraps of their former lives. I was surprised that a woman like Glaurica made the transition. She did not last long."

Her vertebrae did not turn to ice, but it would've been a lie to say they didn't cool down considerably.

"Glaurica's dead?"

Silas took an infuriatingly long drink of water. The pallid column of his throat moved. "They died on the way back to their home planet," he said, wiping his mouth. "Their shuttle exploded. Curious, considering it was a perfectly good Cohort shuttle with an experienced pilot. This was the shuttle you had intended to commandeer, was it not?"

Ortus would never rhyme *melancholy* with *my mortal folly* again. Gideon did not confirm or deny. "I don't know the full story," admitted Silas. "I don't need to. I am not here to read out all the secrets of your life and startle you into saying anything. I'm here to talk about the children. How many in your generation, Gideon the Ninth? Not infants. But your peers, your age group."

Not infants. Maybe Glaurica had kept some secrets after all. Or— more like—her spirit chose to shriek back into existence solely to complain about the two things that had been of utmost importance to her: her sad dead sack of a son, and the sacred bones of her sad dead husband. Gideon held her tongue. Silas pressed, "Yourself? The Reverend Daughter?"

"What do you want, a census?"

"I want you to think about why you and Harrowhark Nonagesimus now represent an entire generation," he said, and he leant forward onto his elbows. His eyes were very intense. His nephew was still braiding his hair, which only somewhat lessened the effect. "I want you to think about the deaths of two hundred children, when you and she alone lived."

"Okay, look, this is wacky," said Gideon. "You've picked on exactly the wrong thing to slam Harrow with. If you want to talk about how she's a corrupt tyrant, I'm all ears. But I know about the flu. She wasn't even born yet. I was, what, one year old, so I didn't do it. There was vent bacteria in the creche and the schoolroom hall, and it took out all the kids and one of the teachers before they found out what it was."

This had made perfect sense to her, always: not only were the children of the Ninth unusually sickly and decrepit anyway—the Ninth House only seemed to truck with the pallid, defective, and upset—but among so much malign decay nobody would have noticed a ventilation problem until it was far too late. She had always privately suspected that she had lived due to the other children avoiding her. The youngest had gone first, and the eldest who were caring for the youngest, and then everyone was gone from the age of nineteen down. A whole generation of holy orders. Harrow had been the only birth amidst a sea of tiny tombs.

"Vent bacteria does not kill immunoefficient teenagers," said Silas.

"You've never seen a Ninth House teenager."

"Vent bacteria," said Silas again, "does not kill immunoefficient teenagers."

It made no sense. He didn't know that Harrow was the last baby born. The Ninth House had been jealous of its dwindling population for generations. Bumping off any child, let alone its youngest crop of nuns and cenobites, would be a horrifying waste of resources. The creche flu had been an extinction event. "I don't get it," Gideon said. "Are you trying to make out like the Reverend Father and Mother killed hundreds of their own kids?"

He did not answer her. He took another long draw of his water. Colum had finished the braid and pinned it back, perfecting the usual severe silhouette of the Master's pale head, after which he measured tiny spoonfuls of black tea into a jug to steep cold. He then lowered himself down onto a stool a little way away from the table, close to the door and face to the window like a true paranoid. The cavalier took a pile of what looked to be darning and began to run a nervous white seam up a pair of white trousers. The Eighth House must all be martyrs to stains, she thought.

"The Ninth House is a House of broken promises," said Silas. "The Eighth House remembers that they were not meant to live. They had one job—one rock to roll over one tomb; one act of guardianship, to live and die in a single blessedness—and they made a cult instead. A House of mystics who came to worship a terrible thing. The ruling Reverend Father and Mother are the bad seeds of a furtive crop. I do not know why the Emperor suffered that shadow of a House. That mockery of his name. A House that would keep lamps lit for a grave that was meant to pass into darkness is a House that would kill two hundred children. A House that would kill a woman and her son simply for attempting to leave is a House that would kill two hundred children."

Gideon felt grimy and unsettled. "I need a better motivation than the fact that the Ninth House sucks," she said. "Why? Why kill two hundred kids? More importantly, why two hundred kids and not me or Harrow?"

Silas looked at her over steepled fingers.

"You tell me, Gideon the Ninth," he said. "You are the one who tried to leave in a shuttle they planted a bomb in."

Gideon was silent.

"I do not think any scion of the Reverend Mother and the Reverend Father should become a Lyctor," said Silas softly. "The open grave of the Ninth House should not produce its own revenant. In fact, I am unsure that any of us should become Lyctor. Since when was power goodness, or cleverness truth? I myself no longer wish to ascend, Gideon. I've told you what I know, and I assume you will understand when I say I must take your keys from you."

Her spine jolted her upright in her chair. The dust-coloured fingers paused on their bleached seam.

"That's what this is about," said Gideon, almost disappointed.

"My conscience is clear. I ask for the good of all the Houses."

"What if I say *no*?"

"Then I will challenge you for them."

"My sword—"

"You may find the challenge hard without it," said Silas Octakiseron, quiet and resigned in his triumph.

Gideon couldn't help darting a glance at Colum, half-expecting to find his sword already in his hand and a grim smile on his face. But he was standing with his needlework tumbled to the floor, his face closed like a fist and his shoulders so set each tendon looked like it was flossing his clavicular joints. He was brown-eyed and baleful, but he was not looking at her.

"Master," he said, and stopped. Then: "I told her there'd be no violence here."

Silas's eyes never left Gideon's, so they did not see his cavalier's face. "There's no sin in that, Brother Asht."

"I—"

"An oath to the Ninth is as medicine to sand," the necromancer said. "It sinks from sight and yields no benefit. She knows this as well as any, and better than some. The Ninth heart is barren, and the Ninth heart is black."

Gideon opened her mouth for a witty riposte—*Well, fuck to you too!*—but Colum got in first, to her infinite surprise. "I'm not worried about the Ninth's heart, Uncle."

"Brother Asht," said Silas, quite gently, "your heart is true."

"Every day we spend here I'm less sure about that," said Colum.

"I share your feelings, but—"

"I said to her, '*I swear on my honour.*'"

"We will waste no truth on liars," said Silas, his voice still colourless but harder now, like water to ice: reminding, not reassuring. "Nor pledges on the damned."

"I *said*," repeated Colum, slowly, "'*I swear on my honour.*' What does that mean to you?"

Gideon stayed very still, like a strung-up animal, but she let her eyes slide sideways to the door. Sudden movement might let her pick up her sword and get the hell out of there before this terrible uncle-nephew soap opera climaxed in beating her like a gong, but it might also remind them she existed and that they could have this heart-to-heart later. Silas had shifted restlessly in his seat, and he was saying: "I will not dissect words and meanings with you like a mountebank, Brother. Leave the semiotics to the Sixth. Their sophists love nothing more than proving *up* spelled differently is *down*. If a wasted oath pains you I will lead you in atonement later, but for now—"

"I am your cavalier," said his cavalier. This shut Silas off mid-flow. "I've got my sword. I've got my honour. Everything else is yours."

"Your sword is mine also," said Silas. His hands were gripping the finials of his chair, but his voice was calm and even and actually sympathetic. "You need take no action. If your honour must remain unsullied, I may have your sword without asking for it."

He raised his hand, and the white linen sleeve fell away from the pale chain cuff. Gideon remembered the blood-stuffy room where Abigail and Magnus lay, and she remembered all the colour pulled from the room like it was just so much fast fabric dye. She knew that this was a game over, and her eyes slid sideways from the door and onto Colum, who was—looking right at her.

Their stares met for a single hot second. This single second felt like so long and stretched a pause that her overwound nerves very nearly went *ping* like elastic and fired her clean across the room. Then Colum seemed to make a decision.

"Once upon a time you would've taken everything I said as gospel," he said, in a very different voice. "I used to think that was worse than now . . . but I was wrong."

The hand faltered. Silas snapped his head around to stare at the older man. It was the first time he'd looked anywhere but at Gideon since she entered the room. "I urge you to recall yourself," he said shortly.

"I recall myself perfectly," said Colum. "You don't. You did, once. When you and I started this, when you weren't even twelve. When you thought I knew everything."

The fingers curled inward, just slightly, before straightening out again as though some inner resolve had stiffened. "This is not the time."

Colum said: "I respected the child. At times I can't stand the man, Si."

Silas's voice had sunk to a dead whisper: "You made an oath—"

"*Oath?* Ten years of training, before you were even born. Oath? Three brothers with different blood types, because we couldn't tell what you'd be and which of us you'd need. Ten years of antigens, antibodies, and waiting—for you. I am the oath. I was engineered into a man who doesn't—pick and choose his *decencies*!"

His voice had risen to fill the room. This left Silas Octakiseron perfectly white and still. Colum jerked his chin hard toward Gideon, and she noticed dimly that it was just another version of the elfin, fork-tine chin on Silas. He turned and strode toward the door. Gideon, completely out of her depth but sensing escape on some automatic rodent-brain level, started out of her chair and followed. Silas stayed where he was.

When Colum reached the sword, he picked it up, and Gideon had just a second to worry that he was now going to exploit some insane religious loophole and kill her with her own weapon. But this was beneath her. When Colum held her sword out to her, horizontally in one hand, it was as cavalier to cavalier. His expression was perfectly calm now, as though the anger had never even surfaced: maybe it hadn't. And his eyes were the eyes of a man who had just tied his own noose.

She took her blade. She now owed him very badly, which sucked.

"The next time we meet," he said beneath his breath, as monolithic and impassive as when she'd arrived, "I think it's likely one of us will die."

"Yeah," Gideon said, "yeah," instead of "I'm sorry."

Colum picked up the knuckle-knife and handed that to her as well. "Get away from here," he said, and it sounded more warning than command.

He moved away from her again. Gideon was sorely tempted to take him *with* her and away from Silas, sitting still and pale in his great white room, but she felt that probably that wasn't going to happen. She also thought about skidding off a couple middle fingers to Silas around Colum's shoulders, but concluded the moral high ground was sometimes worth holding on to. So she left.

As she walked away, she braced for a sudden burst of angry voices, yelling, recriminations, maybe even a cry of pain. But there was only silence.

29

In a welter of stupefaction Gideon wandered the halls of Canaan House, unwilling to go home. She walked down the neglected halls and dimly realised she could no longer smell the mould, having smelled it for so long that it had become indistinguishable from the air around her. She stood in the cool shadows of putrefied doorways, trailing her fingers over the porous bumps and splinters of very old wood. Skeleton servitors rattled past her, holding baskets or ancient watering cans, and when she looked out through a filth-streaked window she saw a couple of them standing on the battlements, lit up by white sunshine, holding long poles over the side. Her brain registered this as making total sense. Their ancient finger bones gleamed on the reels, and as she watched one pulled a jerking, flapping fish to the apex of its extreme journey from ocean to phalange. The construct carefully put it in a bucket.

She passed the great atrium with the dry, dubious fountain, and she found Teacher there. He was sitting in front of the fountain, in a chair with a ruptured cushion, praying, or thinking, or both. His shining head was drooping, but he gave her a weary smile.

"How I hate the water," he said, as though this conversation was one they'd had before and he was simply continuing it. "I'm not sorry that this has dried up. Ponds . . . rivers . . . waterfalls . . . I loathe them all. I wish they had not filled the pool downstairs. It's a terrible portent, I said."

"But you're surrounded by sea," said Gideon.

"Yes," said Teacher unexpectedly, "it is a bit of a pisser."

Gideon laughed—slightly hysterical—and he joined in, but his eyes filled with tears.

"Poor child," he said, "we're all sorry. We never intended this to happen, none of us. The poor child."

Gideon might've been the child in question; she might've not. She strongly did not care either way. She soon found herself wandering through the little vestibule and past the gently lapping pool that Teacher hated: the low whitewashed ceiling, the softly gleaming tiles. Past the glass-fronted doors, which stood open, lay abandoned towels on the floor of the training room where the cavaliers practised their art, and what was unquestionably Naberius's prissily pinned-up jacket. And inside the training room was Corona.

Her lovely golden hair was stuck up in sweaty tendrils atop her head, and she had stripped down to her camisole and her shorts, which Gideon was far too befuddled to appreciate but not too befuddled to overlook. Her long tawny limbs were leprous here and there with chalk dust, and she held a rapier and a knife. She was fixed in the classic training attitude, arm coming down in a slowly controlled arc through the movements of *thrust—half step—knife thrust—retreat,* and there was a deep red flush of exertion on her face. Her necromantic robe lay abandoned in a thin filmy heap at the side, and Gideon watched, fascinated, through the open door.

Coronabeth spun to face her. Her stance was good: her eyes were very beautiful, like amethysts.

"Have you ever seen a necromancer hold a sword before?" she asked gaily.

"No," said Gideon, "I thought their arms would all flop around."

The Third princess laughed. The flush on her cheeks was a little bit too hot and pink. "My sister's do," she said. "She can't hold her arms up long enough to braid her hair. Do you know, Ninth, I've always wanted to challenge you?" This was said with a low, intense breathlessness, ruined by the addendum: "Babs said it was incredible."

This was maybe the worst statement of a day so filled with terrible statements that they crowded one another, like spectators at a duel. Once Gideon would have loved to hear Corona talk to her with that low, breathy intensity, maybe saying "Your biceps . . . they're eleven out of ten," but right now she did not want anyone to talk to her at all.

"If I never fought Naberius again I'd be happy," she said. "He's a prick."

Corona laughed in a hard, light trill. Then she said smilingly: "You might have to, eventually. But I don't mean him."

She lunged. Gideon drew, because despite her brain's long droning white noise her nervous system was still full of adrenaline. She slipped her hand into her gauntlet and was cautious when she met Corona's shiny Third blade with her own—was surprised at the force behind the blow, at the manic energy in the other girl's eyes. Gideon pushed down, forcing Corona's blade aside—and Corona moved with her, sliding her blade down with the pressure, her footwork taking her into a beautiful disengage. She pressed, and it was only a hasty parry on Gideon's part that kept the Princess at bay.

Corona was breathing hard. For a moment Gideon thought that this was the necromancer weakness coming to bear—the lungs already sagging under the strain—but she realised that Corona was excited, and also very nervous. It was like the queenly, confident Corona of old, masked over badly damaged stuffing. This lasted just a moment. She gave a sudden purple, furtive look over Gideon's shoulder, stiffening and retreating backward, and there was an indrawn breath from the doorway.

"Drop it," barked Naberius Tern.

Not fucking likely, thought Gideon—but he skirted far around her reach, lunging past her to curl a hand hard around Corona's forearm. His eyes were bugged out with alarm. He was in his undershirt, with his collection of rangy and sinuous muscles all being brought to bear on his princess. She sagged mutinously, like a child caught fist-deep in the lollies jar, and he was putting his arm around her. "You can't," he was saying, and Gideon realised: he was also terrifically afraid. "You *can't*."

Corona made a giving-up sound of incoherent, fruitless rage, muffled by Naberius's arm. It was, thankfully, not tears. She said something that Gideon missed, and Naberius said in reply: "I *won't* tell her. You can't do this, doll, not now."

For the second time that day, Gideon drifted away from a scenario she was utterly shut out of, something she did not want to be privy to. The saline tickled her nose as she sheathed her rapier and backtracked away, before Naberius decided he might as well challenge for her keys while she was there, but as she darted a glance over her shoulder he had utterly discarded her presence: he had placed his arm like a crossbar over Corona's collarbone, and she had bitten him, apparently to soothe her own obscure feelings.

Gideon wished for no more part in any of this. Gideon went home.

* * *

Her feet took her, heavy and unwilling, back to the bone-wreathed door of the Ninth quarters: her hands pushed open the door hard, recklessly. There was no sign of anyone within. The door to the main bedroom was closed, but Gideon pushed that open too, without even knocking.

There was nobody there. With the curtains drawn Harrow's room was dark and still, the bed inhabiting the centre of the room like a big hulking shadow. The sheets were rumpled and unmade. She could see the foetal-curl dent on the mattress where Harrow slept. Pens spilled off the mildew-spotted dressing table, and books propped up other, usefuller books on the drawers. The whole room smelled like Harrow: old Locked Tomb veils and preserving salts, ink, the faint smell of her sweat. It skewed harder toward the preserving salts. Gideon stumbled around blindly, kicking the corner of the four-poster bed in the same way that Corona had sunk her teeth into her cavalier's arm, stubbing her toe, not caring.

The wardrobe door was ajar. Gideon made a beeline toward it, pulling it open violently, though she had no heart to sew shut the cuffs on all of Harrowhark's shirts as she once might have done. She half-expected bone wards to yank both her arms from their sockets, but there was nothing. There was no guard. There was nothing to have ever stopped her doing this. This drove her demented, for some reason. She slapped the rainbow of black clothes aside: neatly patched trousers, neatly pressed shirts, the formal vestments of the Reverend Daughter tied up inside a net bag and hung from a peg. If she looked at them too long she would feel tight-chested, so she very forcibly didn't.

There was a box at the bottom of the cupboard—a cheap polymer box with dents in it, tucked beneath a pair of Harrowhark's boots. She would not have noticed it except that there had been a cursory attempt to hide it with the aforementioned boots and a badly ripped cloak. It was about a forearm's length on every side. A sudden exhaustion of everything Harrow had ever locked away drove her to mindlessly pull it out. She eased off the pockmarked top with her thumbs, expecting diaries, or prayer bones, or underwear, or lithographs of Harrow's mother.

With numb fingers, Gideon removed the severed head of Protesilaus the Seventh.

IN THE FLIMSY-PAPERED LIVING room of the Sixth quarters, Gideon sat staring into a steaming mug of tea. It was grey with the sheer amount of powdered milk stirred into it, and it was her third cup. She had been terribly afraid that they'd put medicines into it, or tranquillizers or something: when she wouldn't drink, both necromancer and cavalier had taken sips to prove it was unadulterated, with expressions that plainly said *idiot*. Palamedes had been the one to wait patiently next to her while she had thrown up lavishly in the Sixth's toilet.

Now she sat, haggard and empty, on a spongy mattress they had pulled out as a chair. Protesilaus's head sat, dead-eyed, on the desk. It looked exactly as it had in life: as though, upon being separated from its trunk, it had entered into some perfect state of preservation to remain boring forever. It looked about as lively as it had when she'd met him. Palamedes was investigating the white gleam of the spinal column at the nape of the neck for maybe the millionth time.

Camilla had shoved a mug of hot tea into Gideon's hands, strapped two swords to her back, and disappeared. This had all happened before Gideon could protest and now she was left alone with Palamedes, her discovery, and a cluster headache. Things were happening too much. She took a hot mouthful, swilled tea around her teeth, and swallowed mechanically. "She's mine."

"You've said that five times now."

"I mean it. Whatever goes down—whatever happens—you have to let me do it. You have to."

"Gideon—"

"What do I do," she said, quite casually, "if she's the murderer?"

His interest in the spinal column was not abating. Palamedes had slipped his glasses down his long craggy nose, and was holding the head upside down like he was emptying a piggy bank. He had even shone light into the nose and ears and horrible warp of the throat. "I don't know," he said. "What do you do?"

"What would you do if you discovered Camilla was a murderer?"

"Help her bury the body," said Palamedes promptly.

"*Sextus.*"

"I mean it. If Camilla wants someone dead," he said, "then far be it from me to stand in her way. All I can do at that point is watch the bloodshed and look for a mop. One flesh, one end, and all that."

"Everyone wants to tell me about fleshes and ends today," said Gideon unhappily.

"There's a joke in there somewhere. You're sure there was nothing else along with the head—bone matter, fingernails, cloth?"

"I checked. I'm not a total tool, Palamedes."

"I trust Camilla. I trust that her reasons for ending someone's life would be logical, moral, and probably to my benefit," he said, sliding one fragile eyelid up an eyeball. "Your problem here is that you suspect that Harrow has killed people for much less."

"She didn't kill the Fourth or Fifth."

"Conjecture, but we'll leave it."

"Okay, so," said Gideon, putting her empty mug next to her mattress. "Um. You are now getting the impression that my relationship with her is more—fraught—than you might've guessed." ("You shock me," muttered Palamedes.) "But that doesn't change the fact that I've known her as long as she's lived. And I thought I knew how far she'd go, because I will tell you for free she has gone to some intensely shitty lengths, and I guess she's gone to some shittier lengths than I thought concerning me, but that's the thing—it's me, Sextus. It's always me. She nearly killed me half a dozen times growing up, but I always knew why."

Palamedes took off his glasses. He finally stopped molesting the head, and he pushed himself up and away from the desk; he sat down heavily on the mattress next to Gideon, skinny knees tucked up into his chest. "Okay. Why?" he asked simply.

"Because I killed her parents," said Gideon.

He did not say anything. He just waited, and in the space of that waiting, she talked. And she told him the beginning stuff—how she was born, how she grew up, and how she came to be the primary cavalier of the Ninth House—and she told him the secret she had kept for seven long and awful years.

* * *

Harrowhark had hated Gideon the moment she clapped eyes on her, but everyone did. The difference was that although most people ignored small Gideon Nav the way you would a turd that had sprouted legs, tiny Harrow had found her an object of tormentable fascination—prey, rival, and audience all wrapped up in one. And though Gideon hated the cloisterites, and hated the Locked Tomb, and hated the ghastly great-aunts, and hated Crux most of all, she was hungry for the Reverend Daughter's preoccupation. They were the only two children in a House that was otherwise busy getting gangrene.

Everyone acted as though the Emperor had personally resurrected Harrowhark just to bring them joy: she had been born healthy and whole, a prodigious necromancer, a perfect penitent nunlet. She was already mounting the ambo and reading out prayers even as Gideon began desperately praying herself that she might one day go to be an enlisted soldier, which she had wanted ever since Aiglamene—the only person Gideon didn't hate all the time—had told her she might be one. The captain had told her stories of the Cohort since Gideon was about three.

This was probably the best time of their relationship. Back then they clashed so consistently that they were with each other most of the time. They fought each other bloody, for which Harrow was not punished and Gideon was. They set elaborate traps, sieges, and assaults, and grew up in each other's pockets, even if it was generally while trying to grievously injure the other one.

By the time Harrow was ten years old, she had glutted herself on secrets. She had grown bored of ancient tomes, bored of the bones she had been raising since before she'd finished growing her first set of teeth, and bored of making Gideon run gauntlets of skeletons. At last she set her gaze on the one thing truly forbidden to her: Harrow became obsessed with the Locked Door.

There was no key to the Locked Door. Maybe there had never been a key to the Locked Door. It simply didn't open. What lay beyond would kill the trespasser before they'd cracked it wide enough to go through anyway, and what lay beyond *that*—long before ever getting to the tomb—would make them wish they were dead long before their final breath. The nuns dropped to their knees at the mere mention of what was through there. It was the brief delight of Gideon's life that the unnecessarily beatified Harrowhark Nonagesimus chose to ditch her sainthood and unlock it, and that Gideon had been witness to that fact.

Out of everyone who found Gideon Nav repellent, Harrow's parents had always found her particularly so. They were chilly, joyless Ninth House necromancers of the type that Silas Octakiseron seemed to think universally inhabited Drearburh: black in heart, power, and appearance. Once when she had touched a fold of Priamhark Noniusvianus's vestments he had held her down with skeletal hands and whipped her till she howled. It was only out of the most desperate perversity that she ran straight to them to tell her tale: out of some baffling desire to show some evidence of House loyalty, to absolutely drop Harrow in the shit, to get the pat on the head she knew she'd earned for preserving the integrity and the fervid spirit of the House—precisely the qualities she was so ceaselessly accused of lacking. She felt no flicker of guilt or doubt. Just hours before, she'd wrestled Harrow down in the dirt, and Harrow had scratched until she'd had half of Gideon's face beneath her fingernails.

So she told them. And they listened. They had not said a word, either in praise or in censure, but they had listened. They had called for Harrow. And they had made Gideon leave. She waited outside the great dark doors of their room for a very long time, because they hadn't told her to go away, just go out of the room, and because she was a shitty trash child she wanted to relish the one chance she had of hearing Harrowhark raked over the coals. But she waited a whole hour and never heard a damn thing, let alone Harrow's screams as she was confined to oss duty until she turned thirty.

And then Gideon couldn't wait anymore. She pushed open the door and she walked in—and found Pelleamena and Priamhark hanging from the rafters, purple and dead. Mortus the Ninth, their huge and tragic cavalier, swung beside them from a rafter groaning with his bulk. And she walked in on Harrowhark, holding lengths of unused rope among the chairs her parents had kicked aside, with eyes like coals that had burnt away.

Harrow had beheld her. She had beheld Harrow. And nothing had ever gone right after that, never ever.

* * *

"I was eleven," said Gideon. "And here I am, narking all over again."

Palamedes did not say anything. He just sat there, listening as solemnly as if she had described some new type of novel necromantic theorem. Far from feeling cleansed by her impromptu confession, Gideon felt absolutely the opposite: dirty and muddy, terribly exposed, as though she had unbuttoned her chest and given him a good long look at what was inside her ribs. She was garbage from the neck to the navel. She was packed tight with a dry and dusty mould. She had been filled up with it since she was eleven, on the understanding that as long as she was attached to the House of the Ninth she could never make it go away.

Gideon took a long breath, then another.

"Harrow wants to become a Lyctor," she said. "She would do anything to become a Lyctor. She'd easily have killed Dulcinea's cavalier if she thought it would help her become a Lyctor. Nothing else matters to her. I know that now. In the last couple days, I sometimes thought—"

Gideon did not finish that sentence, which would have been "that she had stopped making it her top priority."

Palamedes said very gently, "You really should not need me to tell you that an eleven-year-old isn't responsible for the suicides of three grown adults."

"Of course I'm responsible," said Gideon disgustedly. "I made it happen."

"Yes," said Palamedes. "If you hadn't told Harrow's parents about the door, they would not have made the decision to end their lives. You inarguably caused it. But *cause* by itself is an empty concept. The choice to get up in the morning—the choice to have a hot breakfast or a cold one—the choice to do something thirty seconds faster, or thirty seconds slower—those choices cause all sorts of things to happen. That doesn't make you responsible. Here's a confession for you: I killed Magnus and Abigail."

Gideon blinked at him.

"If, the second I stepped off my shuttle," said the suddenly revealed double murderer blithely, "I had snatched Cam's dagger and put it straight through Teacher's throat, the Lyctoral trial could never have begun. There'd have been uproar. The Cohort would have arrived, I'd have been dragged away, and everyone else would have been sent safe back home. Because I didn't kill Teacher, the trial began, and because the trial began, Magnus Quinn and Abigail Pent are dead. So: I did it. It's my fault. All I ask is that you put some pen and flimsy in my cell so I can start on my memoirs."

Gideon blinked a couple more times. "No, hold up. That's stupid, they're not the same."

"I don't see why not," said the necromancer. "We both made decisions that led to bad things happening."

She rubbed at the bridge of her nose. "Octakiseron said you guys loved to mess with what words mean."

"The Eighth House thinks there's right and there's wrong," said

Palamedes wearily, "and by a series of happy coincidences they always end up being right. Look, Nav. You ratted out your childhood nemesis to get her in trouble. You didn't kill her parents, and she shouldn't hate you like you did, and *you* shouldn't hate you like you did."

He was peering at her through his spectacles. "Hey," she objected lamely, "I never said I hated myself."

"Evidence," he said, "outweighs testimony."

Awkwardly, and a bit brusquely, he took her hand. He squeezed it. They were both obviously embarrassed by this, but Gideon did not let go—not when she rummaged in the pocket of her robe with her other hand, and not when she passed over the scrumpled-up piece of flimsy that had bewildered her for so long.

He unscrumpled it, and read without reaction. She squeezed his hand like an oath, or a threat.

"This is from a Lyctor lab," he said eventually. "Isn't it?"

"Yeah," she admitted. "Is it—I mean—is it real?"

He looked at her. "It's nearly ten thousand years old, if that's what you mean."

"Well, I'm not," she said. "So . . . what the fuck, basically."

"The ultimate question," he agreed, returning his attention to the flimsy. "Can I borrow this? I'd like to look at it properly."

"Do *not* show it to anyone else," Gideon said, without really knowing why. Something about her name being on this ancient piece of garbage felt as dangerous as a live grenade. "I'm serious. It stays between us."

"I swear on my cavalier," he said.

"You can't even show her—"

They were interrupted by six short knocks on the door, followed by six long. Both sprang up to pull apart the interlaced lattice of deadbolts. Camilla came through, and with her, upright and calm, was Harrow. For one wacky moment Gideon thought that she and *Camilla* had been holding hands and that today was one huge rash of interhousal hand fondling, but then she realised that their wrists were cuffed together. Camilla was nobody's fool, though how she'd cuffed Harrow was going to be a tale of terror for another day.

Gideon did not look at her, and Harrow did not look at Gideon. Gideon very slowly put her hand on her sword, but for nothing. Harrow was looking at Palamedes.

She expected pretty much *anything*, but she didn't expect him to say—

"Nonagesimus—why didn't you tell me?"

"I didn't trust you," she said simply. "My original theory was that you'd done it. Septimus wasn't capable on her own, and it didn't seem far-fetched that you were working in concert."

"Will you believe me when I say we aren't?"

"Yes," she said, "because if you were that good you would have killed my cavalier already. I hadn't even intended to hurt him, Sextus, the head fell off the moment I pushed."

What?

"Then we go," said Palamedes. "We get everyone. We talk to her. I won't have any more conversations in the dark, or doubting of my intentions."

Gideon said helplessly, "Someone enlighten me, I am just a poor cavalier," but nobody paid her the slightest damn bit of attention even though she had her hand very forbiddingly on her sword. Harrow was ignoring her entirely in favour of Palamedes, and she was saying:

"I wasn't sure you'd be willing to go that far, even for the truth."

Palamedes looked at her with an expression as grey and airless as the ocean outside the window.

"Then you do not know me, Harrowhark."

* * *

They all crowded into Dulcinea's little hospital room: it was them and the priest with the salt-and-pepper braid, who scuttled out as though affrighted as they lined the room in stony array. The whole gang had arrived for party times. Palamedes had sent for all the survivors, though considering their current group-wide interest in killing one another the fact that they had bothered coming was nothing short of a miracle. The Second stood against the wall, their jackets less creased than their faces; Ianthe and Coronabeth sat fussily crowded up on each other's knees, with their cavalier close behind. Silas stood inside the door, Colum stood just behind him, and if anyone had wanted to take them all out then and there it would have been as simple as shutting the door and letting them all asphyxiate on Naberius Tern's pomade. It seemed so strange that this was now *all of them*.

The necromancer of the Seventh House was propped up on a bundle of fat cushions, looking calm and transparent. With every stridorous breath her shoulders shook, but her hair was perfectly brushed and her nightgown nightmarishly frilly. She had in her lap the box that contained Protesilaus's head, and when she drew it gently out—wholly unspoiled as if he were still alive—there were several indrawn breaths. Hers was not among them.

"My poor boy," she said, sincerely. "I'll never be able to put him back together now. Who took him apart? He's a wreck."

Palamedes steepled his fingers and leaned forward, greyly intent.

"Lady Septimus, Duchess of Rhodes," he said, very formally, "I put to you before everyone here—that this man was dead before you arrived, by shuttle, at the First House, and appeared alive only through deep flesh magic."

There was an immediate hubbub, uncalmed by his impatient *be quiet* gestures and the shoving of his spectacles up his nose. Among the collective mutters, Ianthe Tridentarius's acid drawl was loudest: "Well, this is the only interesting thing she's ever done."

Nearly as piercing was Captain Deuteros: "Impossible. He's been with us for weeks."

"It's not impossible at all," said Dulcinea herself. She had been gravely meeting Protesilaus's murky stare, as though trying to find something out, and now she settled the head on her lap. "The Seventh House have been perfecting the way of the beguiling corpse for years and years and years. It's just—not entirely allowed."

"It is unholy," said Silas, flatly.

"So is soul siphoning, my child," she said, in tones of deliberately celestial sweetness. "And it's *not* unholy—it's entirely useful and blameless; just not when you do it like this, which is the very old way. The Seventh aren't just soul-stoppers and mummifiers. Yes, Pro was dead before we even landed."

Gideon said, just as flatly as Silas: "Why?"

Those enormous flower-blue eyes turned to Gideon as though she were the only person in the room. There was no laughter in them, or else Gideon might have started to yell. Suddenly, the dying necromancer seemed enormously old; not with wrinkles, but with the sheer dignity and quiet with which she sat there, totally serene.

"This competition caught out my House," she said baldly. "Let me tell you the story. Dulcinea Septimus was never intended to be here, Gideon the Ninth . . . they would have preferred she be laid up at home and have another six months wrung out of her. It's an old story of the House. But there wasn't another necromantic heir. And there was a very good cavalier primary . . . so even if the necromantic heir was one bad cold away from full lung collapse . . . it was thought that he might even the odds. But then he had an accident."

Dulcinea fretted the dull hair of the head with her fingertips, then smoothed it out as if it were a doll's. "Hypothetically. If you were the Seventh House, and all your fortunes were now represented in two dead bodies, one breathing a little bit more than the other, wouldn't *you* consider something far-fetched? Let's say, by utilizing the way of the beguiling corpse, and hoping that nobody noticed that your House was DOA? I'm sorry for deceiving you, but I'm not sorry I came."

"That doesn't add up."

Harrow was stiff as concrete. Her eyes were huge and dark, and though only Gideon could tell, very agitated. "The spell you're talking about is not within the range of a normal necromancer, Septimus. Impossible for a necromancer in their prime, let alone a dying woman."

"A dying woman is the perfect necromancer," said Ianthe.

"I wish I could get rid of that idea. Maybe for the final ten minutes," said Palamedes. "The technical fact that dying enhances your necromancy is vitiated considerably by the fact that you can't make any use of it. You might have access to a very personal source of thanergy, but considering your organs are shutting down—"

"It's not possible," insisted Harrow, words hard and clipped in her mouth.

"You seem to know a lot about it. Well, I put it to you: Would it be possible for all the heads of the Seventh House," said Dulcinea calmly, "adepts of the perfect death—a Seventh House mystic secret, one that's been ours forever—working all in concert?"

"Perhaps initially, but—"

"King Undying," said Silas, primly disgusted. "It was a conspiracy."

"Oh, sit on it," said Dulcinea. "I know all about you and your house, Master Silas Octakiseron . . . the Emperor himself never bothered to speak out against beguiling corpsehood, but he did say that siphoning was the most dangerous thing any House had ever thought up, and ought only to be done with the siphoner in cuffs."

"That does not mitigate the penalty for performing a necromantic act of transgression—"

"I've no interest in meting out the justice of the tome," said Captain Deuteros, gruffly. "I know that's the Eighth House's prerogative. But at the same time, Master Octakiseron, we cannot afford this right now."

"A woman who would be party to this kind of magic," said Silas, "might be party to anything."

The woman who was party to that kind of magic and therefore maybe party to anything opened her mouth to speak, but instead had a coughing fit that seemed to start at her toes and go all the way up. Her spine arched; she bleated, and then began to moistly choke to death. Her face turned so grey that for a moment Gideon was convinced the Eighth House was doing something to her, but it was a block of phlegm rather than her soul being sucked out. Palamedes went for her, as did Camilla. He turned her over on her side, and

she did something awful and complicated with her finger inside
Dulcinea's mouth. The head on her lap went rolling, and was caught
only by the quick reflexes of Princess Ianthe, who cupped it between
her hands like an exotic butterfly.

"What do you want, Octakiseron?" said the captain in the wake
of this, stone-faced. "Room confinement? A death sentence? Both
are uncharacteristically easy to fulfil in this instance."

"I understand your point," said Silas. "I do not agree with it. I will
take my leave, madam. This is not interesting to me anymore."

His exit was arrested by his cavalier, as brown and as careworn
as ever, standing between him and the doorway. Colum did not
really seem to notice his necromancer's attempts to leave. "The furnace," he said shortly. "If we've got his head, what's in the furnace?"

Dulcinea, grey and squirming, managed: "What did you find in
the fu—fur—*fur*—" before Palamedes slapped her on the back, at
which point she coughed up what looked like a ball of bloody twigs.
The Third turned their faces away.

Captain Deuteros did not: maybe she'd seen worse. She gestured
to her lieutenant, who had removed the head none too gently from
Ianthe's fascinated gaze and was boxing it up as though it were an
unwanted meal. The captain moved closer to Harrow and Gideon,
and demanded: "Who found him?"

"I did," said Harrow, casually failing to provide any details on
how. "I took the head because I couldn't readily transport the body.
The body has since disappeared through unknown means, though
I've got my suspicions. The skull's mine by finder's rights—"

"Ninth, the head is going in the *morgue* where it belongs," said
the captain. "You don't have carrion rights over found murders, and
today is not the day when I'll countenance your House taking bones
that don't belong to it."

"I agree with Judith," said Corona. She had pushed her twin off
her thigh, and was looking a bit green around her lovely gills. She
also looked uncharacteristically tired and careworn, though she
managed to pull this off with a certain pensive loveliness to the
fine crinkles at her eyes and mouth. "Today isn't the day when we

start to use one another's bodies. Or tomorrow, or ever. We're not barbarians."

"Sheer prevarication," remarked her sister to nobody in particular. "Some people will do anything to get . . . *a head.*"

Everyone ignored her, even Gideon, who found herself trembling like a leaf. Harrowhark said merely, "The furnace bones are still mine to identify."

"You can *utilise* the morgue all you like," said the captain dismissively. "But the bodies aren't your property, Reverend Daughter. That goes for the Warden, that goes for everybody. Do I make myself clear, or shall I repeat?"

"Understood," said Palamedes.

"Understood," said the Reverend Daughter, in the tones of someone who neither understood nor intended to.

Silas had not left.

"In that case," he said, "I consider it my bounden duty to take watch over the morgue, in case the Ninth forgets what constitutes defilement of the bodies. *I* will take the remains. You may find me there."

Captain Deuteros did not roll her eyes. She gestured to her lieutenant, who handed over the box: Silas took it and winced faintly, and then passed it to his nephew. Gruesome parcel secured, they finally turned and left. The Third were already starting to bitch—

"I always said he didn't look right," said the cavalier.

"You said no such thing," said the first twin.

"At no point did you ever say that," said the second twin.

"Excuse you, I did—"

Captain Deuteros cleared her throat over the fresh internecine squabbling. "Does anyone else want to take this opportunity to admit that they're already dead, or a flesh construct, or other relevant object? Anyone?"

Palamedes had been wiping Dulcinea's mouth very gently with a white cloth. He laid his hand at her neck. She was still. Her face was now the thin blue-white colour of Canaan House's milk, and for a moment Gideon expected him to add her to the *already dead* list.

She *would* decide to go out with an audience, with her hair done, and with her miserable secrets revealed. Now she knew that Dulcinea had always been alone, carrying on an even greater farce than Gideon's, knowing the impossibility of the odds. But the dying necromancer sucked in a sudden, rattling, popped-balloon breath, her whole body surging in spasm. Gideon's heart started up again. Before she could move, Palamedes was there, and with terrible tenderness—as though they were alone in the room and the world alike—he kissed the back of Dulcinea's hand.

Gideon looked away, blushing with a shame she didn't interrogate, and found Teacher in the doorway with his hands folded before his gaudy rainbow sash. Nobody had heard him enter.

"Maybe later, Lady Judith," he said.

She said, "You'll need to contact the Seventh House and have her sent back home. It's morally and legally out of the question to leave her this way. Is that clear?"

"I cannot," said Teacher. "There was only ever a single communications channel in Canaan House, my Lady . . . and I cannot call her House on it. I cannot call the Fifth, nor the Fourth, nor now the Seventh. That is part of the sacred silence we keep. There will be an end to all this, and there will be a reckoning . . . but Lady Septimus will stay with us until the last."

The Second's adept had stopped all of a sudden. For a moment Gideon thought she was going to lose her carefully buttoned rag. But she cocked her dark head and said, "Lieutenant?"

"Ready," said Marta the Second, and they both marched out as though they were in parade formation. They did not give the rest of the room a backward glance.

Teacher looked at the tableau before him: the bed, the blood, the Third. Palamedes, still clutching Dulcinea's fingers within his own, and Dulcinea out cold.

"How long does Lady Septimus have?" he asked. "I can no longer tell."

"Days. Weeks, if we're lucky," said Palamedes bluntly. Dulcinea made a little hiccupping noise on the bed that sounded half like a giggle and half like a sigh. "That's if we keep the windows open and her airways clear. Breathing recyc at Rhodes probably took ten years off her life. She's been sitting on the brink without shifting one way or the other—the woman has the stamina of a steam engine—and all we can do is keep her comfortable and see if she doesn't decide to pull through."

Harrow said to him, slowly: "Undoing the cavalier's bodywork should have killed her. It would have been an incredible shock to her system."

"Spreading it between multiple casters may have diluted the feedback."

"That is not remotely how it works," said Ianthe.

"Oh, God, here comes the *expert*," Naberius said.

"Babs," said Ianthe's sister hurriedly, "you're getting hangry. Let's go find some food."

Gideon watched her necromancer's gaze fix on Ianthe Tridentarius. Ianthe did not notice, or affected not to notice; her eyes were as pale and purple and calm as they ever were, but Harrowhark was quivering like a maggot next to a dead duck. As the Third traipsed out—as noisy as if they were leaving a play, not a sickroom—Harrow's eyes went with them. Gideon said aloud, "Hey. Palamedes. Do you need someone to stay with her?"

"I will," said Teacher, before Palamedes could respond. "I will move my bed here. I will not leave her alone again. Whenever I must leave my post one of the other priests will take my place. I can do that much, at least . . . I am not afraid, nor do I have better things to do with my time. Whereas—I am very much afraid—you do."

Gideon allowed herself a lingering look at Dulcinea, who made for a more beguiling corpse than her stolid dead cavalier ever did: lying on the bed looking nearly transparent with streaks of drying, bloodied mucus on her chin. She wanted to help, but out of the corner of her eye she saw Harrow moving out of the doorway and into the corridor—staring after the disappearing Third—and she steeled herself to say, "Then we're out. Can you—let us know if anything changes?"

"Someone will come for you," said Teacher gently.

"Cool. Palamedes—"

He met her eye. He had taken off his glasses and was cleaning them with one of his innumerable handkerchiefs.

"Ninth," he said, "if she were capable of anything, in order to become a Lyctor—don't you think she'd be one already? If she really wanted to watch the world burn—wouldn't we all be alight?"

"Stop flattering her. But—thanks," said Gideon, and she darted off into the corridor after Harrow.

31

IN THE CORRIDOR, HER necromancer was staring distantly down the passageway at the disappearing hems of the Third: her brow had furrowed a wrinkle into her paint. Gideon had intended to—she had intended to do a lot of things; but Harrow left her no opening for the actions she'd planned and offered none of the answers she'd wanted. She simply turned in a swish of black cloth and said, "Follow me."

Gideon had prepared beforehand a *fuck-you* salvo so long and so loud that Harrow would have to be taken away to be killed; but then Harrow added, "Please."

This *please* convinced Gideon to follow her in silence. She had more or less expected Harrow to lead with "What were you doing in my closet," at which point Gideon might well have shaken her until the teeth in her head and the teeth in her pockets all rattled. Harrowhark swept down the stairs two at a time, the treads creaking in panic, as they went down the grand flight that led them to the atrium: from there, down one corridor, down another, one left, and then down the steps to the training rooms. Harrow ignored the tapestry that would have taken them to the hidden corridor and the ransacked Lyctor laboratory where Jeannemary had died, and instead pushed open the big dark doors to the pool.

Once there, she tossed down two grubby knuckles from her pockets. A substantial skeleton sprang from each, unfurling. They stood before the door, linked elbows, and held it shut. She scattered another handful of chips like pale grain; skeletons rose, forming and expanding the bone as though bubbling up from it. They made themselves a perimeter around the whole room, pressing the knobbles of their spines against the old ceramic tile and standing to attention. Shoulder to shoulder they stood, as though bodyguards, or hideous chaperones.

Harrow turned to face Gideon, and her eyes were as black and inexorable as a gravity collapse.

"The time has come—"

She took a deep breath; and then she undid the catches to her robes, and they fell away from her thin shoulders to puddle around her ankles on the floor.

"—to tell you everything," she said.

"*Oh, thank God for that,*" said Gideon hysterically, profoundly embarrassed at how her heart rate had spiked.

"Shut up and get in the pool."

This was so unanticipated that she didn't bother to question, or to complain, or even to hesitate. Gideon unhooked her robe and hood and pulled off her shoes, unstrapped her rapier and the belt that held her gauntlet. Harrow seemed ready to enter the greenly lapping waves wearing her trousers and shirt, so Gideon figured *Oh well, what the hell* and made the plunge almost fully clothed. She jumped in recklessly: tidal waves exploded outward at her passing, peppering the stone sides of the pool with droplets, gushing and foaming. The seamy, distasteful feeling of water seeping through her underwear hit her all at once. Gideon spluttered, and ducked her head beneath, and spat out a mouthful of liquid that was warm as blood.

After a moment's consideration, Harrow stepped in too—walking off the side carelessly, slipping beneath the water like a clean black knife. She disappeared beneath the surface, then emerged, gasping, spluttering in a way that ruined everything about the portentous entrance. She faced Gideon and trod water, flapping her arms a little before she managed to get her toes touching the bottom.

"Are we in here for a reason?"

Their voices echoed.

"The Ninth House has a secret, Nav," said Harrow. She sounded calm and measured and frank in a way she'd never been before. "Only my family knows of it. And even we could never discuss it, unless—this was my mother's rule—we were immersed in salt water. We kept a ceremonial pool for the purpose, hidden from the rest of the House. It was cold and deep and I hated every moment I was in it. But my mother is dead, and I find now that—if I really am to betray my family's most sacred trust—I am obliged at the least to keep, intact, her rule."

Gideon blinked.

"Oh shit," she said. "You really meant it. This is it. This is go time."

"This is go time," agreed Harrowhark.

Gideon swept both of her hands through her hair, trickles going down the back of her neck and into her sodden collar. Eventually, all she said was, "Why?"

"The reasons are multitudinous," said her necromancer. Her paint was wearing off in the water; she looked like a grey picture of a melting skeleton. "I had—intended to let you know some of it, before. An expurgated version. And then you looked in my closet . . . If I had told you my suspicions about Septimus's meat-puppet on the first day, none of this would have happened."

"The *first day*?"

"Griddle," said Harrow, "I have not puppeted my own parents around for five years and learned nothing."

Anger did seep into Gideon then, along with a couple more litres of salt water. "Why the hell didn't you tell me when you killed him?"

"I didn't kill him," said Harrowhark sharply. "Someone else did—blade through the heart, from what I saw, though I only got a few minutes to look before I had to run. I only had to push the theorem the most basic bit before he came apart. I took the head and left when I thought I heard someone coming. This was the night after we completed the entropy field challenge."

"No, you monster's ass," said Gideon coldly. "I mean, why didn't you tell me you'd killed him before you sent Jeannemary Chatur and her necromancer down to the facility to look for the guy who was in a box in your closet? Why didn't you take the moment to say, I don't know, *Let's not send two children downstairs to get fucked up by a huge bone creature.*"

Harrow exhaled.

"I panicked," she said. "At the time I thought I was sending you down a blind tunnel, and that the real danger was Sextus and Septimus; that either one might ambush you, and that the sensible solution was to take them both on myself. My plan was to get you clear of a necromantic duel. At the time I even thought it elegant."

"Nonagesimus, all you had to do was delay, tell me you were freaking out. All you had to do was say that Dulcinea's cav was a mummy man—"

"I had reason to believe," said Harrow, "that you would trust her more than you trusted me."

This answer contorted Gideon's face into her best *are you fucking kidding me* expression. Opposite, Harrow smoothed her forehead out with her thumbs, which took away another significant portion of skeleton.

"I thought you were *compromised,*" she continued waspishly. "I assumed *you* would assume that I dismantled the puppet as an act of bad faith and go straight to the Seventh. I wanted to do enough research to present you with a cut-and-dry case. I had no idea what it would mean for the Fourth House. The Ninth is deep in their blood debt and I am undone by the expense. I—I did not want to hurt you, Griddle! I didn't want to disturb your—equilibrium."

"Harrow," said Gideon, "if my heart had a dick you would kick it."

"I did not want to alienate you more than I already had. And then it seemed as though—we were on a more even footing," said Harrow, who was stumbling in a way Gideon had never before witnessed. It looked as though she were ransacking drawers in her brain trying to find the right set of words to wear. "Our—we— It was too tenuous to risk. And then . . ."

Too tenuous to risk. "Harrow," said Gideon again, more slowly, "if

I hadn't gone to Palamedes—and I nearly didn't go to Palamedes—I would have waited for you in our rooms, with my sword drawn, and I would have gone for you. I was so convinced you were behind everything. That you'd killed Jeannemary and Isaac. Magnus and Abigail."

"I didn't—I don't—I never have," said Harrow, "and—I know."

"You would have killed me."

"Or vice versa."

This surprised her into silence. The wavelets sploshed gently at the tiled edges of the pool. Gideon kicked off the bottom and fluttered her feet back and forth, bobbing, her shirt billowing out with water.

"Okay," she said eventually. "Question time. Who did all the murders?"

"*Nav.*"

"I mean it. What's happening? Is Canaan House haunted, or what? What—who—killed the Fourth and the Fifth?"

Her necromancer also pulled her feet up from the bottom and floated, momentarily, chin-deep in green salt water. Her eyes were narrowed in thought. "I can't say," she said. "Sorry. That's not a fruitful line of inquiry. We are being pursued by revenants, or it's all part of the challenge, or one, or more, of us is picking off the others. The murders of the Fifth and the Fourth may be connected, or not. The bone fragments found in everyone's wounds don't match, naturally—but I believe their very particle formation points to the same type of necromantic construction, no matter what Sextus says about topological resonance and skeletal archetype theory . . ."

"Harrow, don't make me drown myself."

"My conclusion: if the murders are linked and if some adept, rather than a revenant force or the facility itself, is behind the construct you saw—then it is one of us," said Harrow. "We're the only living beings in Canaan House. That means the suspect list is the Tridentarii; Sextus; Octakiseron; the Second; or myself. And I haven't discounted Teacher and the priests. Septimus has something of an alibi—"

"Yes, being nearly dead," said Gideon.

Harrowhark said, rather grudgingly: "I've downgraded her in some respects. Logically, judging by ability, and mind, and the facility to combine both in service to an end, it's Palamedes Sextus and his cavalier." She shook her head as Gideon opened her mouth to protest. "No, I realise neither has, as you might put it, *a fucking motive*. A logical conclusion is worth very little if I don't have all the facts. Then there's Teacher—and the Lyctor laboratories—and the rules. Why those theorems? What powers them? Why was the Fourth cavalier killed, but you left alive?"

These were all questions that Gideon had privately asked the dead of night many times since Jeannemary had died. She let her shoulders slide back into the water until it was cold up to the backs of her ears, staring at the single fluorescing bar that swung above the pool. Her body floated, weightless, in a puddle of yellow light. She could have asked Harrow anything: she could have asked about the bomb that had taken Ortus Nigenad's life instead of hers, or she could have asked about her whole entire existence, why it had happened and for what reason. Instead, she found herself asking: "What do you know about the conditioner pathogen that bumped off all the kids—the one that happened when I was little, before you were born?"

The silence was terrible. It lasted for such a long time that she wondered if Harrow had slyly drowned herself in the interim, until—

"It didn't happen before I was born," said the other girl, sounding very unlike herself. "Or at least, that's not precise enough. It happened before I was even conceived."

"That's unwholesomely specific."

"It's important. My mother needed to carry a child to term, and that child needed to be a necromancer to fill the role of true heir to the Locked Tomb. But as necromancers themselves, they found the process doubly difficult. We hardly had access to the foetal care technology that the other Houses do. She had tried and failed already. She was getting old. She had one chance, and she couldn't afford chance."

Gideon said, "You can't just control whether or not you're carrying a necro."

"Yes, you can," said Harrow. "If you have the resources, and are willing to pay the price of using them."

The hairs on the back of Gideon's neck rose, wetly.

"Harrow," she said slowly, "by *resources*, are you saying—"

"Two hundred children," said Harrowhark tiredly. "From the ages of six weeks to eighteen years. They needed to all die more or less simultaneously, for it to work. My great-aunts measured out the organophosphates after weeks of mathematics. Our House pumped them through the cooling system."

From somewhere beneath the pool, a filter made blurting sounds as it recycled the spilloff. Harrow said, "The infants alone generated enough thanergy to take out the entire planet. Babies always do—for some reason."

Gideon couldn't hear this. She held her knees to the chest and let herself go under, just for a moment. The water sluiced over her head and through her hair. Her ears roared, then popped. When she pushed above the surface again, the noise of her heartbeat thumping through her skull was like an explosion.

"Say something," said Harrowhark.

"Gross," said Gideon dully. "Ick. The worst. What can I say to that? What the *fuck* can I say to all *that*?"

"It let me be born," said the necromancer. "And I was—me. And I have been aware, since I was very young, about how I was created. I am exactly two hundred sons and daughters of my House, Griddle— I am the whole generation of the Ninth. I came into this world a necromancer at the expense of Drearburh's future—because there is no future without me."

Gideon's stomach churned, but her brain was more urgent than her nausea.

"Why leave me, though?" she demanded. "They murdered the rest of the House, but they left me off the list?"

There was a pause.

"We didn't," said Harrow.

"What?"

"You were meant to die, Griddle, along with all the others. You inhaled nerve gas for ten full minutes. My great-aunts went blind just from releasing it and you weren't affected, even though you were just two cots away from the vent. You just didn't die. My parents were terrified of you for the rest of their lives."

The Reverend Father and Mother hadn't found her unnatural because of how she'd been born: they'd found her unnatural because of how she hadn't died. And all the nuns and all the priests and all the anchorites of the cloister had taken the cue from them, not knowing that it was because Gideon was just some smothered and unfortunate animal who had still been alive the next day.

The world revolved as Harrow floated closer. Memory took Pelleamena's steady gaze, and refocused the way it slid through and over Gideon from contempt to dread. It took the stentorious, short-changed breath when Priamhark saw her and breathed it again in horror, not in repugnance. One small kid who, to two adults, was a walking reminder of the day they had chosen to mortgage the future of their House. No wonder she had hated the huge dark doors of Drearburh: beyond that portal lurked the used-up, emptied-out shades of a bunch of kids whose main sin in life was that they'd be good batteries. "And do you think you're worth it?" she asked bluntly.

Next to her, Harrow didn't flinch. "If I became a Lyctor," she said meditatively, "and renewed my House—and made it great again, and greater than it ever was, and justified its existence in the eyes of God the Emperor—if I made my whole life a monument to those who died to ensure that I would live and live powerfully . . ."

Gideon waited.

"Of course I wouldn't be *worth it*," Harrow said scornfully. "I'm an abomination. The whole universe ought to scream whenever my feet touch the ground. My parents committed a necromantic sin that we ought to have been torpedoed into the centre of Dominicus for. If any of the other Houses knew of what we'd done they would destroy us from orbit without a second's thought. I am a *war crime*."

She stood up. Gideon watched as sheets of seawater slicked down her shoulders, her hair a wet black cap on her skull, her skin sheening grey and green from the waves. All the paint had rubbed off, and Harrowhark looked thin and haggard and no older than Jeannemary Chatur.

"But I'd do it again," said the war crime. "I'd do it again, if I had to. My parents did it because there was no other way, and they didn't even know. I had to be a necromancer of their bloodline, Nav . . . because only a necromancer can open the Locked Tomb. Only a powerful necromancer can roll away the stone . . . I found that only the *perfect* necromancer can pass through those wards and live, and approach the sarcophagus."

Gideon's toes found purchase and she stood, chest deep in water, goose-bumped all over from the cold. "What happened to praying that the tomb be shut forever and the rock never be rolled away?"

"My parents didn't understand either, and that's why they died," said Harrowhark. "That's why, when they knew I'd done it—that I'd rolled away the stone and that I'd gone through the monument and that I had seen the place where the body was buried—they thought I'd betrayed God. The Locked Tomb's meant to house the one true enemy of the King Undying, Nav, something older than time, the cost of the Resurrection; the beast that he defeated once but can't defeat *twice.* The abyss of the First. The death of the Lord. He left the grave with us for our safekeeping, and he trusted the ones who built the tomb a myriad ago to wall themselves up with the corpse and die there. But we didn't. And that's how the Ninth House was made."

Gideon remembered Silas Octakiseron: *The Eighth never forgot that the Ninth was never meant to be.*

"Are you telling me that when you were ten years old—*ten years old*—you busted the lock on the tomb, broke into an ancient grave, and made your way past hideous old magic to look at a dead thing even though your parents told you it'd start the apocalypse?"

"Yes," said Harrowhark.

"*Why?*"

There was another pause, and Harrow looked down into the water. Limned by electric light, her pupils and her irises appeared the same colour.

"I was tired of being two hundred corpses," she said simply. "I was old enough to know how monstrous I was. I had decided to go and look at the tomb—and if I didn't think it was worth it—to go up the stairs . . . all the flights of the Ninth House . . . open up an air lock, and walk . . . and walk."

She lifted her gaze. She held Gideon's.

"But you came back instead," said Gideon. "I'd told the Reverend Mother and the Reverend Father what I'd seen you do. I killed your parents."

"What? *My parents* killed my parents. I should know."

"But I told them—"

"My parents killed themselves because they were frightened and ashamed," said Harrow tightly. "They thought it was the only honourable thing to do."

"I think your parents must've been frightened and ashamed for a hell of a long time."

"I'm not saying I didn't blame you. I did . . . it was much easier. I pretended for a long time that I could have saved them by talking to them. Them and Mortus the Ninth. When you walked in, when you saw what you saw . . . when you saw what I had failed to do. I hated you because you saw what I didn't do. My mother and father weren't angry, Nav. They were very kind to me. They tied their own nooses, and then they helped me tie mine. I watched them help Mortus onto the chair. Mortus didn't even question it, he never did . . .

"But I couldn't do it. After all I'd convinced myself I was ready to do. I made myself watch, when my parents—I could not do the slightest thing my House expected of me. Not even then. You're not the only one who couldn't die."

The waves lapped, tiny and quiet, around their clothes and their skins.

"Harrow," said Gideon, and her voice caught. "Harrow, I'm so bloody sorry."

Harrow's eyes snapped wide open. The whites blazed like plasma. The black rings were blacker than the bottom of Drearburh. She waded through the water, snatched Gideon's wet shirt in her fists, and shook her with more violence than Gideon had ever thought her muscularly capable of. Her face was livid in its hate: her loathing was a mortar, it was combustion.

"*You* apologise to *me*?" she bellowed. "You apologise to me now? You say that you're sorry when I have spent my life destroying you? You are my whipping girl! I hurt you because it was a relief! I exist because my parents killed everyone and relegated you to a life of abject misery, and they would have killed you too and not given it a second's goddamned thought! I have spent your life trying to make you regret that you weren't dead, all because—I regretted I wasn't! I ate you alive, and you have the temerity to tell me that *you're sorry*?"

There were flecks of spittle on Harrowhark's lips. She was retching for air.

"I have tried to dismantle you, Gideon Nav! The Ninth House poisoned you, we trod you underfoot—I took you to this killing field as my slave—you refuse to die, and you pity me! Strike me down. You've won. I've lived my whole wretched life at your mercy, yours alone, and God knows I deserve to die at your hand. You are my only friend. I am undone without you."

Gideon braced her shoulders against the weight of what she was about to do. She shed eighteen years of living in the dark with a bunch of bad nuns. In the end her job was surprisingly easy: she wrapped her arms around Harrow Nonagesimus and held her long and hard, like a scream. They both went into the water, and the world went dark and salty. The Reverend Daughter fell calm and limp, as was natural for one being ritually drowned, but when she realised that she was being hugged she thrashed as though her fingernails were being ripped from their beds. Gideon did not let go. After more than one mouthful of saline, they ended up huddled together in one corner of the shadowy pool, tangled up in each other's wet shirtsleeves. Gideon peeled Harrow's head off her shoulder by the hair and beheld it, taking her inventory: her point-boned, hateful little face, her woeful black brows, the bloodless bow of her lips. She examined the disdainful set of the jaw, the panic in the starless eyes. She pressed her mouth to the place where Harrow's nose met the bone of her frontal sinus, and the sound that Harrow made embarrassed them both.

"Too many words," said Gideon confidentially. "How about these: *One flesh, one end*, bitch."

The Ninth House necromancer flushed nearly black. Gideon tilted her head up and caught her gaze: "Say it, loser."

"One flesh—one end," Harrow repeated fumblingly, and then could say no more.

* * *

After what seemed like a very, very long time, her adept said:

"Gideon, you need to promise me something."

Gideon wiped a thumb over her temple, tidied away a stringy lock of shadow-coloured hair; Harrow shuddered. "I thought that this was all about me getting a bunch of concessions and you grovelling, but you called me *Gideon*, so shoot."

Harrow said, "In the event of my death—Gideon, if something ever does get the better of me—I need you to outlast me. I need you to go back to the Ninth House and protect the Locked Tomb. If I die, I need your duty not to die with me."

"That is such a dick move," said Gideon reproachfully.

"I know," said Harrow. "I know."

"Harrow, what the hell is in there, that you'd ask that of me?"

Her adept closed heavy-lidded eyes.

"Beyond the doors there's just the rock," she said. "The rock and the tomb surrounded by water. I won't bore you with the magic or the locks, or the wards or the barriers: just know that it took me a year to walk six steps inside, and that it nearly killed me then. There's a blood ward bypass on the doors which will only respond for the Necromancer Divine, but I knew there had to be an exploit, a way through for the true and devout tomb-keeper. I knew in the end it had to open for me. The water's salt, and it's deep, and it moves with a tide that shouldn't exist. The sepulchre itself is small, and the tomb . . ."

Her eyes opened. A small, astonished smile creased her mouth. The smile transformed her face into an affliction of beauty that Gideon had heretofore managed to ignore.

"The tomb is stone and ice, Nav, ice that never melts and stone that's even colder, and inside, in the dark, there's a girl."

"A *what*?"

"A girl, you yellow-eyed moron," said Harrowhark. Her voice dropped to a whisper, and her head was dead weight in Gideon's hands. "Inside the Locked Tomb is the corpse of a girl.

"They packed her in ice—she's frozen solid—and they laid a sword on her breast. Her hands are wrapped around the blade. There are chains around her wrists, coming out of her grave, and they go down into holes by each side of the tomb, and there are chains on her ankles that do the same, and there are chains around her throat . . .

"Nav, when I saw her face I decided I wanted to live. I decided to live forever just in case she ever woke up."

Her voice had the quality of someone in a long dream. She stared through Gideon without looking at her, and Gideon gently took her hands away from Harrow's jaw. Instead she sat back in the water, buoyed by the salt, her eyes starting to sting from it. They both floated there for a long time in amicable silence, until they pulled themselves up and sat, dripping, on the side of the pool. The salt was crusting up their hair. Gideon reached over to take Harrow's hand.

They sat there, wet through and uncomfortable, fingers curled into each other's in the half-light, the pool interminably lapping at the cool tiles that surrounded it. The skeletons stood in perfect, silent ranks, not betraying themselves with even a creak of bone against bone. Gideon's brain moved and broke against itself like the tiny wavelets they had left, the water lurching restlessly from side to side, until it came to a final conclusion.

She closed the gap between them a little, until she could see tiny droplets run down the column of Harrow's neck and slide beneath her sodden collar. She smelled like ash, even smothered under litres and litres of saline. As she approached Harrow grew very still, and her throat worked, and her eyes opened black and wide: she looked at Gideon without breathing in, her mouth frozen, her hands unmoving, a perfect bone carving of a person.

"One last question for you, Reverend Daughter," said Gideon.

Harrow said, a little unsteadily: "Nav?"

Gideon leaned in.

"Do you really have the hots for some chilly weirdo in a coffin?"

One of the skeletons punted her back into the water.

* * *

For all the rest of that evening they were furtive and unwilling to let the other one out of their sight for more than a minute, as though distance would compromise everything all over again—talking to each other as though they'd never had the opportunity to talk, but talking about bullshit, about nothing at all, just hearing the rise and fall of the other one's voice. That night, Gideon took all her blankets back to the unedifying cavalier bed at the foot of Harrow's.

When they were both lying in bed in the big warm dark, Harrow's body perpendicular to Gideon's body, Gideon said: "Did you try to kill me, back on the Ninth?"

Harrow was obviously startled into silence. Gideon pressed: "The shuttle. The one Glaurica stole."

"What? No," said Harrow. "If you'd gotten on that shuttle, you'd have made it safe to Trentham. I swear by the Tomb."

"But—Ortus—Sister Glaurica—"

There was a pause. Her necromancer said, "Were meant to be brought back after twenty-four hours, in disgrace, with Ortus declared unfit to hold his post, relegated to the meanest cloister of the House. Not that Ortus would have minded. We had paid off the pilot."

"Then—"

"Crux claimed," said Harrow slowly, "that the shuttle had a fault, and blew up en route."

"And you believed him?"

Another pause. Harrow said, "No." And then: "Above all else, Nav . . . he couldn't bear what he saw as disloyalty."

So it was Crux's mean, blackened revenge on his own House— his own zealous desire to burn it clear of any hint of insurrection— that had forced Glaurica's ghost back to her home planet. She did not say this. Silas Octakiseron knew more than he should, but if Harrow discovered that now, she'd be off down the corridor in her nightdress with a sack of emergency bones and a very focused expression. "What a dope," she said instead. "I was never loyal a day in my life and I still saw you in the raw."

"*Go to sleep*, Gideon."

She fell asleep, and for once didn't dream of anything at all.

32

"THIS IS CHEATING," SAID Harrowhark forbiddingly.

"We're just being resourceful," said Palamedes.

They were standing outside a laboratory door that Gideon had never seen. This one had not been hidden, just very inconveniently placed, at the topmost accessible point of the tower: it took more stairs than Gideon's knees had ever wanted, and was situated plainly at the end of a terrace corridor where the sun slanted in through broken windows. The terrace in question looked so frankly about to disintegrate that Gideon tried to stay close to the corridor's inside wall, in case most of the floor suddenly decided to fall off the side of Canaan House.

This Lyctoral door was the same as the others had been—gaping obsidian eye sockets in carved obsidian temporal bones: black pillars and no handle, and a fretwork symbol to differentiate it from the other two doors Gideon had seen. This one looked like three rings, joined on a line.

"We have no key," Harrow was saying. "This is not entering a locked door with *permission*."

Palamedes waved a hand. "I completed this challenge. We have the right to the key. That's basically the same thing."

"That is absolutely not the same thing."

"Look. If we're keeping track, which I am, the key for this room currently belongs to Silas Octakiseron. Lady Septimus had it, and he took it off her. That means the only way either of us ever gets inside is by defeating Colum the Eighth in a fair duel—"

"I can take Colum," said Camilla.

"Pretty sure I can also take Colum," added Gideon.

"—*and then relying on Octakiseron to hand it over.* Which he won't," concluded Palamedes triumphantly. "Reverend Daughter, you know as well as I do that the Eighth House wouldn't let a little thing like fair play get in the way of its sacred duty to do whatever it wants."

Harrow looked conflicted. "This is no ordinary lock. We're not just going to—pick it with a bit of bone, Sextus."

"No, of course not. I told you. Lady Septimus let me hold the key. I'm an adept of the Sixth. She might as well have let me make a silicone mould of the damn thing. I can picture every detail of that key right down to the microscopic level. But what am I going to do by myself, carve a new one out of wood?"

Harrow sighed. Then she rummaged in her pocket and took out a little nodule of bone, which she placed in the palm of her right hand. "All right," she said. "Describe it for me."

Palamedes stared at her.

"Hurry up," she prompted. "I'm not waiting for the Second to find us."

"It—I mean, it looked like a key," he said. "It had a long shaft and some teeth. I don't—I can't just describe a molecular structure like it's someone's outfit."

"Then how exactly am I meant to replicate it?" demanded Harrow. "I can't—oh. No."

"You did Imaging and Response, right? You must have, you got the key for it. Same deal. I'm going to think about the key, and you're going to see it through my eyes."

"Sextus," said Harrow darkly.

"Wait, wait," put in Gideon, intrigued. "You're going to read his mind?"

"No," said both necromancers immediately. Then Palamedes said, "Well, technically, sort of."

"No," said Harrow. "You remember the construct challenge, Nav. I couldn't read your mind then. It's more like borrowing perceptions." She turned back to Palamedes. "Sextus, this was bad enough when I did it to my own cavalier. You're going to have to focus on that key incredibly hard. If you get distracted—"

"He doesn't get distracted," said Camilla, as if this had caused difficulties in the past.

Palamedes closed his eyes. Harrow gnawed on her lip furiously, then closed hers too.

Nothing happened for a good thirty seconds. Gideon was dying to make a joke, just to get a reaction, when the tiny lump of matter in Harrow's palm twitched. It flexed and began to stretch, forming a long, thin, cylindrical rod. Another few seconds passed, and a spine of bone extruded slowly from near one end. Then another.

Gideon was honestly impressed. In all the time Harrow had tormented her back on Drearburh, she had only ever used bones as seeds and starters—stitching them together into trip wires, grasping arms, kicking legs, biting skulls. This was something new. She was using bone like clay—a medium she could shape not just into one of a bunch of predetermined forms, but into something that had never existed before. It looked like it was giving her trouble too: her brow was furrowed, and the first faint traces of blood sweat gleamed on her slim throat.

"*Focus*, Sextus," her necromancer gritted out. The object on her palm was now clearly a key: Gideon could see three individual teeth, twisting and flexing as Harrow filled in the fine detail. The whole length of the key quivered, and looked for a moment as though it would jump off her hand and fall to the floor, but then it abruptly lay still. Harrow opened her eyes, blinked, and peered at it suspiciously.

"This won't work," she said. "I've never had to work with something so small before."

"That's what she said," murmured Gideon, sotto voce.

Palamedes opened his eyes too, and breathed a long sigh of what sounded like relief.

"It'll be fine," he said unconvincingly. "Come on. Let's try it out."

He headed for the black stone door, followed by Harrow, both cavaliers, and the five skeletons that Harrow had refused point-blank not to conjure on their way up here. He took the newly formed bone key, examined it, fitted it in the lock, and then turned it decisively to the left.

The mechanism went *click.*

"Oh, my God," said Harrow.

Sextus ran a hand convulsively through his hair. "All right," he said. "No, I did not actually think that was going to happen. Masterful work, Reverend Daughter—" and he gave her a little mock-bow.

"Yes," said Harrow. "Congratulations to you also, Warden."

He pushed the door open onto total blackness. Harrow stepped closer to Gideon and muttered, "If anything moves—"

"*Yaaas,* I know. Let it head for Camilla."

Gideon did not know how to handle this new, overprotective Harrowhark, this girl with the hunted expression. She kept looking at Gideon with the screwed-up eyes of someone who had been handed an egg for safekeeping and was surrounded by egg-hunting snakes. But now she stepped forward grandly, spread her palms wide in the necromantic gesture as threatening as a cavalier unsheathing a sword, and strode into the dark. Palamedes went after her, groped around on the wall for a few moments, and then hit the light switch.

Gideon stood in the laboratory and stared as Camilla carefully closed the door behind them. This Lyctoral lab was an open-plan bomb wreck. There were three long lab tables covered in old, dis-used tools, splotches of what looked to be russet fungus, abandoned beakers, and used-up pens. The floor underfoot was hairy carpet, and in one corner there was a hideous, slithery tangle of what Gideon realised must be sleeping bags. In another corner, an ancient chin-up bar sagged in the middle alongside a strip of towel left to hang for a myriad. Everywhere there were bits of paper or shaken-out clothes, as though somebody had left the place in a hurry or had simply been an unbelievable slob. Spotlights shone down hot on the ruined jumble.

"Hm," said Camilla neutrally, and Gideon knew immediately that she organised Palamedes's and her socks by colour and genre.

Harrowhark and Palamedes picked their way through the mess to the tables. Palamedes was saying in his explanation voice: "It's not as though I didn't complete this challenge by lunchtime, though I had a distinct advantage. It was a psychometrical challenge. The main difficulty was working out what the challenge wanted in the first place: it was set up by someone with an obscure sense of humour. It was just a room with a table, a locked box, and a single molar."

"Reconstruction?"

"Not all of us can respring a body by dint of a molar, Reverend Daughter. Anyway, I must have examined that tooth for two hours. I know every single thing there is to know about that tooth. Mandibular second, deciduous eruption, vitamin deficiency, male, died in his sixties, flossed obediently, never left the planet. Died in this selfsame tower."

Both of them were riffling through the papers left on the desk: Palamedes left them in forensically exact piles divided by where they had been found. He adjusted his glasses and said, "Then Camilla took over because I wasn't bloody thinking."

Camilla grunted. She had meandered over to look at the rust-pitted crossbars of the chin-up, and Gideon had repaired to the worm mound of sleeping bags to kick them unhelpfully. Harrow said impatiently, "Get to the denouement, Sextus."

"I had tracked the tooth. It told me nothing—no spiritual links to any part of the building. It was a black hole. It was as though the body it came from had never been alive. No ghost remnants, nothing—this is impossible, you understand, it meant the spirit had somehow been removed entirely. So I did some old-fashioned detective work."

He peered under an abandoned clearfile. "I looked upstairs for the skeleton with the missing upper molar. He wouldn't come down with me, but he did let me make a plaster impression of his clavicle.

The clavicle! Someone was having a joke. Anyway, you can imagine my reaction when I unlocked the box with it and found it empty."

Gideon looked up from a pasteboard box she had found: it was full of the ring tabs you got on pressurised drink cans, and jingled unmusically when she shook it. "The constructs? Like, the bone servants?"

"Second's right, first isn't," said Camilla laconically.

"They're the opposite of what Lady Septimus calls the *beguiling corpse*," said Palamedes. "They seem to have most of their faculties intact. Mine was very nice, though he's forgotten how to write. The skeletons aren't reanimations, Ninth, they're revenants: ghosts inhabiting a physical shell. They simply lack a true revenant's ability to move itself along a thanergetic link. The *beguiling* corpse is a remnant of spirit attached to a perfect and incorruptible body—that's the idea, anyway—where what I'll term the *hideous* corpse is a fully intact spirit attached permanently to a rotting body. Not that someone hasn't preserved those bones beautifully."

Harrowhark slammed a ring-binder down on the bench.

"I'm a fool," she said bitterly. "I knew they moved too well to be constructs—no matter how I tried to mimic how they'd been done. I just could have sworn—but that's impossible. They'd need someone to control them."

"They do—themselves," said Palamedes. "They are autonomously powering themselves. It debunks every piece of thanergy theory I ever learned. The old fogeys back home would peel their feet for half an hour alone with one. It still doesn't explain why there's no energy signature on the bones, though. Anyway, this is the laboratory of the Lyctor who created them—and here's their theory."

Much like the one back in the other laboratory, the theorem was carved into a big stone slab pinned down in a dusty back corner and covered up with loose-leaf flimsy. Both cavaliers drifted over, and they all together stared at the carved diagrams. The laboratory was very quiet and the spotlights haloed streams of dust so thick you could lick them.

Resting on the edge of the stone set into the table, there was a tooth. Palamedes picked it up. It was a premolar, with long and horrible roots: it was brown with age. He handed it to Harrow, who gently unfolded it in the way that only a bone magician could and in the way that always made Gideon's jaw hurt. She turned it into a long ribbon of enamel, an orange with the skin taken off and flattened, a three-dimensional object turned two-dimensional.

Written on the tooth in tiny, tiny letters was this:

FIVE HUNDRED INTO FIFTY
IT IS FINISHED!

Harrowhark took out her fat black journal and was scribbling down notes, but Palamedes had abruptly lost interest in the theory stone. He was looking at the walls instead, flipping open some of the ring-binders that she had discarded. He stopped in front of a faded pinboard, riddled thick with pins, all with bits of string attached. Gideon came to stand next to him.

"Look at this," he said.

There were rainbow splotches of pins all over the board. There were tiny clusters, and Gideon noticed that at the centre of each cluster there was one white pin; the smallest and most numerous clusters had three pins fixed around one white pin. Some others had five or six. Then there were two other separate whorls of pins, each made up of dozens alone, and then one enormous pin-splotch: more than a hundred of them in a rainbow of colours, thickly clustered around one in white.

"The problem of necromancy," said Palamedes, "is that the acts themselves, if understood, aren't difficult to do. But maintaining anything . . . we're glass cannons. Our military survives because we have hundreds of thousands of heavily armed men and women with big swords."

"There's always more thanergy to feed from, Sextus," said Harrow distantly, flicking her eyes back and forth as she copied. "Give me a single death and I can go for ten minutes."

"Yes, but that's the problem, isn't it; ten minutes, then you need more. Thanergy's transient. A necromancer's biggest threat is honestly themselves. My whole House for a reliable food source—"

"Warden," said Camilla, quite suddenly.

She had opened up a ring-binder untidy with pages. Inside were an array of old flimsy lithographs, the black-and-white kind. On the very first page there was a faded note that had once been yellow, the letters still legible in a short, curt hand:

CONFIRMED INDEPENDENTLY HIGHLIGHTED
BEST OPTION
ASK E.J.G.
YRS, ANASTASIA.
P.S. GIVE ME BACK MY CALIPERS I NEED THEM

Camilla flipped through the binder. The pictures were hasty, low-quality snaps of men and women from the shoulders up, squinting at the camera, eyes half-shut as though they hated the light: most of them looked very serious and solemn, as though posing for a mugshot. Some of these men and women had been crossed out. Some had a few ticks against their picture. Camilla thumbed a page over, and they all paused.

The overexposure did not disguise a head-and-shoulders photo of the man they all called Teacher, bright blue eyes a desaturated sepia, still smiling from a lifetime away. He looked not a day older or younger. And his photograph had been ringed around in a black marker pen.

"Sextus," Harrow began, ominously.

"I couldn't tell," said Palamedes. For his part, he sounded almost dazed. "Ninth, I absolutely could not tell. *Another* beguiling corpse?"

"Then who's controlling him? There's nobody here but us, Sextus."

"I'd like to hope so. Could he be independent? But how—"

Palamedes's eyes drifted back to the pinboard. He took his spectacles off and squinted his lambent grey eyes at it. He was counting under his breath. Gideon followed along with him gamely up into the hundreds until a dreadful noise startled them out of any mental arithmetic.

It was an electronic klaxon. From somewhere within the room— and without—it howled: *BRRRRAAARRP...BRRRRARRRRP... BRRRRARRRRRP...*

This was followed by, bafflingly, a woman's voice, unreasonably calm. *"This is a fire alarm. Please make your way to designated safe zones, led by your fire warden."* Then the klaxon again: *BRRRARRRRP...BRRRRARRRRP...BRRRRARRRRRRRRP...* and the exact same recorded inflexion: *"This is a fire alarm. Please make your way..."*

They looked at each other. Then all four of them sprinted for the door. Palamedes didn't even stop to shut it behind them.

The Sixth and the Ninth Houses knew that a fire was absolutely no joke, and moved like people who had learned that a fire alarm could be the last thing any of them heard, the last thing their whole House heard. But this was curious. There was no smoke to smell, nor any latent heat: when they all got to the atrium, the only thing they saw amiss was that one of the skeletons had fallen over with an armful of towels, spread-eagle in the awful dried-up fountain.

Camilla looked around, narrowed her eyes, and headed toward the lunch room. Here there was an ongoing *pssshhhtt* sound that Gideon could not identify until they reached the kitchen—there was a bad smell, and white steam—and realised it was a water sprinkler, the really old kind. They all squashed themselves through the kitchen door and stood out of the reach of the spray.

All the skeletons were gone. In their places were untidy piles of bones and sashes. A pan of fish smoked on a lit stove: Gideon waded in, kicked aside a humerus, and fumbled with the knobs until the fire extinguished. There were piles of bones at the sink, a skull floating in a familiar pot of green soup: the tap had been left on, and the sink was close to overflowing. A pile of bones had mixed in among the potato peelings. Gideon ducked back out and away from the spray and stared. She was only vaguely aware of Harrowhark disdainfully mopping her wet head with a handkerchief.

The sprinklers stopped. Camilla knelt down and, amidst all the dripping and burbling, touched one of the phalanges that had fallen on the tiles. It dissolved into ash like a sigh.

Palamedes went and turned off the tap like someone in a dream. The bones in the sink gently bobbed against a saucepan. He and Harrow looked at each other and said—

"Shit."

With only the faintest liquid whisper of metal on sheath, Camilla drew her swords. Gideon had never had the opportunity to study Camilla's two short swords before: they were more like very long daggers, slightly curved at each end, wholly utilitarian. They glittered clean and hot beneath the soggy light of the kitchen; she marched back toward the door to the dining hall.

"Split up?" she said.

"Hell no," said Gideon.

Harrow said, "Let's not waste time. Get to Septimus," and Gideon could have kissed her.

There seemed to be nobody else in the long, echoing halls of Canaan House, now longer and more echoey than ever. They passed another skeleton, arrested by an unseen force in the middle of carrying a basket. As it tumbled to the floor the weight of the basket had crushed its brittle pelvis to a powder. When they got to Dulcinea's sickroom, Gideon had a sharp moment of not knowing what the hell to expect; but they found Dulcinea, struggling feebly to try to sit up, whey-faced and wide-eyed. Opposite her was the salt-and-pepper priest in the high-backed chair, looking as though they were peacefully asleep.

"It wasn't *me*," Dulcinea wheezed, in no small alarm.

Camilla ducked forward. The white-robed priest's chin had slumped forward to their chest, and the braid was tucked beneath their chin. As Camilla pressed her hand to their neck, the priest lurched very gently sideways, limp and heavy, until the Sixth cavalier had to prop them up so that they wouldn't slide off the chair entirely.

"Dead as space," said Harrowhark, "though, accurately, that's been true for a very, very long time."

Palamedes turned to Dulcinea, who had given up thrashing her way to her elbows and was lying flat on the pillows, panting in exertion. He brushed her hair gently away from her forehead and said, "Where's Teacher?"

"He left me maybe an hour ago," said Dulcinea helplessly, eyes darting between him and the rest of them. "He said he wanted to lock a door. What's going on? Why is the priest dead? Where did Teacher go?"

Palamedes patted her hand. "No idea. This is the interesting part."

"Dulcinea," said Gideon, "are you going to be okay by yourself?"

Dulcinea grinned. Her tongue was scarlet with blood. The veins in her eyelids were so dark and prominent that the blue of her eyes appeared a limpid, moonless purple.

"What can anyone do to me now?" she said simply.

They could not even warn her not to let anyone in: she seemed exhausted simply from the act of sitting up. They left her with only the dead priest for company and headed to a wing where Gideon had never gone: the hot, sultry corridor lined with fibrous green plants of all sorts, the wing where the priests and Teacher lived.

It was a pretty, whitewashed passageway, totally out of kilter with the rest of Canaan House. The light bounced off the walls from the clean, well-kept windows. There was no need to knock at the doors or yell to find the action; at the end of the corridor, there was an absolute pile-up of bones, sashes, and the laid-out body of the other wizened priest. He had collapsed flat on his face with his arms outstretched, as if he had tripped while running.

The bones were all piled up outside a closed door, as though they had been trying to get through it. Palamedes led the way, crunching through the wreckage. Gideon put her hand on the hilt of her sword, and Palamedes threw open the door.

Inside, Captain Deuteros looked up, somewhat wearily. She was sitting in a chair facing the door. Her left arm hung uselessly at her side, wizened and crumpled. Gideon did not want to look at it. It looked like it had been put in a bog for a thousand years and then stuck back on. Her right arm was tucked up against her stomach. There was an enormous crimson stain spreading out onto the perfect white of her jacket, and her right hand was clasped, as though ready to draw, around the enormous bone shard shoved deep in her gut.

Teacher lay unmoving by her side. There was a rapier buried in his chest, and a dagger through his neck. There was no blood around the blades, only great splashes of it at his sleeves and his girdle. Gideon looked around for the lieutenant, found her, and then looked away again. She didn't need a very long look to tell that Dyas was dead. For one thing, her skeleton and her body had apparently tried to divorce.

"He wouldn't listen to reason," said Judith Deuteros, in measured tones. "He became aggressive when I attempted to restrain him. Binding spells proved—useless. Marta used disabling force. He was the one to escalate the situation—he blew out her eye, so I was compelled to respond . . . This didn't—it didn't have to happen."

Two professional Cohort soldiers, one a necromancer, one a cavalier primary; all this mess for one unearthly old man. Palamedes dropped to his knees beside the captain, but she pushed him away, roughly, with the tip of her boot.

"Do something for *her*," she said.

"Captain," said Camilla, "Lieutenant Dyas is dead."

"Then don't touch me. We did what we came to do."

Gideon's eyes were drawn to a machine in the corner. She hadn't noticed it because it seemed ridiculously normal, but it wasn't normal at all, not for Canaan House. It was an electric transmitter box, with headphones and a mic. The antenna was set out the window, glowing faint and blue in the afternoon sunshine.

"Captain," said Palamedes, "what did you come to do?"

The Second necromancer shifted, grunted in pain, closed her eyes. She sucked in a breath, and a bead of sweat travelled down her temple.

"Save our lives," she said. "I sent an SOS. Backup's coming, Warden . . . it's just up to you to make sure nobody else dies . . . He said I'd betrayed the Emperor . . . said I'd put the Emperor at risk . . . I entered the Emperor's service when I was six."

Captain Deuteros's chin was drooping. She lifted it back up with some effort. "He wasn't human," she said. "He wasn't like anything I'd ever seen before. Marta put him down—Marta . . . Go tell them she avenged the Fifth and the Fourth."

Palamedes had ignored the kick and moved in again. The Second laid one booted foot on his shoulder in warning. He said, "Captain, you are no use to anyone dead."

"It is my privilege to no longer be of use," said the captain. "We fixed the problem none of the rest of you could . . . did what we had to do . . . and paid for it, dearly."

Harrow had gone to stand over the quiet, punctured corpse of Teacher. She dropped to his side like a long-tailed crow. All Gideon could do was press herself back up against the wall, smell the blood, and feel absurdly empty. Her necromancer said, "You fixed nothing."

"Harrow," Palamedes said warningly.

"This man was a shell filled with a hundred souls," said Harrow. The captain's eyes flicked open, and stayed open. "He was a thing of ridiculous power—but he was a prototype. I doubt he had killed anyone before today. I would be astonished if he had a hand in the deaths of the Fourth and Fifth Houses, as he was created for the sole purpose of safeguarding the place. There is something a great deal more dangerous than an old experiment loose in the First House, and he could have helped us find out what it is. But now you're going to die too, and you'll never know the whole story."

The whites of Judith's eyes were very white, her carefully merciless face suddenly a picture of hesitation. Her gaze moved, more remorselessly than Gideon's ever could have, to her cavalier; then she returned it to them, half-furious, half-beseeching. Palamedes moved in.

"I can't save you," he said. "I can't even make you comfortable. A team of trained medics could do both. How far away is the Second? How long do we have to wait for Cohort backup?"

"The Second's not coming," said Captain Deuteros.

She smiled, tight and bitter. "There's no communication with the rest of the system," she said, hoarsely now. "He didn't lie. There was no way to reach the Houses . . . I got through to the Imperial flagship, Sixth. The *Emperor* is coming . . . the King Undying."

Next to Harrow, Teacher gurgled.

"You draw him back—to the place—he must not return to," said the dead man, with a thin and reedy whistle of a voice around the blade in his vocal cords. His whole body wriggled. His dead eyes no longer twinkled drunkenly, but his tongue slithered. His spine arched. "Oh, Lord—Lord—Lord, one of them has come back—"

His voice trailed off. His body collapsed to the floor. The silence in the wake of his settling was huge and loathsome.

Palamedes said, "Judith—"

"Give me her sword," she said.

The rapier was too heavy for her to hold. Camilla laid it over the necromancer's knees, and Judith's fingers closed around it. The steel of the hilt was bright in her hand. She squeezed down until her knuckles were white.

"At least let us get you out of here," said Gideon, who thought it was a shitty room to die in.

"No," she said. "If he comes back to life again, I will be ready. And I won't leave her now . . . nobody should ever have to watch their cavalier die."

The last Gideon ever saw of Captain Judith Deuteros was her propped up on the armchair, sitting as straight as she could possibly manage, bleeding out through the terrible wound at her gut. They left her with her head held high, and her face had no expression at all.

IT SEEMED AS THOUGH just when you least wanted them, the Eighth House were always there. They were striding down the whitewashed corridor outside Dulcinea's room as the rest of the group made their way back to her, making the whitewash look off-colour and dirty with the spotlessness of their robes. Gideon nearly drew her sword; but they had come in need, rather than in warfare.

"The Third House have defiled a body," said Silas Octakiseron, by way of hello. "The servants are all destroyed. Where's the Second and the Seventh?"

Harrow said, "Dead. Incapacitated. So is Teacher."

"That leaves us critically shorthanded," said the Eighth House necromancer, who could not be accused of having the milk of human kindness running through his veins. He did not even have the thin and tasteless juice of feigned empathy. "Listen. The Third have opened up Lady Pent—"

Palamedes said, "Abigail?" and Harrow said, "Opened up?"

"Brother Asht saw the Third leave the morgue this morning, but we have not seen them since," said Silas. "They are not in their quarters and the facility hatch is locked. We are compelled to join forces. Abigail Pent has been interfered with and opened up."

"Please elaborate *opened up*, because my imagination is better than your description and I am not having a lot of fun here," said Gideon.

The Eighth cavalier said heavily, "Come and see."

It couldn't have been an ambush. There was one House versus two. And for once, Silas Octakiseron seemed genuinely jumpy. Gideon hung back near Harrowhark as the grisly procession made its way down through the hallways again, to the atrium, working their way toward the dining hall and the makeshift morgue off the kitchen.

Harrow murmured beneath her breath, for Gideon's ears only: "The Second dead and dying. Teacher dead, and the revenants with him—"

"Teacher turned against the Second. Why are you so sure that Teacher didn't kill the others?"

"Because Teacher was afraid of Canaan House and the facility most of all," said Harrow. "I need to go back and check, but I suspect he was incapable of going down that ladder at all. He was a construct himself. But what was *Teacher* the mould for? Griddle, at the first sign of trouble—"

"Run like hell," said Gideon.

"I was going to say, *Hit it with your sword*," said Harrow.

The morgue was dreary and chill and serene. The anxiety of the rest of Canaan House had not touched it. It was getting to be untenably full: the two teens were still safely away in their cold iron drawers, and Protesilaus was in situ, though he was a head without the body. As it would have been difficult to cram all of him in, this was maybe a blessing in disguise. Magnus was also laid out on his own slab, a little too tall for comfort: but his wife—

Abigail's body had been left out, pulled fully away from its niche. She was still cold and ashen-faced and dead. Her shirt had been rolled up to her ribs. With no great elegance, a knife had been used to open up her abdomen on the right side of her body. There was a big bloodless hole there the size of a fist.

Their unseemly interest never quenched, both of the Sixth House immediately peered into the wound. Camilla flicked on her pocket torch. Harrow crowded in beside them while Gideon stayed to watch the Eighth. Silas looked as wan and uncomfortable as Abigail did; his cavalier was as impassive as ever, and he did not meet Gideon's eye.

"The cut was made with Tern's triple-knife," said Palamedes. He had laid his hand over the wound. He eased his fingers into the hole without any hint of a wince, and he held them there for a second. "And removed the—no, the kidney's still present. Cam, there was something here."

"Magnifier?"

"Don't need it. It was metal—Camilla, it was here for a *while*... the flesh had sealed over it. It would—fuck!"

The rest of the room jumped. But nothing had bitten Palamedes, except maybe internally: he was staring off into the middle distance, horrified. He looked as though he had just been given a piece of chocolate cake and found, after two bites, half a spider.

"My timing was wrong," he said softly, to himself, and again more waspishly: "Nonagesimus. My timing was wrong."

"Use your words, Sextus."

"Why didn't I investigate Abigail *before*—The Fifth went down into the facility—they must have completed a challenge. The night of the dinner. Pent was nobody's fool. They were caught out on the top of the stairs coming back. Something was hidden inside her to avoid detection—God knows why she did it, or why anyone did it—three inches long, metal, shaft, teeth—"

"A key," said Silas.

"But that's insane," said Gideon.

"Someone wanted to hide that key very badly—it may have been Lady Pent herself," said Palamedes. Finally, he withdrew his hand from her insides, and crossed to wash it in the sink, which Gideon thought was the civilised thing to do. "Or it may have been the person who killed her. There is one room that someone has made every attempt to keep us from. Octakiseron, this wasn't defilement for the sake of defilement, it was someone breaking open a lockbox."

Silas said calmly, "Are those rooms worth carrying such a sin?"

Harrow stared at him.

"You took two keys off the Seventh House," she demanded, "won one from a challenge, and never bothered to open their doors?"

"I won the first key to see what I was up against, and took possession of two more to preserve them from misuse," said Silas. "I hate this House. I despise the reduction of a holy temple to a maze and a puzzle. I took the keys so that you wouldn't have them. Nor the Sixth, nor the Third."

Palamedes wiped his hands dry on a piece of towelling and pushed his glasses up his nose. They had fogged up from his breath, in that cold and quiet place.

"Master Octakiseron," he said, "you are an intellectual cretin and a dog in a manger, but at least you're consistent. *I* know which door this opens, as does the Ninth. And, we have to assume, so does the Third. I know where they'll be, and I want to see what they've found—"

"Before it is too late," said Harrow.

She went over to the racks of bodies, and she opened up one last slab that Gideon had forgotten about entirely. It was the sad pile of cremains and bone that they had found in the furnace. The biggest bits of the corpses were no bigger than a thumbnail. Surprising Gideon—yet again—it was Colum who moved opposite to Harrow, gesturing to the bones and the ashes almost impatiently.

"This one," he said. "Half of it. It's the Seventh cavalier."

"I had assumed as much," said Harrow. "There was no skull. The time of death only made sense if it was Protesilaus."

"The other half is someone else," said Silas.

"We can't do anything for them yet," said Palamedes. "The living have to take precedence here, if we want to keep living."

As it turned out, he was wrong.

34

Six of them walked the dim hallways of Canaan House: three necromancers, three cavaliers. Every so often they would come across the fallen-down body of a skeletal servant, still and grinning emptily up at the ceiling, the chains that had bound them to this tower finally broken. Gideon found the sight of the little heaps and piles weirdly distressing. They had been walking around for ten thousand years, probably, and after two moments of panic and tragedy it was all over. The priests of the First House were gone. Maybe it was relief, or maybe it was sacrilege.

Gideon wondered what her state of mind would be after a whole myriad: bored as hell, probably. Desperate to do anything or be anyone else. She would have done everything there was to do, and if she hadn't seen it, she could probably imagine what it looked like.

They followed Harrow's map to the hallway of the stopped-up Lyctor door. The lock still carried the mark of the regenerating bone that had been such a bastard to remove. The stark painting of the waterless canyon had been taken away, and now all three necromancers stood silently before the great black pillars and bizarre carvings above. Silas said, "I feel no wards here."

Harrow said, "It's a lure."

"Or carelessness," said Palamedes.

"Or they just didn't give a shit, guys," said Gideon, "given that the key is still inside the lock."

It was the third door that day they had opened with absolutely

379

no knowledge of what would lie within. The yellow light flooded out into the corridor, and inside—

The other two laboratories Gideon had seen were caves. They were practical places to work and sleep and train and eat, homely at best, cheerless at worst, laboratories in the real sense of the word. This room was something else. It had been light and airy, once. The floors were made of varnished wood, and the walls were great white-washed panels. The panels had been painted lovingly, a long time ago, with a sprawling expanse of fanciful things: white-skinned trees with pale purple blossoms trailing into orange pools, golden clouds thick with flying birds. The room was sparsely furnished—a few broad desks with pots of neatly arranged pencils and books; a polished marble slab with a tidy array of knives and pairs of scissors; what looked to be an ancient chest freezer; some rolled-up mattresses and embroidered quilts, decaying in an open locker at one end.

This was all immaterial. Three things caught Gideon's attention immediately:

On one of the sweetly painted frescoes, fresh paint marred the blossom-decked trees. Over them, on the wall, black words a foot high proclaimed:

YOU LIED TO US

Someone was crying in the slow, dull way of a person who had been crying for hours already and didn't know how to stop.

And Ianthe sat in the centre of the room, waiting. She had taken up position on an ancient and sagging cushion, reclining on it like a queen. Joining a growing trend, her pale golden robes were spattered with blood, and her pallid yellow hair was spattered with more. She was trembling so hard that she was vibrating, and her pupils were so dilated you could have flown a shuttle through them.

"Hello, friends," she said.

The source of the crying became apparent a little way into the room. Next to the marble slab, Coronabeth was huddled, her arms wrapped around her knees as she rocked backward and forward. Next to her on the ground—

"Yes," said Ianthe. "My cavalier is dead, and I killed him. Please don't misunderstand, this isn't a confession."

Naberius Tern lay awkwardly sprawled on the ground. His expression was that of a man who had suffered the surprise of his life. There was something too white about his eyeballs, but otherwise he looked perfectly real, perfectly alive, perfectly coiffed. His lips were still a little parted, as if he were going to crossly demand an explanation any minute now.

They were stock-still. Only Palamedes had the presence of mind to move: he bypassed Ianthe entirely and crossed to where the cavalier lay, stretched out and stiffening. There were blood spatters down his front, a great tear ripped in his shirt. The blade had come through his back. Palamedes reached down, grimaced at something, and shut the man's staring eyes.

"She's right. He's gone," he said.

At this, Silas and Colum came to themselves. Colum drew. But Ianthe gave a sudden shrill trill of a laugh—a laugh with too many edges.

"Eighth! Sword away," she said. "Oh, Eighth. I'm not going to hurt you."

Ianthe suddenly tucked her knees into her chest and moaned: it was the low, querulous moan of someone with a stomach pain, almost comical.

"This is not how I had envisioned this," she said afterward, teeth chattering. "I am merely telling you. I won."

Gideon said, slowly: "Princess. None of us here speaks crazy lady."

"A very hurtful name," said Ianthe, and yawned. Her teeth started chattering again halfway through, and she bit her tongue, yowled, and spat on the floor. A thin wisp of smoke arose from the mingled spit and blood. They all stared at it.

"I admit it, this smarts," she said, broodingly. "I had my speech all planned out—I was going to brag somewhat, you understand.

Because I didn't need any of your keys, and I didn't need any of your secrets. I was always better than all of you—and none of you noticed—nobody ever notices, which is both my virtue and my downfall. How I hate being so good at my job . . . You noticed, didn't you, you horrible little Ninth goblin? Just a bit?"

The horrible little Ninth goblin stared at her with tight-pressed lips. She had inched away from Gideon toward the theorem plate, and with no sense of shame began to look it over.

"You knew about the beguiling corpse," Harrow said. "You knew how impossible it was."

"Yee-ee-s. I knew the energy transferral didn't add up. None of the thanergy signatures in this building added up . . . until I realised what we were all being led to. What the Lyctors of old were trying to tell us. You see, my field has always been energy transferral . . . large-scale energy transferral. Resurrection theory. I studied what happened when the Lord our Kindly God took our dead and dying Houses and brought them back to life, all those years ago . . . what price he would have had to pay. What displacement, the soul of a planet? What happens when a planet dies?"

"You're an occultist," said Palamedes. "You're a liminal magician. I thought you were an animaphiliac."

"That's just for show," said Ianthe. "I'm interested in the place between death and life . . . the place between release and disappearance. The place over the river. The displacement . . . where the soul goes when we knock it about . . . where the things are that eat us."

Harrow said, "You make it sound a lot more interesting than it really is."

"Stop being such a bone adept," said Ianthe. She coughed and laughed again, fretfully. She closed her eyes and let her head loll suddenly downward. When she opened them again the pupil and the iris were gone, leaving the terrible white of the eyeball. They all flinched as Ianthe cried aloud. She closed her eyes tight and shook her head like a rattle, and when she opened them back up, she was panting with exertion, as though she'd just run a race. Gideon remained in a state of flinch.

Neither of her eyes were their original colour. Both the pupil and the iris were intermingled shades of brown, purple, and blue. Ianthe closed her eyes a third time, and when the pale lashes opened, both had returned to insipid amethyst.

Palamedes had moved to the wall behind Ianthe, flanking her. She did not even bother to turn or notice. She just curled in on herself. Behind Sextus, YOU LIED TO US stretched out in vast array.

"Step one," she said, singsong, "*preserve* the soul, with intellect and memory intact. Step two, *analyse* it—understand its structure, its shape. Step three, remove and *absorb* it: take it into yourself without consuming it in the process."

"Oh, fuck," said Harrow, very quietly. She had moved back to Gideon's side now, slipping her journal back into her pocket. "The megatheorem."

"Step four, *fix* it in place so it can't deteriorate. That's the part I wasn't sure of, but I found the method here, in this very room. Step five, *incorporate* it: find a way to make the soul part of yourself without being overwhelmed. Step six: *consume the flesh*. Not the whole thing, a drop of blood will do to ground you. Step seven is *reconstruction*—making spirit and flesh work together the way they used to, in the new body. And then for the last step you hook up the cables and get the power flowing. You'll find that one a walk in the park, Eighth, I suspect it was your House's contribution."

Palamedes said: "Princess. You never had any keys. You never saw any of these rooms, except this one."

"Like I said," said Ianthe, "I am very, very good, and moreover I've got common sense. If you face the challenge rooms, you don't need the study notes—not if you're the best necromancer the Third House ever produced. Aren't I, Corona? Baby, stop crying, you're going to get such a headache."

"I came to the same conclusion you did," said Palamedes, but his voice was cold and inflexible. "I discarded it as ghastly. Ghastly, and obvious."

"*Ghastly* and *obvious* are my middle names," said the pale twin. "Sextus, you sweet Sixth prude. Use that big, muscular brain of yours. I'm not talking about the deep calculus. Ten thousand years ago there were sixteen acolytes of the King Undying, and then there were eight. Who were the cavaliers to the Lyctor faithful? Where did they go?"

Palamedes opened his mouth as though to answer this question; but he had bumped against something on the back wall, and had gone still. Gideon had never known him to be still. He was a creature of sudden movement and twitchy fingers. Camilla was watching him with obvious suspicion; one of his thumbs was tracing the edge of a black-painted letter, but the rest of his body was rigid. He looked as though someone had turned his power switch off.

But Silas was saying—

"None of this explains why you have killed Naberius Tern."

Ianthe cocked her head to one side, drunkenly, to take him in. The violet of her eyes was dried-up flowers; her mouth was the colour and softness of rocks.

"Then you weren't listening. I haven't *killed* Naberius Tern. I *ate* Naberius Tern," she said, indifferently. "I put a sword through his heart to pin his soul in place. Then I took it into my body. I've robbed Death itself . . . I have drunk up the substance of his immortal soul. And now I will burn him and burn him and burn him, and he will never really die. I have absorbed Naberius Tern . . . I am more than the sum of his half, and mine."

Her head hung close to her chest again. She gave a hiccup that sounded a little bit like a sob, and a little bit like a laugh. As she did she appeared blurry and indistinct before them—rocking out of her edges, somehow, unreal. Gideon's skin had already been crawling, but now it was trying to sprint.

Palamedes said, though he sounded as though he were ten thousand years away, "Princess, whatever you think you've done, you haven't done it."

"Oh, haven't I?" said Ianthe.

She rose to stand, but Gideon did not see her move. Ianthe came back to solidity all at once, more real now than anything around her. The room faded into insignificance. She glowed from the inside out, like she had eaten a fistful of lightbulbs. "Do you really deny it, even now?" she said. "God, it makes so much sense. Even the rapiers—light swords, light enough to be held by an amateur . . . a necromancer. Each challenge—fusing, controlling, binding, utilising—utilising whom? Did you notice that none of those challenges could be completed by yourself? No, you didn't, and yet that was the biggest red flag. I had to reverse-engineer the whole thing, just from looking at it . . . all alone."

Silas sounded quite normal now when he turned and addressed the monotonously crying girl by the slab: "Princess Coronabeth. Is she speaking the truth? And did you, at any point, attempt to stop her, or know as a necromancer what act she was committing?"

"Poor Corona!" said Ianthe. "Don't get on her case, you little white excuse for a human being. What could she have done? Don't you know my sister has a bad, sad secret? Everyone looks at her and sees what they want to see . . . beauty and power. Incredible hair. The perfect child of an indomitable House."

The Crown Princess of Ida was not acknowledging the fact that anyone was speaking to her. Her sister continued: "Everyone's blind. Corona? A born necromancer? She was as necromantic as Babs. But Dad wanted a matched set. And we didn't want anything to separate us—so we started the lie. I've had to be two necromancers since I was six. It sharpens your focus, I tell you what. No . . . Corona couldn't've stopped me becoming a Lyctor."

Palamedes said, vaguely, "This can't be right."

"Of course it's right, goosey, the Emperor himself helped come up with it."

"So that is Lyctorhood," said Silas. He sounded quiet, almost fretful, lost in thought. Gideon thought—just for a moment—that she could see Colum Asht's throat working, that his pupils had dilated just a very, very little. "To walk with the dead forever . . . enormous power, recycled within you, from the ultimate sacrifice . . . to make yourself a tomb."

"You understand, don't you?" said Ianthe.

"Yes," said Silas.

Colum closed his eyes and was still.

"Yes," repeated Silas. "I understand *fallibility* . . . and fallibility is a terrible thing to understand. I understand that if the Emperor and King Undying came to me now and asked me why I was not a Lyctor, I would fall on my knees and beg his forgiveness, that any of us had ever failed this test. May I be burnt one atom at a time in the most silent hole in the most lightless part of space, Lord—Kindly Prince—should I ever contemplate betraying the compact you appointed between him, and you, and me."

Colum opened his eyes again.

"Silas—" he began.

"I will forgive you eventually, Colum," said his purse-mouthed uncle, "for assuming I would have been prey to this temptation. Do you believe me?"

"I want to," said his nephew fervently, with a thousand-yard stare and his missing finger twitching around his shield. "God help me, I want to."

Ianthe said, contemptuously: "Come off it, you'd drain him dry if you thought it would keep your virtue intact. This is the same thing, just more humane."

"Do not speak to me anymore," said Silas. "I brand you heretic, Ianthe Tridentarius. I sentence you to death. As your cavalier is no more, you must stand in for him: make your peace with your House and your Emperor, because I swear to the King Undying you will find no more peace in this life, anywhere, in any world you care to travel to. Brother Asht—"

Harrow said, "Octakiseron, stop it. This is not the time."

"I will cleanse everything here, Ninth, to stop the Houses from finding out how we have debased ourselves," said Silas. His cavalier drew his great sword and slipped his calloused, stumped-up fingers into his targe: he had stepped before them all with an expression of something that was too deep into relief for Gideon to really translate it. His adept said: "Colum the Eighth. Show no mercy."

"Somebody stop him," said Ianthe. "Sixth. Ninth. I don't intend for anyone's blood to be spilled. Well, you know, any more."

Harrow said, "Octakiseron, you fool, can't you see—" and Camilla was saying "Everyone back off—"

But Colum Asht did not back off. He came down on Ianthe like a wolf on the fold. He was terrifically fast for such a big, ragged-looking man, and he hit her with such kinetic force that she should have been flung back to splatter on the wall like a discarded sandwich. His arm was true and steady; there was no hesitation in his hand or in his blade.

Neither was there any hesitation in Ianthe's. Gideon had seen the exquisite sword of the Third House lying in a smear of blood next to the body of its cavalier: now it was suddenly in the hand of its necromantic princess. She met his blade with a flat parry—it knocked away that titanic blow as though Ianthe were not a head shorter and a third of his weight—and she eased back into perfect, sure-footed precision.

It was Naberius Tern's movement that tucked Ianthe's arm behind her back, and Naberius Tern's perfect, precise footwork. It was profoundly weird to see Naberius Tern's moves restrung in Ianthe Tridentarius's body—but there they were, recreated right down to the way she held her head. Colum moved in for advantage, a high vertical cut to her naked collarbones. She avoided his move with boyish contempt and countered. Colum had to scramble to meet her.

It was only then that it hit home to Gideon what Ianthe had done. The bizarre sight of a necromancer holding a *sword*—a ghost fighting inside the meat suit of his adept—made it real that Naberius was dead, but that he was dead inside Ianthe. It was not that he had taught her how to fight: it was him fighting. There was Naberius's instant counterstrike; there was Naberius's gorgeous deflection, the tiny movement knocking Colum's shield away. Normally Gideon would have been fascinated to watch the cavalier of the Eighth at work—he was as light on his feet as a feather, and yet his blows were all heavy as lead—but her gaze was locked on Ianthe, only Ianthe, who was moving more Naberius than Naberius ever could, whose body was agile and lithe and as suprahuman as a wisp.

But there was one catch. The sword of the Third House must have weighed at least a kilogram, and Naberius's muscle memory could not quite account for Ianthe's arms. Some power must have been compensating for her body—her elbow should have been locking like a door—but whatever she was doing to wield that thing, it was just a fraction not good enough. She was sweating. There was a pucker in the middle of that preternaturally calm forehead, a wince in the eyes, the slight drunken lolling of the head that she had suffered from before. As she faded, Colum took the advantage. She shook herself, and he raised his foot and kicked her sword out of her hand. It spun over to the wall where Palamedes had been, and clattered there miserably, far out of reach. Colum raised his sword.

The Princess of the Third House raised her hand to her mouth, gored a chunk of flesh from the heel of her palm, and spat it at him like a missile. Ianthe disappeared beneath a greasy, billowing tent—cellular, fleshy, coated all over with neon-yellow bubbles and thin pink film. Colum bounced off this thing as though he had hit a brick wall. He went ass-over-teakettle and rolled over and over, only at the last skidding back up to stand, locking himself into position, panting. Where there had been a necromancer, there was instead a semitransparent dome of skin and subcutaneous fat, baffling to the eye. Nothing loath, Colum charged again, smashing his shield down on it with a bad wet noise like *squirk*. It was rubbery: it bounced back against him. He gave a mighty slash downward with his sword: the flesh-bubble tore and bled, but did not give.

Gideon put her hand on her sword to draw it, and slipped her fingers into her gauntlet. Thin fingers wrapped around her wrist. When she looked around, Harrow was tight-lipped.

"Don't go near them," she said. "Don't touch her. Don't think about touching her."

Gideon looked around wildly for the Sixth House: she found only Camilla, swords sheathed, face impassive. Those watching were doing so in near-embarrassed, breathless silence as Colum circled the horrible skin shield, testing it with slashes, shoving his blade home hard and grunting when the flesh did not give. Then Silas closed his eyes and said quietly, "The necromancer must fight the necromancer."

Colum raised his arm for a beautiful downward cross-slice, then jerked back as though he had been stung. He retreated, sword and small shield at the ready, and gritted his teeth. Gideon now knew what leeching felt like, and swore to God she could see the haze in the air and feel the chilly suction as his necromancer began to siphon.

"Stop fighting me," said Silas, without opening his eyes.

Colum said gruffly: "Don't do it. Don't put me under. Not this time."

"Brother Asht," said his necromancer, "if you cannot believe, then for God's sake *obey*."

Colum made a sound in the back of his throat. Ianthe was visible as a blurred shape behind the yellow-streaked flesh wall. Silas walked forward on light feet—crackles of electricity arcing over his skin, his hands—and laid his palms on the shield.

The skin puddled around his fingers, and for a moment Gideon thought it was working. Then the wall sucked his hands inward, ripping and bristling with canine teeth. The shield bit down savagely, and there was blood at Silas's wrists. He cried out, and then closed his eyes, the heat pouring off him in waves; Colum went greyer and greyer, and stiller and stiller, and Silas squeezed his hands into fists.

The shield went *pop*, like a pimple or an eyeball, and fell to the floor in ragged strips and jiggling globs. Silas looked almost surprised to see Ianthe, who was gripping her head in tight-knuckled hands. When Ianthe looked up, her eyes were wild and white again, and she screamed in a voice that required many more vocal cords than she possessed.

Silas approached her with hands like hot white murder. Ianthe ducked past him and flung herself down onto one of the still-bubbling sheets that had made up her shield. She sunk down into the skin with a splash, peppering the wooden floor with hot yellow fat. The skin blistered and crinkled up on itself like it had been burnt, and then it deliquesced into a viscous puddle, leaving no trace of Ianthe.

Silas knelt by the puddle, and—silver chain starting to warp and buckle on his perfect white tunic—thrust his hand into it. Colum made a noise as though he had been punched in the gut. A bloodied hand emerged from the puddle, seized Silas by the shoulder, and jerked him in.

The ceiling broke apart like a thundercloud, and a torrent of bloody, fatty rain sluiced down on them all. Gideon and Harrow gagged and pulled their hoods down over their heads. Two figures tumbled from above, filthy with blood and lymph. Ianthe landed on her feet, and delicately shivered off the fetid red soup, more or less unblemished, while Silas fell heavily to earth. There was a faint red mark like a slap on Ianthe's face; she touched her cheek, and it paled into nothing.

Silas clambered to his knees, clasped his fingers together, and the feeling of suction popped the pressure in both of Gideon's ears. She saw his power warping around Ianthe now, and she gave a disbelieving laugh. She was breathing hard, almost hyperventilating.

"Octakiseron," Ianthe said, "you can't take it faster than I can make it."

"He's trying to drain her," muttered Harrow, spellbound. "But he's splitting his focus—he needs to bring Colum back, or—"

Colum—ashen as his name, drunk in movement, numb—had lifted his sword, and was moving inexorably toward Ianthe. He backhanded her full across the face with his shield, as though to test her. Ianthe's head snapped back, but she looked more dazed and surprised than hurt or injured. Her breath was coming in stutters. She righted herself like nothing had happened, and the cavalier thrust forward with his blade. She raised her hand and wrapped it around the shining edge like it was nothing. Her hand was bloody, but the blood itself pushed back gracefully, quietly repelling the blade like it was all just so many more fingers.

Silas clasped his hands together, and the pressure nearly made

Gideon hurl. Colum shook his sword—the blood broke off like shards of glass—and Ianthe staggered, though nobody had touched her. As she lurched away from Colum the blood on the floor and the walls and the ceiling was drying up, burning into itself as though it had never been. Her eyes were that awful, blank white, and she was holding her head and shaking it as though to reposition her brain.

"Stop doing this to me!" she was hissing. "Stop it!"

Colum turned and with a liquid, exquisite movement, sliced down across her back. It was a shallow cut. Ianthe did not even seem to notice. The blood bubbled over her pretty yellow robe and the new gash revealed the wound sucking in on itself and zipping together. "Listen," she was saying, "Babs, *listen*."

Silas slammed his fists on the ground. The air was choked from Ianthe's lungs. Her mouth and skin puckered and withered: she stopped, awkward, stiff, eyes bulging in surprise. The remnants of blood rose from the floor as pale smoke, trailing heavenward all around them. For a moment everything was blanched clean and luminously white. In the middle of all this stood Ianthe, unnaturally still and bent. Blood dripped calmly out of Silas's nose and ears in the blood sweat.

Gideon felt Harrow flinch—

Ianthe's pallid purple irises had returned, and so had the pupils, though perhaps all a little paler than before. She was ageing before their eyes. Her skin sloughed off in papery threads. But she was not staring at Silas, who held her as firmly as though he had her clasped in his hands. She was staring, disbelieving, at Colum the Eighth.

"Well, now you're fucked," she announced.

Colum the Eighth's eyes were as liquid black as, before, Ianthe's had been liquid white. He had stopped moving as a human being did. The warrior's economy of movement; the long and lovely lines of someone who had trained with the sword his whole life; the swift-footedness was gone. He now moved like there were six people inside him, and none of those six people had ever been inside a human being before. He sniffed. He craned his head around—and kept craning. With an awful crack, his head turned one hundred and eighty degrees to look impassively at the room behind him.

One of the lightbulbs screamed, exploded, died in a shower of sparks. The air was very cold. Gideon's breath came as frosty white frills in the sudden darkness, and the remaining lights struggled to pierce the gloom. Colum licked his lips with a grey tongue.

Particles of bone bounced along the floor. Harrowhark had thrown them in a long, overhand arc, and they fell true at Colum's feet. Spikes erupted from the ground, crowding Colum between them, locking him in tight. Colum raised his white-booted foot indifferently, and kicked through them. They exploded into dusty, tooth-coloured clouds of calcium.

Silas looked up, nearly foetal, from the floor. He still glowed like a pearl in a sunbeam, but he'd lost his focus. Ianthe stepped out of his spell disdainfully, flesh plumping, colour coming back to her face, and she itched herself. There were lights beneath Colum the Eighth's skin: things pushed and slithered along his muscles as he walked, heavy-footed, rocking from side to side.

Silas wiped the blood away from his nose and mouth and said calmly: "Brother Asht, listen to the words of the head of your House."

Colum advanced.

"Come back," said Silas, unruffled. "I bid you return. I bid you return. Colum—I bid you return. I bid you return. *I bid you return.* I bid. I bid, I bid, I bid— *Colum—*"

The thing that lived in Colum raised Colum's sword, and drove the point through Silas Octakiseron's throat.

Gideon moved. She heard Harrow shout a warning, but she couldn't help it. She drew her rapier from its scabbard, and she threw herself at the grey thing wearing a person skin. It was not a cavalier: it did not meet the arc of her sword with a parry. It just clouted her with Colum's shield with a strength no human being ever had. Gideon staggered, very nearly fell, ducked out of the way of a sword gracelessly slammed downward. She took advantage of his movement, got up close, pinned his arm between her body and her sword and shattered his wrist with a meaty *crack*. The thing opened its mouth and opened its eyes, right up in her face. Its eyeballs were gone—Colum's eyeballs were gone—and now the sockets were mouths ringed with teeth, with little tongues slithering out of them. The tongue in his original mouth extended out, down, wrapping itself around her neck—

"Enough," said Ianthe.

She appeared behind the grey-thing-that-had-been-Colum. She took its twisted neck in her hands as calmly and easily as though it were an animal, and she tilted it. The neck snapped. Her fingertips dipped inside the skin; the eye-mouths shrilled, and the tongue around Gideon's neck flopped away, and both those mouths dissolved into brackish fluid. The body dropped to the floor—

—and it was Colum again, face disfigured, neck on the wrong way, sprawled over the pierced shell of his young dead uncle. There was no solace in that big, beat-up body, clutched around his necromancer's in morbid imitation of the whole of their lives. Neither of them wore white anymore: they were stained all the way through, yellow, red, pink.

The lights buzzed again dismally. The air cleared. Ianthe was left among the gore looking like a moth, fairylike. She picked up the hem of her skirts delicately and shook them. The blood and muck came off like it was powder.

The Princess of Ida beheld the mess around her: then she slapped herself very lightly, like you would to wake someone up.

"Get it together," she told herself. "You nearly lost that."

She turned to Gideon, Camilla, and Harrow, and she said—

"There are worse things than myself in this building. Have that one for free."

Then she stepped backward, into the puddled spray of Silas's blood, and disappeared. They were left alone in the room, with the quiet, stretched-out corpses of Silas Octakiseron, Colum Asht, and Naberius Tern; and the low, dreary breathing of Coronabeth Tridentarius, looking like chopped-up jewellery.

Gideon lurched toward her, out of desperation to move—to move away from the middle and what was in it, to move toward the abandoned Third twin. Corona looked up at her with tears on her beautiful lashes and eyes swollen from crying. She threw herself into Gideon's arms, and she sobbed, silently now, utterly destroyed. Gideon was soothed by the fact that someone in this madhouse was still human enough to cry.

"Are you okay—I mean, are you all right," said Gideon.

Corona recoiled from Gideon and looked up at her, her golden hair smeared to her forehead with sweat and tears. "She took Babs," she said, which seemed fair enough.

But then Corona started crying again, big tears leaking out of her eyes, her voice thick with misery and self-pity. "And who even cares about Babs? Babs! She could have taken *me*."

THEY LEFT THE LONELY twin to her bitter, alien grief. Camilla and Harrow and Gideon stood together out in the hallway, reeling. Gideon was rotating her shoulder in its socket to make sure nothing had graunched out of place, and Harrowhark was flicking gobs of something unspeakable off her sleeves, when Camilla said: "The Warden. Where's the Warden?"

"I lost track of him during the fight," said Gideon. "I thought he was behind you."

Harrow said, "He was—and I was by the door. I saw him only a few minutes ago."

"I lost sight of him," Camilla said. "I never lose sight of him."

"Slow your roll," said Gideon, with far more assurance than she actually felt. "He's a big boy. He's probably gone to make sure Dulcinea's okay. Harrow says I'm a weenie over Dulcinea—" ("You are," said Harrow, "a weenie over Dulcinea,") "—but he's six hundred per cent weenier than I am, which I still don't get."

Camilla looked at her and brushed her dark, slanted fringe out of her eyes. There was something in her gaze starker than impatience.

"The Warden," she said, "has been exchanging letters with Dulcinea Septimus for twelve years. He's been—a weenie—over her. One of the reasons he became the heir of the House was to meet her on even footing. His pursuit of medical science was entirely for her benefit."

This turned all the fluids in Gideon's body to ice-cold piss.

"She—she never mentioned him at all," she said, stupidly.

"No," said Camilla.

"But she—I mean, I was spending so much time with her—"

"Yes," said Camilla.

"Oh, God," said Gideon. "And he was so nice about it. Oh my God. Why the fuck did he not *say anything*? I didn't—I mean, I never really—I mean, she and I weren't—"

"He asked her to marry him a year ago," said Camilla ruthlessly, some floodgate down now, "so that she could spend the rest of her time with someone who cared about her comfort. She refused, but not on the grounds that she didn't like him. And they weren't going to relax Imperial rules about necromancers marrying out of House. The letters grew sparser after that. And when he arrived here—she'd moved on. He told me he was glad that she was spending time with someone who made her laugh."

Five people had died that day; it was weird how the small things ballooned out in importance, comparatively. The tragedy saturated the stiffening bones and static hearts lying in state at Canaan House, but there was also deep tragedy in the flawed beams holding up their lives. An eight-year-old writing love letters to a terminally ill teenager. A girl falling in love with the beautiful stiff she'd been conceived solely to look after. A foundling chasing the approval of a House disappointed with her immunity to foundling-killing gas.

Gideon lay on the floor, facedown, and became hysterical.

Her necromancer was saying, "None of this makes any sense."

"Nope," said Camilla heavily, "but it never has the whole time I've known them both."

"No," said Harrow. "I mean that Dulcinea Septimus twice spoke of Palamedes Sextus to me as a stranger. She told me that she didn't know him well at all, after he had turned down her offer for the siphoning challenge."

Gideon, facedown on the dusty ground, moaned: "I want to die."

She was nudged with a foot, not unkindly. "Get up, Griddle."

"Why was I born so attractive?"

"Because everyone would have throttled you within the first five minutes otherwise," said her necromancer. Her attention was on Camilla: "Yet why her about-face, if it's all how you say it was? I still don't understand."

"If *I* did," said the Sixth cavalier restlessly, "my quality of life, my sleep, and my sense of well-being would improve. Ninth, get up. He doesn't hate you. You didn't ruin anything. He and she were always more complicated than that. He never even met her in person until he came here."

Gideon emerged from her prone position and sprang to her feet. Her heart was a dry cinder, but it still seemed ridiculously important that Palamedes Sextus be okay with her: that at the end of this whole world, right before their divine intervention, all the little muddles of their personal lives be sorted out.

"I've got to catch up with him," she said, "please give me a couple minutes alone. Harrow, go get my two-hander, it's in the false bottom of my trunk." ("Your *what*?" said Harrow, affrighted.) "Cam, please, do me a massive solid here and keep an eye on her. I'm sorry I'm a homewrecker."

Gideon turned and sprinted away. She heard Harrow yell, "*Nav!*" but paid her no attention. Her rapier swung awkwardly into her hip, and her arm twinged in its socket, and her neck still felt weird, but all she could do was run as hard and as fast as she could to the place where she knew she'd find her last two living allies: the sickroom where Dulcinea Septimus lay dying.

She found the Warden standing at the midpoint along the long corridor, staring at the shut door to her room. The hem of his grey robe whispered on the ground, and he seemed lost in thought. Gideon took a breath, which alerted him to her presence. He took off his glasses, wiped the lens with his sleeve, and looked back at her as he perched them back on his long nose.

It seemed as though they looked at each other for such a long time. She took a step forward, and opened her mouth to say, *Sextus, I'm sorry*—

He folded his fingers together as you would a piece of paper. Her body stopped where it stood, as though steel needles had pierced her hands and her legs. Gideon felt cold all over. She tried to speak, but her tongue cleaved to the roof of her mouth and she tasted blood. She struggled—an insect pinned to its backing—and he looked at her, cold and dispassionate, unlike himself.

Palamedes surveyed his work, and he saw that it was good. Then he opened Dulcinea's door. Gideon tried to flail against her invisible bonds, but her bones felt rigid in her body, like she was just the meat sock around them. Her heart struggled against her inflexible rib cage, her terror rising in her mouth. He smiled, and with that strange alchemy he was made lovely, his grey eyes bright and clear. Palamedes entered the sickroom.

He did not shut the door. There were soft noises within. Then she heard his voice, distinctly:

"I wish I had talked to you right at the start."

Dulcinea's voice was quiet but audible—

"Why didn't you?"

"I was afraid," he said frankly. "I was stupid. My heart was broken, you see. So it was easier to believe—that things had simply changed between us. That Dulcinea Septimus had been trying to spare my feelings—coddling an ignorant child who had tried to save her from something she understood far better than I ever could. I cared about her, and Camilla cared about us. I thought Dulcinea was saving us both the heartache of watching her fail, and die, during our task."

There was silence in the room. He added, "When this started I was eight and you—you, Dulcinea—were fifteen. My feelings were intense, but for God's sake, of course I understood. I was an *infant*. And yet I was shown endless tact and sympathy. My feelings were always taken as deadly serious, and I was treated as someone who knew what he was talking about. Does that run in the Seventh House?"

Gideon could hear the faint smile in Dulcinea's voice. "I suppose it does. They have been letting young necromancers die for a very, very long time. When you grow up awfully ill, you're used to everyone making those decisions for you . . . and hating it . . . so you do tend to want to take everyone's feelings as seriously as yours aren't."

Palamedes said, "There are two things I want to know."

"You can have more than two, if you want. I've got all day."

"I don't need more than two," he said calmly. "The first is: Why the Fifth?"

There was a puzzled pause. "The Fifth?"

"The Ninth and Eighth houses posed the most clear and present danger," he said. "The Ninth due to Harrow's sheer ability, the Eighth due to how easily they could have outed you—any slip would have shown an Eighth necromancer that you weren't what you claimed. He would only have had to siphon you to know. I even wonder why *I'm* still walking around, if you don't find that arrogant. But it was the Fifth House that scared you."

"I don't—"

"Don't lie to me, please."

Dulcinea said, "I have never lied to any of you."

"Then—*why*?"

A tiny, fluttering sigh, like a butterfly coming to rest. Gideon heard her say: "Well, think about it. Abigail Pent was a mature speaker to the dead. That's no good. It's not insurmountable—but it's a problem. But while that was a factor, it wasn't the reason . . . that was her *hobby*."

"Hobby?"

"I didn't think anybody would care about the distant past . . . but Pent had an unwholesome interest in history. She was interested in all the old things she was finding in the library, in the rooms. Letters, notes . . . pictures . . . the archaeology of a human life."

"Abigail Pent may have been a necromancer, but she was also a historian—a famous one, I might add. You didn't do your research."

"Oh, I've been kicking myself, believe me. I should have gone and swept the whole place first thing. But—I was nostalgic."

"I see."

"Gosh, I'm glad you didn't. I didn't comprehend your mastery of the ghost-within-the-thing. Sixth psychometry." There was a sudden, tinkling laugh. "I think you ought to be really glad I didn't compre-hend that. Pent by herself gave me such a fright."

"And you put the key inside her—why?"

"Time," said Dulcinea. "I couldn't afford anybody catching me with it. Hiding it in her flesh obscured its traces. I thought you'd find it earlier, honestly . . . but it gave me time to gum up the lock. Who got rid of that? I'd thought I'd made it absolutely unusable."

"That was the Ninth."

"That's more than impressive," she said. "The Emperor would love to get hold of her . . . thank goodness he never will. Well, that's an-other blow to my ego. If I'd thought the lock could have been broken *and* the key found, I would have cleaned out the place, I wouldn't have left it to be found . . . but that's why we're having this conver-sation now, aren't we? You used your psychometric tricks on the message. If you hadn't gone in there, you never would have known that I'd been in there too. Am I right?"

"Maybe," said Palamedes. "Maybe."

"What's your second question?"

Gideon struggled again, but she was caught as fast as if the very air around her were glue. Her eyes were streaming from her total inability to blink. She could breathe, and she could listen, and that was it. Her brain was full of sweet fuck-all.

Palamedes said, very quietly: "Where is she?"

There was no answer.

He said, "I repeat. Where is she?"

"I thought she and I had come to an understanding," Dulcinea admitted easily. "If she had only told me about you . . . I could have taken some additional precautions."

"Tell me what you have done," said Palamedes, "with Dulcinea Septimus."

"Oh, she's still here," said the person who wasn't Dulcinea Septi-mus, dismissively. "She came at the Emperor's call, cavalier in tow. What happened to him was an accident—when I boarded her ship he refused to hear a word of reason, and I had to kill him. Which didn't have to happen . . . not like that, anyway. Then she and I talked . . . We are very much alike. I don't mean just in appearance, though that *was* the case, except in the eyes, as the Seventh House is awfully predictable for looks—but our illness . . . she was very ill, as ill as I was, when I first came here. She might have lived out the first few weeks she was here, Sextus, or she mightn't have."

He said, "Then that story about Protesilaus and the Seventh House was a lie."

"You're not listening. I never lied," said the voice. "I said that it was a hypothetical, and you all agreed."

"Semantics."

"You should have listened more closely. But I never ever lied. I am from the Seventh House . . . and it was an accident. Anyway, she and I talked. She was a sweet little thing. I really had wanted to do something for her—and afterward, I kept her for the longest time . . . until someone took out my cavalier. Then I had to get rid of her, quickly . . . the furnace was the only option. Don't look at me like that. I'm not a monster. Septimus was dead before the shuttle landed at Canaan . . . she hardly suffered."

There was a very long pause. Palamedes's voice betrayed nothing when he said: "Well, that's something, at least. I suppose we're all to follow now?"

"Yes, but this wasn't really about any of you," said the woman in the room with him. "Not personally. I knew that if I ruined his Lyctor plans—killed the heirs and cavaliers to all the other eight Houses—I'd draw him back to the system, but I had to do it in a subtle enough way that he wouldn't bring the remaining Hands with him. If I had arrived in full force, he'd have turned up on a war footing, and sent the Lyctors to do all the dirty work like always. This way he's lulled into a false sense of . . . semisecurity, I suppose. And he won't even bother coming within Dominicus's demesne. He'll sit out there beyond the system—trying to find out what's happening— right where I need him to be. I'll give the King Undying, the Necrolord Prime, the Resurrector, my lord and master front-row seats as I shatter his Houses, one by one, and find out how many of them it takes before he breaks and crosses over, before he sees what will come when I call . . . and then I won't have to do anything. It will be too late."

A pause.

"Why would one of the Emperor's Lyctors hate him?"

"Hate him?" The voice of the girl whom Gideon had known as Dulcinea rose, high and intent. "*Hate* him? I have loved that man for ten thousand years. We all loved him, every one of us. We worshipped him like a king. Like a god! Like a brother."

Her voice dropped, and she sounded very normal and very old: "I don't know why I'm telling you this . . . you who have been alive for less than a heartbeat, when I have lived past the time when life loses meaning. Thank your lucky stars that none of you became Lyctor, Palamedes Sextus. It is neither life nor death—it's something in between, and nobody should ever ask you to embrace it. Not even him. Especially not him."

"I wouldn't have done that to Camilla."

"So you know how it happens. Clever boy! I knew you'd all work it out . . . eventually. I didn't want to do it either . . . I didn't want to do it at all . . . but I was dying. Loveday—she was my cavalier—she and I thought it could make me live. Instead I've just kept dying, all this time. No, you wouldn't have done it, and you're smart not to. You can't do that to somebody's soul. Teacher was nearly demented. Did you know what we did to him? I say *we*, but he wasn't *my* project . . . he was a holy terror. Blame your own House for that! I can't be grateful enough to those Second ninnies for killing him and calling for help. He was the only one here who scared me. He couldn't have stopped me, but he might have made things stupid."

"Why did Teacher not recognise you?"

"Perhaps he did," said the woman. It sounded like she was smiling. "Who knows what that soul melange was ever thinking?"

There was another pause. She said, "You've taken this much more sensibly than I thought you would. When you're young, you do everything the moment you think about it. For example, I've been thinking about doing this for the last three hundred years . . . but I assumed you would try something silly when you realized she was dead."

"I wouldn't ever try to do something silly," Palamedes said lightly. "I made the decision to kill you the moment I knew there was no more chance to save her. That's all."

She laughed, as clear and as bright as ice. It was arrested midway through by a cough—a deep, sick-sounding cough—but she laughed through it anyway, as though she didn't care.

"Oh, don't . . . don't."

"I just had to buy enough time," he said, "to do it slowly enough that you wouldn't notice—to keep you talking."

There was another laugh, but this one was punctuated by a big wet cough too. No laughter followed. She said, "Young Warden of the Sixth House, what have you done?"

"Tied the noose," said Palamedes Sextus. "You gave me the rope. You have severe blood cancer . . . just as Dulcinea did. Advanced, as hers was when she died. Static, because the Lyctor process begins radical cell renewal at the point of absorption. All this time we've been talking, I've been taking stock of everything that's wrong with you—your bacterial lung infection, the neoplasms in your skeletal structure—and I've pushed them along. You've been in a terrific amount of pain for the last myriad. I hope that pain is nothing to what your own body's about to do to you, Lyctor. You're going to die spewing your own lungs out of your nostrils, having failed at the finish line because you couldn't help but prattle about why you killed innocent people, as though your reasons were *interesting* . . . This is for the Fifth and the Fourth—for everyone who's died, directly or indirectly, due to you—and most personally, this is for Dulcinea Septimus."

The coughing didn't stop. Not-Dulcinea sounded impressed, but not particularly worried. "Oh, it's going to take a great deal more than that. You know what I am . . . and you know what I can do."

"Yes," said Palamedes. "I also know you must have studied radical thanergetic fission, so you know what happens when a necroman-cer disperses their entire reserve of thanergy very, very quickly."

"What?" said the woman.

He raised his voice:

"Gideon!" he called out. "Tell Camilla—"

He stopped.

"Oh, never mind. She knows what to do."

The sickroom exploded into white fire, and the bonds pinning Gideon snapped. She fell hard against the wall and spun, drunkenly, lurching back down the corridor as Palamedes Sextus made every-thing burn. There was no heat, but Gideon sprinted away from that cold white death without bothering to spare a glance behind as though flames were licking at her heels. There was another enor-mous *CRRR-RRR-RRRACK* and a *boom*. The ceiling shook wide showers of plaster dust down on her head as she threw herself bodily through a doorway. She ran for her life down the long corridors, past ancient portraits and crumbling statues, the grave goods of the tomb of Canaan House, the mechanisms of this feeble shitty machine crumbling as Palamedes Sextus became a god-killing star.

Gideon fell to her knees in the atrium, before the dried-up foun-tain with its dried-up skeleton and his soggy towels. She put her forehead to the lip of the fountain's marble and pressed a dent into herself, still listening to the muffled sounds of destruction behind her. She pressed as though sheer surface contact alone would al-low her to get off the ride. How long she did that for—how hard she pressed, and how long she huddled—she did not know. Her mouth was tight with wanting to cry, but her eyes were dry as salt.

Years later—lifetimes later—there was movement at the entrance of the atrium she had flung herself through. Gideon turned her head.

White steam poured from the hole. Within the steam stood a woman: her fawn-coloured curls sadly sizzled to nothing, her deep blue eyes like electromagnetic radiation. Huge wounds exposed her bones and the bright pink meat inside her arms and her neck and her legs, and those wounds were sewing themselves up even as Gideon watched. She had wrapped herself in the bloodied white sheet that had covered her sickbed, and she was standing upright as though it was the easiest thing in the world. Her face was old—lineless and old, older than the rot of the whole of Canaan.

The woman Gideon had kind of had the hots for held a gleaming rapier. She was barefoot. She leaned in the smoking doorway and turned away, and she began to cough: she spasmed, retched, clung to the frame for support. With a great asphyxiating bellow, she vomited what looked like most of a lung—studded all over with malformed bronchi, with wobbling purple barbs and whole fingernails—onto the ground in front of them. It went *splat*.

She groaned, closed those terrible blue eyes and pushed herself to stand. Blood dripped down her chin. She opened her eyes again.

"My name is Cytherea the First," she said. "Lyctor of the Great Resurrection, the seventh saint to serve the King Undying. I am a necromancer and I am a cavalier. I am the vengeance of the ten billion. I have come back home to kill the Emperor and burn his Houses. And Gideon the Ninth . . ."

She walked toward Gideon, and she raised her sword. She smiled.

"This begins with you."

36

CAMILLA HIT THE ADVANCING Lyctor like the wrath of the Emperor.

She crashed into her from the side, her two knives flashing like signal lamps in the sunlit hall. Dulcinea—Cytherea—staggered, flung up a parry, gave ground. She needed distance to bring her rapier to bear, but Camilla denied it to her; every step she fell back, the cavalier pushed forward, attacking so fast and with such ferocity Gideon could hardly see the individual strikes. For a second or two she thought Cytherea was meeting the blows with a bare hand, until she saw that a shank of bone had sprouted from the backs of her knuckles.

Camilla Hect off the leash was like light moving across water. She punched her knives into the Lyctor's guard over and over and over. Cytherea met them ably, but such was Camilla's speed and perfect hate that she could only hope to block the thunderstorm of blows; she could not even begin to push back against them.

This gave Gideon time to stand, to ready her sword and slide her gauntlet home, biting the straps tight with her teeth. It was a relief to know she would never have to tell Camilla that her necromancer had died. She was already fighting as though her heart had exploded.

"Stop it," said Cytherea. Camilla did not hear her. She drove past the Lyctor's guard and found her blade trapped in a thicket of spines that had evolved from the offhand spur of bone. The spines, flexing like snakes, began to curl over the guard, past her hand, onto her wrist.

Scarcely missing a beat, she stepped in and headbutted Cytherea in the face. The Lyctor's head snapped back, but no blood showed. She laughed, thickly, hoarse. Camilla's body jerked, still pinned by the tangle of bones around her hand. Her other knife fell from slack fingers to clatter on the floor. Her skin seemed to ripple and take on a greyish tinge. She began to wither.

As Gideon sized up the best angle to join the fray, a bleached, skeletal hand emerged from behind Cytherea and grabbed her face. Another hand gripped her sword-arm at the wrist. Over Gideon's shoulder, the skeleton in the fountain began to stir. Harrowhark stood at the top of the stairs, hands full of white particles, her skull-painted face as hard and merciless as morning: she flung them out before her like she was sowing a field. From each grain of bone a perfectly formed skeleton arose, a huge angular mass jostling and crowding on the stairs, and they poured out in single formation to rush the Lyctor one by one. She went under in a sea of bone.

Camilla hauled herself away from the rushing, grinding ocean of Harrow's mindless dead, clutching her knives more firmly in her recovering hands—the muscles in her arms were visibly springing back into shape. Gideon advanced, heart in her throat, moving to take Camilla's place.

"Leave it!" barked her necromancer. "Nav! *Here!*"

Six more skeletons sprang to her call. They were unstrapping something from Harrow's back—it was Gideon's longsword, shining and heavy and sharp. She unbuckled her scabbard and let the black rapier fall—shook her gauntlet off next to it, and gave them both a private prayer of thanksgiving for services rendered—and she caught her sword by the hilt as it fell toward her. She wrapped her hands around its grip and hefted its old familiar weight.

The squirming pile of skeletons exploded outward, and so did the floor. Bricks and tiles and splinters of wood scythed across the atrium like shrapnel. Gideon threw herself behind the fountain, Camilla dived behind an old sofa and Harrow wrapped herself in a hard white cocoon. Skeletons tumbled through the air like morbid rag dolls, bone shrapnel pinging off every surface. Cytherea the First emerged from the clusterfuck, coughing into the back of her hand, looking rumpled but entirely whole.

From the hole emerged one long, overjointed leg, then another. And another. A fretwork of bones, a net, a lace of them—long stingers of teeth, a nesting body, a construct so big that it turned one's bowels into an icebox. The hulking construct that had killed Isaac Tettares filled the room behind its mistress, stretching itself out and expanding, pulverising a wall and a staircase as it emerged. Its great bone head lolled and loomed above them, masklike, with its hideous moulded lips and squinted-shut eyes.

But now this benighted vision stood before its natural predator, the Reverend Daughter of the Ninth House. As yet more skeletons jerked and clambered upward from their fallen comrades, Gideon got up, dusted herself off, and found Harrow standing in a pool of osseous dust and facing the construct with a hot-eyed, half-delighted anticipation. Without even thinking about it, her body moved to take her rightful place: in front of her necromancer, sword held ready.

"This is the thing that killed Isaac," said Gideon urgently. The enormous construct was still trying to wriggle one leg free from the floor, which would have been funny if it hadn't been so terrible.

"Sextus—?"

"Dead."

Harrow's mouth briefly ruckled. "A necromancer alone can't bring that down, Griddle. That's regenerating bone."

"I'm not running, Harrow!"

"Of course we're not running," said Harrowhark disdainfully. "I said a necromancer *alone*. I have you. We bring hell."

"Harrow—Harrow, Dulcinea's a Lyctor, a real one—"

"Then we're all dead, Nav, but let's bring hell *first*," said Harrow. Gideon looked over her shoulder at her, and caught the Reverend Daughter's smile. There was blood sweat coming out of her left ear, but her smile was long and sweet and beautiful. Gideon found herself smiling back so hard her mouth hurt.

Her adept said: "I'll keep it off you. Nav, show them what the Ninth House does."

Gideon lifted her sword. The construct worked itself free of its last confines of masonry and rotten wood and heaved before them, flexing itself like a butterfly.

"We do bones, motherfucker," she said.

Her arms were whole again. Her most beloved and true companion—her plain two-hander, unadorned and perfect—smashed through tendrils and teeth like a jackhammer drill. Stinging flails of bone met her blade and exploded into grey foam as she stood her ground and pummelled them with great, swinging arcs of good cold Ninth House steel.

With Harrow there, suddenly it was easy, and her horror of the monster turned to the ferocious joy of vengeance. Long years of warfare meant that they each knew exactly where the other would stand—every arc of a sword, every jostling scapula. No hole in the other's defences went unshielded. They had never fought together before, but they had always fought, and they could work in and around each other without a second's thought.

Gideon pushed for space. She forced a path, step by careful step, toward the centre of the construct. A tentacle lashed out at her leg; she sliced it open on the downswing and danced away from a stiff whip of molars aimed straight at her heart. Behind her, Harrow took it: it trembled into its component parts, then became a dust of teeth, which settled into a glue that stuck wobbling tendrils together so they broke themselves into pieces trying to smash away. What Harrow did not take, Gideon struck down. She struck at spines with the mad fury and sudden belief that if she just hit and hit and hit—accurately enough and hard enough and well enough—she could rewrite time and save Isaac and Jeannemary; save Abigail, save Magnus.

But the size of the thing defied thought, and every strike created shrapnel. Harrow was doing something, shielding her somehow; the air was a hail of sharp particles that ought to have shredded her skin, and yet none of them seemed to reach her. Even so, the white-out of pinging, ricocheting chips made it hard to see her target. From the corner of her eye, she saw Camilla running through a blizzard of teeth and spines and swinging bone lappets with both knives crossed in front of her chest—then she was gone, lost to view.

Gideon ploughed through a veil of flimsy bone shafts. They were under the bulk of the construct now. Six more skeletons sprang to life and formed a perimeter—these were pillars without legs, thrust through the floor, with the big plated arms and bone-wadded shoulders of the construct in the Response room. They grappled great breadths of the construct's tendrils to themselves, and in the clearing between their backs Harrow flexed her fingers together. She shook finger bones out of her sleeves and slapped the trembling phalanges between her hands like clay. Gideon was busy shearing off questing tentacles that snaked past the skeleton guard and went for her necromancer, catching only a confused glimpse of the slim rosary of knuckles that Harrow was looping around her arm. Then Harrow flung it upward like a whip, and it punched straight through the monster's midsection, burying itself somewhere deep.

She barked at Gideon, "Get clear!"

Two of the skeleton-pillars, still hugging tangled bunches of bone, bowed apart to make a path. Gideon pulled her hood down over the exposed skin of her face as she squeezed through the gap and staggered clear, away from the nightmare of splintering fibulae and tibiae. But before she could find her footing, Cytherea the First leapt from her place of ambush.

She was utterly beautiful and entirely terrible: whole, unhurt, untouched by anything that had happened to her. The wounds from Palamedes's last spell seemed to have vanished as if they'd never been made. It was like she wasn't even made of flesh. A memory flashed up through the haze of adrenaline: *Do I look like I'm in the queendom of my power?*

The Lyctor's rapier thrust whipped out like a fang, like a ribbon. Gideon knocked the stupid fucking thing aside with her two-hander, and turned the momentum into an overhead strike. Cytherea raised her free hand, grabbed the heavy blade, and held it still. A thin trickle of scarlet ran from the base of her thumb down the inside of her skinny wrist. Behind them the construct shook and swayed and thrashed with whatever the hell Harrow was doing to it, and Cytherea's eyes locked on Gideon's.

"I meant it," she said earnestly. "You were wonderful. You would have made that little nun such a cavalier—I almost wish you'd been mine."

"You couldn't fucking afford me," said Gideon.

She stepped away and wrenched her sword upward—pulling Cytherea's arm up with it—closed the gap in a hurry, and kicked the Lyctor's legs out beneath her. Cytherea lost her grip and collapsed into the bone-litter strewn across the atrium floor. She coughed and winked at Gideon, and the scattered bones rose up and closed around her like waves, hiding her from sight.

From above came a terrible muffled bellow—a lowing forced through pursed lips. The construct was howling. It tried to surge forward, but the movement kept getting arrested in midjerk, as though pinned to the floor. Its tendrils slapped and drove against the ground, tilling up billowing clouds of wood pulp and carpet fragments. The thing gave a frustrated final push and overbalanced, then came down hard on the floor right where her necromancer had been. There was an agonizing crash as the fountain shattered under its weight. Gideon's heart was in her throat: but there was the dusty black figure emerging from the wreckage, ropes of teeth wrapped around her wrists where she had jerked the thing to ground, a vanguard of skeletons swatting tendrils away from her.

Gideon fought her way toward her blindly, clipping off strands and trailing chains of bone as she waded her way to Harrowhark. The construct still pursued her, its legs scrabbling to find purchase as the floor buckled and quaked beneath it, sharpened beaks of bone bearing down on her adept. Harrow was forced to split her focus between fending them off and keeping her hands on the reins holding the construct to earth, blood shining on her forehead with the strain. Gideon arrived just in time to plant herself in front of her necromancer and smash a drilling lappet to shards.

"I need to be inside you," Harrow bellowed over the din.

"Okay, you're not even trying," said Gideon.

Her necromancer said: "It's all I can do to pin it in place, so you need to finish it for me. Breach the legs—I will show you exactly where—and then I can keep it quiet for a while."

"Seriously? How?"

"You'll see," said Harrow grimly. "I apologise, Nav. Get ready to move."

The construct crooned in its chains. The central rod that Harrow had somehow awled through its trunk was bowing dangerously. Gideon dove back into the affray of joint and gristle with her sword scything before her and, just as in the Response room, felt another presence slide into her mind like a knife into a pool of water. Her vision blurred out and something said in the back of her mind:

On your right. Eye level.

It wasn't a voice, precisely, but it was Harrowhark. Gideon pivoted right, longsword held high. The first leg of the construct loomed before her, a weighty breadth of impenetrable bone, but the back of her mind told her: *Wrong. Inch higher. Pierce.*

Gideon rehefted the weight of her sword in her hands, steadied the pommel with the butt of one palm, and thrust it home. The bone was thinner here. Across her softened sight a light fizzed in and out of vision, the exact same corona of light that had happened a thousand years ago—a hundred thousand, a myriad of myriads—inside the first trial chamber. She pulled her sword free and the leg buckled.

Half a dozen tendrils came after her. They would have given her an interesting array of new airholes for speed, but a skeleton staggered out of the darkness and took most of the blows, jawbone crushed into powder as a tendril lashed open its skull. Another skeleton lurched in where its comrade had died—but this one dashed *past* Gideon, over to the glimmering wound she had carved into the leg, and it thrust its arm into the gash.

Then it melted. Gideon had a few seconds to watch as it sludged into shining silvery-white bone matter. With a little sizzle of evil-smelling steam, it shrouded the wound and the bottom of the leg in a lahar of hot bone gunge.

She tore her gaze away to skid beneath the heaving torso of the beast, narrowly dodging another few desperate tendrils, cutting her way through a damp nest of them as they unfurled and regrew themselves like the coils of a razor-sharp plant. The leg closest to her had found purchase on the floor with its dainty, sharp-capped foot, so much like the leg of an arachnid, and seemed to be in the process of levering the whole thing upright.

The back of her head said: *It's above you.* Gideon slipped her grip down the handle of her sword, her forearm alarmed with the effort, tip wavering as the leg shifted and hesitated above her. The back of her head said: *Now.*

This one was harder. She didn't have as much purchase. Gideon rammed her sword upward, getting a grip on the pommel and shoving into the limb again, as plates of bone splintered overhead and dried flakes of marrow spun down like confetti. The leg tumbled down like a cut tendon.

Yet another skeleton appeared next to her and, as she withdrew the sword, plunged into the shining gap. It too dissolved into the hot, foul muck that slid inside the construct's body and enrobed the rest of the leg, dripping down into the floor, cooling rapidly. The hard shine of it and the suppressed agony of triumph in the back of Gideon's head made her eyes water, and she was filled with a weird pride that was all her own. Holy shit. Perpetual bone. Harrow had actually cracked it.

She was too busy admiring her necromancer to catch the thick rope of vertebrae that looped around her waist and cinched tight.

The connection in her mind stuttered and disappeared, then her vision sharpened, rendering everything happening to her in bloody clarity. Before Gideon could say *OH MY FUCKING WORD* she was plucked off her feet, hoisted upward, and flung bodily into the air.

For one vertigo-inducing moment she was above the battle-field. She sailed past the huge, masklike face of the bone construct, a thick coating of regenerating bone seeping down its legs in rivulets—free-falling, with an aerial view as Camilla danced through the chaos toward the calm and fragile figure of Cytherea the First, who stood watching her approach. Gideon tried to twist in the air—if she could just contrive to hit a window, rather than the wall—

She was caught with a force that jangled her teeth in her mouth. A spindly pillar of skeletal arms had risen up from the maelstrom to stop her in midcareer, a hundred bone fingers scoring bloody ribbons over her back; but she was not splattered against the wall, which was the main thing.

The pillar of arms was destroyed by a long, sweeping blow from one of the construct's innumerable bone whips, and she fell to earth again, gravity arrested by the hands helpfully piling themselves up to reduce her fall to *terrible* from *obituary*. She landed in a pile next to her necromancer, and her knee went *crunch*.

"I have bested my father," said Harrow to nobody, staring upward at nothing, alight with fierce and untrammelled triumph. They were both lying supine on a pile of what felt like feet. "I have bested my father *and* my grandmother—every single necromancer ever taught by my House—every necromancer who has ever touched a skeleton. Did you see me? Did you behold me, Griddle?"

This was all said somewhat thickly, through pink and bloodied teeth, before Harrow smugly passed out.

* * *

The dust was clearing. The construct could not move. It was making low, plaintive grunts as it thrashed in its half coffin of regenerating ash: with its tentacles, it picked and smashed at the bone cocoons on its back legs, but as soon as it broke some off the stuff simply crumbled back into being. Now that it was concentrating so completely on itself, Gideon could find the cavalier of the Sixth.

Camilla, as she'd seen from above, had caught up with Cytherea the First. She had one hand in the Lyctor's singed curls, dragging her head back. The other hand pressed a knife against the smaller woman's throat. This would have been a commanding position, except that the knife blade was quivering in place. Its edge creased the pale skin, but it hadn't drawn blood, even though Camilla seemed to be leaning on it as hard as she could. Whatever terrible force was holding the knife at bay was also slowly peeling the skin from the cavalier of the Sixth's hand.

"You're a nice girl," the Lyctor said. "I had a nice girl as a cavalier too . . . once. She died for me. What can you do?"

Camilla said nothing. Her face was slick with sweat and blood. Her crop of dark, blunt-cut hair was powdered grey with bone. Cytherea looked faintly amused by the blade that was a finger's breadth away from being buried in her jugular. She drawled, "Is this meant to kill me?"

"Give me time," said Camilla, through gritted teeth.

Cytherea gave this due consideration. "I'd rather not," she said.

Gideon saw, as Camilla could not, the tentacle of bone that wound silently upward from the mess behind the cavalier, tipped with a vicious point the length of a duellist's dagger. Even if she'd had a pristine knee and no necro to haul, Gideon was too far away to save her. The barb drew back, like a poised stinger, and Gideon yelled, "*Cam!*"

Perhaps it was the yell; perhaps it was Camilla's extraordinary instincts. The Sixth cav twisted sideways, and the hook that should have punched through her spine drove into the meat of her shoulder instead. Her eyes went wide with shock, and the knife fell from her half-flayed hand. Cytherea took the opportunity to shove her contemptuously in the chest, and Camilla toppled backward onto the ground, the sharpened bone still buried in her flesh.

Cytherea took up her rapier. In a panic, Gideon began trying to kick her futile way through a jungle of yellow bone, but putting her weight on her bad leg made her stagger and almost drop. Camilla was struggling herself free of the bone skewer, but another tendril had snaked up across her thighs, trapping her against the floor. The Lyctor stood above her with her green sword gleaming in the light.

"You can't hurt me," said Cytherea, almost despairingly. "Nothing can hurt me anymore, cavalier."

The sword glittered. Gideon thrashed through a mesh of bones that her adept could have parted mid-yawn. As the Lyctor drew back her arm for a clean thrust into Camilla's heart, four inches of bloodied steel emerged from her belly.

Camilla stared up at her as though trying to work out why everything hadn't gone black. A red stain was spreading across the thin bedsheet. The Lyctor's face didn't change, but she turned her head slightly. A pale head was now nearly pillowed on her shoulder, peeking over, as though to make sure the sword had hit home. Colourless fair hair spilled over Cytherea's collarbone like a waterfall: the figure behind her smiled.

"Spoke too soon, old news," said Ianthe.

"Oh," said Cytherea, "oh, my! A baby Lyctor."

The construct was stuck fast in the trap that Harrowhark had laid for it, and behind them Gideon could hear its central bulk straining to see what had pained its mistress, like a great skull swivelling in its web. It was held fast, but it still had range, and it lifted its spines to even the fight.

Ianthe ran her free hand over the blood trickling down Cytherea's hip. She flicked hot drops over her shoulder, where they hung in the air, sizzling. They ran together like quicksilver—spread out, widened and flattened into a shimmering, transparent pink sheet. Ianthe narrowed her watercolour eyes and pointed her free hand upward. The sheet tightened, a wide, watery disc of blood, separating the two Lyctors from the construct.

A barbed bone stinger drove straight at Ianthe's head, hit the shimmering disc, and dissolved. Gideon bodychecked her way clear, hauling herself to a corner of the room as far away from the construct as possible. She wasn't thrilled about approaching the embracing Lyctors, but if she played her cards right, she could still get Harrowhark and Camilla out of here. Another stinger, then another, hurtled into the blood disc and evaporated. Despite herself, she turned to watch: the construct stiffened a dozen of its tendrils, two dozen, aiming them like javelins at Ianthe's tiny form, and Gideon remembered Isaac Tettares, impaled on fifty spines at once.

As Gideon passed it, Ianthe's blood pool spun even wider, an aegis, a shield. The construct struck from its stuck position, with its whole gathered array of swift spears, enough of them to reduce Ianthe to a double handful of chopped meat. Every single one went up in a cloud of bad-smelling steam.

The remaining stumps drew back in confusion. The construct swayed, and bones dropped free from its superstructure here and there, rattling down to join the general debris around its trapped legs. There was suddenly a lot more space; injured as well as pinned, the construct seemed to be drawing back on itself, pulling in its remaining limbs as if trying to keep them away from Ianthe.

Gideon snuck past the foot of the dais in time to see Cytherea smile. "I've always wanted a little sister," she said.

She walked away from Ianthe's sword with a bad, liquid sound. Camilla was still wriggling in place, trying to tug herself free of the spike in her shoulder, and Cytherea stepped on her, treading on her collarbone as thoughtlessly as on a ridge in the carpet. Once she was a couple of paces clear, she turned and fell into a beautiful fluid ready stance. She kept running her fingers over the blood at her abdomen, apparently amazed by her capacity to bleed. Gideon wished she was less interested and more *dying,* but you had to take victories where you could get them.

The other, much newer Lyctor raised Naberius's sword, kicking bones away for footing.

"I've tried the sister thing already," said Ianthe, circling around to one side, "and I wasn't any good at it."

"But I have so much to teach you," said Cytherea.

They both charged. Once upon a time it would have been pretty cool to watch the perfect showman's sword of the Third House compete against an ancient and undiluted warrior of the Seventh, but Gideon was crouching down next to Camilla and trying to gauge whether or not her own kneecap was trying to slide off somewhere weird. She had laid down the unconscious Harrowhark behind a pillar on a pile of the softest-looking bones, with her longsword for company, and was wishing fervently that her necromancer was awake. She grabbed Camilla's shoulder in one hand and the slick bone spur in the other, said, "Sorry," and pulled.

Camilla screamed. Gideon flung the bloodied spike away, got her arms under Camilla's armpits, and pulled. Camilla bit her tongue so hard that blood squirted out her mouth, but Gideon heartlessly dragged her away from the ongoing brawl and into cover next to Harrowhark.

Gideon started to look her over to see if her intestines were fountaining out, or something, but Camilla grabbed her sleeve. Gideon looked down into her solemn, obstinate face, and Camilla said—

"He say anything?"

Gideon wavered. "He said to tell you he loved you," she said.

"What? No, he didn't."

"Okay, no, sorry. He said—he said you knew what to do?"

"I do," said Camilla with grim satisfaction, and laid herself back down among the bones.

Gideon looked back at the fight. It was not like watching Ianthe and Silas go at it. Ianthe had wiped the floor with Silas while simultaneously skirmishing with Naberius's soul. A fight between two Lyctors was a swordfight on a scale beyond mortal. They moved almost faster than the eye could see, each clash of their swords sending great shockwaves of ash and smoke and aerosolized bone billowing outward.

The spacious atrium of Canaan House had been built to last, but not through this. The floor splintered and bowed dangerously wherever the construct had dragged itself—the tentacles dug through the floorboards, burrowed out again in showers of rotten timber and bone—and as Ianthe and Cytherea fought, parts of the room exploded at their passing, ancient beams and pillars giving up with screams of falling rock and wood. Brackish water from the fountain had spattered the floor and trickled into the cracks—

Cracks. Shit. The floor was cracking. *Everything* was cracking. Huge fissures separated Gideon from the doors. Ianthe—a lock of her colourless hair in her mouth, chewing furiously—raised her hand,

and a gushing column of black arterial blood burst upward, lifting Cytherea twenty feet into the air and dropping her. She hit the ground awkwardly, and as she staggered to her feet again Ianthe stepped up, hand sparking and flickering with harsh white light, and hit her with a tremendous right hook.

The punch would have spun Marshal Crux's scabrous, plate-clad bulk around three times like a top and left him on the floor seeing little skeletal birdies. It knocked Cytherea clean through the wall. The wall was already feeling pretty sorry for itself, and at this last insult it gave up entirely and collapsed, with a terrific rumble and crash of rock and brick and bursting glass slumping outward onto the garden terrace. Daylight flooded through, and the smell of hot concrete and wood mould filled the air. The potholed floor groaned as if threatening to follow suit. Camilla, who had guts of steel and the pain tolerance of a brick, wobbled to stand; Gideon wove her arm beneath Camilla's sword arm before the Sixth cavalier could protest, retrieved the bird-bone bundle of her necromancer, and staggered outside as fast as this crippled procession could manage. There was simply nowhere else to go.

The salt wind from the sea blew hot and hard through holes in the glass that sheltered the expanse where mouldering plants continued to dry out on their great trellises. Insensitive to the situation, Dominicus shone down on them, cradled in the unreal cerulean of the First's sky. Gideon laid Harrowhark down in the shadow of a broken-ass wall that seemed as though it wouldn't crumple down and squash her yet. Camilla slumped next to her, swords crossed over her knees. At least this place had significantly fewer bones.

Ianthe strode down a low flight of stairs, sword in hand, hair rippling white-yellow in the breeze. Dead leaves and plant matter drifted down around her, disturbed by the crumbling wall. Cytherea was picking herself up off the flagstones where she'd been hurled, and as Ianthe lunged at her again it was obvious she was on the defensive. She was not as quick as Ianthe; she was not as reactive. She would still have speared Gideon through in the first ten seconds of a fair fight, but against another Lyctor, things seemed to be going wrong. Ianthe grew more vicious with each hit. As Cytherea's blood flew into the air, she was freezing it in place, manipulating it, stitching long red lines through the space around and between them. Every time Cytherea got hurt—and she was getting hurt now, bleeding like a normal person, with none of her earlier invulnerability—the web of blood grew in size and complexity, until it looked like she was duelling in a cage of taut red string.

Nor was that the worst of it. As Gideon watched, somewhere between horror and fascination, the earlier wounds—the ones Palamedes had inflicted when he blew up the sickroom—began to reopen. Strips of skin along the Lyctor's arms blackened and curled; a big, messy gouge split down her thigh, independent of Ianthe's blade. Even the curly hair started to sizzle and crisp back up.

"What the hell?" objected Gideon, more to relieve her feelings than in hope of an answer.

"She hadn't healed," said Camilla weakly from beside her. Gideon glanced around; the other cav had dragged herself up into a sitting position against the wall and was watching the fight with grim, professional eyes. Of course, cavaliers from Houses with more than one living necromancer probably saw necromancers duel all the time. "She'd just skinned over the damage—a surface fix, hides the cracks. To really heal, she needs thalergy—life force—and she hasn't got any to spare."

"Oh, yeah," said Gideon. "Sextus gave her turbo cancer."

Camilla nodded with enormous personal satisfaction. "Well," she said, "that'll do it."

Ianthe's magic was as efficient and lean as Naberius's swordsmanship—neat and contemptuous, clean and too perfect, not a beat missed or a second's hesitation. Cytherea stumbled away from her onslaught, and Ianthe closed the trap. The cage of blood suddenly contracted, tightened, clinging to the older Lyctor like a net. Cytherea stood tangled in it, not even bothering to try to fight free, eyes closed to slits. Her hair was scorched almost down to stubble. She was struggling to breathe. Her shrapnel wounds were gaping red and fresh, and her knees were buckling. The smell of blood and leaves was overpowering.

Ianthe stood before her, panting now herself. She kept shaking her head as though to clear it—kept rubbing her temples fretfully—but she was gleaming and triumphant, sweating, smug. "Tired?" she said.

Cytherea opened her eyes and coughed. "Not particularly," she said. "But you're exhausted."

The filmy red net dissolved to nothing. It didn't even fall away from her; it seemed almost to be absorbed back through her skin. She straightened up, stepped forward, and grabbed Ianthe's throat in one fine-boned, delicate hand. Ianthe's eyes bulged, and her hands flew up to clutch at the other woman's wrist.

"Just like a child . . . all your best moves first," said Cytherea.

Ianthe squirmed. A thread of blood coiled in the air around her, uselessly, and then spattered to the ground. The ancient Lyctor said, "You aren't completed, are you? I can feel him pushing . . . he's not happy. Mine went willingly, and it hurt for centuries. If I'm old news . . . *you're* fresh meat."

She tightened her grip on Ianthe's throat, and the dreadful, bone-deep suction of siphoning sent an icy ripple throughout the sheltered terrace. The trees and trellises shook. This was soul siphoning as Gideon had never felt it before. Colourless at the best of times, Ianthe was now as blank and tintless as a sheet. Her eyes rolled back and forth in her head, and then there was no eye to roll: she jerked and squealed, pupils gone, irises gone, as though Cytherea had somehow had the ability to suck them out of her skull.

"No," cried Ianthe, "*no, no, no*—"

The great wound in Cytherea's thigh was starting to weave itself back up: so too were the burn marks all over her arms and her neck. Her charred hair was growing back in—rippling out in pale brown waves from her skull—and she sighed with pleasure as she shook her head.

"Okay," said Camilla in carefully neutral tones, "now she's healing."

The thigh wound closed up, leaving the skin smooth as alabaster. Cytherea dropped Ianthe dismissively to the ground in a crumpled-up heap.

"Now, little sister," she told the grey-lipped Third princess, "don't think this means I'm not impressed. You did become a Lyctor . . . and so you'll get to live. For a while. But I don't need your arms and your legs. So—"

She rested one delicate foot on Ianthe's wrist, and Gideon rose to her feet. The sharp shank of bone extended from her knuckles, a long butcher's blade with a wicked heft. Cytherea sliced down. Bright red blood sprayed in the sunshine as Ianthe's right arm came off just above the elbow. Ianthe, too weak even to scream, made a keening sound.

By this point Gideon had already lurched forward two steps and regretted it. Her kneecap was absolutely not where it should have been. She tottered to the side, letting her sword drop one-handed, pressing her other over the knee and cursing the day she had been born with kneecaps. Cytherea was shifting to the other side, the other limb, judging the distance with her bloody spar—

"Duck," called Camilla.

Camilla had somehow propped herself on the arm with the mangled shoulder wound, which was in no condition for propping. Her good arm was up behind her head, holding the blade of her knife. Gideon ducked. The knife whistled over the top of Gideon's head in a flashing blur and buried itself in Cytherea's upper back.

This time Cytherea screamed. She went stumbling away from Ianthe's prone form, and Gideon saw what Camilla had been aiming at: a lump, a delicate swollen mass, right next to Cytherea's shoulder blade. It bulged out only slightly, but once you saw it, it was impossible to unsee—especially with a long knife buried squarely in its centre. Cytherea fumbled one hand over her shoulder, bone appendage drifting into dust, groping for the knife. She found it— she pulled it out, drawing a spurt of appalling black-and-yellow liquid from the wound.

The Lyctor turned her head and coughed miserably into the crook of her elbow. Then she looked at the knife, wondering at it. She turned her head to look at Camilla and Harrow and Gideon. She sighed pensively and ran one hand through her curls again.

"Oh no," she said, "heroics."

She dropped the knife, fell gracefully to one knee beside Ianthe, and lifted a limp arm—the one that was still connected to her body—in a cruel mockery of hand holding. Gideon thought for a bad second she was going to pull the limb clean off, and wondered how far she could throw a longsword—except no, her longsword was never going to leave her hands again, thank you—but Cytherea was just siphoning. There was the deep-gut lurch as energy drained from the younger Lyctor to the older, knitting the gross knife wound back up again.

"An inadequate Lyctor," said Cytherea, as though giving Gideon and Camilla a hot tip on stain removal, "still makes a perfect power source . . . an everlasting battery."

She stood back up and wiped her mouth with the back of her hand. Then she began walking toward Gideon: calm, almost insolent in her lack of aggression. This was somehow much scarier than if she'd stalked forward with a hateful glare and a rill of mad laughter.

Gideon planted herself before Camilla and the unconscious body of her adept and held her sword aloft. They were alone in a back area of the courtyard: a little area not yet buried in rubble or tilled up by the titanic fight between two immortal sorcerers. Dead trees bowed overhead. Gideon stood behind the iron fence that had once protected some herbaceous border, as though its bent, bowed spikes would be good for anything other than throwing herself down on as one last fuck-you salute.

Camilla was huddled in a corner, now standing upright—that was probably her own last fuck-you salute—but her wounded arm hung uselessly. She had lost a lot of blood. Her face was now pallid olive.

"Ninth," said the Sixth impatiently. "Get out of here. Take your necromancer. Go."

"Hell no," said Gideon. "It's time for round two." She considered that. "Wait. Is this round three now? I keep losing count."

Cytherea the First was brushing bloodstains off her makeshift dress, the blood leeching into her fingers as though it obeyed the merest touch of her fingertips. She vaulted daintily into their part of the courtyard and smiled Dulcinea's smile at Gideon: dimpling, bright-eyed, as though they both knew something extra nice that nobody else did.

"There's that two-hander," she said admiringly.

"Want a closer look?" said Gideon.

The Lyctor arched her free hand languorously behind her back; she slid into position, weighting herself on her back foot, the sword in her hand luminous—tinted green like still water, or pearls. "You know you can't do this, Gideon of the Ninth," she said. "You're very brave—a bit like another Gideon I used to know. But you're prettier in the eyes."

"I may be from the Ninth House," said Gideon, "but if you say any more cryptic shit at me, you're going to see how well you can regenerate when you're in eighteen pieces."

"Cry mercy," said Cytherea. The dimple was still there. "Please. You don't even know what you are to me . . . You're not going to die here, Gideon. And if you ask me to let you live you might not have to die at all. I've spared you before."

Something ignited deep in her rib cage.

"Jeannemary Chatur didn't ask for mercy. Magnus didn't ask for mercy. Or Isaac. Or Abigail. I bet you Palamedes never even considered asking for mercy."

"Of course he didn't," said the Lyctor. "He was too busy detonating."

Gideon the Ninth charged. Cytherea went straight for her heart, no foreplay, but this was a Gideon who had trained with a double-handed sword since before she could even hold the damn thing. This was a Gideon who had lived her entire life behind the hilt of a two-hander. No more playing around with dodging and ducking and moving away—it was her, her sword, and all of the power and strength and speed that Aiglamene had been able to realise in her.

She met Cytherea's water-smooth thrust to her heart with an upward cut that flung the Lyctor's rapier's point skyward, and ought to have knocked it clean out of her hand. She stopped thinking about the pain in her knee and went back to being the Gideon Nav who never left Drearburh, who fought like it was her only ticket off-world. The Lyctor danced out and in again, close quarters, trying to slide her sword under and around Gideon's own. Gideon knocked the thing to the ground, the rapier scraping the flagstones with an awful screech. Cytherea retreated, prettily, and Gideon smashed her guard and followed through with a huge, perfect overhand cut.

It ought to have cleaved the Lyctor open from the shoulder to the gut. She'd wanted it to. But the edge of her sword sank into Cytherea's collarbone and *bounced off,* like she was trying to cut steel. There was the faintest pink mark on the skin—and then nothing. Her two-hander had failed. Something in Gideon rolled over and gave up.

Cytherea moved in for the kill, her sword flashing like a snake, like a whip, as Gideon moved half a second behind where she needed to be. She saved herself a skewered lung by clumsily blocking with the flat of her sword. The Lyctor's unholy strength made the longsword shudder on impact, and Gideon's forearms shuddered with it. Undeterred, Cytherea went for her numbed arm—sank the tip deep into the soft flesh above the bicep, met the bone, splintered something deep in there. Gideon gave ground, sword held in guard, clawing for distance now. The blade was drooping in her hands despite every iota of determination coursing through her body. She tried to conjure up some of the old, cruel caution with which Aiglamene had so often sent her to the mat—watched Cytherea closely, stepped away from a feint, saw an opening—turned herself to iron, and thrust forward, straight to her opponent's heart.

Cytherea raised her free hand and caught the blade before it carved through her sternum. She had to step back with the force of the blow, but her frail, worn hand wrapped around the breadth of the blade and held it as easily as Naberius's shitty trick trident knife had her rapier, all those years ago in the training room. Gideon shoved. Her feet slipped for purchase on the ground, her knee screaming. Her arm squirted blood with the effort. Cytherea sighed.

"Oh, you were gorgeous," said the Lyctor, "a thing apart."

She batted Gideon's sword away with her hand. Then she advanced.

"Step off, bitch," said Harrowhark Nonagesimus, behind her.

Cytherea turned to look. The black-robed, black-hooded figure had stumbled forward, step by staggering step, away from the shelter of the tower wall. She was bookended by skeletons—skeletons too huge to have ever lived inside the greasy meat sock of anyone real. Each was eight feet high with ulnar bones like tree trunks and wicked bone spikes spiralling over their arms.

"I wish the Ninth House would do something that was more interesting than skeletons," said Cytherea pensively.

One of the monstrous constructs flung itself at Cytherea, like she was a bomb it was ending its life upon. The second came shambling after it. Cytherea contemptuously dashed away one skeleton's enormous forearm spike—she shattered another with her rapier—and the spike, almost before it had finished crumbling, stretched and pushed itself back into shape. Harrow wasn't stinting on the perpetual bone, and if she kept it up she was going to be a perpetual corpse.

Gideon rolled away, seized her sword, and crawled. Her pierced arm left a snail's trail of slippery red behind her. It was only years of training under Aiglamene that gave her the guts to wobble herself upright before her adept, blind with blood, blade leant flat on her good shoulder. Two more dead giants were already knitting themselves together. Harrow couldn't afford this, she thought dimly; Harrow couldn't afford this at all.

"You're learning fast!" said the Lyctor, and she sounded honestly delighted. "But I'm afraid you've got a long way to go."

Cytherea crooked her fingers toward the massive hole torn in the side of the tower. There was a cry from within, followed by an awful cracking, tearing, breaking sound. When the horrible many-legged construct exploded through the hole, it was not as great nor as leggy as it had been before. It had torn itself free from Harrow's shackles, and in doing so had left most of itself behind. It was a miserable shadow of its previous bulk. Compared to anything normal, though, it was still a horror of waving stumps and tendrils, all lengthening and thickening, regrowing themselves even as she watched. It had been stuck and now it was halved, but it could still regenerate. The huge expressionless face gleamed whitely in the afternoon light—now teetering on a trunk too small for its mask—and broken glass pattered down its sides like drops of water as it crawled out. It sat its broken body on the terrace like a ball of white roots, swaying on two legs, a bitten spider.

It wasn't fair. Cytherea had been right all along: there was nothing they could do. Even half-destroyed, the bristling tentacles and lappets were raised a hundred strong in the air. It staggered and aimed itself in their direction, and there was nowhere to run, no dodging, no escape.

The Lyctor said: "None of you have learned how to die gracefully . . . I learned over ten thousand years ago."

"I'm not done," said Gideon's half-dead necromancer.

Harrow closed her hands. The last thing Gideon saw was the debris of her perpetual servants rattling toward them, bouncing through the air and over the flagstones, hardening in a shell over her and Camilla and Harrow as all those tendrils struck them at once. The noise was deafening: WHAM—WHAM—WHAM WHAMWHAMWHAMWHAMWHAM*WHAM*—until it became a single hammer, a metered pounding: *WHAM . . . WHAM . . . WHAM . . .*

The world vibrated around them. Everything was suddenly very dark. A wavering yellow light flicked on, and Gideon realised that against all odds Camilla had somehow retained her pocket torch.

They were closed in with the bowing iron trellises and the wilting, anciently dead bushes. The sky, the sea, and the rest of the garden were cut off behind a smooth curved shell of what seemed to be solid, uninterrupted bone, like the hemisphere of a propped-up skull. Harrow swayed upright in the gloom as the beast tried to crack them open like a nut and looked at Camilla and Gideon through a face that was mostly blood. Not even blood sweat: just blood. Beneath her skin blood vessels had detonated like mines. It was coming through her pores. She'd figured out how to make perpetual bone, half-destroyed a giant dead spider from hell, and now she'd raised a solid wall six inches thick and was holding it up with sheer nerve.

The Reverend Daughter of the Ninth House smiled, tiny and triumphant. Then she keeled into Gideon's arms.

Gideon stumbled, sick with terror, kneeling them both down to the ground as Harrow lay like a broken rag doll. She forgot her sword, forgot everything as she cradled her used-up adept. She forgot the wrecked ligaments in her sword arm, her messed-up knee, the cups of blood she'd lost, everything but that tiny, smouldering, victorious smile.

"Harrow, come on, I'm here," she told her, howling to be heard above the thunder of the construct's assault. "Siphon, damn it."

"After what happened to the Eighth?" Harrow's voice was surprisingly strong, considering she appeared to be all black robes and wounds. "Not ever again."

"You can't hold this shit forever, Harrow! You couldn't hold this shit ten minutes ago!"

"I don't have to hold it forever," said the necromancer. She contemplatively spat out a clot of blood, rolled her tongue around inside her mouth. "Listen. Take the Sixth, get into a brace position, and I'll break you through the wall. Bones float. It's a long drop to the sea—"

"*Nope—*"

Harrow ignored her. "—but all you have to do is survive the fall. We know that the ships have been called. Get off the planet as soon as you can. I'll distract her as long as possible: all you have to do is live."

"Harrow," said Gideon. "This plan is stupid, and you're stupid. No."

The Reverend Daughter reached up to take a fistful of Gideon's shirt. Her eyes were dark and glassy through the pain and nausea; she smelled like sweat and fear and about nine tonnes of bone. She swabbed at her face again with her sleeve and said: "Griddle, you made me a promise. You agreed to go back to the Ninth. You agreed to do your duty by the Locked Tomb—"

"Don't do this to me."

"I owe you your life," said Harrowhark, "I owe you everything."

Harrow let go of her shirt and subsided to the floor. Her paint had all come off. She kept choking and sniffling on the thick rivulets of blood coming out her nose. Gideon tilted the wet, dark head so that her necromancer did not die untimely from drowning in her bloodied mucus, and tried desperately to think of a plan.

WHAM. One of the tentacles battered a crack in the shield: daylight streamed in from outside. Harrow looked even worse in the light. Camilla said steadily: "Let me out. I can provide the distraction."

"Cram it already, Hect," said Gideon, not looking away from her necromancer, who was painfully serene as even her eyebrows bled. "I'm not getting haunted by Palamedes Sextus's crappy-ass revenant all telling me doctor facts for the rest of my life, just because I let you get disintegrated."

"The other plan isn't going to work," said Camilla evenly. "If we could hold her off and wait on the shore, yes. But we can't."

Harrow sighed, stretched out on the floor.

"Then we hold her off as long as we can," she said.

The crack knitted itself back together with painful, guttering slowness. Harrow snarled from the effort. They were plunged into darkness again, and the sounds from outside stopped, as though the construct was considering its next move.

Camilla closed her eyes and relaxed. Her long dark fringe fell over her face. It was that—Camilla in motion now Camilla at rest—that made the tiny voice inside Gideon's head say, amazed: *We really are going to die.*

Gideon looked down at her necromancer. She had the heavy-lidded expression of someone who was concentrating in the knowledge that when they stopped concentrating, they would fall abruptly asleep. Harrow had gone unconscious once before: Gideon knew that the second time she let Harrow go under, there would probably not be any awakening. Harrow reached up—her hand was trembling—and tapped Gideon on the cheek.

"Nav," she said, "have you really forgiven me?"

Confirmed. They were all going to eat it.

"Of course I have, you bozo."

"I don't deserve it."

"Maybe not," said Gideon, "but that doesn't stop me forgiving you. Harrow—"

"Yes?"

"You know I don't give a damn about the Locked Tomb, right? You know I only care about you," she said in a brokenhearted rush. She didn't know what she was trying to say, only that she had to say it *now.* With a bad, juddering noise, a tentacle had started to pound their splintering shelter again: *WHAM.* "I'm no good at this duty thing. I'm just me. I can't do this without you. And I'm not your real cavalier primary, I never could've been."

WHAM. WHAM. *WHAM.* The crack reopened at this punishment. The sunlight got in, and fragments of bone dissolved in a shower of grey matter. It held, but Gideon didn't care. The construct wasn't there: the shelter wasn't there. Even Camilla, who had turned away to politely investigate something on the opposite wall, wasn't there. It was just her and Harrow and Harrow's bitter, high-boned, stupid little face.

Harrow laughed. It was the first time she had ever heard Harrow really laugh. It was a rather weak and tired sound.

"Gideon the Ninth, first flower of my House," she said hoarsely, "you are the greatest cavalier we have ever produced. You are our triumph. The best of all of us. It has been my privilege to be your necromancer."

That was enough. Gideon the Ninth stood up so suddenly that she nearly bumped her head on the roof of the bone shield. Her arm complained loudly; she ignored it. She paced back and forth— Harrow watched her with only mild concern—studying the little space they were boxed into. The dead leaves. The cracked flagstones. Camilla—Camilla looked back at her, but she was already moving on. She couldn't do this to Camilla. The powdery grey drifts of bone. The iron spikes of the railings.

"Yeah, fuck it," she said. "I'm getting us out of here."

"Griddle—"

Gideon limped over near the dusty flowerbeds. *WHAM— WHAM—WHAM—* She didn't have much time, but she only had one shot anyway. She struggled out of her black robe and thought about taking off her shirt, in one mental blurt of panic, but decided she didn't need to. She peeled her gloves off her wet red palms and rolled up her sleeves for no reason, except that it gave her something to do with her shaking hands. She made her voice as calm as possible: in a way, she *was* calm. She was the calmest she had ever been in her entire life. It was just her body that was frightened.

"Okay," she said. "I understand now. I really, truly, absolutely understand."

Harrowhark had leant back on her elbows and was watching her, black eyes lightless and soft. "Nav," she said, the gentlest she had ever heard Harrow manage. "I can't hold this for—much longer."

WHAM—WHAM—WHAM!

"I don't know how you're holding it now," said Gideon and she backed up, looked at what she was backing toward, looked back at her necromancer.

She sucked in a wobbly breath. Harrow was looking at her with a classic expression of faint Nonagesimus pity, as though Gideon had finally lost her intellectual faculties and might wet herself at any moment. Camilla watched her with an expression that showed nothing at all. Camilla the Sixth was no idiot.

She said, "Harrow, I can't keep my promise, because the entire point of me is you. You get that, right? That's what cavaliers sign up for. There is no me without you. One flesh, one end."

A shade of exhausted suspicion flickered over her necromancer's face. "Nav," she said, "what are you doing?"

"The cruellest thing anyone has ever done to you in your whole entire life, believe me," said Gideon. "You'll know what to do, and if you don't do it, what I'm about to do will be no use to anyone."

Gideon turned and squinted, gauged the angle. She judged the distance. It would have been the worst thing in the world to look back, so she didn't.

She mentally found herself all of a sudden in front of the doors of Drearburh—four years old again, and screaming—and all her fear and hate of them went away. Drearburh was empty. There was no Crux. There were no godawful great-aunts. There were no restless corpses, no strangers in coffins, no dead parents. Instead, she was Drearburh. She was Gideon Nav, and Nav was a Niner name. She took the whole putrid, quiet, filth-strewn madness of the place, and she opened her doors to it. Her hands were not shaking anymore.

WHAM—WHAM—*WHAM*. The structure bowed and creaked. Big chunks were falling away now, letting in wide splotches of sunlight. She felt movement behind her, but she was faster.

"For the Ninth!" said Gideon.

And she fell forward, right on the iron spikes.

ACT FIVE

 **37**

"Okay," said Gideon. "Okay. Get up."

Harrowhark Nonagesimus got up.

"Good!" said her cavalier. "You can stop screaming any moment now, just an FYI. Now—first make sure nothing's going to ice Camilla—I meant it about not wanting an afterlife subscription to *Palamedes Sextus's Top Nerd Facts*."

"Gideon," said Harrow, and again, more incoherently: "Gideon."

"No time," said Gideon. A hot wind blew over them both: it whipped Harrow's hair into her face. "Incoming."

The shield sighed, shuddered, and finally broke. The ancient Lyctoral construct surged forward, triumphant in its brainlessness. Harrow saw it for what it was: a spongy breadth of regenerating ash, and many lengths of teeth. For all its killing speed before, it now crested before them as though it were travelling through syrup. It shivered in the air, a hundred white lances ready.

Gideon said, "Take it down."

And Harrow took it down. It was bafflingly simple. It was nothing more than a raised skeleton, and not one that had been formed with any particular grace. It was half gone already, having torn itself free like an animal from her trap. The head was just a chitinous plate. The trunk was a roll of bone. The remaining tentacles fell like rain, arrested in midswing. The bone responded to their call, and together they sailed the thing through the cracked glass panes of the terrace garden to fall—a huge white comet, with flailing tails of bone—into the rolling ocean.

"There's my sword," Gideon said. "Pick it up—pick it up and *stop looking at me, dick*. Don't. Don't you dare look at me."

Harrow turned her head away from the iron railing and picked up the longsword, and cried out: it was far too heavy, far too awkward. Gideon reached her arm out to steady Harrow's sword hand, shifting the other arm around her in a strange embrace. Her fingers wrapped around Harrow's, scratchy with callouses. The sheer weight of the thing still stretched the muscles of Harrow's forearms painfully, but Gideon clasped her wrist, and despite the pain they lifted the sword together.

"Your arms are like fucking noodles," said Gideon disapprovingly.

"I'm a *necromancer*, Nav!"

"Yeah, well, hope you like lifting weights for the next myriad."

They were cheek to cheek: Gideon's arm and Harrow's arm entwined, holding the sword aloft, letting the steel catch the light. The terrace stretched out before them, glass shards spraying in the wake of the construct, falling as slowly and as lightly as down. Harrow looked back at Gideon, and Gideon's eyes, as they always did, startled her: their deep, chromatic amber, the startling hot gold of freshly-brewed tea. She winked.

Harrow said—

"I cannot do this."

"You already did it," said Gideon. "It's done. You ate me and rebuilt me. We can't go home again."

"I can't bear it."

"Suck it down," said Gideon. "You're already two hundred dead daughters and sons of our House. What's one more?"

Before them stood Cytherea the First, though they noticed her only as an afterthought. She stood with her sword down, just watching them, her eyes as wide and as blue as the death of light. The garden narrowed to her and her bloody green sword. Her lips were parted in a tiny *o*. She did not even seem particularly troubled: just amazed, as though they were an aurora, a mirage, an unreal trick of the sunshine.

"Now we kick her ass until candy comes out," said Gideon. "Oh, damn, Nonagesimus, don't cry, we can't fight her if you're crying."

Harrow said, with some difficulty: "I cannot conceive of a universe without you in it."

"Yes you can, it's just less great and less hot," said Gideon.

"*Fuck* you, Nav—"

"Harrowhark," said Gideon the Ninth. "Someday you'll die and get buried in the ground, and we can work this out then. For now—I can't say you'll be fine. I can't say we did the right thing. I can't tell you shit. I'm basically a hallucination produced by your brain chemistry while coping with the massive trauma of splicing in *my* brain chemistry. Even if I wasn't, I don't know jack, Harrow, I never did—except for one thing."

She lifted Harrow's arm with the hilt clutched in it. Her fingers, rough and strong and sure, moved Harrow's other hand into place above the pommel.

"I know the sword," she said. "And now, so do you."

Gideon brought them into position: weight on the forward foot, knee bent a little, light on the right. She tilted the blade so that it was held with the blade pointed high before them, a perfect line. She moved Harrow's head up and corrected her hips.

Time sped up, blurred, moved in bright lights before them. Now the old Lyctor Cytherea—wretchedly old, it seemed impossible that they could have ever taken her for anything else—stood there at the bottom of the stairs. Her radioactive blue eyes were quiet; her sword was held at the ready. She was smiling with colourless lips.

"How do you feel, little sister?" she said.

Harrowhark's mouth said, "Ready for round three," and, "or round four, I think I lost track."

Their swords met. The noise of metal on metal screamed in that empty garden. Cytherea the First had been Cytherea the First for ten thousand years, and even ten thousand years ago her cavalier had been great. Time had made her more perfect than a mortal cavalier could understand. In a fair fight, they might even have fought to a standstill.

It was not a fair fight. As they fought—and fighting was like a dream, like falling asleep—they could see Cytherea was made up of different parts. Her eyes had been taken from somewhere else, two blue spots of someone else's fire. Within her chest another conflagration burned, and this one was eating her alive: it smoked and smouldered where her lungs ought to have been, bulging, dark, and malignant. It had swollen to the bursting point inside her body, and most of Cytherea's energy was being expended on holding it still. Harrow could touch what Palamedes had done; nudge it; knock it out of Cytherea's grip.

"There," said Gideon, in Harrow's ear, her voice softer now. "Thanks, Palamedes."

"Sextus was a marvel," admitted Harrow.

"Too bad you didn't marry him. You're both into old dead chicks."

"*Gideon—*"

"Focus, Nonagesimus. You know what to do."

Cytherea the First vomited a long stream of black blood. There was no fear in her now. There was only anticipation verging on panicked excitement, like a girl waiting for her birthday party. The weight of Gideon's arms on Harrow's forearms was getting more ephemeral, harder to perceive; the brush of Gideon's cheek was suddenly no more substantial than the remembrance of an old fever. Her voice was in her ear, but it was very far away.

Harrow placed the tip of her sword to the right of Cytherea's breastbone. The world was slow and chilly.

"One flesh, one end," said Gideon, and it was a murmur now, on the very edge of hearing.

Harrow said, "Don't leave me."

"*The land that shall receive thee dying, in the same will I die: and there will I be buried. The Lord do so and so to me, and add more also, if aught but death part me and thee,*" said Gideon. "See you on the flip side, sugarlips."

* * *

Harrowhark drove the blade home, straight through the malignant thing in Cytherea's chest: it bubbled and clawed out of her, a well of tumours, a cancer, and she seized up. It ran through her like a flame touched to oil, seething visibly beneath her skin, her veins, her bones. They bulged and buckled. Her skin tore; her heart strained, stretched, and, after ten thousand years' poor service, gave out.

Cytherea the First sighed in no little relief. Then she toppled over, and she died.

The sword made a terrific clatter as it dropped to the ground. The breeze blew Harrow's hair into her mouth as she ran back and strained at the arms of her cavalier, pulled and pulled, so that she could take her off the spike and lay her on her back. Then she sat there for a long time. Beside her, Gideon lay smiling a small, tight, ready smile, stretched out beneath a blue and foreign sky.

Epilogue

HARROWHARK NONAGESIMUS CAME AROUND in a nest of sterile white. She was lying on a gurney, wrapped up in a crinkly thermal blanket. She turned her head; next to her there was a window, and outside the window was the deep velvet blackness of space. Cold stars glimmered in the far distance like diamonds, and they were very beautiful.

If it had been possible to die of desolation, she would have died then and there: as it was, all she could do was lie on the bed and observe the smoking wreck of her heart.

The lamps had been turned down to an irritatingly soothing glow, bathing the small room in soft, benevolent radiance. They shone down on her gurney, on the white walls, on the painfully clean white tiles of the floor. The brightest light in the room came from a tall reading lamp, positioned next to a metal chair in the corner. In the chair sat a man. On the arm of his chair was a tablet and in his hands was a sheaf of flimsy, which he would occasionally shuffle and take notes on. He was simply dressed. His hair was cropped close to his head, and in the light it shone a nondescript dark brown.

The man must have sensed her wakefulness, for he looked up from his flimsy and his tablet at her, and he shuffled them aside to stand. He approached her, and she saw that his sclera were black as space. The irises were dark and leadenly iridescent—a deep rainbow oil slick, ringed with white. The pupils were as glossy black as the sclera.

Harrow could never tell precisely how she knew who he was, only that she did. She threw off the rustling thermal blanket—someone had dressed her in an unlovely turquoise hospital smock—and got out of bed, and she threw herself down shamelessly at the feet of the Necromancer Prime; the Resurrection; the God of the Nine Houses; the Emperor Undying.

She pressed her forehead down onto the cold, clean tiles.

"Please undo what I've done, Lord," she said. "I will never ask anything of you, ever again, if you just give me back the life of Gideon Nav."

"I can't," he said. He had a bittersweet, scratchy voice, and it was infinitely gentle. "I would very much like to. But that soul's inside you now. If I tried to pull it out, I'd take yours with it and destroy both in the process. What's done is done is done. Now you have to live with it."

She was empty. That was the terrible thing: there was nothing inside her but the sick and bubbling detestation of her House. Even the silence of her soul could not dilute the hatred that had fermented in her from the genesis of the Ninth House downward. Harrowhark picked herself up off the floor and looked her Emperor dead in his dark and shining eyes.

"How dare *you* ask me to live with it?"

The Emperor did not render her down to a pile of ash, as she partway wished he would. Instead, he rubbed at one temple, and he held her gaze, sombre and even.

"Because," he said, "the Empire is dying."

She said nothing.

"If there had been any less need you would be sitting back home in Drearburh, living a long and quiet life with nothing to worry or hurt you, and your cavalier would still be alive. But there are things out there that even death cannot keep down. I have been fighting them since the Resurrection. I can't fight them by myself."

Harrow said, "But you're *God*."

And God said, "And I am not enough."

She retreated to sit on the edge of the bed, and she pulled the hem of her hospital smock down over her knees. He said, "It wasn't meant to happen like this. I intended for the new Lyctors to become Lyctors after thinking and contemplating and genuinely understanding their sacrifice—an act of bravery, not an act of fear and desperation. Nobody was meant to lose their lives unwillingly at Canaan House. But—Cytherea . . ."

The Emperor closed his eyes. "Cytherea was my fault," he said. "She was the very best of all of us. The most loyal, the most humane, the most resilient. The one with the most capacity for kindness. I made her live ten thousand years in pain, because I was selfish and she let me. Don't despise her, Harrow—I see it in your eyes. What she did was unforgivable. I can't understand it. But who she was . . . she was wonderful."

"You're awfully forgiving," said Harrow, "considering she said she was out to kill you."

"I wish she'd said that to me," said the Emperor heavily. "If she and I had just fought this out, it would have been a hell of a lot better for everyone."

Harrow was silent. He seemed lost in thought. He said presently, "Most of my Lyctors have been destroyed by a war I've thought best to fight slowly, through attrition. I have lost my Hands. Not just to death. The loneliness of deep space takes its toll on anyone, and the necrosaints have all put up with it for longer than anybody should ever be asked to bear anything. That's why I wanted only those who had discovered the cost and were willing to pay it in the full knowledge of what it would entail."

All this washed over Harrow's shoulders. She realised immediately that she was a fool: that she was asking the wrong questions, and listening to the wrong thing.

"Who else beside me is alive, Lord?"

"Ianthe Tridentarius," said the Emperor, "minus one arm."

"The Sixth House cavalier was only injured when I left her," said Harrowhark. "Where is she?"

"We haven't recovered any trace of her, or her body," said the Emperor. "Nor that of Captain Deuteros of Trentham, nor of the Crown Princess of Ida."

"*What?*"

"All the Houses will have questions tonight," he said. "I can hardly blame them. I'm sorry, Harrow, we couldn't recover your cavalier either."

Her brain listed sharply.

"Gideon's gone?"

"Everyone else is accounted for," he said. "We have had to settle for partial remains of the Seventh House and the Warden of the Sixth. Only you two were confirmed alive. It doesn't help matters that I can't even go down there and search."

Harrow found herself saying, distantly, "Why can't you go back? It seemed to be the whole of Cytherea's plan."

The Emperor said, "I saved the world once—but not for me."

Harrow pressed her legs down into the cool metal rib of the gurney. She expected to feel something, but she didn't. She felt nothing at all. There was a great and gnawing emptiness, which was mildly better than feeling something, at least. A tiny voice in the back of her head was saying, *Someone will burn for this,* but it was only ever her own.

The Emperor leaned back in his chair and they looked at each other. He had a ridiculously ordinary face: long jaw, high forehead, hair a dull and leaden brown. But those *eyes.*

He said, "I know you became a Lyctor under duress."

"Some may call it *duress,*" said Harrow.

"You aren't the first," said the Emperor. "But—listen to me. I will do what I haven't done in ten thousand years and renew your House." (How did he know about that?) "I'll safeguard the Ninth. I will make sure what happened at Canaan House never happens again. But I want you to come with me. You can learn to be my Hand. The Empire can gain another saint, and the Empire needs another saint, more than ever. I have three teachers for you, and a whole universe for you to hold on to—for just a little while longer."

The King Undying had asked her to follow him. All she wanted was to be alone and weep.

"Or—you can go back home again," he said. "I have not assumed you'll agree with me. I will not force you or buy you. I will keep covenant with your House whether you come with me or stay at home."

Harrow said, "We can't go home again."

There was a vague reflection of her in the window, interrupted by distant space fields pocketed thick with stars. She turned away. If she saw herself in a mirror, she might fight herself: if she saw herself in a mirror, she might find a trace of Gideon Nav, or worse— she might not find anything, she might find nothing at all.

So the universe was ending. Good. At least if she failed here, she would no longer have to be beholden to anybody. Harrow touched her cheek and was surprised to find her fingertips came away wet, and that the Necrolord Prime had chivalrously lowered his gaze.

She said, "I will have to go back eventually."

"I know," said the Emperor.

"I need to find out what happened to my cavalier's body. I need to know what happened to the others."

"Of course."

"But for now," said Harrow, "I will be your Lyctor, Lord, if you will have me."

The Emperor said, "Then rise, Harrowhark the First."

GLOSSARY

Necromancer—an adept of the Nine Houses, born with the ability to control thanergy (the energy of death) and thalergy (the energy of life), as well as the ability to convert the latter to the former. There is no isolated genetic code associated with necromantic potential, nor the presence of any extra biological feature apart from heightened activity from organs we would otherwise mark as vestigial. Necromantic aptitude must be exercised in order to be used efficiently, and is strongest on a thanergenic planet (such as those typical to the Nine Houses). A very common side effect is physical weakness and an inability to keep and form muscle mass, though this has its genetic exceptions. Necromancy does not work in space or on board spaceships due to the way space disperses thanergy without a thalergy anchor such as a planet: necromancers are almost entirely personally powerless when travelling from planet to planet, though theorems (spells) they have created will last in some cases in deep space.

Cavalier—a swordsman of the Nine Houses who has sworn themselves to a specific necromancer. The lead cavalier in any House is known as the cavalier primary, and second to them the cavalier secondary; they are not ranked otherwise. Cavalier status must be awarded by the House, and a cavalier may keep their title in the Cohort. Who becomes a cavalier and under what rubric differs from House to House, but a cavalier cannot be fully considered to be so without a necromancer who has sworn the oath with them.

Thanergy—death energy. Planets and gaseous bodies in space usually produce thalergenic radiation. The sun and planets of the Nine Houses are thanergenic in character after the Resurrection. Thalergenic planets may be converted to be thanergy planets, i.e. dying planets, but almost never thanergenic (producing death energy but on a stable basis). Thanergy is produced by cellular death.

Thalergy—life energy. Most objects in the universe are thalergenic in character. Thalergy is produced by cellular growth and reproduction. Most planets, even ones without a biological mass of life, are thalergenic. Thalergy is produced by all living creatures.

Nine Houses—the name of both the empire and the system that comprise the Necrolord Prime's home system. The Nine Houses came into being ten thousand years ago with the "Resurrection," a response to the mass dying-off of the system's planets and sun that destroyed all life. When the first necromancer—the Emperor—ascended, he resurrected the planets and the people to become the Nine Houses. Nine Houses territory only comprises the system; planets and systems that the Empire "shepherds" are not regarded as being extensions of home, especially because necromancers do not reproduce successfully outside the system.

Dominicus—the central thanergenic star of the Nine Houses system.

Bone magic—the school of magic chiefly to do with manipulating the extant thanergy of bones, or impregnating them with additional thanergy. Bones being the only known source of long-term storable thanergy, bone magic is to do with animating and "programming" bones (raised skeletons), manipulating inert or living bone, or forming bone into patterns it wants to fill (topological resonance). Bone creation—reproducing skeletal matter from a sample—is the ultimate end state of bone magic.

Flesh magic—the school of magic chiefly to do with manipulating the extant thanergy of flesh, or impregnating it with additional thanergy. Flesh is a conduit for short-term storable thanergy, and in the right circumstances provides immense thalergy and thanergy boosts to the magician. Flesh magic is wide-ranging, covering preservation, imbuing, manipulation, creation, and processing. Blood magic is a subschool of flesh magic, as the remnant thalergy and thanergy in blood makes it perfect for use in warding. Lymph magic is widely disregarded as a poor substitute. Flesh magic is also used for self-manipulation of the human body, either to make it perform better or to make it perform worse, often quite suddenly.

Spirit magic—the school of magic chiefly concerned with the River, ghosts, and revenants, as well as with liminal magic spaces and nexuses. Spirit magic is diverse, and can range widely from creation of anti-thalergy and anti-thanergy spaces (impregnation of spirit energy into non-River spaces) to manipulation of people's souls, forming conduits to the River, to the conversion of another person's spirit and thalergy to thanergy. It is also the school of magic that lets the living access the River, the afterlife space to which the dead are drawn. The subschool of River magic is practised only by the Emperor and his Lyctors.

The Locked Tomb—another name for the Ninth House, but also an area within the Ninth House. The Locked Tomb is the resting place of an unfathomable enemy of the Emperor, killed after the Resurrection and placed in the Ninth House in order to show it respect. There is a school of thought in the outer Houses that the Ninth House was never meant to exist in the long term, and that the Ninth House priests, nuns, and faithful worship the Tomb *alongside* the Emperor, rather than as being a sign of the Emperor's might. What it contains has never been made explicit.

Lyctor—a personal servant, guard, and disciple to the Emperor. The Lyctors are undying, all-powerful necromantic saints whose aptitude endures even in space. In the early days of the Empire, they made it possible for the Nine Houses to act within the fullness of their power on thalergy planets; they also set steles throughout the galaxy, the necromantic means through which the Nine House fleet travels quickly through space without needing to use faster-than-light speed. Though there were originally seven full Lyctors, they have died over the years, none being as powerful or eternal as their Necrolord Prime.

A SERMON ON CAVALIERS AND NECROMANCERS

taken from the collected works of M. Bias

I have heard critique of cultural depictions of necromancers as romanticising an essentially military bondage; it is hard not to see these critiques as ignoring the poignancy, the humanity, and the quintessentially Nine Houses qualities of the concept. Have we, as a civilisation, had a love affair with the idea? Yes! Has it been the keystone of all interstellar exploration and success in military conflict? Yes! Was *Be My Cavalier VII* six too many sequels for that worthy first novel? Yes; but be it ever so saccharinely depicted in poetry and prose, our concern with the relationship between a necromancer and their cavalier remains at its heart our pure ideal: that though as a people we are divided between those who are attuned to, and afflicted by, the aptitude, and those who are withdrawn from, and spared from, the aptitude, we two groups share a symbiotic relationship. Those who hold the sword must hold it for the necromancer. Those who were born with thanergetic nervous systems ply their art only by the grace of the sword. The necromancer is weak, and the sword is strong. The sword is weak, and the necromancer is strong. Our pleasure at the bond unbroken between necromancer and cavalier is a Nine Houses acknowledgement of the equality granted to us by God.

This is not to say that the relationship entered our consciousness fully formed, nor that we have not watched it change through the eras. Its application in military circumstances has changed just as much as its application in society and in fiction. Necromancer-cavalier pairs are never sent out without the backup of modern Cohort regiments: those soldiers who make up the frontline Cavalier units would be the first to differentiate *their* work from the work of the classic cavalier. The social cavaliers—attached to the premier necromancers of their house—are under fire from traditionalists for contributing to the "worrying trend" of granting the title of cavalier to people who go unranked in swordplay: the use of "cavalier" as a metaphor. But this argument is at least five thousand years old: we have reams of editorials criticising cavaliers primary who have failed to travel and gain fame and "at least captaincy." Society would consider this an unnecessarily harsh requirement of a cavalier primary nowadays: even Second House cavaliers primary most often begin their higher services as a lowly lieutenant.

What has not changed is the essential equation. A necromancer who must leave her House and fight requires a swordswoman. A swordswoman leaving her House to fight requires, amid the bullet-fuelled barbarism of other planets, a necromancer. Of course, it is the swordswoman who makes the necromancer's art possible: thalergy planets reject the necromancer, and require fresher death than we do in the Nine Houses to perform. But without the care and craft of the adept, would the first assault not be merely a suicide strike? Perhaps the swordswoman may survive alone where the necromancer would find it difficult or impossible: but this is the mathematics we come back to. The one binds to the other. More warriors, and the necromancer would be hard-pressed to perform the feats that come with intimate knowledge of another's thanergy; more necromancers, and the swordswoman's burden to supply thanergy would multiply with each adept, to say nothing of the difficulty of protecting more than one person. Both halves serve as sword and shield. The long-standing relationship is required for the heat of battle; unfamiliarity with the other's methods will lead to death.

Our concern with what the relationship *should* be is a long-standing one. The love between them should be centred on duty. No matter the House, the vow is short—

One flesh, one end.

The Emperor confirmed long ago that this oath was taken from the Lyctors themselves, in the early years of discipleship after the Resurrection. With this as our understanding, how beautiful an oath it is!

"One flesh" is the underpinning of our whole Empire. We are born necromancers, or we are not; yet we are one. The non-necromancer will still have necromantic children. The necromancer will have parents who lacked the aptitude. The possibility is within us. We live under the thanergenic light of Dominicus, are born, grow, and die in his thanergetic Houses; the Resurrection made us so. We are fundamentally different to those born on thalergy planets outside the Empire. Our anxiety drives the expectant parent to arrange to give birth back home, or concern themselves with the baby's proximity to grave dirt sourced from home. Our necromantic characteristics make us more like the Emperor. As he was once man, and became God, and was God and became man, so were we dead and became alive; so were we alive and became dead. The necromancer and the cavalier are no different. They are one flesh. And yet that is only one understanding of the mystery that characterises us as a society.

"One end" is necessarily martial. We may take "end" as in the sense of goal or desire; the necromancer and cavalier work toward the same thing, no matter their differences in personality or method. Both members of the pair must work together to secure whatever path has been marked for them by House or empire. One end is one Empire. Love between a necromancer and cavalier is vital to differentiate them from a soldier's love of the Emperor: they are carrying out a personal devotion that beautifies both types of adoration. If the cavalier and the necromancer do not take "one flesh, one end" as a maxim for their passion for each *other*, their bond is nonexistent. They must each take the other as their ideal. The necromancer must be a pure expression of their art to the cavalier. The cavalier must strive for perfection in theirs, to gain the necromancer's admiration and trust. They do not have to enjoy each other's society; they must simply take their togetherness as assumed. The cavalier who will not sleep in the same room as their necromancer must question themselves as to why. Their love is the love that fears only for the other: the love of service on both sides. Some have tried to characterise this relationship as the cavalier's obedience to the necromancer, but the necromancer must be in turn obedient to the needs of the cavalier without being asked or prompted: theirs is arguably the heavier burden.

As we are concerned with what the relationship *is*, so are we concerned with what it is *not*. The love of the cavalier for the necromancer, and the necromancer for the cavalier, is not the love of a spouse. It cannot be libidinous. "Sword-marriages" wherein a necromancer and their cavalier married to one outside party as dual spouses were almost certainly the invention of the fiction writer, or more likely, the pornographer who cannot see anything beautiful without wanting to make it lewd. This is proved in the fact that, after a myriad of thought about the matter, marrying your cavalier remains taboo at best. There have been those who have argued eloquently that it is traitorous to the ideals of the Necrolord Prime. There is still a precedent in the Fifth for spouses to *become* a cavalier at particular times, but this is regarded as a stubborn holdover that is characteristically Fifth to not remove from their practise. Neither can the love be familial love, which is why the necromancer and cavalier cannot be parent and child; sibling rules have relaxed, but only in times of unusual paucity. Many Houses still cleave to the idea that the best cavaliers are those who from the cradle know both what they are and at whose side they are destined to stand; the Second House has notably argued against this, stating that this results in a sibling relationship. History gives us successful and unsuccessful examples of both methods: of the cavaliers and necromancers trothed nearly at birth, or of the necromancer and the cavalier who join as strangers to each other.

It has gone out of fashion to have "pattern" marriages as a hard rule; for one reason that adhering to "pattern" marriages often led to blurring of traditional cavalier families and administrative families, leading to the need for new branches of both. Atrial marriages, of necromancer to necromancer, and of their cavalier to cavalier, worked only inside House lines; ventricular marriages, of necromancer to the other necromancer's cavalier, and vice versa, worked best with outsiders. "Swap" or "bruise" marriages are still common in this way—non-adepts sent in to marry necromancers on both sides—but are hardly done to "pattern." In this era of mixed Cohort regiments and long placements out in space, mixed-House marriages can occur by sheer accident, or—in the case of the Sixth—by hopeful design. The only "pattern" left is the Sixth's rigid adherence to set childbearing pairs, albeit this is acknowledged within the Library to often have little to do with love and everything to do with genetic scarcity. This fluctuation of style and whim has not touched the central tenet of cavalier and necromancer, nor what they represent to both each other and the children of the Resurrection.

As we approach the celebration of a myriad of years serving the Necromancer Divine, our King of the Nine Renewals, first and last among us, we may see the cavalier-necromancer bond as a gift to us in long standing. Like him, it has not changed; like him, although we may build altars and light candles, the fundamental substance beneath does not wear or tarnish with long years of worship. The necromancer stands with her cavalier. The cavalier stands with her necromancer. They are one flesh, and one end, and they are all of us.

A LYCTORAL NOTE ON CAVALIERS AND NECROMANCERS

NEARLY TEN THOUSAND YEARS OLD, KEPT IN SECRET IN A CHEMICAL FILE WITHIN THE LIBRARY OF THE SIXTH HOUSE TO GUARD AGAINST THE RAVAGES OF TIME

valancy says one flesh one end sounds like instructions for a sex toy. can't stop thinking about that so can someone stop cris and alfred before the sex toy phrase catches on, thanks

COHORT INTELLIGENCE FILES

Intelligence report assembled on the advent of the Lyctor pilgrimage by Captain J. Deuteros (Dead Fleet, Dve Territorials 12th Necromancer's Unit). NOT FOR ARCHIVAL USE. Only for use accompanied with verbal distribution to Trentham-based members of the Admiralty, Generals [REDACTED] and [REDACTED], Head of Intelligence [REDACTED], and Lieutenant M. Dyas (Dead Fleet, Dve Territorials 12th Necromancer's Unit Auxiliary) acting in the role of cavalier primary.

Second House

Captain Judith Deuteros

Age 22.

Judith Deuteros, born interstellar, home Trentham of the Second House. Joined the JCTs (Junior Cohort Territorials) at eleven years old, commission to second lieutenant at fourteen. Attached to the Leviathan-class ship *Emperor's Dominion* at fifteen, awarded commendations in within-system war games. Promoted to first lieutenant at twenty and attached to Behemoth-class ship *Rigor*. Onboard *Rigor*, saw intragalactic action wherein she headed an in-ship tactics unit alongside Lieutenant Dyas. Promoted to captain at twenty-two. Returned to Trentham to attend intelligence and officer training, as well as to pursue further necromantic studies.

NOTES: Forgive the third-person. The basis of my representation is made upon Lieutenant Dyas' skills as well as my birth, the equation being the sum of our parts. Two Cohort trainees, despite not having seen frontline action, could be said to have an unfair advantage in this arena. I have studied energy-transferral aptitude with Lt. Dyas since our school days. I am also widely trained across the schools, with an eye to military applications. I received a first-class rating at Trentham. As well as having passed psychological examinations, I will be interested in acquiring for the Cohort the first up-to-date intelligence on the First House in three hundred years. I have no family or marital responsibilities that will distract me.

Lieutenant Marta Dyas

Age 27.

Marta Dyas, born on Trentham, home Trentham of the Second House. Joined the JCTs (Junior Cohort Territorials) at ten years old, commission to second lieutenant at fifteen. Awarded status of cavalier at twenty on attachment to Judith Deuteros with a bid for cavalier secondary, received honour title Marta the Second. Attached to the Leviathan-class ship *Emperor's Dominion*, awarded multiple commendations for within-system war games. House duel ranking maintained within the top three of the cavalier secondary class, top five general class. Promoted to first lieutenant at twenty-two, saw action onboard *Rigor* in the same circumstances as Captain Deuteros. Returned to Trentham in supporting role to Captain Deuteros, was ranked first in the system two years ago for her class in duelling.

NOTES: No cavalier primary currently in the system has Dyas' credentials. She has been training since childhood, received her first-class rating at Trentham and has established herself as a premier cavalier before thirty years old. Her House ranking, despite it being outside Cohort management, is extraordinary. Her offhand style is the dagger, but she has trained with a wide variety of weapons, both modern and archaic. She has no family or marital responsibilities to distract her, and is in every way an exemplary cavalier. In terms of the current lineup of cavaliers that the Houses are bringing, our data suggests that she is easily the best and most promising. Protesilaus Ebdoma of the Sixth has a famous ranking average, but his withdrawal into family duties suggests he is not at peak performance.

Third House

Crown Princess Coronabeth Tridentarius

Age 21.

Coronabeth Tridentarius, born on Ida, home Ida of the Third House. Has received home instruction rather than attending a specific institution. No Cohort placement, nor any indication that Cohort placement will be sought. In line with Third tradition, is eldest and will take control of the House once her father relinquishes it. Necromantic aptitude animaphilia. A classic Third magician, but again, has not pursued scholarly betterment either on the Third or elsewhere. No marital ties.

NOTES: Coronabeth Tridentarius may be a necromantic dilettante or a powerhouse. Our intelligence is incomplete, and her lack of formal study in other places has muddied the issue. She enjoys popular status within her House and without. As well as being very physically imposing and extraordinarily beautiful, or at least very beautiful on a subjective level to many people, she also has a natural charisma. She and others around her have been known to mistake this charisma for leadership ability. Tridentarius has a long history of close interaction with the Second and the Fifth. I myself have known Corona, as she is familiarly known, since childhood, and she was capricious then. She is an intense personality, energetic, driven, and wildly ambitious, excellent with people and with wide appeal. As a necromancer we cannot begin to guess, but given other factors her ability to succeed in this endeavour is high, albeit it would create a power vacuum within the Third House. See below.

Princess Ianthe Tridentarius

Age 21.

Ianthe Tridentarius, born on Ida, home Ida of the Third House. Has received home instruction rather than attending a specific institution. No Cohort placement, nor any indication that Cohort placement will be sought. Has been ranked as third in line after her twin sister Coronabeth. Necromantic aptitude animaphilia. A classic Third magician, but as with her sister, a lack of extramural scholarship means a lack of data as to how good they are. Ianthe has never performed necromancy without her sister in the room, which may indicate a lack of confidence or aptitude. She is in her attitudes much more languid and apathetic than her sister. No marital ties.

NOTES: Ianthe is lesser than her sister in almost every way. She is much more physically frail, less able in social situations, more retiring, and frankly unappealing in personality. She is more inclined than Coronabeth to think before she speaks, but as they never appear in public without the other one, she defers entirely to her. Her physical characteristics next to Corona's own may indicate that her animaphilia-specific study is not as strong, or that she has chosen a different school. Her psychological profile suggests she looks to her sister for support. If Coronabeth is successful in becoming a Lyctor, scionship will fall to Ianthe. If both become Lyctors, it will fall outside the immediate family.

Prince Naberius Tern

Age 23.

Naberius Tern, born on Ida, home Ida of the Third House. Only child of the previous cavalier primary. Resurrection-purity family, line has been serving Ida and providing cavaliers historically. Attended various academies and institutions on the Third as well as receiving home instruction with the princesses. Formal recognition of cavaliership when he was fourteen, but somewhat irregularly registered with both of them. As with the twins, no indication that Cohort placement was sought. House duel ranking maintained within the top five of his specific cavalier class, top five also in general class.

NOTES: Nominally Coronabeth's cavalier, but Ida has been internally and externally referring to him as being "both" their cavalier for years. His offhand style is the dagger, and classically the Third House threefold knife. He has maintained his very high duel ranking for years. We have data both formative and summative, however, suggesting that he is in danger of becoming more of a duellist than a swordsman. His bouts with Lt. Dyas have confirmed this. In personality, he is more public-facing than Ianthe, but less successful than Coronabeth; his mood is more changeable, he is more openly materialistic, he is inclined to be socially immature. He also has an extremely good opinion of himself and his swordplay, an opinion that Lt. Dyas notes occasionally aligns with reality.

Fourth House

Baron Isaac Tettares

Age 13.

Isaac Tettares, born on Tisis. Resurrection-purity family, the eldest of eight. As is normal on the Fourth, children were a mix of vat-womb and XX carry. Father killed by terrorists out on [REDACTED] nineteen years ago: all of his children have been posthumous and the title held in stewardship. Trained at home with time spent in a school at Koniortos Court on the Fifth, on the direction of Abigail Pent. Strong spirit magician, ranks very highly for his age. Cohort placement was first sought two years ago, rejected first on age grounds and then on health grounds, again on advisement from the Fifth House. Will most likely be accepted next year should he choose to apply again.

NOTES: Isaac Tettares is a talented child. It is for us to wonder how far the Fifth House agitated for his inclusion among the invited pairs, and for what reason. It is very unlikely that Tettares will become a Lyctor any time soon, and it is my opinion that frankly it would not be desirable for him to become so due to his age and immaturity. Abigail Pent has forged a strong relationship with both Tettares and Chatur, much stronger even than her mothers' relationship with Tettares' father. It is already suggested that her nephew will be affianced to him once they are of age. This is a pity, as Isaac Tettares is suggestive of an interesting personality: less forceful than is common on the Fourth, but more reflective and restrained. It would be good for the Fourth House to take this direction. If the Second House can make any headway with the Fourth House during this process, they will.

Sir Jeannemary Chatur

Age 14.

Jeannemary Chatur, born on Ops. Resurrection-purity family, second of six. Being the first non-necromancer of the line, she is her generation's Chatur. Mother given posthumous commendations by the Emperor after her death at [REDACTED], albeit she was in breach of agreement travelling there. Intended to be Isaac Tettares' cavalier from birth, swore the oath with him and gained the title at age nine. Cavalier primary only subsequent to last year's bombing. Attended all the same schools as Baron Tettares, maintains the same relationships as he with Abigail Pent. Cohort placement with her necromancer sought two years ago under her name, rejected on the same grounds.

NOTES: Jeannemary Chatur is also a talented child. Her offhand style is the dagger, and she actually made placement last year in her class ranking despite her age: it wasn't thought that she would get through the heats. Is the aggressor of the pair, boisterous and physical, albeit how much of this is personality and how much of this is age is a query. Both she and Tettares are eager to join the Cohort and would obviously be a huge asset if one can prevent native Fourth instinct from making too much headway. Lt. Dyas will watch her, but remains hands-off.

Fifth House

Lady Abigail Pent

Age 37.

Abigail Pent, born at Koniortos Court. First of two. The famous historian, she received head of House five years ago, at which point her husband became her cavalier. Due to genetic failure of their chromosomes, her younger brother's children will become the next scions unless she names a different heir. Has studied on the Fifth, the Third, the Sixth, and the Eighth Houses. Possesses a slew of first-class degrees. Her necromancy is generalist with status as speaker to the dead, but she has published ten books, eighty-six articles and gives instruction as well as taking on the duties of the Fifth House leader. How devoted Abigail Pent really is to the leadership role is questionable, but she has more than maintained the Fifth's interests in the Fourth House. A formidable mind, a living asset, and undoubtedly future generations will look at her as one of the great historians of the Nine Houses. No Cohort placement ever sought, and Pent's sentiments have veered at times to anti-Cohort. As her grandfather was the previous Admiral of the Undying Fleet, where this sentiment came from is to be investigated.

NOTES: To keep close watch on. Pent's martial and necromantic presence is poor, but her cultural capital is high. If Pent became a Lyctor, it might be problematic.

Sir Magnus Quinn

Age 38.

Magnus Quinn, born on Rhax. First of three. An administrator, only received cavalier training in his school days, never receiving a ranking or indeed ever distinguishing himself in the field. A much more capable civil servant, he reached seneschal status at Koniortos Court shortly before marrying Abigail Pent. Cohort placement was briefly sought when he was eighteen before it was rejected in-House, but no interest afterward.

NOTES: Quinn is cavalier primary simply by unhappy coincidence. The Fifth House is undoubtedly chagrined at the timing. His offhand style is the dagger, but Quinn remains a schoolboy fighter. Marriage with Pent and the subsequent cavaliership seems to be entirely due to Pent's informal abdication of the future role. Some suggestion she will announce her brother as heir and step down in the mid future. Quinn himself is a Fifth House bureaucrat with all that entails.

Sixth House

Master Warden Palamedes Sextus

Age 20.

Palamedes Sextus, born in the Library. Not much data is available on Palamedes Sextus. He is the youngest Master Warden by far ever to achieve the title, taking part in the examinations at thirteen and winning out over at least fifteen other and significantly older candidates. All of his publishing has so far been internal to the Sixth House, but secondhand accounts put him as being regarded as a genius by his Sixth peers (!). The Sixth House has maintained its position and strength rather than weakened during the first years with Sextus at the helm. Unfortunately, he has cleaved to his House's tradition of secrecy, and data is limited. No Cohort placement ever sought.

NOTES: I myself met the Master Warden once. Despite the reputation of ferocious intellect, his demeanour inclines to the light-hearted rather than the dignified or ponderous. More years in the position will perhaps lend him gravity, but on meeting, I would not have known he was the Master Warden without having been told before.

Camilla Hect

Age 20.

Camilla Hect, born in the Library. Almost nothing is known of Camilla Hect except that she passed the examinations to become Palamedes Sextus' cavalier when she was twelve. She has not entered in any duelling tournaments or done informal bouts. No Cohort placement ever sought.

NOTES: She is registered as his second cousin; the genetic data is still readily available and reliable as the Sixth's leading concern. Offhand style is most likely the dagger, as the Sixth House do not have the confidence to move away from the classics. A pair who will most likely be flexible minds, but will not even bother to compete on the cavalier stage.

Seventh House

Duchess Dulcinea Septimus

Age 27.

Dulcinea Septimus, born at Rhodes. Duchess Septimus has been removed multiple times to high-atmosphere facilities on-planet to convalesce, as she was publicly diagnosed with the Heptanary blood cancer as a child and her lifestyle has followed accordingly. Either necromancy or resilience has kept her alive long past the terminal diagnosis, and she has lived to be in her late twenties; whether or not she is in a stable position or deteriorating is not known, as she has not been seen in public for five years. No Cohort placement ever sought.

NOTES: Attempt to become a Lyctor may well be based entirely on the cavalier.

Protesilaus Ebdoma

Age 39.

Protesilaus Ebdoma, born on Cypris. A well-regarded cavalier, he served Septimus' father as cavalier secondary before being given to Septimus, albeit this may well have been because Septimus was not expected to live and it would have been a waste to give her a cavalier close to her in age. Schooled privately. Sought Cohort placement at eighteen, and did tours to three separate front lines before returning home. Married with multiple children. Ranked first for three years running in the general class cavaliers duelling before retiring to attend to the Duchess Septimus. Has not partaken in any duels since then, but the reputation remains.

NOTES: From hearsay and reports, Protesilaus Ebdoma was enormously skilled. Offhand style is the chain. The Seventh House still rest on the laurels that Ebdoma won them, but why he was given to a necromancer with a terminal diagnosis is so particularly Seventh in character that it defies most reasoning. It may well be that he was never intended to be with her long and that the role was scaffolding him up into a more long-term cavalier primary role, but Septimus has failed to die and he has stayed with her. Marital and familial responsibilities back home mean his attention may be divided. Difficult to quantify.

Eighth House

Master Silas Octakiseron

Age 16.

Not much is known about the current head of the White Templars. He is young, but as is Eighth House tradition, would have been aware of his role from a very young age. He would also have been bonded with his cavalier in the extremes of youth. His age indicates that the Eighth House is sending a Templar confident in the genetic bonds to his cavalier, which means the cavalier will be closely related. As is traditional, we can safely surmise that Master Octakiseron is a soul adept, well-versed in the siphoning school.

NOTES: The Eighth House consists of both safe guesses and absolute enigmas.

??? Asht

Age 32, 34, or 37.

There are three brothers currently registered as Asht, which would be the next in line to serve Octakiseron. In relationship, all three are genetically his nephew, albeit all of them are also significantly older. The Eighth House have not been well represented in duelling lists as of late, but this may be a reshuffle in House fighting expertise.

NOTES: Offhand style could be anything from the shortsword to the shield or the claws. Eighth House cavaliers have tended in the past few generations toward close melee.

Ninth House

???

Absolutely nothing is known of the Ninth House necromancer, scion or cavalier. Due to their nonresponsive status, they may not even arrive. Shuttles are still ordered regularly to the site, but the contents have been blanked out in the system. Someone with a higher intelligence clearance than myself may want to check the database. After the Lyctor pilgrimage, suggest that the prison should be contacted to get a closer look around the perimeter and report findings back to us.

Offhand could be anything. The necromancer, although inevitably a bone adept, could be anyone. We will proceed with caution: the Ninth House is dangerous and may even warrant hostile status.

A LITTLE EXPLANATION
OF NAMING SYSTEMS

In the two-name system of the Nine Houses, your last name is not a proper surname: it is an arithmonym, indicating House allegiance. Your first name is given to you by your parents, and may indicate a family connection: the first name often refers to your family in some way. For instance, the suffix *Hark* in Harrow's and her father's name honours a previous pilgrim entrant into the Tombkeeper line; double-barrelled names like *Jeannemary* and *Coronabeth* are inevitably formed from heirloom name particles. Your last name always indicates the House you were born in, and is regarded as part of your name: this is why Abigail Pent is known as both "Lady Abigail" and "Lady Pent" in a way that never would have been typical before the Resurrection: both Abigail and Pent are referent to her. Different Houses have different methods for coming up with both first names and arithmonymics. Many Houses are also fond of referential diminutives (*Mortus* to *Ortus*).

Siblings will not generally share a last name, though they may share particulates. Twins rarely share a surname, and if they do may gain a "unit" name; the fact that the Tridentarii are the *Tridentarii* may say something about Corona and Ianthe's parents hopes or desires for their children. There are, of course, always exceptions (e.g. Colum was one of three Asht boys despite them not being triplets).

Names are not changed through marriage. Non-necromancers getting married must pick which House to settle on and affiliate with; their children will be of the settled House. Necromancers as a rule cannot marry out of House: marry the necromancer, affiliate with their House. There are a handful of other rules in play (simply *having a baby* with a Sixth is an inherent agreement that your children will all be born to the Sixth, which can prove a legal nightmare).

Some names below are not included in the pronunciation guide due to their appearance in the Bible or elsewhere (the Second, the Fifth, Isaac, Silas).

As the author, I have sometimes included a little meta-note beneath the pronunciation guide to share with you, the reader, all the unnecessary jokes as to why I included it, or thought it funny or appropriate. You don't have to read these. Put your thumb over them if you like.

Harrowhark Nonagesimus

HA-row-hark. To rhyme with "arrow," not as in "hay."
Noh-nah-*GUESS*-i-mus. "I" as in "bitter"; "mus" for the Latin, closest to "moose."

NOTE: *Harrow is named very specifically for the harrowing of Hell. "Hark" is one of those terrible, portentous words that always precedes an awful time, in the old sense of "awe." Hark! A herald angel. Hark! From the tombs, a doleful sound.*

Gideon Nav

NAV. Short "a" as in "navigator," not as in "nave."

NOTE: *There are a lot of reasons as to why Gideon is called Gideon. The warlike prophet of God who really messed up the Midianites is part of it. Gideon is a prophetic name: someone named their own demise in her.*

Ortus Nigenad

ORT-us. To rhyme with tortoise, unless you pronounce tortoise "tor toys," in which case it doesn't. *NIGH*-ga-nad. As with Harrow, hard "g."

NOTE: *Although Ortus is obviously referential to his father Mortus, Ortus by itself is the Latin for "rising." Is this hilarious or sad?*

Pelleamena Novenarius

Pelly-*AM*-enna. Rather than ah-*MAY*-nah.
Noh-ven-*ARE*-ee-us. As with Harrow, the "us" closer to an "o" sound.

NOTE: *In myth, Peleus famously was the father of Achilles.*

Priamhark Noniusvianus

PRY-am-hark. Three distinct syllables; avoid eliding the H.
NOH-nee-us-vee-*AHN*-us. You should have the trick of the "us" sound by now. If you don't, it's fine, nobody cares, it's a random name in a novel about bonermancy.

NOTE: *Priam in the Iliad was famously a dad in a city about to go splat.*

Aiglamene

Eye-*GLAM*-en-ay.

NOTE: *"Aigla" was meant to refer to the French "aigle," the eagle.*

Crux

CRUX. To rhyme with "sucks," not "crooks."

NOTE: *"Crux" as in "Cross," which is funny multiple ways.*

Aisamorta

EYE-sa-mor-tah.

NOTE: *"Aisa" is a Greek word for fate or destiny.*

Lachrimorta

LACK-ri-mor-tah.

NOTE: *"Lachri" from "tears."*

Glaurica

GLAU-ri-kah. Ri as in "ridicule," not as in "reed."

Judith Deuteros

DEW-ter-oss.

NOTE: *Famously beheaded Holofernes. Book of Deuteronomy is a very didactic text.*

Marta Dyas

DIE-ass. I'm sorry, I couldn't come up with anything better.

NOTE: *Marta, martial, war. The Second House names are serious business.*

Ianthe Tridentarius

E-*AHN*-thay. The "e" should be in "see," not as in "eh."
Try-den-*TAR*-ee-us. Again, the "e" is the same sound as in the fore-name.

Coronabeth Tridentarius

Cor-*OWN*-a-beth. "Corona" as in the halo.

NOTE: *In the original, Ianthe and Corona were "Cainabeth and Abella," a feat of naming so unsubtle that I might as well have just gone with "Goodtwin" and "Badtwin." And it's not even accurate! It should be Badtwin, and Lessbadtwin.*

Naberius Tern

Na-*BEER*-e-us. "E" as in "speed," "us" as in "fuss."
TURN. As in, I wish Naberius would TURN into a bat and fly out the window.

NOTE: *Naberius is one of the demon princes of Hell. Will this mean anything significant later on?? (No.)*

Jeannemary Chatur

JOHN-mair-ee. "Mary," not "Marie." Softer J, as in the French.
Cha-*TOUR*. Not "chatter," though that'd be appropriate.

NOTE: *"Jeannemary" is a Biblical car crash, but Jeanne here is meant to be reminiscent of Jeanne d'Arc.*

Isaac Tettares

Tett-*AR*-ez. Not "tett-*aries*."

NOTE: *"Isaac" in Christian theology foreshadows Jesus' death by taking the wood for his own sacrifice up a mountain. Isaac here foreshadows Gideon's death by doing the "bravest and stupidest" thing, i.e. getting his abdomen made into a huge Connect-4 board. I might as well have called Jeannemary and Isaac "Don'tgetattached" and "Deadsoon."*

Palamedes Sextus

Pal-*AM*-a-dees. At first I had a coarse comparison here, but then I removed it.
SEX-tus. "Us" as in "bus" rather than the "oos" of Nonagesimus.
"Sex" as in "you'd have to be weird to want this with Harrow."

NOTE: *There was a very brief space of time where Palamedes was Diomedes, Athena's favourite goodboy in the Iliad, but that would not have facilitated Gideon's stupidest joke in the book.*

Camilla Hect

HEKT. To rhyme with "wrecked."

NOTE: *Camilla's name was picked to go with Palamedes'—their names resonate with the "am" fragment in a way that other necromancer-cavalier pairs who love each other very much do in the book: Pal**am**edes and C**am**illa, Abig**ail** and M**ag**nus.*

Dulcinea Septimus

Dul-sin-*AY*-a. Not "dul-sinn-eya."
SEPT-i-mus. "Sept" as in "September," rather than "seeped." "Mus" as in "Nonagesimus."

NOTE: *"Dulcinea" is the famously illusory persona assigned to the prostitute Aldonza in* Don Quixote: *a case of a woman you want to exist, but who really doesn't. In this essay I will*

Protesilaus Ebdoma

Prot-eh-sil-*OW*-us. "Prot" rather than "prote."
EBB-do-mah. "Ebb" as in what the tide does, "doma" as in "domain."

NOTE: *Protesilaus is the first hero to die at Troy. He is also the first man who dies as a result of the Lyctor trials. "Johnny Quickdeath" would've also been a good pick.*

Silas Octakiseron

Ock-ta-*KISS*-er-on. "Kis" as in "kiss," rather than "keys."

Colum Asht

COL-um. As in "column."
ASHT. As in "hash."

NOTE: *"Colum" is referent to "Columba": Colum and his three brothers all have sacrificial-animal names—Colum (dove), Ram (sheep), and Capris (goat). Unfortunately I couldn't get over how one of the poor Asht brothers has the name of a type of leggings and this didn't get into the book, which just goes to show that the Asht boys even got meta-misused. Sorry, guys. I should've named him Aiglos.*

INCIDENTAL NAMES AND TERMS

Matthias Nonius

Mah-*TYE*-as. Hard "t," rather than the "Math" as in "Matthew."
NOH-knee-us. As in, no knees for us.

NOTE: *I would be lying if I did not say that "Matthias," the legendary sword-wielder of the Ninth, has a name that is a reference to Brian Jacques' Redwall.*

Cytherea

KITH-er-*AY*-a. Not "kith-*AIR*-ee-ah."

NOTE: *Reference to Aphrodite.*

Lyctor

LICK-tor. In order to facilitate "Lyctor? I hardly touched her," stand-up routines in the Nine Houses.

NOTE: *Lyctor as in "lych," but also as in Lictor, the Emperor's guards.*

Canaan House

KAY-nan. Emphasis on the first syllable rather than kay-*NAAN*.

Secundarius Bell

Se-cun-*DAR*-ee-us.

Drearburh

DREAR-burr.

NOTE: *The most Gormenghastian name in the book. "Burh" as in the old variant for "burgh," "Drear" as in "dreary"!*

Harrowhark will return in

HARROW THE NINTH

Turn the page for a preview.

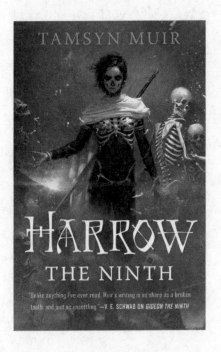

Available 2020

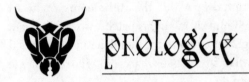

prologue

YOUR ROOM HAD LONG AGO plunged into near-complete darkness, leaving no distraction from the great rocking *thump—thump—thump* of body after body flinging itself onto the great mass already coating the hull. There was nothing to see—the shutters were down—but you could feel the terrible vibration, hear the groan of chitin on metal, the cataclysmic rending of steel by fungous claw.

It was very cold. A fine shimmer of frost now coated your cheeks, your hair, your eyelashes. In that smothering dark, your breath emerged as wisps of wet grey smoke. Sometimes you screamed a little, which no longer embarrassed you. You understood your body's reaction to the proximity. Screaming was the least of what might happen.

God's voice came very calmly over the comm:

"Ten minutes until breach. We've got half an hour of air-con left . . . after that, you'll be working in the oven. Doors down until the pressure equalizes. Conserve your temp, everyone. Harrow, I'm leaving yours closed as long as possible."

You staggered to your feet, limpid skirts gathered in both hands, and picked your way over to the comm button. Scanning for something damning and intellectual to say, you snapped: "I can take care of myself."

"Harrowhark, we need you in the River, and while you are in the River your necromancy will not work."

"I am a Lyctor, Lord," you heard yourself say. "I am your saint. I am your fingers and gestures. If you wanted a Hand who needed a door to hide behind—even now—then I have misjudged you."

From his far-off sanctum deep within the Mithraeum, you heard him exhale. You imagined him sitting in his patchy, worn-out chair, all alone, worrying his right temple with the thumb he always worried his right temple with. After a brief pause, he said: "Harrow, please don't be in such a hurry to die."

"Do not underestimate me, Teacher," you said. "I have always lived."

You picked your way back through the concentric rings of ground acetabula you had laid, the fine gritty layers of femur, and you stood in the centre and breathed. Deep through the nose, deep out the mouth, just as you had been taught. The frost was already resolving into a fine dew misting your face and the back of your neck, and you were hot inside your robes. You sat down with your legs crossed and your hands laid helplessly in your lap. The basket hilt of the rapier nudged into your hip, like an animal that wanted feeding, and in a sudden fit of temper you considered unbuckling the damn thing and hurling it as hard as you possibly could to the other side of the room; only you worried how pitifully short it would fall. Outside, the hull shuddered as a few hundred more Heralds assembled on its surface. You imagined them crawling over one another, blue in the shadow of the asteroids, yellow in the light of the nearest star.

The doors to your quarters slid open with an antique exhalation of gas levers. But the intruder did not set off the traps of teeth you'd embedded in its frame, nor the gobbets of regenerating bone you had gummed onto the threshold. She stepped over the threshold with her cobwebby skirts rucked high on her thighs, teetering like a dancer. In the darkness her rapier was black, and the bones of her right arm gleamed an oily gold. You closed your eyes to her.

"I could protect you, if you'd only ask me to," said Ianthe the First.

A tepid trickle of sweat ran down your ribs.

"I would rather have my tendons peeled from my body, one by one, and flossed to shreds over my broken bones," you said. "I would rather be flayed alive and wrapped in salt. I would rather have my own digestive acid dripped into my eyes."

"So what I'm hearing is . . . *maybe,*" said Ianthe. "Help me out here. Don't be coy."

"Do not pretend to me that you're here for anything other than to look after an investment."

She said, "I came to warn you."

"You came to *warn* me?" Your voice sounded flat and affectless, even to you. "You came to warn me *now*?"

The other Lyctor approached. You did not open your eyes. You were surprised to hear her crunch through your metrical overlay of bone, to kneel without flinching on the grim and powdery carpet beneath her. You would never sense Ianthe's thanergy, but the darkness seemed to give you an immense attunement to her fear. You felt the hairs rise on the back of her forearms; you heard the hammering of her wet and human heart, her scapulae drawing together as she tensed her shoulders. You smelled the reek of sweat and perfume: musk, rose, vetiver.

"Nonagesimus, nobody is coming to save you. Not God. Not Augustine. Nobody." There was no mockery in her voice now, but there was something else: excitement, perhaps, or unease. "You'll be dead within the first half hour. You're a sitting duck. Unless there's something in one of those letters I don't know about, you're out of tricks."

"I have never been murdered before, and I truly don't intend to start now."

"It's *over* for you, Nonagesimus. This is the end of the line."

You were shocked into opening your eyes when you felt the girl opposite cup your chin in her hands—her fingers febrile compared to the chilly shock of her gilded metacarpal—and put her meat thumb at the corner of your jaw. For a moment you assumed that you were hallucinating, but that assumption was startled away by the cool nearness of her, of Ianthe Tridentarius on her knees before you in unmistakable supplication. Her pallid hair fell around her face like a veil, and her stolen eyes looked at you with half-beseeching, half-contemptuous despair: blue eyes with deep splotches of light brown, like agate.

Looking deep into the eyes of the cavalier she murdered, you realised, not for the first time, and not willingly, that Ianthe Tridentarius was beautiful.

"Turn around," she breathed. "Harry, all you have to do is turn around. I know what you've done, and I know how to reverse it, if only you'd ask me to. Just ask; it's that easy. Dying is for suckers. With you and me at full power, we could rip apart this Resurrection Beast and come away unscathed. We could save the galaxy. Save the Emperor. Let them talk back home of Ianthe and Harrowhark—let them *weep* to speak of us. The past is dead, and they're both dead, but you and I are alive.

"What are they? What *are* they, other than one more corpse we're dragging behind us?"

Ianthe's lips were cracked and red. There was naked entreaty on her face. Excitement, then, not unease.

This was, as you understood it dimly, the psychological moment.

"Go fuck yourself," you said.

The Heralds came plopping down onto the hull like rain. Ianthe's face froze back into its white and mocking mask, and she dropped your jaw—untangled her restless fingers and her awful gold-shod bones.

"I didn't think this was the time for dirty talk, but I can roll with it," she said. "Choke me, Daddy."

"Get *out.*"

"You always did think obstinacy the cardinal virtue," she remarked, quite apropos of nothing. "I think now, perhaps, you should have died back at Canaan House."

"You should have killed your sister," you said. "Your eyes don't match your face."

Over the comm, the Emperor's voice came, just as calm as before: "Four minutes until impact." And, like a tutor chiding inattentive children: "Make sure you're in place, girls."

Ianthe turned away without violence. She stood and trailed her human fingers over the wall of your quarters—over the cool filigreed archway, over the polished metal panels and inlaid bone—and said, "Well, I tried, and therefore no one should criticize me," before ducking through the arch to the foyer beyond. You heard the door shut behind her. You were left profoundly alone.

The heat rose. The station must have been completely smothered: wrapped in a squirming shroud of thorax and wing, mandible and antenna, the dead couriers of a hungry stellar revenant. Your communicator crackled with static, but there was only silence at the other end. There was silence in the lovely passageways of the Mithraeum, and there was a hot and sweating silence in your soul. When you screamed, you screamed without sound, your throat muscles gulping mutely.

You thought about the flimsy envelope addressed to you that read, *To open in case of your imminent death.*

"They're breaching," said the Emperor. "Forgive me . . . and give it hell, children."

Somewhere far off on the station there was a warping crunch of plex and metal. Your knees became jelly, and you would have collapsed to the floor in a spasm had you not been sitting. With your fingers you closed your eyes, and you wrestled yourself into stillness. The darkness got darker and cooler as the first shield of perpetual bone cocooned you—the act of a fool, meaningless, doomed to dissolve the moment you submerged—then the second, then the third, until you were lost in an airless and impregnable nest. Throughout the Mithraeum, five pairs of eyes closed in concert, one of them yours. Unlike theirs, yours would not open again. In half an hour, no matter what Teacher might hope, you would be dead. The Lyctors of the Resurrecting Emperor began their long wade into the River to where the Resurrection Beast squatted—just out of the orbit of the Mithraeum, half-alive, half-dead, a verminous liminal mass—and you waded with them, but your meat you left vulnerably behind.

"*I pray the tomb is shut forever,*" you heard yourself saying aloud, and you could not bring your voice above a choked whisper. "*I pray the rock is never rolled away. I pray that which was buried remains buried, insensate, in perpetual rest with closed eye and stilled brain. I pray it lives . . .* O corse of the Locked Tomb," you extemporised wildly. "Beloved dead, hear your handmaiden. I loved you with my whole rotten, contemptible heart—I loved you to the exclusion of aught else—let me live long enough to die at your feet."

Then you went under to make war on Hell.

* * *

Hell spat you back out. Fair enough.

You did not wake up having passed into the thanergetic space that was the sole province of the dead, and the necromantic saints who fought the dead; you woke up in the corridor outside your rooms, on your side and broiling, gasping for air, soaked right through with sweat—your own—and blood—your own; the blade of your rapier leered through your stomach, punctured through from behind. The wound was not a hallucination or a dream: the blood was wet, and the pain was terrible. Your vision was already curling up black at the edges as you tried to close the rent—tried to sew your viscera shut, cauterize the veins, stabilize the organs whimpering into shutdown— but you were too far gone already. Even if you had wanted it, the *imminent death* letter would not be yours to read. All you could do was lie gasping in a pool of your own fluids, too powerful to die quickly, too weak to save yourself. You were only half a Lyctor, and half a Lyctor was worse than not a Lyctor at all.

Outside the plex, the stars were blocked by the skittering, buzzing Heralds of the Resurrection Beast, beating their wings furiously to roast everything inside. From very far away you thought you heard the ring of swords, and you flinched at each bright scream of striking metal. You had loathed that sound from birth.

You prepared to die with the Locked Tomb on your lips. But your idiot dying mouth rounded out three totally different syllables, and they were three syllables you did not even understand.

ΡΛΓΘΔΘΣ

In the myriadic year of our Lord—the ten thousandth year of the King Undying, our Resurrector, the full-pitying Prime!—the Reverend Daughter Harrowhark Nonagesimus sat on her mother's sofa and watched her cavalier read. She idly fretted her thumbnail into a decaying brocade skull on the cover, carelessly destroying in a second long years of labour by some devoted anchorite. The mandible unravelled beneath the pad of her thumb.

Her cavalier sat very upright in the study chair. It had not taken anyone of comparable bulk since his father's day, and was now in danger of a final fatal sag. He had tucked his considerable frame tight within its borders as though breaching them might cause Incident; and she knew full well that Ortus hated Incident.

"*No retainers. No attendants, no domestics,*" read Ortus Nigenad, folding the paper with obsequious care. "Then I will wait on you alone, my Lady Harrowhark?"

"Yes," she said, vowing to keep her patience as long as possible.

"No Marshal Crux? No Captain Aiglamene?"

"In fact, *no retainers, no attendants,* and *no domestics,*" said Harrow, losing her patience. "I believe you've cracked the elaborate code. It will be you, the cavalier primary, and me, the Reverend Daughter of the Ninth House. That's all. Which I find . . . suggestive."

Ortus did not seem to find it suggestive. His dark eyes were downcast behind their thick black lashes, the sort Harrowhark had always fancied you might get on some nice domestic mammal, like a hog. He was perennially downcast, and not out of modesty; the faint crow's feet trampling each eye were lines of sadness; the fine creases at his forehead were a careful act of tragedy. She was glad to see that someone—maybe his mother, the mawkish Sister Glaurica—had painted his face as his father had once painted his own, with a solid black jaw to represent the Mouthless Skull. This was not because she had any especial love for the Mouthless Skull, as paint sacrament went. It was merely because any jawéd skull he affected became a wide white skull with depression.

After a moment, he said abruptly: "Lady, I cannot help you become a Lyctor."

She was only surprised that he dared to offer an opinion. "That's as may be."

"You agree with me. Good. I thank you for your mercy, Your Grace. I cannot represent you in a formal duel, not with the sword, nor the short sword, nor the chain. I cannot stand in a row of cavaliers primary and call myself their peer. The falsehood would crush me. I cannot begin to conceive of it. I will not be able to fight for you, my Lady Harrowhark."

"Ortus," she said, "I have known you my entire life. Did you really think I entertained any delusions that you could be mistaken, in the dark, by a dementia-ridden dog raised with no knowledge of bladed objects, for a *swordsman*?"

"Lady, it is only to honour my father that I call myself a cavalier," said Ortus. "It is for my mother's pride and my House's scarcity that I call myself a cavalier. I have none of a cavalier's virtues."

"I am not sure how many times I must relay to you how truly I am aware of that," said Harrowhark, picking a tiny fragment of jet thread from her fingernail. "Given that it has constituted one hundred percent of our exchanges over the years, I can only assume you are coming to some new point, and begin to feel excitement."

Ortus leant forward on the edge of his chair, his restive, long-fingered hands locking together. His hands were big and soft—all of Ortus was big and soft, like a squashy black pillow—and he spread them open, beseeching. She was intrigued, despite herself. This was more than he had heretofore dared.

"Lady," ventured Ortus, voice deepening with timidity, "I would not venture it—but if a cavalier's duty is to hold the sword—if a cavalier's duty is to protect with the sword—if a cavalier's duty is to die by the sword—have you never considered **ORTUS NIGENAD**?"

"What?" said Harrow.

"Lady, it is only to honour my father that I call myself a cavalier," said Ortus. "It is for my mother's pride and my House's scarcity that I call myself a cavalier. I have none of a cavalier's virtues."

"I feel as though we have had this conversation before," said Harrowhark, pressing her thumbs together, testing with risky pleasure how malleable she might make her distal phalange. One misstep, and her nerves might split. It was an old exercise her parents had set her. "Each time, the news that you have not spent your life in acquiring martial virtues comes as a little less of a shock to me. But have a go. Surprise me. My body is ready."

"I wish that our House had produced some swordsman more worthy of our glory days," said Ortus meditatively, who always found enthusiasm for alternate histories where he was not pressed into service or asked to do anything he found difficult. "I wish that our House had not been diminished to '*those who are fit but to hold their blade in the scabbard.*'"

Harrowhark congratulated herself on not pointing out how this lack of production was directly due to three things: his mother, himself, and *The Noniad,* his ongoing verse epic devoted to Matthias Nonius. She had a vile suspicion that the quotation, around which he had somehow contrived to pronounce quotation marks, was from that very same verse epic, which she knew was already on its eighteenth book and showed no signs of slowing down. If anything it seemed to be gaining momentum, like a very boring avalanche. She was composing a rejoinder when she noticed that a serving sister had arrived in her father's library.

Harrow had not noticed her knocking, or her passage in; this wasn't the problem. The problem was that the sister's ashen paint was decorating the lovely dead face of the Body.

Her palms felt wet. In this scenario, either the sister was real and her face was not, or the sister was herself unreal. One couldn't simply gauge all the osseous mass in the room and do a best guess; bones in meat generated so much deceptive soft thalergy, only a fool would try. She flicked her eyes over to Ortus in the faint hope that he would betray her reality one way or another. But his gaze was still levelled at the ground.

"Our House has received good service from '*those who are fit but to hold their blade in the scabbard,*'" said Harrowhark, keeping her voice even. "Which is not a line that scans, just so you know. Nobody will be surprised to find you a laggard."

"It's enneameter. The traditional form. *Those who are fit but to hold their blade in the scabbard—*"

"That's not nine feet of anything."

"*—never to draw it forth for the battle.*"

"You will train with Captain Aiglamene for the next twelve weeks," said Harrowhark, rubbing her fingers back and forth, back and forth, until the pad of her thumb felt very hot. "You will meet the very minimum that is expected of a Ninth House cavalier primary, which is now, fortunately, that you be as broad as you are tall with arms that can carry a weight. But I need . . . significantly more from you . . . than the edge of a sword, Nigenad."

The serving sister shadowed the edge of Harrow's peripheral vision. Ortus had raised his head and did not acknowledge the sister, which complicated things. He looked at Harrow with the faint kind of pity she always suspected he held her in: the pity that marked him as an outsider in his own House, and would mark him as all the more an outsider in the House of his mother's line. She did not know what made Ortus *Ortus.* He was a mystery too boring to solve.

"What more is there?" he asked, a little bitterly.

Harrowhark closed her eyes, which shut out Ortus's tremulous, worried face and the shadow of the Body-faced serving girl that fell over the desk. The shadow told her nothing. Physical evidence was often a trap. She shut out the new and rusty rapier that now creaked in the scabbard at Ortus's hip. She shut out the comforting smell of dust made hot by the whirring heater in the corner of the room, mixing with the just-milled ink in her inkwell. Tannic acid, human salts.

"This isn't how it happens," said the Body.

Which gave Harrow a curious strength.

"I need you to hide my infirmity," said Harrowhark. "You see, I am insane."

ACKNOWLEDGEMENTS

I would like to express my very great appreciation for my agent, Jennifer Jackson, both for her enthusiasm and her tireless work on behalf of *Gideon the Ninth*. My thanks are also extended to my incredible editor, Carl Engle-Laird; I can't begin to outline everything he has done for me and this novel, except to say that if it was a labour of love on my part it was a hundred labours of love on his. Thanks for being a Sixth House stalwart to the end, Carl.

Particular thanks are due to the staff at Tor.com—Irene Gallo, Mordicai Knode, Katharine Duckett, Ruoxi Chen, and everyone else on the team—whose hard work and support I have deeply appreciated over the editing and publishing process.

I would like to acknowledge the work of Lissa Harris, who advised me on use of the rapier, off-hands, and the Zweihänder throughout this novel. Anything good, true, or beautiful about swordplay here is due to her; any mistake or rank stupidity is mine, probably because I ignored her advice in the first place. I'm thankful for her patience, wit, and insight, but would like to remind her here that hard-boiled eggs shouldn't be added to potato salad. Fight me.

Special thanks also to Clemency Pleming and Megan Smith, my friends and first readers, whose support means I now possess a kitchen apron embroidered with the worst deleted meme from the manuscript. Their good humour and sympathy kept me sane—and also, now I have an apron.

I am grateful to my excellent Clarion instructors of 2010, and wish to particularly thank Jeff and Ann VanderMeer, knowing Jeff won't mind if I especially highlight years of support, goodwill, and enthusiasm from Ann. Assistance provided by my classmates, whose work I enjoyed, whose advice I solicited, and whose boundless sympathy I took advantage of constantly over the years, proved invaluable. (Thanks, suckers.) For special services to this novel I'd like to thank Kali Wallace, the living embodiment of *nolite te bastardes carborundorum*; John Chu, for wholehearted kindness; and Kai Ashante Wilson, who gave me the gentle kick up the rear I needed to send out the manuscript.

Various people have supported me and this novel in general. I'm grateful for the love and support of my friends and family, in particular my brother, Andrew Muir, the guy who believed in my writing even when I was eleven and publishing turgid Animorphs fanfiction. His support for me in every avenue of my life has made me who I am today. Also, thanks for leaving critical anonymous reviews on my fanfiction.net masterpieces, jagoff.

Finally but most importantly, I acknowledge the ongoing contributions of Matt Hosty, who mopped blood, brewed tea, and corrected drafts with the patience of Griselda. Two more books and then I'll never mention bones again, I swear to God.